I0664419

A Dog Return To Its Own

A Dog Among Thorns, Volume 3

Joshua Fields

Published by Joshua Fields, 2023.

Table of Contents

"'OUR FATHER WHO IS IN heaven, hallowed be your name, your kingdom come, your will be done, on earth as it is in heaven. Give us this day our daily bread. And forgive us our debts, as we also have forgiven our debtors. And do not lead us into temptation, but deliver us from evil . . . .'" (Excerpt from the Gospel of Mathew 6:9-13).

Miriam repeated the Lord's prayer a second time as the terrifying and chilling blackness soaked her being. The unctuous evil of Ba'al Zeboul's realm sought to silence her, its efforts including a crescendo of the pained cries and wild clicking sounds that echoed in her soul.

"Our Father who is in Heaven," Miriam uttered in her spirit, the demon summoning every last drop of her strength in the attempt. The power of the Abyss intensified each time she finished a recitation of the prayer but pulsed away each time she began the next one. The two pinpricks of light that appeared when she first resorted to the words of Christ blazed furiously.

"Our Father who is in Heaven," Miriam implored God, her prayers lasting for what seemed an eternity but, with each individual plea, the blackness retreated and morphed into ever lighter shades of gray. The volume of the horrible, incessant noises decreased.

"And do not lead us into temptation . . . ."

An all-encompassing flash of white light suddenly broke the duskiness and, in an instant, Miriam was free from the Abyss. Shunted into the material world, she lay face-down on a hard, undeterminable surface. She rolled onto her back despite her emotional and spiritual exhaustion.

". . . but deliver us from evil," Miriam gasped as her ability to perceive the material world gradually returned. She recognized earthly skies floating above and the peak of Mount Borgia towering over her. She stretched out her arms, wiggled her fingers and then scratched the hard surface with her claws. The resulting noise sliced through the afternoon air.

"I'm back," Miriam said with a soft smile of jagged teeth. She lay on a small sepulcher of pristine white stone with small grains of luminous minerals embedded in it. They sparkled each time the sun emerged from the clouds passing overhead. Surrounded by a sloping, manicured green lawn on the western side of the mountain, the sepulcher held a special place in Miriam's heart.

The demon's smile faded as she sat up and studied her body. She no longer wore a red dress but a white, full-length gown of silk. Running her hand through her long hair, she pulled it into her field of vision and scanned it with her black eyes.

"I can feel it again," Miriam said. An image of Jacob arose in her mind and she panicked. Miriam paid no further heed to her appearance and, determined to find him, vanished into thin air.

TAKING ADVANTAGE OF the relative evening warmth, Jacob drank his coffee on the roof of the tower and watched the westering sun. The coffee would have been overly bitter not so long ago but, after going without for several months, he relished it.

"It's gonna be hell when it runs out," Jacob thought as he sipped from his mug. The observation station in which he resided had been abandoned shortly after being resupplied and there was no shortage of basic goods like coffee. A chilling wind swept past the tower, the breeze causing Jacob to shiver despite his heavy winter clothing and mutter, "Warmer still means cold."

Comprised of brown stone blocks of varying shades, the station was a one-story building to which was attached the five story, cylindrical tower. The top level of the tower contained rectangular windows around its entire circuit while a four-foot wall encircled the roof and allowed for open-air observations on days when the weather cooperated. Numerous antennas clung to the building and erupted from its roof. Some of their support lines had broken and many of them were showing signs of neglect.

The sun soon dipped behind one of the snowy mountains. The bright orange light from it splintered into a thousand shards as it reflected off the contours of the clouds rushing on a frantic journey to the southeast. Tinges of pink touched the cacophony of orange streaks; together they made the clouds appear as if they burst into flames.

It was at this point that Jacob would usually laud God on his creation of such beauty. Yet his relationship with God had frayed since his arrival at the station. The valley it overlooked seemed a godless, religion-free zone where an unfettered spirituality flowed from a mystic spring below the mountains. It bathed the soul in tranquility and security.

"Maybe this is it," Jacob said as he reveled in both the inner and outer peace the station offered. The last warm glows of the sun bathed the sky.

"Hello, Jake," a familiar voice greeted him. Those words, spoken in that voice, once nauseated Jacob every time he heard them. His emotions were so blunted by their repetition, however, that they garnered no emotional response.

"Maybe not," Jacob said with sinking spirits. He glanced over his shoulder and uttered, "I don't have it in me today so you're getting a free pass. Put on your little performance and then go the fuck away."

The corpses of Jacob's stepdaughters, which appeared as they did at the time of their deaths, visited him often with taunts, threats and temptations. He would charge the demon-possessed marionettes with words of spiritual banishment upon each visit but, without exception, they escaped his attempts. His constant failure to free Vanessa and Mallory was wearing on him.

"You fucked up, Gottschalk, you fucked up!" shrieked Marcion with his usual delight. The sniveling demon caused Mallory's body to perform a bizarre dance and sang his usual tune: "You fucked up!"

Before her demise, seventeen-year-old Mallory stood on the cusp of womanhood. She was pretty and willowy with olive-hued skin, wispy, light-brown hair and curvaceous hips.

The brutal death she experienced, however, marred her physical form. Mallory's right eye was a gruesome gunshot wound, her clothing was a mess of dried blood and her internal organs were visible through a large, gnarled hole in her chest. She still wore a thin silver chain around her neck though it was sullied with gore.

"I must speak with you, Jake," said Assarion as she placed a hand on Mallory's shoulder. Marcion ceased his humanly vessel's dance as Assarion added, "Alone."

"What?!" exclaimed Marcion. He shoved Assarion away but she did not retaliate.

"Leave, now," ordered Assarion. Marcion launched into a profanity-laced objection but, whether intentional or not, he faded from view and disappeared.

Entrenched in the physical form of Vanessa, Assarion hazarded a few cautious steps towards Jacob. The beautiful nineteen-year-old shared much with her mother in life: the coffee-hued hair, the muted green eyes, the pale skin, the height. Their voices were nearly identical and Jacob found that when he watched Vanessa speak it still unnerved him. He turned away and seethed, tortured by the sagging, grey flesh hanging from her bones.

"Look, I've got your number, cunt," Jacob warned.

"Jake, please, there's no need for hostility," replied Assarion innocently. She moved even closer to him but he avoided her approach. Accepting his coldness, Assarion explained, "I'm simply protecting myself until the moment is right. If I make a move prematurely, my Master will know and I'll never get another chance. But changes are coming."

"Oh, bullshit," Jacob scoffed. Gesturing emphatically as he spoke, he said, "You're runnin' around, playing both sides and causing as much havoc as you can and then, *when the moment is right*, you'll strike. I'm sure you've done it a thousand fucking times before but I'm finally on to you so just get the fuck outta here and go back to whatever Abyssal shithole you crawled out of."

Jacob's words stung Assarion and she pondered her next move in silence. Frustrated with her continued presence, Jacob shook his head and turned to walk away.

"Is that any way to speak to the mother of your child?" asked Assarion in an injured tone, the combination of her bizarre question and Vanessa's voice stopping Jacob's retreat. He turned around and laughed.

"You're in the wrong Nicks, you goofy bitch," Jacob responded incredulously. Thoroughly amused by Assarion's desperation, he ridiculed her, "Damn, you've lost your touch."

"What makes you think I'm referring to a Nicks?" asked Assarion with a pensive expression. Jacob's mind jumped to his sexual encounter with Sarah but, before he could respond, Assarion fled into the spirit world with Vanessa's body. The demon's scandalous assertion prickled him.

"She's a bullshitter of the highest order and you know it," Jacob said aloud. Dismissing Assarion's questions as a subterfuge, he turned back to enjoy one last glimpse of the sunset. When he did, the magnificent end of day had died, its light extinguished and replaced with dead, grey clouds and the darkening sky of oncoming night.

The stairwell door suddenly opened behind Jacob. He sighed.

"Get in here," demanded Sophie with flat affect as the wind tussled her long, pale-blonde hair. She let it grow when the pair left Kaiser, her locks straightening as they lengthened.

"Not right now," Jacob replied. He turned to see she wore only a pink t-shirt and jeans, the cold causing her nipples to harden and become clearly visible through the fabric. He ogled her lean frame before chastising her, "I've told you a thousand times, Soph. You gotta wear a fucking coat when you come outside. Do you know how quick you can get frostbite in this climate?"

"I want to fuck," said Sophie, "so get in here."

Trapped between two cold winds, Jacob relented and shook his head. He experienced a small sense of dread but swiftly shook free of it and drained his mug.

"Fine," Jacob replied bitterly, "let's fuck."

· · · ·

JACOB GRASPED SOPHIE'S curvy hips and squeezed the tiny deposits of baby fat on them as she gyrated on his erection. Sexual gratification drove her earlier command from his mind and, in a surge of sensual energy, he thrust upward several times into her womanhood. She shivered with pleasure but then slapped him.

"*I said stop it*," insisted Sophie as she grinded on him in a dominating, circular motion.

"I said don't hit me," Jacob snapped.

"Shut the fuck up," Sophie growled, their spat failing to interrupt her efforts. Jacob surrendered and permitted Sophie to work her magic uninterrupted.

He knew that Sophie was seducing him but to what end he did not know. Yet, whether it was her intention or not, her insatiable sexual appetite was fueling his own and sapping him of his will to free his stepdaughters. Jacob began to wonder if it even mattered. Vanessa and Mallory were dead after all, and to free them was simply to drive the evil ones from their bodies so that they could be returned to Kaiser for proper burial.

Kaiser.

His brain-dead wife, Elizabeth, lay in a hospital bed in that Hell, the former love of his life serving merely as a human incubator for his unborn child.

Hell.

It was there that the demonic "woman" who ruined his marriage now served a life of eternal punishment thanks to the spiritual banishment he wrought on her. He thought also of the Ursuline nun Sarah, the last woman with whom he had intercourse prior to Sophie.

"Sarah was possessed by a demon at the time, dumbass. She ain't interested," Jacob scolded himself.

Sophie, though not without her faults and foibles, was eager and seemingly wanted him. She also roiled with a wild sexual energy and paid no mind to his drinking which, given the paucity of liquor at the station, was an infrequent occurrence.

"Sophie's an easy decision," Jacob told himself with a grim face. Sophie noticed that his presence waned and wrenched his penis within her. The pain caused him to grimace.

"Pay attention," she snapped while ejecting his penis from her body. She quickly spun around, reinserted him into her vagina and vigorously resumed her efforts.

"Sometimes, anyway," thought Jacob. His mind drifted to an earlier time in their relationship . . . .

. . . .

SOPHIE KNEELED ON THE floor of a small, dingy hotel room and fellated Jacob in her usual hyperactive manner, his crazed paramour making it difficult for him to restrain his orgasm. The room, situated on the second floor of a dilapidated inn, contained nothing but the chair in which Jacob sat, a bed and a broken dresser.

"We shouldn't stay here," Jacob warned Sophie as he looked to the dirty window. She responded by biting one of his testicles, the pain prompting him to recoil and shout, "Ow! Damn it, Soph!"

The pain warded off his impending ejaculation but not his concerns about the small settlement in which they found themselves. Located to the northeast of Kaiser but outside its zone of influence, the desert town was loosely governed by ill-tempered ruffians. Sophie immediately drew their deviant sexual attention and only an intervention by their leader prevented a violent attack.

"Miriam would've loved ripping those fuckers to shreds," Jacob thought, "especially that cocky, big-nosed fuck."

He regretted his words and chastised himself.

"*Stop thinking about her*, asshole."

Sophie recognized that Jacob's mind wandered and gave his testicles a punitive squeeze. He winced and grimaced, made eye contact with her and, satisfied with his response, she returned her full attention to his penis.

"More time to think, I guess," Jacob thought as Sophie again interrupted his orgasm. His statement proved incorrect as a forceful blow rocked the door. Sophie stood up and whirled around, her naked body on full display while Jacob yanked up his pants and said, "What the fuck?!"

A second blow tore the door from its hinges and broke it into several pieces. A corpulent, bald-headed man burst through the doorway, easily tossed the bed into the far wall and seized Sophie by the hair. A lifted knee to his crotch interrupted his assault for but a second before he turned and hurled her into the dresser. It crumbled on impact and Sophie fell to the floor.

"Sophie!" Jacob exclaimed as he tore through his shock and, sweeping up the chair, slammed it into the behemoth. It had little effect and exploded into a hail of wood.

"Marcus!" bellowed a nasally voice. Jacob instantly recognized it as the ruffian leader. He attempted to move to Sophie who lay motionless on the floor but the monster of a man blocked his path.

"Marcus! Stand down," the leader ordered as he entered the room. Wearing a long, black trench coat and drab, gray clothing, he was a tall man with small green eyes, a huge nose and a pudgy, evil face. He glared at Jacob and stated, "I'm pressed for time so I will make this short."

He glanced at Sophie longingly and then looked back to Jacob. The fat man seethed but remained still.

"I've decided I am taking this young woman from you," explained the leader. Stepping toward Sophie, he continued, "You will collect your things and leave this place, never to return again . . . or you will simply never leave this place"

Jacob perceived the next several moments in slow motion. Sophie rose with incredible celerity and, with a powerful swing of her baseball bat, hit the leader in the face. The force of the blow obliterated his huge nose, caved in the front of his skull and broke the bat. He tumbled over backward into the corner as his minion rotated around to face the new threat. Sophie closed on him in the blink of an eye and thrust the splintered half of the bat into his throat.

"Holy shit," Jacob gasped in awe. Blood spilled from the man's wound as he remained standing and grabbed the piece of bat with both hands. Sophie swiftly recovered the other piece and began using it as a hammer to pound the wooden shard deeper into the man's neck. He stumbled backwards and fell to the floor.

Jacob pressed himself against the wall to avoid the carnage. Sophie turned, flipped the bat so that she gripped it by its rounded end and offered it to him.

"Go kill him," instructed Sophie with a nod over her shoulder. Jacob looked at the bat, peeked around Sophie at the leader's seemingly lifeless body and then looked at her.

"I think he died when you caved in his face, Soph," Jacob replied, his head still spinning from Sophie's violence of action. The fat man stirred while gurgling and choking on his own blood. Sophie ignored him and instead extended her arm to its full length and poked Jacob with the bat's jagged end.

"He's still breathing," said Sophie. She closed her eyes, tilted her head to one side and then the other, saying, "I can hear it and it's irritating me."

The fat man's movements, while still slow, became more pronounced and he put forth one last effort to breathe. Jacob noticed and stepped away from him.

"How can you hear him over all of that?" Jacob asked with a point towards the man and a disgusted mien. Sophie pressed the bat into Jacob again with more force and he felt a twinge of pain. Whisking the bat out of her hands, he barked, "Stop it!"

"You'd better learn to kill," droned Sophie. Jacob's displeasure failed to daunt her.

"Learn to kill?" Jacob replied with incredulous eyes. Looking over Sophie, he noticed the spatters of blood clinging to her skin. They stretched from her face to her shins and even her breasts and her tuft of blonde pubic hair were tinged with red. A normal, sane human being would have made some effort to clean and clothe themselves. Sophie did not. Jacob thought, "It's almost as if she's more comfortable that way."

Sophie waited for his next move patiently with her arms hanging at her sides. Jacob's face hardened with a sobering realization.

"I've taken up with another demon," he said to himself. The fat man's moan derailed his thoughts. Acting with sudden conviction, Jacob approached him and held his foot on his throat until his futile struggles ceased. He wiped a bloody shoe on the fat man's protruding belly.

"Clean yourself off and get dressed," Jacob instructed Sophie without looking at her. She watched him intently but showed no emotion. Brushing past her, Jacob walked to the leader and studied him closely. He detected weak respiration.

"She was right," Jacob thought, "he's still alive."

Without hesitation, Jacob ended what little of the leader's life remained with a thrust of the wooden shard into his throat and a sickening, crackling squish. Jacob released the bat and turned around. It stuck straight up like a makeshift gravestone.

"I said clean up and get dressed," Jacob growled. Sophie procrastinated but eventually wiped the blood from her body with the bedsheets.

"There are more of them," warned Sophie, "and they have guns."

"*I don't care anymore*," Jacob snapped.

· · · ·

SOPHIE CAME IN THE usual manner, the twentysomething bucking on Jacob's erection and moaning on her way to complete satiation. Her vigorous movements ushered him to the edge of his own climax.

"In me!" screamed Sophie. It was the first time Jacob's younger paramour made such a demand. Her sensual movements intensified and she screamed again, "In me!"

Jacob, despite the prurient effect of Sophie's reckless desires, managed to withdraw from her and ejaculate on her back at the last possible second. Sophie undulated several more times before falling onto her stomach as Jacob finished the deed. Breathless and sweaty, he laid on his back next to her.

"What the hell was that all about?" Jacob inquired sharply when he recovered from his orgasm. Sophie turned her head to look at him.

"I want a baby," deadpanned Sophie.

"Are you fucking crazy?" Jacob asked. Sophie's behavior was bizarre, even for her, and it irked him. He raised himself up on an elbow and prepared to berate her for her foolishness. She placed an index finger on his lips.

"Clean up your mess so I can go to sleep," instructed Sophie. Standing up, Jacob grabbed a towel off the nightstand and tossed it onto her back.

"Do it yourself," Jacob snapped. Sophie, acting as if Jacob were not present, threw off the towel, turned onto her back and immersed herself in the covers. He watched in disbelief as she snuggled into them and quickly fell asleep, her deep breaths bordering on light snores within thirty seconds. Jacob shook his head and commented blithely, "That girl could sleep through a fucking plane crash."

Jacob and Sophie moved into one of the station's small bunkrooms upon their arrival but they spent little time in it during their non-sexual waking hours. Fortunately for them, the station's power supply relied on several sources, including solar panels, and would continue to produce electricity indefinitely. Jacob intended to stay at the station for the foreseeable future though he had yet to convey that intention to Sophie.

"She doesn't need to know," Jacob assured himself. He collected his rumpled clothes, exited the room and quietly closed the door behind him, adding, "Hell, she probably doesn't even care."

Jacob pointed himself in the direction of the shower room. However, a strange sound reached his ears. Moving to the window of the bunkroom across the hall, he looked out but saw nothing. The noise continued to develop as it neared the station.

"Holy shit," Jacob said, "that's a plane."

Quickly donning his clothes as he stumbled down the hallway, he proceeded towards the main entry doors. He hastily slid on some boots and attempted to grab a coat. The attempt failed.

"Damn it!" Jacob shouted as he cast open the doors and charged outside into the cold, dark night. The sound of the plane grew louder as he ran through the four-pillared entrance and into the station's empty parking area. Spinning around in circles, he searched the sky for any visible sign of an airplane. Its echoes in the mountains played tricks on his ears and he could not determine the direction of the plane's approach.

"Where the fuck is it?" Jacob said as he ran farther away from the station. An explosion rocked the mountains followed by the whine of a rapidly descending airplane and the deafening roar of engines.

"Oh, fuck," Jacob said. Turning to the station, he watched a dark-gray cargo plane round the mountainside. Its left wing clipped a rocky outcropping and was shorn from its body, the force of the blow altering the plane's trajectory and hurling it towards the station. Jacob whirled around and took a few steps but he was too late. The flaming plane slammed into the station and detonated in a fiery blast of debris that illuminated the vicinity of the station in an orange glow.

The explosion thrust Jacob into the trees at the far end of the parking lot and his body bounced off one of their trunks. Snow from the trees cascaded down upon him and buried him in a frozen grave. His conscious faded: his last vision was of fire, his last thought was of Sophie.

2

UPON FERRETING OUT Jacob's presence in Kaiser, Miriam expected to materialize in the quaint ranch house where he resided with Sarah. It was there that Jacob banished her to the Abyss and she believed it was there that her redemption would begin. Her expectations were immediately shattered.

"Why would he be here?" Miriam said aloud. She stood in a small room with beige walls, a white ceiling and sheet-vinyl flooring in a woodgrain pattern. A counter-topped shelving unit beneath the window formed an L-shape at the far end and a closed door behind Miriam led to the bathroom. Sunlight streamed through a space between two heavy, blue curtains and fell on a long female form lying on a platform bed. Miriam initially tensed but, sensing no threat, she relaxed her body.

"Welcome back, Miriam," said Sarah. She rose up slowly, eased her legs out of the bed and placed her feet on the floor. Miriam could see that her classic beauty remained but her chocolate-hued hair was disheveled, her face was worn with care and her olive-toned skin was dull. Her deep blue eyes, however, lost none of their luster and shone from her tired face.

"You're pregnant," Miriam said in astonishment when she noticed a pronounced belly interrupted Sarah's otherwise lean figure. She attempted to stand but thought better of it and sat back down on the bed.

"Yes, Miriam, I am pregnant," replied Sarah. Studying Miriam closely, she smiled and said, "And I see that He has blessed you as well."

A security officer passed outside, his head visible through the two-foot, rectangular window embedded in the door. Knowing that he could not see Miriam, Sarah waved to him while maintaining her smile. He waved back at her before disappearing.

"Where's Jake?" Miriam asked forcefully. She suddenly felt his presence, spun around and grabbed the door handle.

"Miriam!" beckoned Sarah in a low, stern voice, the nun anticipating her violent response. Miriam paused. Softening her tone, Sarah explained, "If you tear the door from its hinges, the guards will hear it and come to investigate. You and I have much to discuss and I would prefer to do so without any interruptions."

"Always so wise," Miriam said while fighting the urge to rip the door from its frame. Turning the handle after a moment of reflection, she opened it. Her emotions fluttered but then fell when she realized the bathroom was empty. She still perceived Jacob's spirit but it was not in front of her.

It was behind her.

"The last time I stood in one of these rooms with Jacob's unborn child and its mother, I bounced Elizabeth's head off a wall and put her in a coma," said Miriam in a flash of anger. The consequences of her unrestrained violence struck her, however, and her hatred vanished.

"Well, if you wish to do that to me, I am right here," said Sarah without fear. Guilt wracked Miriam and she bowed her head.

"No," Miriam replied after twenty seconds of silence. She turned around, acquired Sarah's face with her black eyes and said, "I don't want that."

Sarah watched Miriam with great wonder. It buttressed her faith that God placed Miriam on the path to redemption; yet she knew that she would face many challenges, expected and unexpected, on the journey.

"The greatest of which may very well be Jacob," thought Sarah. Her expression became one of pity.

"Where is he?" Miriam inquired, the determination evident on her face.

"I don't know," said Sarah sadly. The concern she radiated for the father of her child prickled Miriam but, with great difficulty, she managed to keep her jealousy at bay. Sarah again attempted to rise and this time successfully stood up as she continued, "He left Kaiser about seven months ago with Sophie to find his stepdaughters. His aim was to free them from their possessors and properly lay them to rest but I fear that is an impossible task. There has been no contact since."

"Sophie," Miriam muttered with the slightest hint of the demonic. Her regression startled Sarah but, before she could address it, Miriam gestured towards her distended stomach and asked, "Does he know?"

Sarah mulled over the proper response in her head but could not find the words. She placed a hand on her hip and shuffled towards the bathroom.

"I feel so big I think I'm carrying triplets," quipped Sarah with a wince and a smirk. Miriam sidestepped and blocked her advance.

"Does he know?" Miriam demanded.

"I must use the restroom, Miriam," advised Sarah, the immediacy of her urge plain for all to see. Miriam stood her ground and glared at the nun.

"There are many things he does not know," said Sarah forebodingly. Realizing that the road to relief ran through Miriam, she sighed and finally admitted, "And my pregnancy is one of them."

Sarah hurried past her and into the bathroom. The door slammed shut and Miriam heard her urinating. The emotion bled from her face.

"I guess she did have to go," Miriam said with a shrug.

· · · ·

MAKING HERSELF INVISIBLE to human eyes, Miriam slithered through the hospital hallways in search of the perfect prey. She discovered it within minutes.

"I'm burnt, you guys," said a dark-haired doctor whose body type aligned closely with Miriam's petite figure. She offered a group of nurses a single wave and added, "I'm gonna grab some sleep. See ya' later."

"She'll do," Miriam thought. The doctor turned and walked away to a chorus of "byes" and "laters". Miriam waited for her to pass and then followed her to a small room in the next corridor. The doctor opened its door and entered but Miriam allowed it to close, saying to herself, "Just kill her and stash her. It's easier that way."

Staring at the door handle, she did not move as the urge to simply slay the doctor flickered within her. She heard Jacob's voice.

"You say it's His will but can you accept His will in your life?"

Miriam remembered the promise she made to Jacob. She also remembered that no such promise had been required of her upon her parole from the Abyss.

"It doesn't matter," Miriam thought. She became stone-faced and added, "He'll know."

A nurse approaching with a full medical cart interrupted Miriam's ponderings and she refocused on her task. Reaching out with clawed hands, she plucked a bottle of sedative and an individually-wrapped syringe from the cart. She became entirely spiritual and walked through the door. The doctor lay on a twin bed, the rising and falling of her chest evidencing that she slept soundly.

Miriam unscrewed the cap of the sedative bottle, set it on the nightstand and then unwrapped the syringe. Despite her claws, she deftly inserted the syringe in the bottle and wrinkled her nose.

"How much do I give her?" Miriam asked aloud. Her quick search of the bottle did not reveal any instructions. She exhaled in frustration and said, "Jake really hates it when I kill civilians."

The doctor stirred and rolled over to face Miriam. She quickly filled the syringe and moved to the doctor's side.

"Why can't you just let me sleep?" asked the doctor groggily as she opened her eyes. Miriam placed her hand over the woman's mouth and was promptly bitten. Though she felt no pain, the violent desire to crush the doctor's skull struck her. Her arm shook as she fought to repress it.

"Be. Still," Miriam commanded in her demonic voice. The monstrous tone paralyzed the doctor and she gazed at Miriam with wide, frightened eyes. Gaining control of her homicidal impulses, she stopped shaking and said, "I'm not going to hurt you but you're going to take a *long* nap for me. You need one anyway."

The doctor's expression melted into confusion. Miriam held up the bottle in the fingers of her off hand.

"This is Pheno-barbi-tal," Miriam said slowly. Placing the bottle on the table, she then held up the full syringe and continued, "And this is a zero-point-five milliliter syringe. Now, if I give you all of this, will you die?"

The doctor hesitated but then shook her head in the negative. Miriam applied firmer pressure to hold her in place and, without hesitation, stuck the needle in her arm and injected the Phenobarbital. The doctor screamed into Miriam's hand and lost consciousness.

Miriam swiftly went to work, tossing aside the empty syringe and pulling off her gown. Examining her naked body, she realized that the hideous spider bite on her abdomen, once purplish and swollen, was gone. She smiled a smile of jagged teeth.

"It's gone," Miriam said with satisfaction. She remembered the stormy night at Crestfallen, a restaurant in Kaiser owned by the late crime lord

Agatha Moriarty. It was there that she revealed the bite to Jacob, the site of the wound interrupting his rapt attention as she unveiled her body to him.

Turning her own attention back to the doctor, she threw the blanket aside and assessed her body. Miriam removed her dark-rimmed glasses and set them on the nightstand.

"Jake would like her," Miriam told herself jealously. She removed the doctor's white coat while saying, "The brown hair, the brown eyes. She's slender, and tight. Pretty, too, though maybe a little old for my pervert."

Miriam laughed joyously as she thought about Jake's penchant for drunken, sexual mischief. She imagined he was in the room with her.

"He'd enjoy watching me do this," Miriam said aloud as she tugged the doctor's blouse out of her slacks and unbuttoned it. She removed the blouse and then her bra. Miriam studied the difference in breast size between she and the doctor. She said proudly, "My tits are bigger."

Miriam removed the doctor's shoes and her socks, unzipped her slacks and slid them off her body, and then worked her panties down her legs and over her feet. Standing nude with her arms at her sides and the doctor's panties in her right hand, she compared her body to the form of the slumbering doctor. Miriam stated eerily, "If he'd like her, then he definitely likes me."

A sudden wave of remorse swept over Miriam and an elusive anxiety arose within her. She swiftly dressed in the doctor's clothing.

"You'll be fine," Miriam said to the doctor who responded with a snore. Searching the room with her black eyes, she settled on a pile of hospital gowns. She put one of them on the doctor and pulled the blanket over her. Miriam donned the doctor's glasses and, as she faded from view, said earnestly, "Your part in all of this is over and you're still alive. *You're welcome.*"

· · · ·

SARAH EXITED THE BATHROOM while tying her hair into a ponytail. She no longer saw or sensed Miriam yet she looked around the room as if she might be hiding from view.

"Miriam?" said Sarah. She waited for Miriam to appear for several minutes but, uncertain if she would return, she showered and dressed for the monotony of another day of confinement. The nun started when Miriam reappeared. She sat at the foot of the bed with her legs folded beneath her.

"Put these on," Miriam said as she shoved a pile of clothes at Sarah. She wore the doctor's clothing but also donned a slim gold chain nearly identical to the one she once wore.

"Is that an order, doctor?" asked Sarah with grin. She noticed that Miriam's necklace lacked a charm.

"Yes, so put them on," Miriam replied. Looking at Sarah's pink maternity nightgown, she again shoved the clothes at the nun and said, "And get rid of that ugly thing."

"They won't fit, Miriam," countered Sarah.

"Yes, they will," Miriam said through clenched teeth. Standing up and thrusting the clothes into Sarah's arms, she added, "You're not the only pregnant woman in this hospital."

"Shoes?" asked Sarah.

A curse word arose on Miriam's lips but she choked it down. She crouched and held out her hand.

"Foot," Miriam replied. Sarah chuckled.

"I can't do that, not in this condition," said Sarah. Miriam scowled and examined Sarah's feet. Fading into nothingness, she journeyed into the spirit world.

Sarah used Miriam's absence to slide out of her nightgown and into her new outfit. She looked herself over with approval: the clothes were surprisingly stylish for maternity jeans, a white blouse and a loose, navy-blue sweater. Several minutes later Miriam reappeared with a pair of red shoes.

"Sit," Miriam ordered Sarah.

"What are you doing?" inquired Sarah as she plopped onto the bed.

"Putting on your shoes," Miriam stated flatly. She grabbed one of Sarah's ankles and abruptly lifted it. The nun almost toppled over but managed to catch herself.

"You know what I mean," said Sarah. Miriam unlaced the first shoe.

"I'm getting you out of here," Miriam said while slipping on the shoe. She began tying the laces.

"And exactly why are you doing that?" asked Sarah. Miriam finished tying the laces and picked up the second shoe. She looked to Sarah.

"Because I'm going to find Jake, and, when I do, we're going to go as far away from this fuck- . . . *this place*, as we can," Miriam answered sharply. She untied the laces of the second shoe and slid it onto Sarah's other foot, saying, "But he won't go with me if he knows his brat . . . *his kid* . . . is still here. So we're all going on a permanent family vacation."

"And what of his other child?" asked Sarah as, uncertain of the extent of Miriam's knowledge, she decided to test it. The reformed demon did not immediately respond as she finished affixing the shoe to Sarah's foot.

"I can't sense any other Gottschalk blood in the city," Miriam said with a grim, knowing expression. Sarah bowed her head and sat before her in silence. Unwilling to wait any longer, Miriam lifted Sarah's chin with a single finger.

"Jacob lied to you," confessed Sarah. Miriam squeezed her foot and, as if the pressure forced the words from the nun's mouth, she expounded, "He lied to you to defuse your anger and protect me. Though Elizabeth was brain dead, her body endured and the baby was still alive."

"*Was* still alive?" Miriam inquired curtly.

"The reason you cannot sense Elizabeth's child is . . . is . . . she and her unborn child were murdered shortly after your . . . *departure*," said Sarah sadly.

"I didn't murder the baby," Miriam objected.

"I know," Sarah replied as she pulled her foot from Miriam's uncomfortable grasp, "but Darby believes you did. And she believes you killed Elizabeth and Tara as well."

Miriam offered Sarah, who appeared on the verge of tears, a horrid glower. The accusations angered and confused her.

"Spill it," Miriam demanded with her demonic voice bleeding into her human one. Sarah exhaled with a shudder.

"Someone stabbed Tara and Elizabeth to death with a knife at the hospital," explained a nauseated Sarah. She became woozy and began to cry, continuing with difficulty, "Elizabeth's body was . . . was mutilated . . . and the baby . . . *the poor baby* . . . was cut from Elizabeth's womb and smashed on the floor."

Sarah wept. Miriam pondered. Time passed.

"It was all so terrible," gushed Sarah after composing herself. Sniffling and wiping her eyes, she said, "The evil scourge of the demonic world destroyed a family . . . a grandmother, a mother and three children."

"It's unfortunate," Miriam said without emotion, "but it makes my situation less complicated."

"*Miriam*," scolded Sarah. Miriam's callous words blunted her grief.

"If there's anything you want to take with you, get it *quickly*," Miriam advised her without another thought about the Nicks family. She gradually turned the door handle until her demonic strength twisted it free. Easing it partway from the door, Miriam warned, "Because I'm about to ring the alarm."

· · · ·

THE HALLWAY GUARD DUTIFULLY came to inspect the clanging sound of door hardware hitting the floor. When he arrived at Sarah's room, he pushed it open and ducked his head inside.

"Sister Sarah?" he called out. He extended his neck too far and his mistake allowed Miriam to grab him by it with one hand. Dragging him into the room, she effortlessly picked him up and slammed him onto Sarah's bed. The sudden attack knocked the breath from his lungs.

"Just kill him," said a voice from within Miriam, a cruel voice that was once her own. The guard struggled and attempted to shout but all that came from his efforts was a weak gurgle. Recovering his breath, he managed to slap her face and knock off her glasses. They clattered as they struck the floor.

Unharmed but enraged by his attack, Miriam repositioned herself by grasping both of his wrists, pinning him to the bed and pressing her right knee into his throat.

"Stop moving," demanded Miriam in her demonic voice. The guard continued to squirm despite the futility of his resistance so she lifted her knee into his chin and warned, "I swear, I'll shove your jaw right into your fucking brain."

The bathroom door opened. Miriam's head snapped around and she stopped Sarah with an evil glare.

"God help you! Miriam!" Sarah exclaimed when she noticed the guard's precarious position. The mention of God gradually defused Miriam's vitriol and she lowered her knee to his chest. Balling her right hand, she punched him across the face and knocked him unconscious.

"I told you to stay in there," snarled Miriam in her human voice.

"It's a good thing I did not," Sarah countered. Miriam slithered off the guard and stood before her. She pressed her palm into Sarah's mouth.

"*Be quiet*," whispered Miriam. Drawing herself out of the emotional state that accompanied her killing frenzies, she lowered her hand and said, "Now let's go."

Sarah looked to the guard with pity in her eyes. She exhaled in relief when she saw his chest rise and fall and offered Miriam the smile of a proud mother.

"You've learned to control your evil impulses, at least somewhat," Sarah lauded her. She gently grasped Miriam by the cheeks and placed a kiss on her forehead. The affection, to Miriam's great surprise, did not sear her skin. She pulled away from Sarah nonetheless.

"I said let's go," grumbled Miriam. Sarah retrieved a small brown bag from the bathroom while Miriam used the blanket to bind the guard in a cocoon of cotton. She tied the pillowcase around his head to muzzle him.

"Is that necessary?" Sarah asked as Miriam threw the guard over her shoulder. She ignored Sarah while stashing him in the bathtub, closing the shower curtain and shutting the door. Miriam then plucked her glasses from the floor and slid them onto her face.

"Act like a patient," said Miriam. Taking Sarah by the arm, she led her into the hallway, shut the room door and then adjusted her coat. She also turned the doctor's identification badge so the picture could not be seen. The pair strolled down the hallway without incident, Miriam hiding her claws and lowering her gaze each time they passed someone. They stopped upon reaching a bank of elevators and Miriam pushed the "Down" button.

"Are we just going to walk out the front entrance?" Sarah asked skeptically as they waited for the elevator.

"Yes," answered Miriam. A "ding" alerted them to the elevator's arrival. The doors slid open and Miriam, turning to Sarah, said, "I bet no one knows who the hell you are except for a few guards and nurses, and maybe a doctor."

"That's correct," conceded Sarah. She and Miriam boarded the elevator in silence. Seconds later, the doors closed and they began their descent. Sarah looked to Miriam and asked, "And, after the lobby, where do we go?"

Miriam withdrew inside herself and did not answer.

3

"WHAT THE FUCK IS THAT!?" Darby Nicks bellowed as she threw open the bulletproof glass doors and marched to the edge of the balcony. The whistling of artillery shells hurtling earthward followed by thunderous explosions emanated from the southern slums. Sirens blared, streams of smoke curled into the sky and fires sprung up amongst them. Darby drained the glass of whiskey in her hand and threw it off the balcony, grumbling, "They get closer to the fucking wall every day."

Darby rued her role as Acting Constable and the demands it placed on her. Perhaps, had Elizabeth's former Chief of Staff, Sören Walter, survived, she could have handled it with his aid. She clenched her hands into fists and said to herself, "But that German fuck's dead. Thanks, *Mom*."

Stomping back into the office which once belonged to her sister, Darby threw a pointed finger in the direction of the doors. She shook with rage and her light-blue eyes blazed with intensity.

"*This*," said Darby with a horrid scowl. She slammed the doors shut and continued her tirade, barking, "This fucking bullshit. My scheming bitch of a mother and Liz could deal with it. Hell, they *liked* dealing with it. But not me. See, I can stamp out these little fires but *they* could stop them from starting. I'm not a fucking administrator or negotiator or whatever the fuck."

Darby walked towards her desk. Seeing her muscled, five-foot-eleven-inch frame in a wall mirror, she appraised what she had become since the destruction of her family. Her long, light-brown tresses were now short, blonde and set in a wispy style that she hated for its disgusting cuteness. She was unwilling to do more than don a leather jacket despite being Constable and was normally seen in blue jeans and tank tops. Her sleeveless shirts revealed that the tattoos of the hideous, screaming gargoyles on her shoulders now extended to her wrists, her body art displaying the twisted, demonic stuff of her dreams.

"And my reality," Darby thought.

"What are you then, Ms. Nicks?" queried a deep, composed voice, the words wresting Darby from her reverie. She gazed at its owner.

"An enforcer," Darby replied. Becoming acutely aware of the fifty-caliber pistol holstered on her hip, she uttered without emotion, "A killer."

"Are you certain you wish to leave the City?" asked the man known simply as Niu. He sat in a chair in the sitting area of Darby's office and drank black coffee. Flanked by two suit-clad bodyguards, he said, "Your skills are known far from this city and I am well aware of your reputation. You could serve me in much the same role as you served the Constable and I will guarantee you substantial freedom in conducting your duties."

"I'm done serving," Darby growled with a glare.

"Fair enough," said Niu. He defied the stereotypes of small Chinese men, the portly man standing nearly as tall as Darby and weighing over three hundred pounds. He possessed great strength, even given his size, and was well-named as his moniker meant "ox" in Chinese.

Mentally, however, he was no ox.

"Moving, then, to the matter at hand . . . you're offering me this City and all its vast resources for, as they used to say here, pennies on the dollar," began Niu. His black Van Dyke was thin and meticulously trimmed and he occasionally tapped his beard with his finger as he spoke. He sipped his coffee and reasoned, "The price is suspiciously low even given the rebel groups operating in the area. That begs the question: What else?"

Retrieving a second glass from her desk, Darby poured more whiskey into it from a crystal decanter. She set the glass down, swigged from the decanter and then let it fall to her side.

"Do you believe in demons, Mr. Niu?" Darby inquired, her fey mood troubling his bodyguards. She plopped down in her chair and threw her feet up on her desk.

"My people have many rich traditions involving the spiritual world dating back thousands of years," answered an undaunted Niu, "but I do not subscribe to them."

Darby laughed a long, disturbing laugh. Niu gave her a dubious look and set his coffee cup in its saucer.

"I mean it," Darby said as her mirth faded, "I'm talking actual, real-as-fuck demons."

Niu, though he could not see his bodyguards' faces, sensed their growing disquiet. He studied Darby's countenance.

"Out," ordered Niu suddenly with a nod towards the main office doors. His bodyguards obeyed, albeit slowly, and soon exited the room. The doors, constructed of tinted bulletproof glass that allowed Niu to see his underlings outside, were then closed.

"So, tell me about your demons," requested Niu. He freshened his coffee and sipped from his cup again.

"My demons," Darby said while staring into the decanter. She soon took another drink from it and explained, "Well, there are two ways we can do this."

Darby paused for Niu's reaction. He made her wait for twenty seconds.

"Go on," said Niu.

"You see, I can tell you about my demons," Darby said, her bizarre mood deepening, "which is really fucking boring, or I can show you my demons, which is dangerous as fuck but so much more fun."

Niu smiled. Darby was not a kindred spirit but in some strange way he identified with her. Setting down his coffee and standing up, he motioned towards the door.

"Then by all means," replied Niu. Darby belched and rose to her feet.

"I was hoping you'd say that," Darby said.

• • • •

DARBY SPED THROUGH the streets of Kaiser with her usual recklessness and flashing red light affixed to the roof of her car. Nui sat next to her and two of his bodyguards sat in the backseat. Four more bodyguards traveled in the escort car that tailed Darby with difficulty.

"Do you always travel without your own security retinue?" asked Niu. Though his bodyguards struggled to stay stationary through the screeching turns and abrupt changes in speed, Niu's girth kept him centered and in his seat.

"They slow me down," Darby answered while gazing into the rearview mirror. It pleased her that the escort car became entangled in traffic and fell far behind. She added sharply, "And I hate being slowed down."

An intersection approached where a street entered the main road from Darby's left but did not continue to her right. A white van pulled into the intersection and appeared to stall.

"Shit," Darby griped. Pushing the accelerator to the floor, she warned, "Hold on, assholes."

"What're you doing?!" demanded Niu while quickly engaging his seatbelt. One of the bodyguards protested Darby's actions in Chinese.

"Eat it, fuckers," said Darby as she rammed her sedan into the van. The impact flipped it over and it rolled several times, the vehicle finally landing on its roof. Darby again accelerated and pushed the van farther down the road before shifting into reverse and, turning to look out the back window, sped away from it.

"Please get your guns out, boys," Darby requested in a tone of feigned politeness. The white van exploded and the resultant debris peppered the sedan. Darby clicked on her windshield wipers.

Gunfire erupted from the storefronts to the right, the assault prompting Darby to stop the vehicle with its rear end pointing towards the attackers. Niu ducked down as best he could given his rotundity and his bodyguards returned fire through the shattered back window.

The escort car entered the fray, its driver turning it perpendicular to the assault. All four bodyguards immediately exited the vehicle and opened fire on the assailants. A bullet struck one of them in the leg and he tumbled to the ground. His comrades pulled him to safety behind the shield of the car.

Darby exited the sedan and stood facing the opposite direction of the gunfire. Acquiring a second van careening towards them from the side street, she calmly drew her pistol and fired two shots. The first shattered the windshield while the second blew out the front passenger-side tire. The vehicle swerved to the right, hit a streetlight pole and exploded.

Ignoring the gunfire behind her, Darby approached the burning van. She watched the dancing flames as if hypnotized and felt the heat of the fire pressing against her body.

Sirens behind her drew her attention and she saw Kaiser's internal security force arrive. The officers' submachine guns, in conjunction with Niu's bodyguards, overwhelmed and dispatched the attackers in a matter of minutes.

Walking back to her ruined sedan, Darby watched Niu extract himself from it and brush broken glass and other debris from his suit. The scene swarmed with security officers, some of whom attended to Niu's wounded bodyguard.

"Was that for you or for me?" inquired Niu. The attack raised his ire but he restrained it.

"Do I look like a fucking psychic?" Darby snapped, her mood fouled even further by the assault. She ejected the clip from her pistol and replaced the two bullets she expended. Reinserting the clip and chambering a round, she holstered her pistol and said, "You're the fucking genius. You figure it out."

• • • •

LEAVING THE CLEANUP efforts and investigation to her underlings, Darby procured another vehicle – one of her sister's beloved M1114 Humvees – and shuttled Niu and two of his bodyguards outside the city walls and into the slums. Their comrades remained behind.

"Your demon leaves his gates open," commented Niu as Darby rolled through large metal gates affixed to high stone walls.

"You should've seen this joint when Agatha ran it," Darby said. Driving slowly through the parking lot, she drifted into another time and reminisced, "But it's all gone now . . . the concertina wire, the cement barriers, the kill zones . . . the machine gun nests and the dogs . . . all of it."

"Why is that?" inquired Niu. He knew of Agatha Moriarty, the crime lord who once controlled the slums of Kaiser under Elizabeth's watchful eye. Studying Darby once again, Niu wondered at her odd behavior.

"There aren't many humans who they fear," Darby said cryptically, "and the ones who they do fear don't come here anymore."

The courthouse was massive, the building standing ten stories tall and constructed to overlook the city to the northwest. Built primarily of granite and limestone, limestone blocks composed its façade. The basement and first two stories formed the base of the building while the remaining eight floors formed a separate section. Square windows set in pilasters dotted the base except at the entrances while the upper section contained vertical, rectangular banks of windows.

"Fuck," Darby grumbled as she stopped the vehicle, "not this bitch again."

Three square limestone pillars formed the main entrance behind which there was a recess and granite steps leading up to four sets of double glass doors. An attractive black woman with raven hair styled in a bun and smooth, rounded facial features stood at the top of the stairs. Dressed in the garb of a high-priced attorney, she clasped her hands in front of her stomach.

"Stay here," Darby instructed her passengers as she exited the Humvee. Niu signaled his bodyguards to be on higher alert by raising his hand and snapping his fingers once.

"Greetings, Ms. Nicks," said Adedewe melodiously with her usual inviting smile. Darby slammed her door shut after which the demon asked, "To what do we owe the pleasure of your visit?"

"Fuck this 'we' shit," Darby replied. Marching across the sidewalk and up to the bottom step, she demanded, "I need to see your boss, *now*."

"That is not possible today, I am afraid," said Adedewe. She gracefully descended the steps and asked, "Perhaps I can assist you?"

"*Demons*," said Niu in astonishment as he peered through the windshield and noticed Adedewe's black, spectacled eyes, clawed fingers and serrated teeth. His guards, deeply disturbed by their first taste of the spirit world, glanced at each other.

"Perhaps I should go get the nun and bust some demon heads," Darby threatened. Her mind conjured up a desire for Jacob and his exorcist expertise. The thought vexed her greatly.

"Come now, Ms. Nicks, we both know her condition does not permit that," said Adedewe with a tilt of her head and a dismissive expression. Darby seethed but, resigned to her powerlessness in the matter, composed herself. Adedewe softened her countenance and continued, "But such hostility and violence is not necessary. I assure you, should you share your concern with me, I will make certain that it comes to Aaron's attention promptly."

"Kaiser's changing hands, bitch," Darby announced while folding her arms. Niu stirred in his seat and waited patiently for a resolution. Mustering all the condescension she could, Darby expounded, "So, I thought, hey, I should probably do a little meet and greet with the new owner and Aaron. Ya' know, talk transition because you fucks are gonna be neighbors. But I guess Aaron can figure it out on his own."

Darby turned her back on Adedewe and returned to the Humvee. The demon lowered her eyes and remained still as if listening intently. Darby heard nothing as she opened the vehicle's door.

"My Master will see you now," advised Adedewe pleasantly. A slow smile came to Niu's face. Darby once again slammed her door.

"No shit," Darby grumbled.

• • • •

ADEDEWE WASTED NO TIME in bringing the guests to her Master, the demon guiding them through a dim, cold stairwell and up many flights of stairs. Darby kept a close eye on Niu given his corpulence but he showed no signs of slowing. His footfalls remained heavy and strong throughout the entire journey.

"Big Phat Phuck's in pretty good shape," Darby said to herself. She, like Niu, was cognizant that the haunting route upon which Adedewe led them was a psychological tactic. Despite that fact, she asked, "What, is the fucking elevator broken?"

"This is the most direct way to Aaron," answered Adedewe while leading the group farther upward and letting her hand elegantly slide along the handrails. She added with a hint of hauteur, "At least for your kind."

"Fucking cunt," Darby muttered, her slight ignored by Adedewe. She felt the demonic presences swirling around them and it irked her. Darby took several swigs of whiskey from her flask during the ascent, each pull garnering disapproving looks from Niu's bodyguards. Niu himself paid her drinking little attention and remained mute.

"Chemical agents causing psychosis," thought Niu. The inadequate lighting often flickered and the whispers of the spirits made noises he attributed to drafts in the stairwell. Unwilling to surrender his disbelief, he lauded his host, "This Aaron is very much advanced in his tactics. I must be cautious."

All four humans felt relief when they emerged onto the roof of the courthouse, its height and position providing a spectacular view of Kaiser. Aaron stood at its northwest edge and gazed out over the City like his Master showing Christ all the kingdoms of the world.

"Darby Nicks, the violent and incorrigible sister of Elizabeth Nicks, former Constable of the City of Kaiser," Aaron announced. Darby squelched the urge to charge Aaron and throw him from the roof. Sensing her desire, he turned around, grinned haughtily and said, "I understand the new Queen is not enjoying her reign."

The six-foot-five-inch Aaron was the definition of masculinity. He possessed the entire package: a lean, muscular frame; brown, stylishly mussed hair; sharp facial features and prominent cheekbones. Aaron's brown eyes penetrated each soul he looked upon and immediately set about seducing it. A modest growth of neatly manicured stubble covered the lower part of his face.

"Her reign is about to end," Darby replied, her hatred cooling into a grimness that struck even Aaron. Already tiring of the affair, she motioned to Niu and said, "This is Niu and I'm selling the City to him."

Niu stepped forward and greeted Aaron with a deep bow of his head. The demon returned it but quickly looked back to Darby.

"And how does the City feel about that?" inquired Aaron. Niu's bodyguards bristled at the role to which their employer was relegated in the conversation but Niu remained quiet and noncommittal.

"I'm no administrative genius like my sister," Darby said as she folded her arms and put her foot up on an air conditioning unit, "but I can tell you that the city administration is weak. It suffered when my bitch of a mother whacked Sören Walter and, after she and Liz were murdered, most of the senior staff resigned."

"You permitted that?" asked Aaron coyly. Darby sneered at him. She dropped her hands to her sides and clenched her fists.

"By resigned I meant disappeared," admitted Darby, the words bitter on her tongue. Moving the conversation away from the mass defections, she said, "But that may not be the biggest problem. There are at least two higher-ups in the security force that are contemplating separate coups, though they think I'm clueless about it. *Dumbasses.*"

"That doesn't answer my question," interjected Aaron. Darby marched up to him, her crazy eyes awash in blue flames.

"Fuck you, you fucking demon fuck," growled Darby while poking Aaron in the chest. Bested by his own anger, he allowed his demonic traits to bleed out of his human façade. Niu's bodyguards began to draw their weapons but a raised hand from their master stopped them.

"You have no power here, Darby," growled Aaron in his demonic voice. Pushing her pointed finger down, he warned, "I could slaughter you and every human in the City in a matter of hours. *I could take Kaiser for my own.*"

Niu's bodyguards shook with fear but he remained unmoved by the conflict erupting before him. He pointed with two fingers at the other side of the roof and they hurriedly followed his order. Darby suddenly composed herself.

"You could," Darby said with a smirk, "but then you'd have no one to tempt into damnation, and you'd be outta business. Plus the nun's carrying Jake's kid and I'm the one watching out for her. You kill me, and something happens to her, he'll come looking for you, *Aaron.*"

"Gottschalk," thought Niu. He decided at that moment to learn more about the former Constable's ex-husband. Meanwhile, Aaron's demonic appearance faded and his humanness returned. He turned his gaze to Niu.

"My apologies for such a poor welcome," said Aaron with a polite bow. Moving past Darby, he walked to Niu and extended his hand, "As I'm sure you can tell, there is little love lost between Ms. Nicks and I. My name is Aaron."

Darby rolled her eyes and turned to watch the pleasantries. Niu took Aaron's hand in an iron grip.

"Niu," replied the portly Asian. The demon nodded as if he already knew the name.

"It is a pleasure to meet you, Niu," said Aaron. They ended their handshake and he continued, "I am looking forward to our partnership . . . that is, if you wish to continue the status quo. I think you will find it an exquisitely-crafted and symbiotic relationship."

"Ms. Nicks provided the details of your arrangement with her mother and I believe that can serve as a foundation for our negotiations," replied Niu.

He surveyed Kaiser and said, "Though I do not anticipate any disruptions. They are bad for business."

"Excellent," Aaron said.

Darby procured her flask. She exhaled dramatically to draw their attention.

"Well, I'll let you two finish jerking each other off," Darby said before emptying her flask. Sauntering past Aaron and Niu, both of whom watched her movement, she stowed the flask and said, "I'll send a car for you, Niu."

Darby brushed Adedewe's shoulder as she passed her but the demon suffered the affront without a reaction. Disappearing into the enclosed stairwell, she slammed the door behind her.

"I am sure you would like to kill her as much as I would, and would agree that it would normally be best to dispose of such a chaotic force," Aaron said while staring at the door, "but, in this unique situation, I think it best to simply let her leave . . . and take the nun and Gottschalk's child with her."

"My thoughts exactly," replied Niu.

4

JACOB WOKE TO FIND himself in a reclining hospital bed raised into a sitting position. The room was dimly lit by a small lamp in the right far corner.

"Where the hell am I?" Jacob asked himself.

His eyes slowly focused on a dark, blurry figure sitting at his bedside. He thought he discerned a ponytail and his mysterious visitor seemed tall despite being seated.

"Damn, woman, you found me all the way up here?" grumbled Jacob. He said with a weak chuckle, "And buried in the fucking snow even. You must really wanna kill me, huh?"

There was a brief silence.

"I merely wish to speak with you," said a woman in a measured yet strong voice and a light accent that betrayed her Russian heritage. She stated without emotion, "I am not here to kill you."

Jacob's "fight-or-flight" reflex triggered and he attempted to jump from the bed. He quickly realized his ankles and wrists were strapped into restraints.

"Who the fuck are you?" Jacob asked as he futilely fought against the restraints, his movements revealing the soreness in his muscles. His vision gradually improved and he determined the woman was not Darby.

"I believe the more important question is who did you think I was?" said the woman. Realizing the hopelessness of his predicament, Jacob ceased struggling and let his steadily improving eyes size up his captor.

Straightlaced and tall, the woman walked the line between slender and gaunt with surprisingly large breasts for one of her thinness. She was wrapped tightly in a blue skirt suit with a hem that brushed her shins and an impossibly white blouse.

"The crazy bitch that is my sister-in-law," Jacob answered while suspiciously examining the woman. He thoughts turned to Elizabeth and he muttered, "*Was* my sister-in-law."

The woman lifted her chin as if she read more into Jacob's words than he intended them to convey. She had but one prominent feature above the neck: a pointed, witch-like nose. Everything else was subdued, from the light freckles that dotted her face (as Jacob would later discover, they sometimes faded into the paleness of her skin); to her dull, auburn hair that struggled to retain its reddish tinge and was pulled into a tight ponytail; to her weak green eyes that bordered on a light gray when sitting behind her black glasses. The first traces of age lines appeared on her angular face, their presence causing Jacob to believe, correctly, that she was in her middle forties.

"You are safe here, at least for the time being," advised the woman matter-of-factly. She slid her chair back, scraping its legs against the floor, and warned, "However, that will depend in no small part on your intentions and your honesty."

The woman stood up and whirled around. Clasping her hands behind her back, she walked away from the bed.

"So this is the part where you try to figure out who the fuck I am and why the fuck I showed up in the cold, snowy hell you call home," Jacob replied. The failures, losses and deaths of the last year of his life flooded his mind and he found himself caring nothing for the future. He relaxed his tense muscles and expounded, "Well, let me save you the time and a whole lotta grief. I'm nothing... not worth the effort you're putting into me. If you're smart – and I think you are – you'll let me the fuck outta here and send me on my way as fast as you can."

"Let us not be so hasty," replied the woman. She turned around to face Jacob and stated, "As a preliminary issue, your language is horribly profane and I would ask that you refrain from such vulgarity while you are here."

"Eat a bag of shit and die, fucking cunt," Jacob replied. He closed his eyes. The woman did not react to his verbal assault.

"I would prefer you call me Dr. Zhukova," said the woman. She approached the bed and placed her hand on the wooden footboard, inquiring, "And what may I call you?"

"A dead man," Jacob said. Withdrawing into himself for a moment, he paused and then added softly, "Or at least I should be."

Dr. Zhukova said nothing. After lingering at the foot of the bed for a few more seconds, she moved back to the chair and sat down. Jacob thought more acutely of Sophie and his mood darkened.

"Were there any other... survivors?" he asked.

"What would you say if I removed your restraints?" asked the Doctor while evading his question. Jacob opened his eyes and looked at her with amusement.

"I'd say you're fucking crazy," Jacob answered. He feigned a lunge at Dr. Zhukova, though she did not react, and said, "You have no idea who the hell I am or what I could do to you, *Doc.*"

"So then you would agree that the restraints are a reasonable precaution for someone in my position," said Dr. Zhukova, "especially given that I do not know 'who the hell' you are?"

Jacob stared at Dr. Zhukova and felt his blood begin to boil. His anger, however, was short-lived and his sneer melted into a smirk. He laughed.

"Okay, Doc, you got me," Jacob said with a sigh. Consequences be damned, he confessed, "The name's Jacob Gottschalk."

"May I ask from where you hail, Mr. Gottschalk?" queried Dr. Zhukova. Jacob rolled his eyes.

"I only ask you these questions to determine who you are. I would like to remove your restraints as we seek to be hospitable hosts to those visitors who mean us no harm," explained Dr. Zhukova, "but perhaps you would be more comfortable if we continued our *quid pro quo*. I shall first, therefore, tell you more about myself."

"Knock yourself out, Doc," Jacob replied. He closed his eyes again and settled into his bed as if to sleep. Dr. Zhukova offered him a muted, knowing smile and, untroubled by his sardonic attitude, sat up straight.

"I am the chief elder of the Christian religious community in whose territory you now find yourself," said Dr. Zhukova, her proper posture and primness making sense in light of her revelation.

"Oh, that's fucking fantastic," Jacob said, the sudden reappearance of religion a most unwelcome development. Dr. Zhukova absorbed his sarcasm without reaction.

"I take it that you disapprove of the Christian faith," said Dr. Zhukova, "or perhaps you have had negative experiences with religion in the past. However, we are-,"

"I'm not joining any cult," interjected Jacob, his use of the word "cult" causing a brief flash of anger in Dr. Zhukova's eyes. She quickly extinguished it and became stone-faced.

"Membership, while always encouraged for those who are deserving, is never required for those who genuinely need our assistance, Mr. Gottschalk," stated Dr. Zhukova with a weak smile.

Jacob paused to examine the Doctor and detected nothing but sincerity. His face became grave as his self-preservation instinct returned.

"So, what denomination is your little Church?" Jacob inquired. He decided to stall.

"Let's not ruin the surprise," said Dr. Zhukova, her tone almost playful. Jacob's puzzled expression amused her and she stated, "Everything will be explained to your satisfaction when you meet with the Community Council, I assure you."

"And when will that be?" Jacob asked. Dr. Zhukova's smile widened and became one of satisfaction.

"As soon as you are able," answered Dr. Zhukova. She stood up, straightened her suit jacket and said, "Given that you are now conscious, and assuming you continue to regain your strength, you will be able to travel to the Community tomorrow or the day after tomorrow."

"I feel fine, Doc," Jacob said. He struggled against his restraints again and demanded, "*Let's do it right now.*"

"It is late. Your restraints will be removed tomorrow, if you act like a respectful guest," replied Dr. Zhukova firmly. Abruptly standing up, she turned from him and walked to the door.

"Tomorrow?!" Jacob objected. Dr. Zhukova grasped the handle of the door and paused. She did not turn to face him.

"If there were any others at the station with you, Mr. Gottschalk," replied Dr. Zhukova grimly, "I can only say I hope they are with the Lord now."

Dr. Zhukova swiftly exited the room and closed the door. Tears welled in Jacob's eyes.

"*Fuck,*" he muttered angrily.

. . . .

JACOB AWOKE OUT OF a nightmare which immediately faded from his memory. Covered in sweat, he squirmed uncomfortably in the bed and was reminded of his restraints.

The door to his room stood ajar and allowed an intense sliver of light to slice into the darkness. He heard hushed voices outside though they argued in a language with which he was not familiar.

"Anya, nem!" exclaimed one of the voices.

"Csendes!" Dr. Zhukova scolded. The voices fell silent briefly but then resumed. All that Jacob could discern was that Dr. Zhukova admonished a younger female subordinate. Unable to understand the source of their disagreement, Jacob could not keep his eyes open and fell asleep.

The opening of the door awoke him several hours later. His stomach churned with hunger, his mouth was dry and his bladder was full.

"Mr. Gottschalk?" called out a sweet voice as the door was slowly opened wider. It belonged to whoever argued with Dr. Zhukova in the night. She turned on the lamp.

A large pair of the sharpest, bluest eyes Jacob had ever seen acquired him and, for a moment, they were all he saw. Their owner gradually came into view, a beautiful woman approaching with swaying hips. The raven-haired angel smiled, albeit nervously, and said, "Good morning. I am Boyka. Welcome to Station Genesis."

Perfection in human form, she possessed five-feet-six-inches of a slender-yet-curvaceous figure with flawless, glowing skin, healthy tresses that fell past her shoulders and full, pink lips. Boyka dressed similarly to Dr. Zhukova save for the Doctor's suit jacket. Undeterred by Jacob's licentious attention – or perhaps unaware of it – the exotic beauty extended her hand.

"I am pleased to meet you," said Boyka.

"This is a little obvious, don't ya' think?" Jacob said. Despite his realization that the young woman was bait, he could not deny that she thoroughly aroused and instantly attracted him. Jacob called out as if speaking to an unseen person in the hallway, "Well played, Doctor. *Well played.*"

"I, I do not understand, Mr. Gottschalk," said Boyka as she offered him a puzzled expression and her gaze alternated between Jacob and the door. She withdrew her hand.

"Where's that accent from?" Jacob asked.

"I am Hungarian," answered Boyka with pride as she straightened into a statuesque pose and her eyes glittered.

"I didn't realize they were making girls like you over there," Jacob remarked with a dubious smirk. The Hungarian princess failed to take his meaning and, for several seconds, stared at him blankly.

"Dr. Zhukova wishes you to meet with the Community Council soon, Mr. Gottschalk," advised Boyka as she shook off her confusion and gestured to an unknown location, saying, "so, if you please, Charles and I are here to escort you to the Community."

"Charles?" Jacob asked with raised eyebrows and a fading smile.

"Hello, Mr. Gottschalk," said a twenty-something man who resembled a movie star playing a secret service agent: trim-figured, clad in a crisp suit and brimming with good looks. His hair was manageably-wild and his stubble dark.

"Well hello, Charlie," Jacob said. Boyka's Stepford Wives vibe emanated from her male counterpart as well, their quirkiness enough to tick up his alert level. He thought, "Attractive, submissive and polite. That's an odd combination, especially in the young."

"Please release Mr. Gottschalk, Charles," requested Boyka as she motioned to the restraints. The pair let their gazes linger on each other for a second and then Charles dutifully obeyed. He first freed Jacob's arms.

"What a story a second can tell," Jacob said to himself while rubbing his sore wrists. An image of Dr. Zhukova appeared in his mind and he thought, "Inserting me into a love triangle right off the bat. Now what purpose does that serve, my bony little Russian?"

• • • •

JACOB DISCOVERED HIS prison was a long brick building with central hallways running from end-to-end. It resembled a two-story version of the observation station that he occupied with Sophie though it lacked a tower and its function appeared to be the guarding of the road.

Boyka disappeared before Charles loosed the restraints on Jacob's ankles and, with the young man lurking nearby, he was permitted to shower and given new clothes appropriate for the subarctic climate. He was then taken to a small dining room with one long table in its center. He and Charles spoke very little and there was clearly a tension between the two men.

"Little soon to be chasing tail, don't ya' think?" Jacob scolded himself as his grief over Sophie crept into his heart. A corner of his mind, however, took solace in the convenient appearance of another young woman on whom to rest his affections. He thought, "God I'm a scumbag."

"Please, have a seat, Mr. Gottschalk," requested Charles as he motioned to the table. Jacob maneuvered to his left and chose a middle seat while Charles banked to the right and exited into the kitchen. Wonderful smells wafted from it.

"I forgot how hungry I am," Jacob said when his stomach emitted an angry growl. Charles emerged from the kitchen minutes later with a plate of eggs, sausage and wheat pancakes and set it in front of Jacob. He again went into the kitchen and returned with a carafe of coffee and a mug.

"Got coffee, huh?" Jacob said. The drink's abundance in a remote area well after the fall piqued his interest and he pondered the copiousness of the area's foodstuffs. His thoughts were interrupted when Charles, who never responded to his question, sat down across from him. The two men stared at each other.

"Go get the girl," Jacob said after an awkward minute of silence.

"What?" asked Charles with a quick tilt of his head. His suspicion growing, he said, "Why?"

"Because you've stalked me enough today, Charlie," Jacob replied with a sardonic grin, "and I'd rather stare at her than you."

Charles barely restrained his indignation but, mastering his emotions, rose and left the room. Jacob filled his mug with coffee and appraised his breakfast with satisfaction.

"Where are they getting all this?" Jacob inquired with a shake of his head. Thinking of the cargo plane, he sipped his coffee and began his meal. He chewed a mouthful of food and said through it, "Eh, right now, who the fuck cares?"

"Is something wrong, Mr. Gottschalk?" asked an anxious Boyka as she swept into the dining room.

"Not a thing, sweetheart," Jacob answered. He thought his use of the word "sweetheart" was peculiar but amusing. Gesturing towards the chair across from him, Jacob said, "Please, join me."

"Thank you, Mr. Gottschalk, but I have already eaten," declined Boyka, the Hungarian unnerved by the invitation. Her stunning eyes emitted their usual luminescence nonetheless.

"Then have some coffee," Jacob countered. Boyka fidgeted.

"I have had my morning coffee as well," replied Boyka with a nervous smile and a backward step. Jacob took another drink from his mug and then set it down.

"Then at least keep me company while I eat," Jacob said while motioning to the chair a second time. He surprised himself with his aggressive pursuit of Boyka given his lack of confidence with women in the past.

"There is much to do before our departure," pleaded Boyka, her body squirming anxiously yet sensually. Jacob held her with his gaze and she lingered. He decided on a different strategy.

"Fine, then get fuck out," Jacob said with mock incredulity. He turned back to his food and resumed his meal.

"Mr. Gottschalk, I-," began an apologetic Boyka.

"Get out!" Jacob demanded. Boyka hesitated with watery eyes. Uncertain of what to do, she bowed her head and swiftly scurried from the dining room. Jacob instantly felt remorse and doubted his new uncaring attitude, thinking, "What the hell is happening to me?"

He ate the rest of his meal in solitary silence.

· · · ·

"FUCK IT'S COLD OUT here," Jacob griped as he and Boyka stepped onto the wide porch of Station Genesis. Darkness reigned outside the range of the station's floodlights, the spring sun still hiding beneath the horizon. The steady wind caught his breath and whisked it away and the hair in his nostrils froze.

"You will adapt to the cold," said Bokya with an encouraging smile. Despite Jacob's poor treatment of her at breakfast, she remained positive and helpful but still unsettled in his presence.

"Yeah, we'll see about that," Jacob muttered though the only part of his body that was cold was his face. Boyka provided him with the same state-of-the-art cold-weather gear that she and Charles wore. Jacob wondered about the source of the equipment and thought, "This little cult's outfitted pretty well post-apocalypse. I wonder if that ex-wife of mine was profiting from it."

Glancing up, he saw Charles sitting at the wheel of a Ford E-Series Van modified with two rear wheels on each side. Everything about the van seemed larger than normal.

"Holy shit," Jacob said as he walked around it with Boyka dangling at his tail. Running his gloved hand along its side, he asked, "Where the hell did you get this?"

"My people were here long before the fall," said Boyka in an eerie tone, "and we were ready."

Jacob completed his circuit around the van, making sure to shoot Charles a sharp glance, and then began a second. When he reached the passenger side door a second time, he saw Boyka pull a long, black leather strap over her head. It was connected to an insulated holster designed for a semi-automatic handgun.

"*You've* got a gun?" Jacob asked with a smirk. A Hungarian-Christian princess with a firearm amused him.

"Yes, I have gun," asked Boyka while forgetting the need for the article "a". She guided Jacob to the rear of the van.

"Can I have gun?" Jacob inquired. Boyka opened the back doors and motioned for him to embark.

"I am sorry, but no," replied Boyka. She was apologetic but clearly unwilling to budge. Shrugging off her denial, Jacob boarded the van and took a seat in the first of two chairs to his left. Boyka smiled at him and closed the doors, the click of the locking mechanism echoing in his head.

The sky turned from black to dark gray in the first hour of the trip. It proved to be an almost spiritual experience as Jacob observed the vast mountainous terrain, boreal forest and constant, light snow showers. The peaceful feeling it engendered made him uncomfortable.

"Calm before the storm," Jacob muttered as he cast his eyes to the northeast and unsuccessfully attempted to peer into his future. It seemed, in an eerie way, as if the two-lane road led away from his past and into an entirely different world.

"Pardon me, Mr. Gottschalk," said Boyka. Jacob turned his attention from the winter scenery to her comely face.

"Eh, never mind, kid," Jacob replied. Intent on plying Boyka for information, he said, "So, tell me about this Church of yours."

"I am very sorry, Mr. Gottschalk, but I am not permitted to speak of it before you have met with the Council," said Boyka slowly as she carefully chose her words. Charles glanced at Jacob via the rear-view mirror.

"And why's that?" Jacob pressed her. His inquiries made Boyka uncomfortable and she squirmed under his gaze. Charles, too, seemed nervous and again glanced in the rearview mirror.

"I cannot say," stated Boyka as she shook her head in the negative and turned away from him. Her palpable distress caused Jacob to abandon his inquiry.

"They've instructed her to keep her mouth shut on pain of some serious punishment. That's Religious Cult 101," he thought. The next hour of the journey became one of the rising sun, uncomfortable silence and occasional small talk. Charles remained stonily silent.

The hours gradually melted away until the road ascended to a mountain pass, leveled out for a mile and then descended again. Jacob straightened up.

"What the hell is that?" he asked. Two towers arose out of the swirling snowflakes before them, towers that supported a suspension bridge traversing a narrow river valley. Boyka's anxiousness became fear as they approached it and that fear radiated from her. Unbuckling her seatbelt, she moved toward the back of the van.

"Boyka!" snapped Charles as he grabbed her arm. She flailed against him and broke his grasp to which he responded, "Come back here! You're being ridiculous."

"Hey, why don't you pay attention to the fucking road?" growled Jacob. They shared a quick glower before Charles did just that. Boyka ignored the spat and seated herself in the chair next to Jacob as he asked her, "How the hell is a bridge like that still intact in a place like this?"

Boyka did not answer his query but instead grabbed his hand. The road leveled out again as it approached the bridge and Charles stopped the van before reaching it. He cleared his throat.

"I will open the gate," he stated gruffly. Looking through the windshield, Jacob noticed an iron-barred gate blocking access to the bridge. Boyka shuddered when Charles added, "Be ready."

"Ready for what?" Jacob asked while feeling the sweatiness of Boyka's palm. Charles exited the van and slammed the door.

"It is very scary to me," replied Boyka. She lowered her eyes to the floor and scooted closer to Jacob. Squeezing his arm, Boyka added ominously, "It moves."

Jacob looked to the bridge. A stiff wind blew through the valley and it did indeed cause a perceptible sway.

"It is moving now," whispered Boyka as she cuddled into his body. Jacob wrapped his arm around her shoulder to comfort her but he, too, felt an uneasiness.

"Something's not right," Jacob thought, ". . . but what?"

• • • •

JACOB HELD A TREMBLING Boyka in his arms for several minutes. During that time, Charles opened the gate, drove the van onto the bridge and then closed it. Boyka began trembling uncontrollably when Charles returned to the vehicle.

"C'mon, Boyka," Jacob implored her. The van coasted forward and easily cut a path through the mounting snow. Boyka refused to look at Jacob, prompting him to encourage her, "I can't even feel any movement. And before you know it, we'll be across."

The van eased to a halt with its engine rumbling. Charles shifted the vehicle into park, exited via the driver side door and then quietly closed it. Jacob raised his head.

"Why are we stopping in the middle of the fucking bridge?" he asked. Boyka shuddered yet again and her grip on Jacob tightened. He attempted to ease himself out of her grasp but she resisted. Jacob urged her, "Hey, *let go.*"

The rear doors of the van opened. Charles appeared with a semiautomatic pistol in his hand, the young man framed by a winter scene of intensifying snow and howling wind. He aimed the gun at Jacob and gestured for him to exit the van.

"Come with me, Mr. Gottschalk," he instructed Jacob firmly. He avoided eye contact with Boyka and said, "May God forgive me but you cannot be allowed to enter the Community."

"Must we do this?" whimpered Boyka. Using only his eyes, Jacob glanced down at her.

"Yes, Boyka, we must," Charles rebuked her. His hot breath steamed into the frozen air as he explained, "It's for the good of the Community. You know this. Now move away from him."

Boyka reluctantly stood up but, instead of moving out of the line of fire, she kept herself between Charles and Jacob. She battled tears and drew her gun.

"No," refused Boyka flatly. The firearm shook in her hand but she could not bring herself to raise it. She mewled, "It is sin!"

"It's okay, kid," Jacob assured her as she glanced at him over her shoulder, "I'm sure God'll forgive ya' one murder, and I'm ready to get the fuck off this shithole planet anyway."

Jacob's morbid reasoning sent tears streaming down Boyka's twitching face. He understood the play. Someone inside the Community did not want him there but needed a plausible, non-homicidal cause of death.

"Move, Boyka!" demanded Charles. He became increasingly agitated as Boyka's doubt delayed his plan and his gun, though meant for Jacob, was aimed at her.

"All right, Charlie, take it easy," said Jacob, his adrenaline pumping through his veins. His plan formulated, he rose from his seat, locked his gaze on Charles and stated pointedly, "I didn't peg Dr. Zhukova as a murderer, or you either for that matter, but I guess you gotta follow the Doctor's orders."

Charles's puzzlement over Jacob's words gave him the answer he wanted and the distraction he needed. Grabbing Boyka and using her as a human shield, he charged towards Charles. The young man hesitated, unwilling to shoot his beloved. Jacob launched himself from the van and hurled himself and Boyka onto Charles.

"Fuck you, Charlie!" a crazed Jacob bellowed. The crash of bodies sent all three combatants sprawling in the snow. The back of Charles's skull smacked into the ice of a worn tire track while Boyka tumbled into the retaining wall.

The initial impact knocked the breath from her lungs and she gasped for air but she managed to retain her grip on her gun.

Jacob recovered first, shook the snow from his body and scooped up Charles's firearm. Despite his precarious situation, the cold air and his adrenaline seemed to give him supernatural clarity.

"I don't feel any fear," Jacob said aloud. He walked towards Charles and stated, "This must be how Miriam felt."

The pace of the snow slackened briefly. Jacob looked down to Charles whose head lay in a growing pool of blood, its dark redness contrasting starkly with the whiteness of the snow.

"Sorry, Charlie, but you're not gonna make it," Jacob said. Though he had no intention of ending Charles's life, he pointed the pistol at his face and added, "Not with that crack in your skull."

"Stop! Stop!" shouted Boyka. Jacob glanced at her, the young woman struggling to lift herself into a crouching position despite the pain that wracked her body. Breathing heavily, she pointed her gun at Jacob. Her black hair absorbed many of the swirling snowflakes and fluttered in the wind like a multitude of flailing arms. She yelled again, though with less gusto, "Don't kill him!"

Jacob steadfastly stood against the wind. He wondered at his continued lack of emotion and fear in the face of the firearm aimed at his head. Tossing his gun onto Charles's chest, he walked towards Boyka with slow steps.

"Whatever you say, sweetheart," Jacob replied dryly. Despite the threat of death, the tense situation became a game to him. He nodded over his shoulder and said, "But unless you've got some surgical equipment and spare blood hidden somewhere in the van, Charlie's done for no matter what the fuck I do."

Boyka looked at Charles as he lay lifeless in the snow. She sobbed.

"So if this is gonna work, you've got to be the one to pull the trigger, I'm afraid," Jacob advised Boyka. He stopped three feet from her and patted his chest, taunting her, "Right here. Center mass. Do it."

Boyka faltered. She never approved of the plot to dispose of Jacob and certainly never intended to become his murderer.

"Throw him off the bridge," ordered Boyka as she holstered her weapon. She wiped away tears and occasionally winced as she moved.

"Don't you want to take the body back?" Jacob inquired. She rose up and brushed past him as he said, "Maybe come clean on this little fifth column thing you've got going? They might go easy on you if you do."

"No," replied Boyka curtly. The storm released another wave of fury with strong gusts of wind and thousands of larger snowflakes. Boyka surveyed it grimly.

"Why not?" Jacob asked.

"Throw him off the bridge!" pleaded Boyka with panic in her voice. She hurriedly collected Charles's firearm and hurled it from the bridge. Rummaging around in one of several containers in the van, she soon found that for which she searched and directed Jacob, "Wrap him in this."

Boyka thrust a thick blanket at Jacob. He reluctantly took it.

"He is dead?" asked Boyka. Jacob checked Charles's breathing and pulse.

"Yeah, he is dead," Jacob advised her using a mock Hungarian accent.

"Please, you must do it now," begged Boyka. Jacob took the blanket and wrapped Charles' body while taking great pains to avoid the blood oozing from his head. Boyka provided him with cords and he used them to tightly tie the blanket to the corpse.

"Okie dokie," Jacob muttered. Using the last of his adrenaline surge, he slung Charles over his shoulder. Jacob trudged through the snow, across the oncoming traffic lane and to the edge of the bridge. He laid Charles's slumping body on the wall and turned to take Boyka's temperature on the matter one last time.

"Please!" squeaked Boyka with a wave of her hand. Bursting into another crying fit, she scurried to the van and jumped into the driver's seat. Jacob shrugged.

"Happy landings, *Charles*," Jacob said as he pushed the body forward. It slid over the wall and disappeared into the mists below the bridge. Feeling morally slimy, Jacob made his way to the van and said, "Broads and bodies. Now all I need is booze and it's a normal day in the life of Jacob Gottschalk."

When Jacob climbed into the van's passenger seat, he saw Boyka resting her head on the steering wheel. He slammed the door and she snapped to attention. Jacob peered piercingly into the depths of her bleary eyes.

"Why did I just chuck Chuck off the bridge?" Jacob asked.

"The storm will be bad," warned Boyka. Turning her attention to the road ahead, she shifted the van into drive and said, "It is you and I, Mr. Gottschalk, who must now get off the bridge."

5

JACOB AND BOYKA SPOKE little during the half hour they journeyed east from the bridge. The road eventually cut through a large shoulder of land and it was there that Boyka pulled the van off the road. The high cliffs on either side of it created a small oasis and sheltered the vehicle from the raging storm.

"We're stopping here?" Jacob asked. The last vestiges of daylight bled away.

"I cannot see the road . . . and it is almost dark," replied Boyka, the disquiet evident in her voice as she gripped the steering wheel with both hands. Staring through the windshield at the curtain of white before her, she explained, "This is the best place to stay until the storm ends. I will prepare food now."

Sliding out of her seat, Boyka tried to slip past Jacob without touching or looking at him. He thwarted her attempt by grasping her arm and pulling her to him. Boyka made no effort to escape.

"We need to talk about what happened back there," Jacob demanded. Guiding Boyka back to her seat, he glared at her and said, "I don't want you changing your mind and putting a bullet in my brain while I'm sleeping tonight."

"I could never kill a person," claimed Boyka. The entire affair distressed her greatly and she began to cry. She mewled, "I could never kill you."

"Who wants me dead?" Jacob inquired.

"I do not know," insisted Boyka. Jacob lunged forward, grabbed her by her coat with both hands and shook her.

"Who the fuck is it?!" Jacob barked. Though she struggled against him, he managed to keep Boyka in the driver's seat.

"I do not know!" pleaded Boyka. Her blue eyes dazzled Jacob as she cried, "Charles knew. I do not."

"Well that's convenient because he's dead," Jacob replied as he released Boyka. He slumped into his seat and muttered, "Fucking asshole."

Boyka suddenly propelled herself into Jacob. She kissed him forcefully but with great passion. Jacob resisted her attempt at a longer, sultrier kiss.

"You do not want me?" whimpered Boyka, the young woman clearly surprised by the rejection of an older man. Pawing at him, she asserted, "It is the wish of Dr. Zhukova."

"*It's what*?" Jacob replied. Attempting to derail Boyka's sexuality, he forced her back into the driver's seat and reasoned, "Look, Boyka – and, trust me, I can't believe I'm saying this – we need to set this sex shit aside for now. Charlie said your partners in crime don't want me in the Community so they'll probably try to off me again and-."

"Not if I provide them a reason to keep you alive," interjected Boyka, the Hungarian irked by Jacob's implication that she played a major role in his planned assassination.

"What the hell does that mean?" asked Jacob indignantly.

"I will prepare a place for us," cooed Boyka without answering Jacob's question.

"What the hell does that mean?!" asked Jacob again. Boyka quickly moved to the cargo area of the van and removed her winter overclothing. The vehicle was designed to serve as a refuge for weeks if the subarctic weather required it and she busied herself with constructing their sleeping quarters.

"This girl certainly has a god, and she seems righteous," he prayed silently. Remembering he had not read a single verse of Scripture in over six months, Jacob said, "But I'll ask you this: Am I?"

· · · ·

INHABITING MALLORY'S teenage form, Marcion appeared on the roof of the van and crept forward like a spider. He lowered his head over the windshield to peer inside. Mallory's hair danced wildly in the fierce gale but Marcion paid it no attention.

"What're we doing, *Gottschalk*?" asked the demon, his hatred for Jacob evident in his tone. Jacob did not perceive his material or spiritual presence and wallowed deeply in his contemplations. Marcion sneered, "I should kill you, kill you now and end all of this foolishness."

"If you did, Aaron would send you back to the Master," warned Assarion as she materialized next to him. Her spirit continued to reside within

Vanessa, the young woman's body sitting on the van's roof with her legs folded beneath her.

"Aaron wants Gottschalk out of Kaiser," Marcion argued with a hateful glance. He returned his gaze to Jacob and said, "Dead is the same thing."

"Why do you think your pathetic powers are any match for Jacob Gottschalk? He's defeated you before and exposed you for the useless imbecile you are," replied Assarion. Marcion waved a dismissive hand at her but kept his eyes on Boyka. The Hungarian surveyed the finished sleeping area with approval, clicked on a battery powered heater and then sat down on an air mattress supported by four short, stout columns.

"I am ready for you," beckoned Boyka as she unbuttoned her blouse.

"I am ready for you. I am ready for you," cooed Marcion mockingly as he sensed both humans' heightened sexual desire. He crawled backward on the roof and asked, "How does this loser get so much ass?"

Assarion sat quietly. Marcion's head turned on a swivel and he studied her closely.

"Together. Together we could kill him," Marcion suggested in a hushed tone, "and maybe gain favor with the Master. There are rumors that Aaron's days are numbered and a greater one is coming."

"Perhaps," said Assarion as the gears of her mind quickened. Marcion laughed an evil, hideous laugh.

"I have bad news, Gottschalk!" Marcion exclaimed with wicked delight. Inside the van, Boyka had stripped down to her bra and panties and moved cautiously towards Jacob.

"Be patient, Marcion," advised Assarion in a sugary tone, "and wait for the opportunity to present itself. It will not be long."

• • • •

WHILE BOYKA ATTENDED to their accommodations, Jacob sat facing the driver's seat with his elbows on his knees and his hands clasped in front of him. Thoughts of what lay behind, what lay ahead and the fate of his stepdaughters intermingled in his ponderings and he made little progress on any front.

"I am ready for you," beckoned Boyka. Returning to the present, albeit slowly, Jacob finally turned his head and caught his breath.

"Holy shit," Jacob said. The young woman stood before him in nothing but her underclothes and, despite their modest nature, she was a vision of youth and attractiveness. She moved to him.

"It is time for bed," said Boyka, the kindness and care of her tone tugging at his heartstrings. His sex with Sophie had been frequent yet animalistic and he had not made love to a woman since Sarah.

"Sarah," Jacob said to himself. He remembered the way she once warned him about Miriam and envisioned her providing the same admonishments about Boyka.

"*Mr. Gottschalk*," said Boyka insistently when she noticed Jacob mentally drifting. She placed a reassuring hand on his shoulder but he politely removed it.

"Boyka, we've known each other less than twenty-four hours. During most of that time, you were part of a plot to kill me," Jacob argued with emphatic gestures. Standing up and backing Boyka towards the bed, he continued, "And now you want me to forget about all that and sleep with you because Dr. Z *wants* us to do it. Do you realize how fucked up that is?"

"You make things too complicated," scolded Boyka gently. Reaching behind her, she unhooked her bra and let it drop to the floor. Her flawless breasts froze Jacob's tongue as she said, "I am a woman. You are a man. I want you. Do you not want me?"

Boyka's blunt assessment unwound Jacob's arguments and forced his surrender. He pulled her into him and they engaged in another fervent kiss, Jacob running his hands over her remarkable body. Boyka, meanwhile, removed his outer clothing and began working on his shirt buttons.

"Your skin feels fantastic," Jacob gushed while trailing kisses down her neck. She shivered with excitement as he massaged her breasts, saying, "And you smell even better."

"Dr. Zhukova says you are strong in the Spirit," said Boyka as she sucked on Jacob's ear. His arousal overwhelmed his judgment and he let her assertion pass unchallenged.

"Yeah, sure," Jacob replied as he and Boyka simultaneously kissed and stripped off the remainder of his clothes. Taking a fistful of her cotton panties, he ripped them from her body and cast them away.

"Mr. Gottschalk!" exclaimed an astonished Boyka. Jacob gave her little time to absorb the shock of his aggressiveness; she shuddered and mewled as he entered her. Several hard thrusts later she cried with pleasure, "Mr. Gottschalk!"

"Jake," he said in her ear, "call me Jake."

Their sexual encounter progressed unabated for twenty minutes, Jacob dictating a strong yet loving pace and Boyka capitulating to his physical direction. His failure to use a condom was on his mind but the fantastic sensation of Boyka around him overruled any exercise of caution.

"Just take it easy," Jacob told himself.

"No, no, faster!" begged Boyka when she felt him slow his thrusts. She bit her lip to repress her cries of ecstasy.

Boyka's request refueled Jacob's deviance. He increased the tempo of his penetrations and bounced the Hungarian about like a rag doll, the idea that he could impregnate her heightening the pleasure he experienced.

"Mr. Gottschalk!" yelled Boyka as she bucked wildly and a powerful orgasm rocked her body. Despite her climax, she kept up the torrid pace.

"Slow down, I'm gonna pop," Jacob grunted through heavy breaths as his own orgasm approached. Boyka locked herself onto Jacob.

"Stop!" Jacob protested. His objection was too late, however, and he finished deep inside her. The paramours wrestled each other, Jacob attempting to disengage Boyka from his body and Boyka trying to soak up every last drop of his seed. He yelled, "What the fuck're you doing?!"

Jacob finally gained the upper hand and flipped Boyka onto her back. Pinning her to the bed, he lowered his face to hers.

"Push it out!" he ordered her. Boyka, to his great surprise, slammed her legs into his sides and then wrapped them around his torso. The impact knocked the wind from Jacob and he struggled for air. Boyka eventually released him and he fell to the bed next to her.

"What the fuck did you do that for?" griped Jacob with a grimace. He rubbed his sides.

"I am sorry, but I cannot do as you wish," said Boyka. Kissing him on the cheek, she departed the bed and began dressing. He watched her cover her alluring figure as she stated, "Now, you rest while I prepare our dinner."

"You know how babies are made, right?" Jacob inquired. He attempted to sit up but, due to his aching ribs, he only managed to prop himself up on one elbow. Boyka stopped buzzing about and held her hand to her stomach.

"They will never harm a member of the Community, and they certainly would not harm his father," explained Boyka. She smiled lovingly at Jacob and then continued her work. Jacob laid down.

"What is it with these girls wanting to be knocked up," Jacob thought, "and why the hell do they want *me* to do it?"

The answer to his question did not present itself. Jacob closed his eyes and fell asleep to the pungent smell of canned stew.

• • • •

THE VAN EXCEEDED ITS function as a temporary shelter and possessed the basics for a comfortable stay: heat, light, food, water, even toilet paper. Performing like the quintessential housewife, Boyka prepared their generic yet passable meal and then tidied up afterward. Jacob pried Boyka for information on several topics, including her decision to risk bearing his child, but she deflected on all of them. Instead, she told him of her lonely childhood in Hungary.

"But now, I have a family," said Boyka happily. She gave Jacob a loving kiss, cuddled into him and promptly fell asleep.

"We gotta be more careful," Jacob scolded himself with a glance at his penis. After Boyka flipped over and descended into a deeper sleep, Jacob picked up one of several Bibles stored in the van and flipped through it.

"You and I haven't spoken much, have we?" he said quietly to God. Laying the Bible face up on his chest, he placed his hands behind his head and thought, "I guess sex, violence and profanity will do that. On the bright side, I haven't had a drink in a few days."

Jacob desired a shot of whiskey the second the words fell from his lips. He wondered if he would ever taste it again.

"I don't imagine a bunch of Christian cultists allow booze," Jacob sighed. He closed his eyes and dozed.

Assarion materialized between Jacob and Boyka with her back to the Hungarian and her head supported on her right hand. Observing him through Vanessa's eyes, she let her left forearm lay on the curve of her hip. Neither Jacob nor Boyka stirred.

"I think your instincts are correct, my dear Jake," Assarion whispered in his ear. The mention of his name caused Jacob to adjust his body and drop his hands to his sides. She began turning pages of the Bible and continued, "You need to get your head back into the Book."

Marcion appeared behind the curtain that Boyka hung between the van's passenger compartment and its front seats. He pulled it aside just enough to spy on Assarion with Mallory's good eye though, as a spirit, his perception was not limited by the physical disabilities of his host.

"Second Peter, Chapter Two," whispered Assarion in Jacob's ear. He exhaled as his awareness returned, his sudden wakefulness causing Assarion and then Marcion to disappear. Jacob looked at Boyka and listened to her heavy breathing.

"She's out," he said before yawning. Tilting the Bible upward so he could read it, Jacob stated, "I guess I should start reading this again."

He flipped a page out of habit. The start of the next section captured his attention.

"The Second Letter of Peter," he read aloud. He felt drawn to the epistle and delved into it, swiftly dispensing with the first chapter. He continued reading the second, "'But false prophets also arose among the people . . . .'" (2 Peter 2:1).

The words swept over Jacob and drowned him in a sullen tide. They laid bare the state of his relationship with God.

"' . . . then the Lord knows how to rescue the ungodly from temptation, and to keep the unrighteous under punishment for the day of judgment, and especially those who indulge the flesh in its corrupt desires and despise authority, '" Jacob said. (2 Peter 2:9-10). He did not need to travel far into his sordid past to know if he deserved rescue or punishment: the memory of Sophie and the sight of Boyka lying next to him were enough. Though he knew it in his heart, his mind finally comprehended the gulf that grew between he and God. Jacob asked grimly, "Was there ever a time I did not despise His authority?"

Assarion materialized at the foot of the bed, the smirking demon reveling in Jacob's angst. She made Vanessa's body visible to Jacob but he was so enthralled with Scripture he failed to notice her. He continued to read its words until Assarion interrupted him.

"'For if, after they have escaped the defilements of the world by the knowledge of the Lord and Savior Jesus Christ, they are again entangled in them and are overcome, *the last state has become worse for them than the first*,'" recited Assarion haughtily. (2 Peter 2:20-21). A pall of defeat settled over Jacob and he raised his blue eyes to her. Watching his former stepdaughter testify to his doom, he listened as she continued, "'For it would be better for them not to have known the way of righteousness, than having known it, to turn away from the holy commandment handed on to them.'"

Jacob lowered his eyes and quietly considered his circumstances. His smile of resignation shocked Assarion.

"Well, then, it seems I'm no longer any use to you, sweetheart," Jacob said as the gravity of his guilt waned, "or to anyone, really. Can't save the girls now, can I? Ah, my final failure as a stepfather. *That's that.*"

Assarion hesitated, the demon uncertain of her next move. She summoned her demonic voice and traits for a final play.

"It is unwise to surrender your faith when the demon world hates you as it does," warned Assarion.

"I probably don't have my Jesus superpowers anymore so I'll just ask you to leave," Jacob replied. Motioning towards the rear doors of the van, he said, "So, if you would."

Tossing the Bible to the floor, he wrapped Boyka in his arms and began kissing her neck. She awoke and eagerly accepted the affection. An emotionless expression on her face, Assarion dropped her hands to her sides and faded into nothingness. Jacob saw the final words of the chapter in his mind's eye as he again entered Boyka:

"'*A DOG RETURNS TO ITS OWN VOMIT*,' and '*A sow, after washing, returns to wallowing in the mire.*'" (2 Peter 2:22).

· · · ·

BOYKA, WITH THE BOUNDLESS energy of youth, doted on Jacob like a jealous housewife the next morning. Her work ethic and eagerness to please left little for him to do other than re-read The Second Letter of Peter. Its words sunk deeper into his soul.

"We will arrive at Station Exodus this morning," explained Boyka while pulling the van onto the road, "and my sister Paliki waits for us there."

"How Biblical," Jacob responded. The storm lessened overnight as it rumbled to the northeast and only the last remnants of it dropped light snow. The swirling winds, as if directed by the hand of God, left enough of a trough through the snow for the van to venture forward.

"What about Charlie?" Jacob asked. Boyka went pale and her smile evaporated.

"I told you," replied Boyka without looking at Jacob, "that he was blown off the bridge by a powerful gust of wind. Because I was sitting in the front seat, I saw it. You were in the back seat and did not see it."

"Convenient," Jacob remarked with a dubious expression. Boyka's color soon returned and she began peppering him with questions about his life.

"Do you have a family?" inquired Boyka gingerly after a string of innocuous queries, the possibility that Jacob was married touching her mind for the first time. Jacob stared out the window, his eyes glazing over and turning the white landscape into a blur.

"Not anymore," Jacob answered grimly. Reading his dismay, Boyka altered her tack and returned to questions on more benign matters.

"Tell me of Kaiser," requested Boyka. Turning his attention back to the newest woman in his life, Jacob forced a weak smile and spoke to her of his post-apocalyptic home. The account was heavily censored and always steered away from Elizabeth, their baby and his stepdaughters.

"Dr. Zhukova spoke of another woman . . . who was with you when the old station was destroyed," offered Boyka carefully. She watched Jacob in her peripheral vision.

"Looks like we're here," Jacob interrupted her, the relief evident in his voice. Their arrival at Station Exodus saved him from the uncomfortable topic of Sophie and her untimely demise.

"Yes, we are," replied Boyka. She drove the van along the lane that ran by the station and stopped in front of its stone porch. Except for small cosmetic differences, Station Exodus was built in the same manner as Station Genesis. Her mood became bubbly and she said, "And there is my sister!"

A six-foot-five-inch woman with a swimmer's body stood on the stone steps. The young brunette, whose long tresses were tied in a curly ponytail, locked her light-green eyes on Boyka and hurried to the van. Boyka lowered her window.

"I wonder who gets to climb that," Jacob thought as he appraised the woman's lengthy form. She was not as attractive as Boyka, though she dressed in the same bland manner, and possessed more of a girl-next-door look than his Hungarian princess. Despite her leanness, the cold seemed to affect her little.

"Szia-szia!" exclaimed Paliki as the sisters shared light kisses on their cheeks. Noticing Jacob, her demeanor became more formal.

"Welcome, Mr. Gottschalk. I am Paliki," said the woman with what sounded like a Hungarian accent though, to Jacob's ears, it was much gentler than the one used by Boyka. She waved her hand for them to disembark and said, "Come inside, into the warmth. Lunch will be ready soon."

Boyka gave her sister a pointed look though Jacob did not see it. Paliki's formal demeanor became one of deep concern.

"Where is Charles?" asked Paliki. Jacob looked away.

Boyka, with a strange air of command, immediately ousted Jacob from the van while ordering Paliki inside. Irritated but kept warm by his winter-weather gear and the emerging rays of the sun, he waited impatiently on the porch as the Hungarians conversed in the van. Jacob occasionally heard Paliki's voice rise in astonishment but could not discern her words. Ten long minutes later, Paliki emerged from the van.

"Szia-szia, puszi-puszi," said Boyka as Jacob approached them. Paliki repeated the words.

"Pussy, pussy?" Jacob asked with a chuckle. The sisters turned to him with puzzled expressions, Paliki tilting her head like a confused child. Jacob sighed and said, "Never mind."

"Go now, while the sun smiles on us," urged Paliki as she surveyed the rapidly fraying clouds and the beautiful blueness of the sky.

"Wait, you're not staying?" Jacob queried. He insinuated himself between Boyka and Paliki.

"I must go," said Boyka, her distress growing as she explained, "and you must stay here tonight with Paliki. You will travel with her to the Community tomorrow."

"Where the hell are you going?" Jacob replied suspiciously.

"I must return to Station Genesis," answered Boyka. Her eyes watered and she slid on a pair of sunglasses to conceal them.

"Why can't you and I grab some lunch here and then *you* can drive me the rest of the way," Jacob protested. He acutely felt Dr. Zhukova's manipulation of his libido and loathed the forced ouster from Boyka's present, saying angrily, "Just tell Dr. Z that I insisted."

"You will be safe here with Paliki," replied Boyka. Jacob's angst fueled her nervousness. Paliki placed a reassuring hand on Jacob's arm and offered him a sympathetic look but his angry glare prompted her to remove it. Boyka felt his hostility and begged, "Please, this is what Dr. Zhukova has instructed and others may be watching us. You must trust me."

"I hate being a pawn, especially when I'm being used by both sides," Jacob snapped. Boyka hesitated for a fraction of a second, a fraction that seemed to pass like an hour. She surveyed the area and, satisfied that no one else watched them, quickly kissed Jacob.

His surprise caused him to miss Paliki's wince, the scent of Boyka's skin and the touch of her lips overwhelming Jacob and rendered him mute. She handed him the Bible from which he read.

"Do not dwell on The Second Letter of Peter," Boyka warned him gravely as he took the Book from her, "because it is not for you."

"How did you know . . . . ?" Jacob asked without finishing his question. He attempted to grab her but she evaded him, raised the window and swiftly drove away. Jacob watched the van rejoin the main road and disappear into the surrounding forest.

"Let us go inside, Mr. Gottschalk," said Paliki sheepishly. He glanced at the Bible and then allowed her to guide him inside Station Exodus.

"How did she know?" Jacob asked again.

6

SARAH WALKED CAREFULLY and quietly through the refuse and broken glass strewn across the floor of Stonechurch. Knowing the former church had been abandoned by the living, she searched there for the lock opened by the key Jacob gave her. She found nothing.

The one-room church was constructed of cobblestone walls; support columns erected of irregular, earth-toned rocks and whitish-gray mortar; and square beams made of heavy wood that rested atop them. Oversized window frames held stained-glass windows.

"It's not here," Miriam thought. She never visited Stonechurch during its days as a place of Christian worship. She instead discovered it after the stained-glass windows were painted with viscous, black paint, the choir loft was converted to a DJ booth and the handcrafted wooden doors were replaced with massive, riveted ones of steel. Miriam spent many a night hunting her prey amongst the crowds practicing deviance and debauchery in the club that Stonechurch became. Jacob confessed to her his frequent visits and she learned that he, too, spent many a night there.

The latest stage of the building's history was one of decay. Several windows were broken, the electronic equipment was gone and vulgar graffiti covered the walls and columns. One of the huge steel doors was even torn from its hinges. The entropic environment heightened Sarah's worry and she became impatient.

"Miriam," called out Sarah, "where are you?!"

Miriam, perched on one of the wooden beams above Sarah, watched the nun pace and shout her name but did not answer. She stewed over Sarah's deep intrusion into her relationship with Jacob until her attention turned to an approaching presence in the vicinity of the building. Miriam recognized it and permitted it to enter.

"Now why would you be calling for that little bitch, Sister Sarah?" Darby asked as she aimed her monstrous pistol at the nun. Sarah spun around and pressed herself against a support column.

"Darby!" exclaimed a startled Sarah as Darby walked towards her.

"You told me Jake tossed her ass into Hell. Remember that?" Darby inquired sharply. Her eyes burned like light-blue coals.

"H-h-he did," said Sarah with quivering words, "but s-she's returned."

"She never left. You fucking lied to me," Darby chastised Sarah. Shaking her head in disgust, she said, "I should've killed you months ago, baby or no fucking baby. After all, it's only a Gottschalk."

"I had no involvement whatsoever in the murders of your sister, your nieces or your mother," explained Sarah earnestly. She composed herself and took a cautious step towards Darby, declaring, "I have always counseled Miriam against violence, Darby. *Always.*"

"You're such a good fucking Christian," Darby chuckled with disdain. She pulled her familiar silver flask from her jacket, the one engraved with "Fuck You", and unscrewed it with two fingers while holding it with the others. She took a drink and said, "Of course, all that holier-than-thou bullshit didn't stop you from getting knocked up by Jake."

The urge to slay Darby – a familiar impulse – erupted within Miriam but, remaining true to her fledgling faith, she squelched it. That faith also wrestled with her jealousy as the time to intervene on Sarah's behalf approached.

"Darby, we've discussed this before," Sarah pleaded, "and I told you our child's conception was the result of demonic possession. I swear it."

Darby reaffixed the lid to her flask and stowed it. Raising her pistol and extending her arm, she leveled the gun at Sarah. The Ursuline began to cry.

"Please, if for nothing else, spare me for the sake of this innocent child," begged Sarah through tears as she placed her hands on her pregnant belly. Her sadness struck Miriam as she continued, "She does not bear anyone's sins, let alone those of Miriam or those of her father."

Darby hesitated. She struggled with the sympathy she felt for Sarah.

"So long, Sister Sarah," Darby said after choking down her unexpected moral impulse. She pulled the trigger and the handgun lurched with a flash and a rolling boom. Miriam simultaneously appeared in front of Sarah and caught the bullet between her left index finger and thumb. Darby lowered her pistol.

"I knew it!" she snarled.

Miriam momentarily studied the bullet, rolled it further down her thumb and then flicked it aside. Darby, unwilling to concede, lifted the gun again and fired several rapid shots in succession. Sarah huddled against the column in terror.

The nun's fear, however, proved unwarranted. Miriam swatted aside each bullet with otherworldly speed, the pings of the bullets echoing as they struck the floor and walls. Darby paused and then fired the last round in her clip. Dispatching of it in the same manner, Miriam remained stone-faced and immovable.

"You're not going to hurt her," Miriam advised Darby. Receiving a scowl in response, she ignored it and said, "So put the gun away."

"You know the brat's Jake's, right?" Darby asked with a smirk. She ejected the clip from her firearm and replaced it with a new one.

"Yeah, I know," Miriam answered while averting her eyes from Darby's glare. Her face twitched and her anger boiled within her. Sarah placed her hand on Miriam's shoulder.

"Trust Him, Miriam," pleaded Sarah. Miriam shrugged away from her touch and returned her eyes to Darby.

"So, you also know, since he's been with you, he's fucked Elizabeth *and* Sarah," Darby said with evil delight.

"Literally and figuratively, right?" Miriam replied, her response wiping the smile from Darby's face.

"I'm sure he's fucking that little blonde, too," Darby said, the disdain thick on her tongue, "probably every chance he gets, and if he hasn't knocked her up yet, it won't be long."

"Miriam, no!" shouted Sarah but she was too late. Disappearing and rematerializing before Darby, she crushed her fifty-caliber pistol like a toy. Darby managed to withdraw her fingers in time but the force of her retreat caused her to fall backwards. Miriam dropped the remnants of the gun and approached her, the former demon looming over where she lay defenseless.

"Go ahead, do it," Darby growled defiantly. She sat up. Reaching into her jacket, Darby pulled out her flask and unscrewed it, saying with a renewed smirk, "I don't fucking care anymore."

Darby swigged her whiskey and watched Miriam while Sarah anxiously spectated. The assault they both anticipated, however, did not occur. Miriam grasped the lapels of Darby's jacket, lifted her up and set her on her feet. She took the flask from Darby's hand, crushed it so that the whiskey inside ran over her hand and then tossed it away.

"Hey," Darby objected, "what the hell're you doing?!"

"Going to find Jake," Miriam answered, "and you're coming with me." Sarah exhaled in relief.

"The fuck I am!" Darby barked as Miriam ushered her forward by her jacket. She struggled futilely, her punches and kicks failing to injure or deter Miriam. She slipped out of her jacket and yelled, "I said I'm not fucking going!"

Miriam grasped Darby's arm before she could escape, twisted it behind her back and again forced her forward. Sarah watched her escort the much larger human towards the door as the latter spewed a hateful, profanity-laced stream of threats. She allowed herself the slightest hint of a smile despite the violence to which Miriam resorted and followed the pair from the church.

"Seven months ago she would have killed her," thought Sarah as she marveled at God's handiwork in molding the toughest and unlikeliest lump of clay.

· · · ·

"MIRIAM, THERE IS NOTHING here that can be unlocked with a key," said Sarah in exasperation as she completed a circuit around the sepulcher. Exhausted and sweaty, she threw herself onto the green lawn, the trek up the mountainside draining her energy and shortening her patience.

"This is the only place left that meant anything to him," Miriam countered while circling the sepulcher and occasionally running her hand over an area that appeared different from the surrounding stone. She abandoned the doctor's clothing for a pair of stonewashed jeans, black, high-heeled boots and a solid black top with white designs on its sleeves. Reaching the spot where Sarah sat, she complained, "You should've asked him what the key opened when he gave it to you."

"There was so much happening at the time it escaped me," admitted Sarah, her mood already improving in the shade of the sepulcher. Her respiration slowed and she closed her eyes, saying, "Perhaps he did not want me to know the location."

"That doesn't make any fucking sense," Miriam countered bitterly. She walked around the sepulcher again but saw nothing resembling a lock.

"A lot of things don't make any sense," said Darby as she strode towards Sarah with a long sledgehammer in hand, "like when Sarah said Jacob chucked the homicidal hussy into Hell, and that she couldn't have killed Liz and the baby."

Miriam instantaneously materialized between Sarah and Darby, her appearance stopping Darby in her tracks. The two beings glared at each other with a fierce hatred fueled by past grievances.

"*Miriam*," Sarah blurted, the nun intent on avoiding a bloody conflict. She struggled to stand as she contended with her pregnant belly.

"He did chuck the homicidal hussy into Hell," Miriam replied in defense of Sarah. Straining against her desire to slaughter Darby, she said threateningly, "But I'm back."

"Oh, just tell her, Miriam," pleaded Sarah. She was too tired for subtleties.

"It doesn't matter," Miriam protested. She turned to address Sarah, saying, "She's not gonna believe me."

"Tell me what?" asked Darby.

"*Tell her*," urged Sarah.

"I didn't kill your sister or the baby," Miriam said. She kept her back to Darby

"Fucking bullshit!" shouted Darby. Her grip on the sledgehammer's handle tightened as she ranted, "Even if you didn't kill her body, which I don't believe for one fucking second, you sure as shit killed her brain."

Miriam growled at Darby. Grasping her shoulder, Sarah encouraged her to retreat a few steps. Miriam surprised her by accepting the guidance and placing a yard of distance between herself and Darby. Sarah then stepped into the void.

"The two of you need to end this war," stated Sarah. Before she could continue, however, Darby lunged forward with a scream and swung the sledgehammer. Sarah ducked as the hammer's head passed harmlessly over her, the strike meant for Miriam.

Miriam dodged the attack with ease. Leaping like a panther over Sarah, she landed upon Darby and knocked the sledgehammer from her hands. Miriam pinned her to the ground with uncanny strength, lifted the claw of her right index finger and held it mere millimeters from Darby's right eye. She moved with such celerity and violence of action that Sarah could not admonish her and stood dumbstruck.

"I don't need a knife to kill," Miriam said. Darby watched the claw intensely as she expounded, "I have ten of these, and they'll slice through flesh, stone, steel . . . or even your thick skull, Darby. Yeah, I killed your sister's brain, and your niece . . . and . . . and I'm . . . ."

Darby's focus left the claw and moved to Miriam's face. She clearly struggled with her emotions.

"I'm sorry for that," Miriam said with difficulty. Shaking free of her inner conflict, she stated resolutely, "But I didn't finish off your sister, or kill her baby or your mother. *It wasn't me.*"

The apology astonished Darby and stifled her rage. Miriam relented and, as she stood up, helped Darby to her feet.

"Jacob said you'd be a threat to the baby," said Darby.

"Miriam has changed," replied Sarah. Wrapping an arm around her shoulder, she said, "She prayed to God to release her from the Abyss, what you call Hell, and, in exchange for her repentance, her sins were forgiven and she was freed from that terrible place."

Watching each other warily, Miriam and Darby ceased their hostilities. Sarah nodded to the sledgehammer.

"What is that for?" asked Sarah.

"Right before Jacob bailed with his *new girlfriend,*" began Darby, "he left me his Bible."

"Darby, please," scolded Sarah. Miriam's mood darkened but she remained quiet and still. Darby picked up the sledgehammer.

"I never read the fucking thing, of course, because I don't believe in all that Jesus bullshit," explained Darby as she walked to the rear of the sepulcher, "that is, until last night. And right there, on the back page, were the directions to this place and a shitty sketch of the tomb."

Darby inspected the sepulcher's back wall. Finding that for which she searched, she looked to Miriam.

"As soon as I heard you talking about the key, I knew what that asshole meant," added Darby. She wiggled a finger at Miriam and ordered, "Come here."

"Why?" Miriam snapped suspiciously. She bristled at the command but a nudge from Sarah sent her on her way.

"I need this moved," said Darby. She pointed to a small yet thick-limbed bush planted near the sepulcher's base.

Firing Darby a dubious look, Miriam kneeled down and grasped the bush by its trunk. Yanking it upward, she rose to her feet and ripped the bush from the earth. Her efforts revealed a tangled, gnarled root system. Miriam threw it aside.

"Now what?" Miriam asked sharply.

Darby immediately swung the sledgehammer at a large blemish in the wall once hidden by the bush. It crumbled easily, the area proving to be thinner than the rest of the tomb's walls. Miriam fell upon the hole in the sepulcher and brushed aside the stone debris. Reaching inside, she pulled out a long, heavy lockbox and laid it on the lawn.

"Jacob obviously wanted the two of you to work together," said Sarah with a hopeful smile. She held up the silver key.

"Fuck off," Miriam and Darby replied in angry unison. Sarah shook her head in disapproval, unlocked the box and removed its lid.

"My goodness," gasped Sarah as gold ingots sparkled in the sunlight and illuminated the three faces that gazed in wonder upon them.

"That son of a bitch," said Darby. She begrudgingly added, "He's a sneaky fuck for hiding it from Liz but it was a smart move."

"Why's that?" Miriam asked.

"Because some things never change," Darby stated while staring at the precious metal. Standing up and folding her arms, she said, "Anyone anywhere will take gold. It was his ticket out."

. . . .

"THIS IS IT," SNEERED Darby as she shifted the Humvee into Park. The warehouse, old yet sturdily built of brick and stone, blended into the urban decay of Kaiser's slums. Its outside walls were awash in graffiti and uncut weeds.

"This is what?" Sarah asked. She sat in the front passenger seat while Miriam sat in the back seat with her legs folded beneath her and a scowl etched on her face.

"The grocery store for those stupid fucking assholes who are insistent on leaving civilization to chase a deviant drunk across the wastelands," griped Darby while getting a glimpse of Miriam in the rearview mirror. Miriam ignored the slight and exited the vehicle.

"Let's go," she said. Sarah disembarked with difficulty but Darby hesitated, her hatred for Miriam still burning within her.

"If only I could kill you," muttered Darby while glaring at Miriam. She watched her approach the warehouse's main doors which, when open, provided access to the street. They also possessed a "door-within-a-door" so its occupants could enter without lifting them. Miriam turned to face Darby.

"Open the door or I'll break it down," Miriam ordered. She and Darby exchanged chilling looks.

"Honestly, you two, *stop it*," scolded Sarah. The constant travel and stress of her rescue rendered her uncomfortable in her own skin and uncharacteristically irritable. Sarah hobbled back to the Humvee and placed her hand on it to rest, imploring Darby through the open window, "Darby, please, we need your help."

"Fine," snapped Darby. She exited the Humvee and slammed the door to convey her displeasure. Folding her arms, Miriam stepped aside from the entry door and waited for Darby. Sarah hurried to interpose herself between them.

Darby produced a key and unlocked the door. Thrusting it open, she stepped back and gestured for Miriam and Sarah to enter.

"After you, ladies," said Darby with feigned politeness. Miriam and Sarah accepted her invitation and, after the three of them were inside, Darby simultaneously lifted three switches and cast light throughout the warehouse. Constellations of girders hung above the concrete floor and two equidistant rows of iron support columns formed a skeleton hallway down its center. High windows lined the long sides of the building and a small office was built into its far left corner. The afternoon light filtered through the windows and illuminated a sea of unmarked crates of all sizes and several tarped vehicles.

"How about a bathroom?" Sarah asked urgently. Darby rolled her eyes and pointed towards the office.

"Over there," she uttered. Placing her hands on her hips she added, "Door's unlocked."

"Thank you," said Sarah as she scurried away and deftly tackled the maze of crates and vehicles.

"I don't understand why you need me anyway," grumbled Darby as she watched Sarah disappear into the bathroom. Turning to Miriam, she continued, "Just take whatever shit you need and get the fuck outta my life."

Darby straightened up when she realized Miriam was gone. Miriam rematerialized on top of a tall vehicle with one leg tucked beneath her and the other hanging off its roof.

"If something happens to me, there'll be no one to take care of Sarah," Miriam replied. Darby turned her head abruptly to reacquire her.

"I thought you were invincible," said Darby as she walked to Miriam and gazed up at her.

"I thought that too, once," Miriam said, "but God and Jake had other ideas and I found out I wasn't. I don't think anyone in this realm is."

Darby folded her arms and shifted her weight to her right foot. She observed Miriam closely.

"How do you know that, if something does happen to you, I won't just off her and toss her and that brat in a fucking ditch?" inquired Darby. Miriam grinned with a frightening display of jagged teeth and the pinpricks of light arose in her black eyes.

"If I can make it back here from the shithole of the Abyss," Miriam announced with confidence, "then I can make it back here from anywhere. And as long as Jake's here, I'll always make it back."

Darby took the hint and a hit from her flask. She was developing a grudging respect for Miriam and it irked her.

"With God's help," Miriam conceded though the admission tasted bitter on her lips. Darby snickered.

"With God's help," scoffed Darby. She drank from her flask again and then stowed it, saying, "That's just fucking great."

"What are we talking about, ladies?" asked Sarah upon her return.

"God and violence, Sister Sarah," Darby replied while Miriam remained silent, "God and violence."

. . . .

DEFERRING TO DARBY'S strongly worded wishes, the trio passed the rest of the day and most of the next at the warehouse. Sarah attempted to rest on the uncomfortable couch in the office while Darby puttered around the building's long aisles and tinkered with odds and ends. Miriam skulked about the rafters and obsessed over Sophie's unfettered access to Jacob.

Darby reconvened them in the evening as darkness settled over the warehouse. A single hanging light above the desk illuminated the office and beneath it Miriam sat with her legs folded like a child.

"Niu's goons started tailing us when we reentered Kaiser," explained Darby, "but I let them find me and Niu knows it. He'll allow us to leave but, if he intends to off us, he'll do it outside the city."

"I can handle that," Miriam said though, as soon as the words passed her lips, she wondered what they meant given her new outlook on morality. Sarah, still resting on the couch, struggled into a sitting position.

"As much as I'd like to see you slaughter those assholes, you won't need to," said Darby. She seated herself in a chair against the wall, let her arms hang limp at her sides and stretched out her long legs. Once her indulgent display was complete, she added, "They're not going to see us leave."

"Which means?" asked Sarah. The prospect of crawling through sewers was on her mind.

"Which means we're not leaving through the front door," said an annoyed Darby. Despite knowing the answer, she asked, "And, while we're on the topic of leaving, where the hell are we going?"

Sarah looked expectantly towards Miriam who bowed her head. She did not immediately answer.

"I don't know," Miriam admitted. Wiggling her fingers in front of her face and examining her claws, she said, "I was able to sense the baby – I thought it was Jake – but I don't know where he is."

"If that cocksucker's even still alive," said Darby dismissively though she knew in her heart he endured.

"*He's alive,*" Miriam insisted with a trace of the demonic in her tone. Sarah observed her with concern.

"I thought you couldn't sense him," countered Darby. She threw Miriam a dubious look.

"I said I don't know where he is," Miriam argued, "but I can still feel his spirit. He's out there, *alive.* I think . . . *I don't know.*"

"What is it, Miriam?" asked Sarah. She heaved herself to her feet and approached the desk.

"Nothing," Miriam snapped. Darby's annoyance burgeoned but Sarah waited patiently for her to speak. She placed her hand on Miriam's shoulder, the touch encouraging her to continue, "It's just, I think . . . I think I'll know as we follow him, like, I'll know the way when I see it."

"How fucking romantic and stupid," grumbled Darby. Clasping her hands behind her head, she said, "Well, until you figure it the fuck out, I've got an idea where he went."

"You do?" said Miriam. She squirmed away from Sarah's touch and scooted to the end of the desk. She let her legs dangle from it and grasped its edge with both hands.

"Yeah, I do," replied Darby in a snarky tone. Looking to Sarah, she advised, "You might want to sit back down."

Sarah shrugged and returned to the couch. Miriam rested her elbows on her thighs, one arm draped over her knees and the other held straight up so she could rest her chin in her palm.

"Liz and I always knew, despite our best efforts, that this could all go to shit, and go to shit fast," began Darby, her general irritation turning to a dutiful seriousness, "so we built a network of escape routes all over this city. Only she and I knew about them, well, until dumbass showed up. She made us memorize them so that if anything happened to her and Kaiser fell, one or both of us could get Ness' and Mal out. I never thought I'd be the only one left to use them."

Taking a moment to digest that reality, Darby grew grim and silent. Sarah allowed her the moment of reflection. Miriam did not.

"And?" demanded Miriam. Darby unexpectedly let the affront pass.

"Our escape plans don't stop at the wall, Blondie," said Darby. She sat up and, as Jacob often did, let her elbows rest on her knees and joined her hands in front of her. She stared at the floor as she elaborated, "We had routes going everywhere, some shorter, some longer. Liz even had a boat on the Pacific coast to make a run to Hawaii for fuck's sake. And every route had supply stations along the way – food, water, gas, whatever the fuck we'd need."

Miriam hopped off the desk and approached Darby. Sarah tensed but, before she could intervene, Miriam crouched down harmlessly in front of her and looked her squarely in the eyes.

"Do you know where he went?" Miriam asked. Darby shook her head in the negative.

"No, I said I have an *idea* where he went," replied Darby. Sarah watched her and Miriam with wonder, the two women comically mismatched in every way but engaging in somewhat civil conversation. Darby explained, "If Marcion's leading him away from Kaiser like you say he is, he could've gone anywhere and then we'll either get lucky or, most likely, be fucked. But, if that little bastard let Jake pick the direction, then he probably took one of the northern routes into Canada. Liz always preferred that direction and told us to take the girls that way unless there was a clear reason not to."

"Why is that?" asked Sarah. Miriam returned to her seat on the desk.

"We know a lot more about it, and there's some civilization that way, plus there are more supply depots," answered Darby, "and if you can survive the winters, the weather and the terrain are good buffers . . . against the remaining dregs of humanity at least."

"Then what are we waiting for?" Miriam asked as she stood up.

"Hold on there, Princess of the Damned," said Darby. She rose to her feet and placed her hand on a file cabinet next to the chair, saying, "Niu runs his guys in twelve-hour shifts. We'll move at shift change. And you'll have to sweep for beasties."

"Okay," Miriam replied despite her urge to charge out the front doors of the warehouse and run due north. Her desire to see Jacob became an uncomfortable pulsation in her spirit. She thought about his provisions for his child's escape and inquired, "What about the gold?"

"Leave it, cuz' we'll never get it out of the Humvee without giving ourselves away," said Darby. Running her hand along the top of the file cabinet, she continued, "We won't need it, anyway."

The planned abandonment of Jacob's ingots troubled Miriam. She faded away from the material world with gold on her mind.

"How stable is she?" queried Darby, her eyes still on the spot where Miriam once stood.

"You are alive, are you not?" Sarah answered with a muted grin.

• • • •

DESPITE THE LOGIC BEHIND Darby's request, it made Miriam nervous to leave Sarah with her and reconnoiter outside the warehouse. She passed invisibly through the night and learned that Niu did indeed replace his men every twelve hours. She did not detect any of her own kind.

"Am I even still one of them?" Miriam asked herself. She left the question unanswered and hurried back inside.

"Second shift's here," Miriam announced as she materialized in a large, metal shipping container. She was relieved to find Sarah hunkered inside it with Darby, the pair illuminated by a small lantern sitting next to a large duffle bag.

"Demons?" inquired Darby. Miriam shook her head in the negative.

The empty container concealed a manhole cover in the floor which Darby removed with considerable effort. Much to her consternation, Miriam took it from her and set it aside with ease.

"Thanks," Darby said with a sneer. She scooped up the duffle and handed it to Miriam, saying, "Now take this."

Miriam, silenced by a look from Sarah, accepted the burden with a scowl. Turning her attention back to the hole, Darby reached inside it and flicked an unseen switch. A dusky, neon blue light shone through it and illuminated the container.

"Liz always thought this color light fucked with people's heads," said Darby as she turned off the lantern.

"Yes, I've received that hospitality before," said Sarah. Swinging her legs over the hole and dropping them inside it, Darby leapt down with the lantern in hand.

"Now Sarah," she called. Miriam held the duffel in one arm while lowering Sarah with the other and, once the nun was inside the tunnel, Darby helped her the rest of the way.

Miriam stepped over the hole and floated downward. She pulled the manhole cover into place with her opposite hand before dropping below the level of the floor.

"That's so fucking weird," said Darby as Miriam's feet touched ground. The unlikely trio stood at the beginning of a rectangular, concrete tunnel running into the distance. The lighting system was comprised of equidistant light fixtures and thick, insulated wires. Darby drew her gun, an identical replacement for the one Miriam destroyed.

"Let's go," she beckoned. Leading the way, she proceeded down the tunnel. Sarah followed several paces behind while Miriam lagged in the rear and felt very much like a pack animal.

"This is certainly not the place for a claustrophobe," commented Sarah with one uncertain hand before her and the other resting on her pregnant belly. She was not claustrophobic but felt apprehension with each step into the eerie, hazy blueness. Darby's confidence bolstered her, however, and she managed to keep pace with her long strides.

The tunnel branched at several intersections but Darby maintained a straight course until the fifth one emerged. She stopped and ushered Sarah past her.

"There's a boat moored at the end of this tunnel," instructed Darby as she threw a pointed finger down the left branch. Holding out her hands to receive the duffel bag, she said, "Untie it and let it out into the river."

"Do you really think they're gonna buy a boat crash?" Miriam inquired as she hugged the duffel into her body. She expected trickery from Darby and, as before, was reluctant to part from Sarah.

"No, but it will cost them time and that helps us," replied Darby. She chuckled and said, "You know, we never told Jake, but the original plan was to bring down fresh corpses and put them in the boat."

"I often wonder which race is eviller, demon . . . or human," uttered a disgusted Sarah. The baby stirred in her womb.

"My sister was a realist," snapped Darby, "a realist who knew there're few people in life you can trust and even fewer you can count on."

"Isn't that the same thing?" Miriam asked. The lighting system flickered and died before Darby could reply.

"*Shit*," griped Darby as blackness overtook them. Clicking the lantern to life and setting it on the floor, she said, "They're in the tunnel."

"Five of them," Miriam confirmed. Her old violent instincts awakened within her as she asked suspiciously, "How'd they know we left?"

"Fuck if I know," replied Darby testily. She holstered her firearm and attempted to grab the duffel from Miriam but missed, saying, "They could have thermal imagers . . . or maybe they have one of you."

"They don't," Miriam scoffed. She threw the bag at Darby who caught it at the cost of several backward steps.

"So what are we going to do about them, ladies?" inquired Sarah sharply. The inane bickering between Darby and Miriam continued to test her patience.

"Make them regret setting foot down here," Darby answered. Dropping the duffel to the floor, she unzipped it and removed an explosive device. She affixed the device to the wall and keyed in a code. It beeped three times. Darby glanced at Miriam as she pulled another device from the bag and chided her, "Well, get her outta here."

"No," Miriam said in her full demonic tone. Its use briefly stunned Darby who glared at her as she ordered, "*You* get her outta here."

"Miriam, do not surrender to old instincts," warned Sarah. Darby recovered quickly and, accepting Miriam's command, affixed the device on the wall opposite its counterpart. Miriam turned and walked several slow paces, her silence prompting Sarah to ask, "Where are you going?"

"To make them regret setting foot down here," Miriam said as Darby punched in the code and the second device chimed three times.

"Miriam, wait," begged Sarah but her plea was too late. Miriam was gone. Darby grasped Sarah's arm.

"She can take care of herself," advised Darby. Forcing Sarah forward, she drew her pistol and said, "And we have less than ninety seconds until the motion sensors kick on, so let's get the fuck outta here."

· · · ·

MAKING NO EFFORT TO conceal their pursuit, Niu's minions entered the tunnel with guns drawn and flashlights beaming. They were all suit-clad Asian men of varying ages and swept the tunnel with rapidity and efficiency.

"There is nothing for you here," Miriam called out to Niu's men, her words echoing in the tunnel. The group halted and pointed their guns forward. The lead man's flashlight swiftly acquired Miriam who stood before them with her eyes closed and her hands clasped behind her back. She warned them, "Go back."

"On the floor," demanded the lead man with a Chinese accent. Miriam shook her head in refusal of his order.

"Go back or you will never leave this place," replied Miriam. The lead man fired a shot that whizzed past Miriam's ear.

"On the ground! Now!" he shouted. Lunging toward the group, Miriam opened her eyes and bared her claws and teeth with a bone-rattling roar.

Flabbergasted by the display, Nui's men hesitated but then opened fire on Miriam. Their bullets careened throughout the tunnel, the multitude of projectiles pulverizing sections of concrete and shattering lightbulbs as they struck. When the shooting ceased, Miriam was nowhere to be seen.

"É mó," said one of the men. His eyes frantically searched the tunnel.

"Chén mò," the lead man hissed. The blue lighting abruptly resumed though, with several fixtures destroyed, it cast weird shadows in the tunnel. Miriam appeared behind the men.

"É mó," Miriam said in a confirmatory and monstrous tone. The men whirled around and fired wildly at her. She flashed through their midst at blinding speed, her movements causing a hail of friendly fire that killed all but the lead man. He shrewdly dropped to the floor the second the shooting began.

"Get up," Miriam ordered him. He responded by firing two shots into her chest. The bullets whizzed through her and ricocheted down the hallway.

Stepping on the man's throat, Miriam applied just enough pressure to block his breathing. She growled at him and said, "Fine, asshole, stay down there."

The man struggled mightily against Miriam by grabbing her ankle with both hands and attempting to wrench her foot from his neck. The effort was futile as were the violent movements of the rest of his body. Miriam pointed in the direction of Darby and Sarah.

"Death," she said demonically. She then pointed towards the tunnel entrance and stated in a human voice, "Life."

Nearing unconsciousness, the man faltered and ceased his escape attempts. The odd, blue light began to fade from his vision and darkness crept over his eyes.

"Always so difficult," Miriam complained.

7

WHEN NIU ARRIVED AT the warehouse, there were no lights, or sirens, or commotion. The second five-man team remained on site after being relieved by the first and managed the scene without reinforcements. Two of them assisted the only survivor of Miriam's appearance, the man cut and bruised but not seriously wounded. The other three underlings tracked their prey deeper into the tunnel system.

Niu's driver disembarked and opened his door. He swiftly exited the vehicle and closed the distance between it and his wounded subordinate. Seeing his portly superior standing before him, the man disentangled himself from his comrades and struggled into an upright position.

"É mó?" asked Niu. A surge of adrenaline broke the man free from his woozy state and he inhaled deeply and dramatically. Wide-eyed, he exhaled his answer.

"É mó."

There was a sudden subterranean explosion as if the man's very words triggered Darby's motion sensors. The ground shook and he passed out, the unconscious man caught at the last second by his escorts. Niu waved dismissively and he was carried away.

"Motion sensors, no doubt," Niu announced. His driver and his bodyguard, clad in suits as the rest of his men, flanked him and listened attentively. Niu ordered, "Clear the rubble, extract our people and pursue them. I want to know where Ms. Nicks is going."

The driver hurried to the car and used a short-wave radio to communicate with Niu's central command. His bodyguard followed him into the warehouse.

"These sisters possessed state of the art technology," he said to himself, "but they did not get it from me. That is concerning."

Sitting above Niu on the edge of the warehouse's roof, Miriam studied him and his men. She swung her legs like a bored child and let her heels gently bump the side of the building. Miriam waited for the driver to complete his task and follow his master.

"It's about time," she complained when at last he entered the warehouse. She began to dematerialize but, with an odd desire to remain in the physical world, she returned to it. She pushed herself off the roof and descended to the ground like a feather on a gentle breeze. When her boots touched the earth, Miriam wiggled her clawed feet and said aloud, "I hate shoes."

Confident in her senses, Miriam deemed that no humans were near and walked to Darby's Humvee. She opened the rear passenger door, reached inside the vehicle and grabbed the lockbox's handle.

"I don't care what anybody says, I'm not leaving this behind," Miriam said in a dig at Darby. Despite the weight of the lockbox, she effortlessly lifted it and removed it from the Humvee. She closed the door quietly and, instead of returning to the warehouse, she walked into the surrounding neighborhood in full view of human eyes.

The former demon appeared comical as she traveled the streets of Kaiser dressed like the spoiled teenager of a wealthy family. Miriam hugged the lockbox to her torso like an infant but her compulsion to protect Sarah and her child ebbed as she thought of how that child came to be.

"I wish it was just me and him," she said sadly. Unable to be with Jacob, Miriam decided to settle into the solitude she knew before him and continued her aimless walk in the dregs of Kaiser. She arrived at a city park and stopped in front of a large, wooden sign. Setting down the lockbox on the sidewalk, she read the sign's engraved, painted lettering. It hailed Elizabeth's generous gift of the park to the community.

"Lying, conniving bitch," Miriam grumbled through clenched teeth. Feeling vile, she uttered with a faint trace of the demonic in her voice, "I wasted so many chances to end her."

Remorse hit Miriam like an unexpected smack on the cheek. She felt God's elusive presence and, with a sour expression, bowed her head.

"I know, I know. I'm sorry," Miriam muttered. Her focus moved to the word "Elizabeth". Shrieking like a *daimoniou*, she lunged forward and shattered the sign with a single, powerful strike. Standing back to appraise her work, she sneered, "I'm *not* sorry about that."

Miriam retrieved the lockbox which, though she did not realize it, was becoming a representation of Jacob. Carrying it to a swing set, she carefully laid it on the ground and settled into a swing. Pumping her legs back and forth, she thrust the swing into motion. The chains attached to the crossbar squeaked with each pass.

"Lady Lizzie and her brat are dead," Miriam said as she contemplated the potential difficulties in her renewed quest for Jacob, "and he could still blame me for that. But she's out of the way at least."

Miriam accelerated her speed and the swing climbed steadily higher with each pendulum-like motion. Her clawed hands gripped the chains though her supernatural balance rendered the precaution unnecessary.

"She's been replaced by Sarah and her baby, though, and Sophie's had months to dig into him," Miriam reasoned as her heart dipped. She let her legs hang limp and the swing decelerate as she continued, "This 'good girl' shit is complicated. In the old days I could just murder everyone and be done with it."

Old urges percolated within her and she found herself wondering about the extent of God's forgiveness. The swing came to a stop. Miriam hopped off it and stood up while simultaneously ripping down one of the swing chains. She detached it from the rubber seat.

"This'll work," Miriam said. Instinctively knowing the center point of the chain, she pulled the middle links apart and created two shorter chains. She stuck her hand in her back pocket and said, "Good thing I swiped this."

Miriam held up the lockbox key. She then crouched down, unlocked the box and removed its lid. Using her right index finger, Miriam poked four holes in the lid, two on either side eighteen inches apart.

A cold wind arose as two sedans rushed past the park at breakneck speed. Miriam watched them and then lifted her emotionless black eyes to the thickening clouds.

"I'd better get back," she said. Returning to her work, Miriam inserted one of the chains into the top hole, ran it down the back of the lid and pulled it through the bottom hole. She then twisted its broken link onto the unbroken link at the other end to create a strap. She repeated the process for the second chain and reaffixed the lid to the lockbox.

Miriam crumpled the lockbox key into a ball. She held it aloft briefly to look at it and tossed it into the grass.

"That should do it," Miriam declared as she stood up, slid her arms into each loop and pulled on her makeshift backpack. Passing into the spiritual world, she said, "I'm coming, Jake . . . and, fuck Darby. I'm bringing the gold with me."

. . . .

THE TUNNEL INTO WHICH Darby and Sarah fled terminated at a single door permitting access to a large storm drain. A foul odor hung within it but, fortunately for Sarah, they did not travel far before ascending a metal ladder embedded in the wall. Despite leaving the putrid stench behind, she vomited once more into the sewer opening. Darby held her arm to prevent her from falling.

"Praise God," Sarah sighed as she wiped her mouth with her sleeve. Her normally olive skin carried a greener tint and her breathing was labored. She stumbled over to a lamppost and slumped against it. The cold drizzle on her face felt refreshing.

"Save the kudos until we get outta here," replied Darby as she closed the sewer hatch. The burden of a pregnant and puking Sarah was an unwelcome one and it raised her ire. She removed several ammunition pouches from the duffle bag and affixed them to her belt.

"Where are we?" Sarah asked, the nun scanning her surroundings. The pair stood at one end of a well-lit, two-lane bridge spanning a tributary of the San Joaquin River. Globes of mist surrounded the streetlights as the drizzle continued.

"Northeast quadrant of the city," Darby said while throwing the duffle bag into the river. Pointing to the west, she explained, "The storm drain leads up to the city wall in the northwest quadrant, so they'll expect us to go that way if they're checking the sewer maps, which I fully expect from Niu."

"Where the fuck is this?" Miriam asked as she appeared behind Darby and Sarah. Darby flinched as if to draw her firearm.

"Sorry, you little bitch, but you missed the briefing," sneered a bristling Darby. She rotated around slowly and glowered at Miriam.

"She shouldn't be out in the rain," Miriam replied while barely restraining the profane word on her tongue. She noticed Sarah's pathetic state and approached her, saying, "What's wrong?"

"Really? You brought the gold?" scoffed Darby when she noticed Miriam's metal backpack.

"Forget about the fucking gold," Miriam said. She lifted Sarah's chin with her index finger and examined her weak eyes. She asked, "*What's wrong?*"

"The smell in the storm drain was . . . *unpleasant*," Sarah answered with a sickly smile, the mere remembrance of the malodorous tunnel causing her stomach to churn. She grabbed Miriam's hand and moved it away from her face, saying, "But the fresh air is helping. I'll be fine."

Miriam whirled around.

"We're miles from the wall," Miriam admonished Darby. She marched up to her and insisted, "She can't keep walking all night in the rain."

The instant Miriam said "rain" a gust of freezing wind raced over them. The precipitation became mixed with the addition of small snowflakes.

"I'm fine, Miriam," lied Sarah while standing up straight. She shivered and felt exhaustion creeping up her legs and over her eyelids.

"This isn't shit," replied an abnormally even-keeled Darby as she held out her hands. Headlights appeared as several vehicles entered the bridge at the far end. Darby glanced at them and added with smug satisfaction, "Besides, she won't have to."

"The cavalry?" asked Sarah as she again leaned into the lamppost for support.

"More like the last train out," grumbled Darby. Miriam returned to Sarah and stood between her and the approaching column of armored vehicles, many of which were Humvees. Darby walked to the center line of the road and waited for it to arrive. The column rolled to a halt with the lead Humvee stopping where she stood.

"You're late, asshole," Darby snapped after its driver rolled down the window.

"We had a little disagreement with the new administration," said a blonde woman who, despite having an age-worn face, was attractive. Darby rested her arms, one atop the other, on the edge of the window.

"What's the score?" Darby inquired in a hushed tone.

"All units except us are outside the city and accounted for. We were the first team to hit resistance, and it was token," reported the woman. Her nose was small and pointed and her eyes were a weak green. Catching a glimpse of Sarah and Miriam, she chuckled and said, "Pick up some strays?"

"Don't ask," answered Darby. Looking to the man who rode in the front passenger seat, she nodded to the next Humvee and ordered, "Get out."

"Yes, Ma'am," he replied and dutifully exited the vehicle. Like all members of Kaiser's security force, he was boot-clad and dressed in black with a submachine gun slung over his shoulder. Darby walked around the front of the Humvee and hit the hood twice.

"Well, get in," ordered Darby. Concerned with Sarah's condition, Miriam led her to the Humvee and assisted her into her seat. She then traveled to her own seat via the spiritual world.

"What the hell?!" exclaimed the woman after witnessing Miriam's disappearing act and seeing her demonic traits. Her hand fell to her sidearm.

"Just fucking relax," said Darby while climbing into the Humvee. Feeling like she might choke on the words, she slammed the door and uttered, "She's with me."

· · · ·

THE COLUMN TRAVELED unmolested to the wall and departed Kaiser through a small utility gate. It was still held by Darby's loyalists when she and her caravan arrived but the guards soon abandoned their posts and joined them.

"Leave the gate open," Darby instructed the guards as her Humvee drove past them. She threw an extended middle finger over her shoulder and said, "It'll serve that asshole right for hassling us on the way out."

Journeying northeast on a winding, dirt road, the column skirted the lower slopes of Mt. Baldwin. Kaiser disappeared behind them as they penetrated the surrounding wilderness. Sarah quickly fell asleep, the expectant mother sapped of her strength by their flight from the city. Miriam found an emergency blanket and covered her with it. She also removed her makeshift backpack and quietly set it on the floor.

"Sleep while you can," Miriam whispered. Ever distrustful of Darby and her minions, she remained vigilant and ready to defend Jacob's child and its mother. Miriam soon learned that a select group of security personnel were part of Elizabeth's escape plan and that they now traveled to a secret rendezvous location.

"How far to the first marker?" asked the woman. The wipers squeaked repeatedly as they cleared the slushy snow from the windshield.

"Just keep driving, Petra," Darby answered. She fell into a fey mood with her eyes forward and the gears of her mind spinning. Petra shrugged off Darby's bitterness.

"Okay, Boss Lady," replied Petra. Her question was answered fifteen minutes later when the caravan passed the first marker and then the second and the third. The column slowly traversed winding seasonal roads made treacherous by the dark, the weather, sharp curves and steep descents.

The day dawned cloudy and dim with intermittent showers of light rain and snow. Quickly changing from the greenness of the forested mountains into the brownness of an arid, mountainous desert, the landscape emanated a dreariness that all save Miriam felt in their bones as the caravan headed northeast. There were no signs of civilization or life save for the occasional rabbit or coyote and hungry carrion birds.

"There's the road," announced Darby. The column turned north onto a dirt road in much better condition than the ones between it and Kaiser. It allowed the vehicles to race northeast at greater speed and soon Darby's minions struck an east-west, four-lane highway.

"Right turn?" inquired Petra. Darby responded with a finger pointing directly ahead. The paved road she chose meandered aimlessly through small, long-abandoned towns before reaching two successively larger highways as her course turned in an easterly direction.

"Someone's coming," Miriam warned while dropping to her knees and positioning herself between Darby and Petra like a child on a Sunday drive with her parents. The proximity unsettled Petra.

"I don't see anything," Petra replied.

"No, she's right," Darby said. A single headlight appeared in the oncoming lane on the edge of the humans' vision. It raced towards the column at a blistering speed.

"Stop," Darby ordered. Petra grabbed the radio microphone and held it to her mouth.

"All units halt," said Petra. The line of vehicles slowed to a crawl and then ceased its movement. Sarah awoke when Darby exited the Humvee and slammed the door.

"What's wrong?" asked a groggy Sarah.

"I don't know," Miriam answered. She kept a close eye on Darby who drew her fifty-caliber pistol and walked down the center of the highway. She abruptly straightened her body and blurted, "I have to go."

"Go where?" asked a befuddled Sarah. Petra glanced at Miriam but started when she realized she was gone.

"You'll get used to it," remarked Sarah.

"Whatever you say, Sister," replied Petra with a dubious expression.

· · · ·

DARBY WAITED FOR THE motorcyclist with her firearm held at her side and ignored the light assault of ice pellets that bounced off her body. The rider stopped the motorcycle by turning it sideways and skidding up to her. Darby did not flinch.

"Little shit," she muttered.

The tiny rider pulled off her helmet and revealed herself to be a young woman with a disproportionately-large head and bulging eyes that bordered on black. She wore a jumpsuit with copious buckles and pockets stuffed full of miscellaneous gear and a gun belt sporting numerous ammunition pouches and a sidearm. The mass of clothing and equipment she wore failed to hide her gaunt frame.

"Ya gonna shoot me, Boss?" asked the girl, who styled her hair in an uncomfortably tight ponytail. She exuded a palpable cockiness that prickled Darby.

"What the hell are you doing here, Magg?" Darby demanded. She holstered her pistol and continued, "You're supposed to be on your way to Jarbidge. *Everybody's* supposed to be on their way to fucking Jarbidge."

"They are," replied Magg. She hung her helmet on one of the handlebars and added, "Well, almost everybody."

Darby lunged at Magg, grabbed the front of her jumpsuit with both hands and hoisted her off her motorcycle. Holding the young woman in the air, she brought their faces to within inches of each other. Magg's bike crashed to the pavement as did her helmet which rolled across the road.

"What the fuck is going on, you little twat?" Darby growled. Magg remained undaunted but looked comical with her thin legs dangling above the ground.

"Darby, that was a new bike," advised Magg as she struggled to turn her body and look over her shoulder.

"I swear, I'll snap your fucking neck right now and leave your body lying on this *fucking* highway for the vultures to pick clean," Darby threatened Magg with a rough shake.

"All right, all right," conceded Magg. Darby held her aloft with no sign of relenting as she said, "It'd prooooobably be better if I showed you."

"Yeah, and why the fuck is that?" Darby inquired sharply. She set Magg on the ground but did not release her jumpsuit. Her underling displayed a rare seriousness.

"Because you wouldn't believe me if I told you," answered Magg. Darby's eyes narrowed as she studied the girl's face.

"You look like absolute fucking shit," Darby said as she noticed the dark circles under Magg's big eyes. She then released her subordinate and appraised her skinniness. Scowling in disgust, Darby added, "You're nothing but fucking bones, Magg. Eat a fucking sandwich or something."

Undaunted by Darby's scathing remarks, Magg simply shrugged. She quickly retrieved her helmet and picked up her bike.

"So what about Tonopah?" Darby asked. The two women looked to the east. The wind died and all that could be heard was the humming of idling engines.

"Not a chance," answered Magg as she rolled her motorcycle towards Darby, "but there's a fuel truck at Millers that never made it there before, well ... *you'll see.*"

"All right," Darby said. Placing her hands on her hips, she surveyed her troops and continued, "We'll leave 'em all at Millers to fuel up while you and I go figure out what the hell's going on."

• • • •

MAGG LED THE COLUMN to Millers, a roadside oasis of green trees and interconnected driveways that once accommodated travelers on the highway. It was fifteen miles from Tonopah, a small unincorporated town prior to the fall that now served as an eastern outpost of Kaiser.

"Usual defensive setup, though I doubt anyone will fuck with you this close to the road," Darby instructed Petra once they arrived. The pair walked a short distance from the cover of the trees and Darby pointed to a one-lane dirt road heading north, saying, "If we're not back by the time you've refueled, take the road until it reaches the hills. And before you go rig the tanker to blow up. I'm not leaving any freebies behind."

"Got it," answered Petra. She folded her arms and kicked a rock.

"There are some abandoned businesses up that way," Darby explained as she aimed her finger at the point where the rocky hills met the horizon, "but stay frosty because sometimes we get strays who think they're bad asses. Believe it or not, those little fuckers *will* hit an armored column. Anyway, there's a huge bay on the north end of the hills. Hole up there until we get back."

"And if you don't get back?" queried Petra bluntly.

"Then do whatever the fuck you want," Darby replied as she stared into the distance, "because I won't give a fuck what you do."

"What about the civilians?" asked Petra. Darby turned to face her.

"Watch out for the blonde," Darby advised blithely. They returned to the oasis without further comment and Darby mounted her own motorcycle, one of several transported with the caravan for scouting purposes. Magg joined her and the two women sped onto the highway and out of sight.

· · · ·

PETRA DID NOT RETURN to the vehicle, Darby's lieutenant instead supervising the refueling efforts and obsessively surveying the horizon with binoculars. Sarah, ravenously hungry after the first leg of their trip, consumed an MRE. Miriam reappeared during her meal.

"Welcome back," said Sarah.

"Whatever," replied Miriam. Sarah sensed an agitation in her but decided to pursue greater matters.

"Miriam, now that we have some time, we must discuss Jacob," advised Sarah as she finished the MRE and neatly packed the refuse into its pouch.

"No," Miriam said flatly. She suddenly felt the baby's presence like a knife in the kidney. Sarah set the pouch aside and moved to the edge of her seat to get closer to Miriam.

"The two of you parted on violent terms," said Sarah. She rested a hand on her pregnant belly and tried to touch Miriam's shoulder. Miriam dodged the attempt.

"Uh, yeah, he threw me into, into the . . . ," said Miriam before trailing off. A dark cloud passed over her and she shuddered, uttering with difficulty, "*Abussos.*"

The mere mention of the Abyss petrified Miriam and she became like stone. Sarah gave her a moment and then spoke.

"And, though warranted by the circumstances perhaps, he led you to believe you killed his child," recounted Sarah. Miriam became life-like once again as Sarah stated, "*He lied to you.*"

"Tryin' to convince me I don't want him," asked Miriam with a suspicious smirk, "so maybe somebody else can have him?"

"Miriam, I care for Jake," explained Sarah, "but I do not love him and I do not believe he truly loves me."

Miriam punched through her seat's backing. Sarah scooted back in her own seat and gave Miriam a look of disapprobation.

"Sorry," Miriam grumbled despite not feeling apologetic.

"I cannot have any romantic relationship with Jacob, even if I did love him, which, as I explained, I do not," continued Sarah as she squirmed and tried, despite her pregnancy, to assume a comfortable position. Finding the least uncomfortable posture, she declared, "My sisterly vows forbid it."

"Your vows didn't stop you from fucking him," Miriam countered snidely. Sarah grew cross.

"Miriam, I was not in control of my own body when that happened and I refuse to battle with you over it any further," argued Sarah. The pair engaged in an optical battle as she expounded, "In any event, it is not for my sake that I raise these issues, but for yours. Justified as Jacob's actions were, those experiences were unpleasant at best and traumatic at worst for you."

Miriam bowed her head and relived the pain of her last encounter with Jacob. Sarah leaned forward.

"Can you accept Jacob's reasons for them and set aside any grievances you have against him?" asked Sarah. Miriam pondered Sarah's words before meeting her stern gaze.

"Yes," Miriam answered with a conviction that surprised Sarah. She granted the nun a temporary respite from her negative emotions and cognitions and said forlornly, "It wasn't Jake's fault. I reaped what I sowed. I just want him back."

Sarah offered Miriam a small yet proud grin. Miriam returned it albeit with some uncertainty.

"See, that wasn't as bad as you thought," Miriam taunted Sarah.

"It astounds me how, after hundreds or thousands of years, demons can become so well-versed in some areas of human nature and yet so naïve in others," replied Sarah while maintaining her stunted smile. Her commentary befuddled Miriam and she received no response when she asked, "What of your sins against Jacob?"

Miriam returned to her stony state. Sarah's smile evaporated.

"You murdered Elizabeth's mind if not her body, mutilated and murdered poor, innocent Mallory and forced the man you claim to love to cast you into the Abyss," said Sarah. She squirmed again, her movements caused more by emotion than physical discomfort, and continued, "And there are other considerations, too, Miriam. He's traveled with Sophie for months now. I hate to say it but they've probably had sex and he may even have developed feelings for her. Strong feelings. She may not give him up willingly and may fight to keep him."

"That won't last long," Miriam stated without affect.

"I don't mean physically and you know it," replied Sarah. She gestured with clenched fists and said, "Sophie could force you into a choice between your newfound faith in God and your love for Jacob. Are you ready to make it?"

Sarah wrapped her arms around her belly as if to protect her baby from a physical blow. Miriam remained unemotional on her surface but her feelings boiled within her.

"This child presents complications as well," said Sarah, "because, when Jacob learns that I'm pregnant he may feel a certain . . . *obligation* to me. Or he may think you present a threat to the baby."

"What's your fucking point?!" Miriam bellowed in a demonic voice, her emotional explosion rocking the Humvee. A spiritual field of force erupted from Sarah, hurled Miriam into the door behind her and then disappeared as quickly as it surged into existence.

"Fuck!" Miriam roared as she picked herself up from the floor of the Humvee. Darby's shocked security personnel aimed weapons at the vehicle but none fired. Petra, wary of Miriam but loyal to her superior, intervened.

"Stand down! Stand down!" ordered Petra. The security personnel hesitated but resumed their duties when she shouted, "You heard me! Get back to it. We're outta here as soon as that last rig is full. Move!"

"*My point*," explained Sara as Miriam slithered back into her seat, "is that Jacob may not readily accept you back into his life and, if he doesn't, you may have to-."

"I'm not giving him up!" Miriam interrupted with monstrous traces in her tone. Sarah looked more worn and frazzled by the minute but still waited for the flames of Miriam's feelings to burn low.

"I was going to say *be patient*," replied Sarah, her own patience waning. She felt tired despite her earlier slumber.

"I have to go," Miriam snapped. Fearful of Sarah's intense spiritual ward and terrified of losing Jacob, she noisily put on her backpack and faded from view.

"Of course you do," sighed Sarah as Miriam vanished. She kicked the seat in front of her in a rare flash of anger and sighed, "I'm seven months pregnant, in my forties, and the mother of a rage-filled, homicidal teenager. Forgive me Lord, but . . . *fuck*."

· · · ·

THE MOTORCYCLES GRADUALLY decelerated as they passed sites of long-demolished roadside buildings and came to a stop less than two miles from the heart of Tonopah. Darby removed her helmet and held it in the crook of her arm.

"What the fuck?" Darby asked in astonishment as she viewed Kaiser's outpost. Magg took off her helmet and hung it on the bike's right handlebar.

"That's what I said," uttered Magg. She folded her arms and, when Darby did not speak, she asked with a hint of nervousness, "What is that?"

It seemed as if the sun illuminated Tonopah with eerie, red rays which cast an amorphous curtain of light around the town. An area of duskiness surrounded the curtain, nibbling on the very light of day and dimming the landscape for several thousand feet.

"Did you send anyone in?" Darby asked. Her mood was dark yet void of anger.

"They've been MIA for hours," answered Magg. She offered Darby an uncertain look and asked, "Think they're still alive?"

"This is Big Phat Phuck's problem now," Darby declared before donning her helmet with both hands. Gunning her motorcycle, Darby whirled it around and, after a jarring squeal of her rear tire, she roared back to Millers. Magg threw a quick look at Tonopah before speeding off in pursuit of Darby. When the sound of their engines faded and the wind died, Miriam appeared.

The world grew quiet.

"'When it is evening, you say, 'It will be fair weather', for the sky is red, '" Miriam recited in a chilling tone as she watched the red light in the east, "'And in the morning, 'There will be a storm today', for the sky is red and threatening.'" (Excerpt from Matthew 16:2-3).

Miriam walked ten feet farther down the road. She gazed into the distance with a grimness etched on her pale face.

"Take what you can," Miriam said aloud, "but you can't have it all back. Not all of it. *I won't let you.*"

8

DINNER PROVED A SUFFICIENT though temporary balm for Jacob's angst. The main course was broiled pickerel and he rapidly consumed his meal while attempting to keep his contemplations on small matters. He managed to chase thoughts of certain problems from his mind - his braindead wife, her unborn child and his missing, demon-possessed stepdaughters – but others weighed heavily on him – Sophie's death, her replacement by a doting Boyka and his sudden insertion into Dr. Zhukova's theocracy.

"Fuck, that's a lot of problems," Jacob said in a neutral tone. He sipped coffee in his small room after dinner, the wayward traveler sitting quietly and gazing out the window. The mug was soon set aside and its contents grew cold. Jacob asked himself, "What the fuck do I do now?"

The winning idea was a nap, and, when he awoke from it, night had fallen. Bored and no longer tired, Jacob wandered out of his room. The other inhabitants of the station were friendly but also reserved, Dr. Zhukova's minions seemingly instructed to avoid prolonged contact with him. Unable to find Paliki, he found himself desiring a stiff drink.

"I haven't had a good, comfortable buzz in days," said Jacob. The advantage of his involuntary isolation was that he could scrounge unnoticed. Chasing a plain, fortysomething woman from the kitchen with his mere presence, he began his search.

"What do we have here?" Jacob asked when he found a small closet that served as a wine cellar. He eagerly checked each of the bottles but, to his dismay, they were all of one homemade variety. He sighed, "Cherry wine. All they got is fucking cherry wine."

Jacob absconded with two bottles and soon set about uncorking one of them. He sampled its contents and grimaced.

"God, that's terrible," he griped. Taking the corkscrew and the bottles, he wandered back to his room, muttering, "It'll hafta' do."

Quickly polishing off the first bottle, Jacob's boredom burgeoned while his judgment waned. He donned his winter weather gear, started on the second bottle and returned to the wine cellar to obtain more wine for the journey. The fortysomething woman, rendered less plain by the alcohol coursing through Jacob's blood stream, interrupted his second raid.

"Mr. Gottschalk, you are not permitted to drink that!" exclaimed the woman in horror.

"Just put it on my tab," Jacob replied while stuffing the bottle in a deep pocket of his snowsuit. Appraising the woman's average build, he drank from the open bottle and said, "I'm going walkabout. Wanna come with?"

Rendered speechless by Jacob's heathenism, she fled the kitchen in a flustered huff. He shrugged off the rejection and made his way to a rear door of Station Exodus.

"Mr. Gottschalk!" called out an older man. Approaching Jacob cautiously, he pleaded, "You cannot go out there, especially not in your condition."

Jacob spun around to face him. The older man stopped.

"Yeah, and what condition is that!? Kidnapped?!" Jacob yelled angrily. The plain woman rounded the corner but the fury of his gaze froze her. Jacob opened the door and said, "If you're gonna stop me, then stop me. Otherwise, I'm leaving . . . *assholes*."

He paused and waited for them to act. When they did nothing but gape at him, Jacob stepped outside and slammed the door behind him.

• • • •

"WHISKEY GOES BETTER with water," Jacob complained as he looked out across a steaming lake from the top of a ridge and choked down the cherry wine. The wind blew steadily, pushing thin wisps of cloud across the sky, and the bright full moon illuminated the landscape. Jacob muttered, "Damn, that's bad."

A well-worn trail descended from the ridge's crest and led Jacob to the water's edge. Initially hidden from his view, a bay was carved into a rock wall to his right, the steam curling against its roof and rolling away into the night. A narrowing, naturally-formed walkway ran along the interior of the bay.

Jacob took another swig of the wine. He noticed a pile of clothes and cold-weather gear neatly-folded at the entrance to the walkway. His eyes then traveled across the windswept waves and he detected movement many yards off shore. Squinting to see in the moonlit dimness, Jacob recognized human arms repeatedly rising out of the water and dipping into it again.

"That's ballsy," Jacob lauded the swimmer. He was amazed that anyone would brave the lake alone in the cold and darkness. Intrigued, Jacob walked to the bay. The constant introduction of heated water and steam created a sauna-effect inside it and a perspiring Jacob quickly shed his outer clothing. Once finished, he again looked to the lake and uttered, "Holy. Fucking. Shit."

Paliki's tall, willowy form arose from the depths as she trudged through gentle waves. Aroused by the athletic prowess and lean figure of Paliki and fueled by a growing alcohol buzz, Jacob indulged in a long study of her body. She froze when she spotted him.

"You're quite the swimmer," Jacob said. Water flowed around Paliki's knees and the rising breeze swirled the steam around her. She shivered.

"Mr. Gottschalk, what are you doing here?!" exclaimed Paliki in a combination of shock and embarrassment. She wore a dark, one-piece swimsuit with an open back and matching goggles. Her hair was stuffed into a white swim cap.

"Watching you swim in freezing temperatures . . . at night," Jacob replied. Paliki continued shivering as the cooler air forced forward by the wind rushed over her wet body. Admiring her dedication in the face of Mother Nature, Jacob said, "I'm impressed."

"Hot springs feed the lake and keep it warm enough to swim throughout the year," Paliki explained as she removed her goggles and approached the shore. Jacob gulped from the wine bottle to her great dismay.

"You must not drink that!" admonished Paliki.

"Wanna nip? It'll warm you up," Jacob said while holding out the wine bottle. He shook it, realized it was empty and tossed it into the snow outside the bay. Producing the third bottle, he proudly displayed it and said, "Don't worry, sweetheart, I always come prepared."

Paliki refused to look at the bottle and hurried into the bay, past Jacob and to a towel placed next to her clothing. She quickly dried herself.

"We only drink wine on special occasions and never from the bottle," advised Paliki. She noticed the way Jacob hawked her figure and requested curtly, "Please do not look at me like that."

"Then don't dress like that," Jacob countered.

"I am sorry, Mr. Gottschalk," gushed a mortified Paliki *sans* her normal level of calm collectedness. She motioned for Jacob to turn his back and begged, "Please give me a moment to dress."

"What would Dr. Z think if she caught you wearing a suit like that?" Jacob inquired. He gawked at her and added, "Though it's a little one-piece for my liking."

"She would consider my swimsuit immodest and inappropriate, especially when I am outside the Community, and my neglect of my duty to escort you to be inexcusable," admitted a distressed Paliki. She wrapped the towel around her body to shield it from Jacob and stated, "I would be punished by the Council."

Paliki lowered her head. Jacob attempted to take another drink but realized the bottle was still corked.

"I *deserve* to be punished," said Paliki, her guilt as thick as the humidity in the air. She hugged herself and stated, "I have disobeyed the Council and neglected my duties. I must seek their forgiveness, and God's."

"You must really like to swim to risk the wrath of Dr. Z," Jacob said. Though his libido and his intoxication prodded him, his mind righted the ship with thoughts of Boyka and he turned his back on Paliki. She removed her towel.

"*I love to swim,* but what they would have me wear slows me down," insisted Paliki as the devil on her shoulder interjected. She removed her swim cap and freed her long, brown hair.

"Well, if you don't say anything, I won't either," Jacob said. A teary Paliki observed Jacob respectfully gaze downward instead of peeking at her as she expected. She smiled but then bit her lip and became anxious.

"I promised Boyka," thought Paliki. Despite her angst, she strode forward, turned Jacob around and kissed him. He initially hesitated, the sheer force of her kiss and her towering height stunning him, but he soon recovered and melded into her body. The press of Jacob's hardening erection on Paliki's thigh brought her to her senses.

"No!" yelled Paliki. She shoved Jacob away and the power behind her rejection nearly sent Jacob into the lake. Whisking up her towel and wrapping herself in it, she huddled against the wall with her back to Jacob.

"What the fuck?!" Jacob shouted back. Paliki trembled and refused to look at him as he barked, "You started it!"

"Go back to the Station, please," pleaded Paliki while weeping. Guilt prickled Jacob but so did ire.

"What the fuck's the matter with you?" Jacob replied.

"Please go!" wailed Paliki.

"Fine," Jacob snapped. He swiftly re-clad himself in his cold-weather gear with frequent glowers at Paliki. She again refused to look at him.

Beginning his trek to the sound of Paliki's sobs, Jacob marched forward on the trail. He looked back on her and saw she had already donned a body-length, long-sleeved shirt. She continued dressing without acknowledging him so he used the corkscrew to open the third bottle of wine. Chucking the cork at Paliki despite knowing it would come nowhere near her, he then tipped up the bottle and took a drink. His aggravation fizzled.

"Well, at least this one didn't try to kill me," Jacob said.

. . . .

IT WAS NOT PALIKI BUT the plain woman, whose name Jacob learned was Anne, that awoke him before dawn. A fitful night's sleep and a hangover ruined the first hour of his day and his excessive drinking the night before caused him to experience alternate states of malaise and mild panic. His morning improved, albeit slightly, after a hot shower and his first cup of coffee.

Anne dutifully assisted Jacob in his preparations for the journey to the Community and he found her presence to be pleasant and calming. She spoke little, however, and watched him with curious eyes.

"That cherry wine is terrible," Jacob said with a smirk as she served him breakfast.

"I would not know," said Anne without affect. Jacob's smile faded when she added, "I practice temperance."

"Sorry about all the trouble last night," Jacob apologized, his usual post-bender anxiety amplifying his guilt.

"I forgive you, Mr. Gottschalk, as any true Christian should," replied Anne as she freshened his coffee, "but I must urge you to submit to the yolk of Dr. Zhukova. You have many demons and only the Community can save a man such as you."

Taken aback by Anne's sudden torrent of profound words, Jacob sat still and mute and made no effort to start his meal. She smiled meekly and then returned to the kitchen.

"Well, she's right about the demon part," Jacob said after several minutes of contemplation. He ate his meal alone and in silence.

. . . .

PROPERLY CLOTHED AND equipped for the bitter, windy morning, Jacob followed Anne to the front doors of Station Exodus. He saw another retrofitted van awaiting him in the drive and wondered if Paliki was inside.

"Well, thanks for the grub and the send-off, Anne," Jacob said with a grin. He extended his hand to her and she took it with an unexpectedly firm grasp.

"Remember me," said Anne with a quick twinkle of adoration in her eyes. Jacob knew her expression conveyed a greater meaning but what that meaning was he did not know.

"I will," Jacob said with the earnest intent to grant Anne's wish in return for her hospitality. Walking through the door that she held open for him, Jacob proceeded down the front steps and pulled on his hat. He hurried towards the van and uttered, "Fuck it's cold out here."

He rounded the rear of the van to avoid a confrontation with Paliki as long as possible. Stopping short of the front passenger-side door, he gripped its handle and exhaled in a visible jet of hot breath.

"Here we go," Jacob thought while opening the door and climbing inside the van.

"I am so very sorry, Mr. Gottschalk," gushed Paliki the second Jacob closed the door. The noise and vibration tweaked his aching head and he winced.

"Let's just forget all about last night," Jacob said as he pressed two fingers into his temple, "and be very, very quiet."

"But I promised Boyka-," insisted Paliki while pawing at him.

"Hey, I'm alive and not permanently damaged," Jacob interrupted her. He pushed away her attempts to touch him and said, "And any temporary damage is self-inflicted. So we're all good."

Paliki struggled with her promise to Boyka and her discontent was evident to Jacob. He nonetheless settled into his seat and stared through the windshield.

"Let's just get on the road," Jacob said with a forward gesture. Paliki's gaze lingered on him for several seconds but his coldness forced her surrender. Shifting the van into gear, she steered it down the drive and onto the main road.

The next hour of their journey was unpleasant. The pair remained silent though Paliki occasionally stole a quick glimpse of Jacob. He retreated into his head and pondered his impending arrival at the Community. Somewhere in the pathways of his mind, he stumbled across a stray thought and turned to Paliki with a furrowed brow.

"Boyka didn't ask you to whack me, did she?" Jacob asked. He bit the callous on the inside of his cheek. Paliki threw him a puzzled, sidelong glance.

"What does it mean, 'whack'?" said Paliki

"*Kill*," Jacob enunciated.

"No!" exclaimed Paliki with a horrified look. She glanced at the road ahead and then back to Jacob.

"Then what did you promise her?" Jacob demanded. Paliki's eyes widened and she snapped her head forward. Slamming on the brakes, she caused the van to skid to a halt. Jacob's momentum hurled him into the dashboard.

"Fuck!" he yelled as he fell to the floor. Shaking his head to clear it, he then rose to his knees and said, "What the hell are you doing?"

"*Zombik*," droned Paliki in Hungarian. She was dumbstruck.

"What?" Jacob asked in disbelief. Climbing back into his seat, he peered outside. Paliki unsnapped her holster and began to draw her pistol but Jacob waved off her attempt.

"Put that away," he said as he opened his door, "and stay here."

"Mr. Gottschalk!" bellowed Paliki. She lunged at him but failed to grasp him as he departed. He turned and pointed at her.

"Stay there!" Jacob ordered. Bristling with anger, he slammed the door and then approached Paliki's zombies.

"I warned you, *Ass*-arion," Jacob growled. Assarion and Marcion dangled the possessed shells of Mallory and Vanessa several yards ahead.

"Did you really?" asked Assarion. Speaking in Jacob's voice, she said, "'I probably don't have my Jesus superpowers anymore . . . .'"

"Gottschalk!" shrieked Marcion hideously. He charged Jacob with bulging eyes, the demon snarling and slavering the entire way. Two gunshots pierced the air and struck Mallory in the back, the force of the bullets knocking her to the ground. She lay still.

"Paliki, get back in the van!" Jacob ordered her. She stood behind the driver-side door with her arms extended through the open window and her gun aimed at Marcion.

"Nem! Menj vissza a furgonba!" shouted Paliki, her fear causing her to revert to her native language. She switched her aim to Vanessa who watched the scene with a satisfied smile but did not move.

Marcion leapt to his feet and cackled with delight. Paliki screamed and his sudden revival caused her to drop her firearm and gape at him in amazement.

"I waited long for this, Gottschalk, waited long!" exclaimed Marcion with wicked delight and a brief, bizarre dance. He abruptly stopped it and straightened up his body, lolled his head towards the paralyzed Hungarian and said in a monstrous tone, "But it will cause more pain if she goes first! More pain!"

"Marcion!" yelled Jacob in a commanding tone, the Holy Spirit exploding within him and petrifying the demon. He instructed Marcion grimly, "I command you, go back to the Abyss and do not return here again."

An unseen force wracked Mallory's body and it convulsed as if struck by lightning. Its puppeteer caused it to emit a final, horrible roar before it twitched one last time and collapsed in a heap on the pavement. Jacob looked to Vanessa whose host still grinned with approval.

"It seems you have not completely fallen out of His favor," posited Assarion. She folded her arms and took three small steps toward Jacob, continuing, "Though perhaps He was only allowing you to save the girl's life, or permitting you one last exorcism before you are stripped of your spiritual authority."

Jacob glowered at Assarion but did not assault or speak to her. He had no intention of testing her theories.

"Take advantage of the lull in the hostilities and lay your stepdaughter to rest, Jacob Gottschalk," advised Assarion, "because a new war is coming."

Ten seconds later she was gone. Jacob felt a presence close to him and threw a glance over his shoulder. Paliki, her gun in her hand, stood a few feet behind him.

"Mr. Gottschalk," said Paliki sheepishly.

"I told you to get back in the van," Jacob grumbled. He moved to where Mallory's mutilated corpse lay and, kneeling down, he scooped her into his arms. Jacob rose to his feet and turned around.

"What is happening?" asked a terrified Paliki. She trembled and shed tears as she observed Mallory's body.

"Trust me, kid, you don't want to know," Jacob answered. Carrying his dead stepdaughter, he walked past Paliki without saying another word.

• • • •

GRIEF WREATHED JACOB as he wrapped Mallory's dead body in bedsheets with great care. Paliki offered her assistance but he refused and she was only able to learn that Mallory was his stepdaughter. Frightened that the *zombi* might reanimate, she sat on a huge roadside rock some distance from the van and uneasily watched Jacob.

"Sorry I can't do better than this, Mal," Jacob said as he caressed Mallory's head through her makeshift shroud. He made no effort to conceal his tears and added mournfully, "Sorry about all of it."

Hopping out of the van, Jacob closed both rear doors. He kept his hands on the handles and rested his hat against its cold metal. Paliki yearned to comfort him but could not bring herself to get closer to Mallory.

Jacob lifted his head and looked into the woods on the opposite side of the highway. Just within his field of vision he noticed a clearing containing several stacks of logs. He stood up straight and wiped away his tears.

"I *can* do better," Jacob said aloud. Walking into the middle of the road, he pointed at the stacks and asked Paliki, "What happened there?"

"What happened where?" asked Paliki. She slid off the rock and approached Jacob.

"There," Jacob said with another emphatic point.

"The logs?" replied Paliki. Wilting under Jacob's intense, impatient gaze, she explained, "A, uh, a storm overturned trees and they blocked the highway. We cut them into shorter, shorter . . . *lengths* and stacked them there."

"Fucking perfect," Jacob said. He opened the van doors and, after sliding Mallory's body halfway out, he threw it over his right shoulder.

"What are you doing!?" inquired Paliki, the Hungarian discomfited by Jacob's bizarre behavior. She stepped back.

"Making sure those demonic bastards never touch her again," Jacob said confidently. He carried Mallory's corpse across the road and into the trees.

"Wait, Mr. Gottschalk!" begged Paliki as she trudged behind Jacob. She arrived at the clearing shortly after he did and was met by his tenacious countenance.

"Clear off that first row of logs," Jacob ordered her. Moving slowly at first but quickly picking up speed, Paliki rolled log after snow-covered log off the largest stack. Jacob supervised her closely and, when she cleared the last log, instructed her, "Now clear off the rest of the snow."

Paliki obeyed. Once her task was completed, Jacob gently laid Mallory on the stack of logs. He then charged back towards the highway.

"Where are you going?!" shouted Paliki while throwing up her arms in exasperation. Jacob's erratic behavior flustered her and she uttered, "Magdolna was right. Americans *are* crazy."

Jacob soon returned with one of the spare cans of gasoline and a Bible. Realizing what he intended, Paliki interposed herself between Jacob and the pyre.

"Do not burn her," said Paliki with pity for both Jacob and Mallory. Gesturing as she spoke, she suggested, "We will take her to the Community and there we will bury her. It is a holy place and she will be protected."

Jacob smirked. His smirk soon broke into a laugh.

"Is that so?" Jacob said as he set the gas can on the ground. Unscrewing its cap, he asked, "How many demons have you seen in your precious Community?"

"Démonok?" said Paliki.

"That's right," Jacob replied. Making his voice harsh, he said, "*Démonok.*"

Paliki's fear returned and she moved away from the pyre. Jacob's fey mood caused her to instinctively place her hand on her holster.

"See, if you pull that gun from your holster, and fire two bullets into my chest, I die," Jacob said while approaching the pyre. Lifting the gas can above Mallory's lifeless body, he drenched both she and the logs in gasoline and expounded, "But, like you saw with Mal, if you pump two rounds into me when I'm demon-possessed, I keep right on movin', even if I'm dead."

Jacob produced a book of waterproof matches. He lit one and held it out to Paliki.

"Demons are spiritual beings that enter into and dominate a physical body," Jacob explained. He tossed the match onto the pyre while stepping backward. Mallory burst into flames. Paliki flinched.

"No physical body," said Paliki sadly, "no possession."

"Exactly, my dear," Jacob confirmed as he tossed the matchbook into the fire. The flames engulfed Mallory's body and within minutes the whole pyre roared with fiery light and heat. Though Jacob held the Bible in his hands, he did not open it but instead recited from memory, "'... but One is coming who is mightier than I, and I am not fit to untie the thong of His sandals; He will baptize you with the Holy Spirit and fire ...'" (Excerpt from Luke 3:16).

· · · ·

A LIGHT SNOW FELL AS stands of evergreen trees closed on the road and made Jacob feel claustrophobic. Paliki seemed lost in a dream though she never let the van stray from the road. The funeral pyre still burned in Jacob's mind when she brought the van to a halt at the Community's front gates. Paliki smiled warmly at them as if they were the very gates of Heaven.

"The gates are always open," said Paliki proudly. Turning to Jacob with love and hope in her eyes, she gushed, "We are home."

The depth of the emotion in Paliki's voice perplexed Jacob. It was as if she experienced an adrenaline rush merely by returning to the Community. The smallest flame of homesickness arose in his spirit but, remembering his lack of a home, he extinguished it.

"*You're* home, sweetheart," Jacob replied, "*you're* home."

An arched, polished sign above the gates read "Welcome to the New Oneida Community", the letters a stark white against the black iron. It was remarkably clean despite the weather. The gates were attached to square, red-bricked columns but, to Jacob's surprise, no fences extended away from them into the surrounding trees.

"No fences, no walls, no wire," Jacob said aloud while tapping his fingers on the armrest. Looking about with a thoughtful expression, he stated, "You're not keeping the world out or the faithful in."

"Why would the faithful want to leave?" asked Paliki in disbelief. She allowed the van to roll forward and inquired, "And why would we not open up our arms to all those who seek Christ and the coming of God's kingdom?"

"Why indeed?" Jacob said with a shrug and a goofy grin. Paliki's faith was great; his, on the other hand, became a greater question each and every day. He said to himself, "Six months is about the limit of my faith . . . but he *is* still letting me kick demon ass."

The road plunged downward into the western end of a valley before jaunting east around the skirts of a mountain. It then took a large turn south, the bend gradual at first but then sharply running in that direction. The van trundled along at ten miles an hour.

"Ho-ly shit," Jacob said as they arrived at a large eastward bend in the road. Springing up from the ground, ground which contained massive, snow-covered lawns and now-dormant gardens, was a humongous, red-bricked mansion. It looked like a building one might find on a university campus or a sprawling nineteenth century estate.

"Such language is not permitted here," scolded Paliki gently. Jacob was too astonished to respond and simply gawked at the massive estate as they passed it. Smaller buildings constructed in the same style occupied the south side of the road, the structures forming a large village that bordered a glassy alpine lake. Despite the cold, Jacob rolled down the window and observed the Community.

"So these are your people," Jacob said as he watched bundled residents attending to tasks like shoveling snow or towing laden carts with snowmobiles.

"They are my family," insisted Paliki. Reaching the near end of a circular drive that ascended the slope to the mansion, she turned onto it and approached the front entrance. Six ornate, white columns supported the overhang extending from the top of the first story. Paliki stopped the car in front of large, forest green double doors topped with semicircular windows and bookended by long, green benches.

Dr. Zhukova stood at the top of the steps leading to the doors with her arms folded, the matriarch remaining as still as a statue but emanating the most foreboding of energies. Glancing at her through the open car window, Jacob waved and smirked.

"Helluva place ya' got here, Dr. Z," Jacob complimented her as his mind conjured up images of a vast treasury in the mansion's basement and pondered all the illicit activities that served to fill it.

"You, as a man, expect a certain measure of deference and respect in your own home, do you not, Mr. Gottschalk?" inquired Dr. Zhukova without the slightest display of emotion. Jacob assumed her position at the higher vantage point was intentional.

"Deference and respect are two things I don't get much of," Jacob answered while bracing for the intellectual fencing to follow. Mallory's impromptu funeral still soured his mood and lowered his tolerance for much of anything.

"Well, if I were in your home, would you expect anything less than a measure of deference and respect?" she continued. He stifled a laugh and looked up to her with a sneer.

"I don't have a home, *Doctor*," Jacob countered.

"Nonetheless, Mr. Gottschalk, I ask, humbly and respectfully, that you afford me a measure of deference and respect in my home," requested Dr. Zhukova politely. She folded her hands in front of her and held them against her body.

"You're good," Jacob remarked. Dr. Zhukova's face softened and she offered him a gentle smile. Patting Paliki on the thigh to jab at the Doctor, he said, "Thanks for the ride, sweetheart."

Paliki blushed at the attention and offered a sheepish grin in reply. Jacob disembarked from the car but then ducked his head back into it.

"We don't need to tell anyone about Mallory for now," Jacob said under his breath. She nodded in assent. He closed the car door and climbed the stairs.

"Hello, *Dr. Zhukova*," Jacob said as he offered her his hand. The discovery of polite, rational civilization after the fall and in a remote land amused him.

"Welcome to New Oneida, Mr. Gottschalk," replied Dr. Zhukova with a firm handshake.

"New Oneida?" Jacob asked. Dr. Zhukova released his hand and addressed Paliki.

"Paliki, please take Mr. Gottschalk's baggage to the guest house we have prepared for him," instructed Dr. Zhukova while passing over his question.

"Yes, Doctor," droned Paliki in a hauntingly robotic manner. She immediately obeyed her superior and drove down the driveway.

"What, I don't get to stay in the mansion?" Jacob asked while watching the car turn onto the main drive.

"The mansion house is strictly for Community members and not visitors," advised Dr. Zhukova, the smallest hint of a taunt in her tone. Jacob proceeded to the front door and began to open it for her as she stated, "While we happily receive and encourage peaceful visitors, we do not permit unfettered access to the Community."

"But I still get to go in, right?" Jacob asked. Dr. Zhukova swiftly closed the distance between the top of the stairs and the doors and placed her hand on his hand. The physical contact created the oddest of sensations on his skin and instantly aroused him.

"Visitors are allowed in the mansion house only with the express permission of the Community Council," Dr. Zhukova said politely yet firmly. The look Jacob gave her caused her to yank back her hand and retreat a step. He closed the door.

"First chink in the armor," Jacob thought while reveling in the good Doctor's unwitting mistake. His sexual success with Sophie and Boyka buoyed his confidence with women. Sizing up her sexual potential, if indeed there was any, Jacob inquired, "So, Doctor, when do we get down to it?"

Dr. Zhukova straightened up and composed herself to ward off Jacob's sexual energy. She apparently succeeded.

"You will meet with the Council early tomorrow morning," said Dr. Zhukova. Gesturing southeastward, she explained, "That meeting will take place at our Visitor Center. In the meantime, I will take you to your guest house. I have assigned you a hostess for the duration of your stay and she is preparing a hot meal for you."

"Boyka?" Jacob inquired stupidly before balling his hands into fists. Handing even little victories to Dr. Zhukova was foolish especially given her policy of seducing him with younger women. He thought, "Slow it down, dumbass, or she'll be leading you around by your cock before you know it."

"No, I'm afraid," Dr. Zhukova replied, the expression on her drawn face conveying her satisfaction with Jacob's reaction. Leading him back down the steps, she said, "Boyka has other duties to which she must attend as does Paliki, if you were going to inquire about her. But do not worry, Mr. Gottschalk, you will have the opportunity to visit with them again if you so wish. "

"So Jacob gets another deferential young hottie to whet his appetite, sit on his cock and scramble his brain," Jacob said to himself. Chewing on the callous inside his cheek, a habit he had avoided for months, he glanced at the sky and thought, "Now you're sending me girls *with* gods. Wonderful."

9

ONEIDA'S GUEST HOUSES were built in the same general style as the mansion house though they were longer and narrower, the faces of the two-story buildings resembling miniature versions of the main entrance. Each house sported a green, rectangular front door with a semi-circular window above it and was flanked by wide, rectangular windows. Two white pillars on a cement porch supported a white balcony accessed by miter-shaped French doors.

"How quaint," Jacob said in jest. Guests were greeted by two symmetrically placed flowerpots on three-foot pillars and a red-brick walkway bordered by lanes of small, white stones. Another set of the flowerpots guarded the single cement step leading to the porch. The entire entrance area was meticulously cleaned of snow and ice.

"You will find it surprisingly spacious and comfortable," countered Dr. Zhukova. She led Jacob down the brick walkway and continued, "We go to great lengths to ensure that our guests have pleasant stays."

"Get a lotta guests way out here?" Jacob asked. Dr. Zhukova did not answer and, before they completed the short journey down the walkway, the front door opened. Dr. Zhukova's next lure appeared but, unlike her other tempting minions, the five-foot-two-inch blonde was buxom with glowing, honey-colored skin. Undaunted by strangers, or at least by Jacob, the young woman gazed on him with strong, wide eyes of rich brown.

"Mr. Gottschalk, please meet Rahela, your hostess during your stay," said Dr. Zhukova. Rahela wore the usual skirt-and-blouse-uniform of New Oneidan women with a navy blue apron over them. She attempted to brush off the telltale signs of work in the kitchen as Dr. Zhukova continued, "She will attend to all of your daily needs, including the preparation of your meals."

"I am pleased to meet you, Mr. Gottschalk," said Rahela without a Hungarian accent. She struggled to contain herself and trembled.

"Likewise," Jacob replied. He marveled at how the New Oneidans seemed little affected by the extreme cold. Extending his hand with the intention of kissing hers, he asked flippantly, "You Hungarian, too, sweetheart?"

The word "sweetheart" broke Rahela's resolve. She charged off the porch and nearly tackled Jacob to the ground with a desperate embrace.

"Is that a yes?" Jacob asked while returning her ardent greeting. The feel of her ample breasts pressing into his body awoke his penis so he rotated to prevent it from poking her. Dr. Zhukova noticed his maneuver and the reason for it.

"Please forgive Rahela's impetuousness," said Dr. Zhukova with a chill in her voice that caused Rahela to release Jacob, step back and come to attention like a soldier.

"I am sorry, Doctor," said an embarrassed Rahela. Clasping her hands behind her back, she turned to address Jacob and said, "And my apologies to you as well, Mr. Gottschalk. You are my first guest and I am anxious to be a good hostess. But come, let us get you out of the cold."

"There's nothing to forgive," Jacob replied with a dismissive gesture. He fired a few optic daggers at Dr. Zhukova and, feeling puckish, looked to Rahela with a wide, mischievous smile and said, "That was one helluva welcome. You're gonna make a *damn* good hostess."

Rahela's face lit up and she stifled a smile but a glower from the good Doctor thrust her right back into line. Dr. Zhukova's treatment of the good-natured Rahela vexed Jacob.

"From this point forward, I ask that you remain here at the guest house unless Rahela is with you or, in her absence, another member of the Community," said Dr. Zhukova.

"House arrest, nice touch," Jacob replied. The restrictions on his movement within the Community screamed cult loudly and clearly in his mind. He gazed on Dr. Zhukova sternly but said, "Whatever you say, Doctor."

"I have prepared a special meal for you, drágaságom," cooed Rahela. Jacob wondered if her fervent hospitality was real or feigned but scolded himself privately, "Doesn't matter, idiot. Either way, Zhukova's using her to manipulate you."

"Ez helytelen volt, Rahela," snapped Dr. Zhukova.

"Bocsánatot kérek," replied an ashamed Rahela. Jacob's chivalrous instinct reared its head.

"Hey, why don't you back off?" Jacob growled. The dust-up between he and Dr. Zhukova distressed Rahela but, with the buffering abilities of a caring mother, she deftly intervened. Insinuating herself between them, she grasped his hands.

"Come, let us get you out of the cold," repeated Rahela, her caring attention easing his irritation. Generating an earnest smile and squeezing his hands tightly, she advised, "Your meal is ready."

"Rahela," beckoned Dr. Zhukova.

"Yes, Doctor Zhukova," replied Rahela in a tone of deference, her grin evaporating.

"Legyen tudatában," said Dr. Zhukova with a hard expression.

"Igen, Orvos," replied Rahela with a bowed head. Squeezing Jacob's hands in a much gentler manner, she soon disengaged from him and disappeared into the guest house.

"I will return at sunrise tomorrow to escort you to the Visitor Center so please be ready," stated Dr. Zhukova. The Russian ostensibly content to sacrifice Rahela to Jacob, she added, "Have a blessed night, Mr. Gottschalk."

Dr. Zhukova, with a nod but without another word, whirled around with measured grace and walked towards the mansion house.

"What about a key?" Jacob said in a raised voice, his mind recovering from Rahela's sex appeal and turning to suspicion and security.

"We do not lock our doors at New Oneida, Mr. Gottschalk," answered Dr. Zhukova.

"That's fan-fucking-tastic," Jacob said while shaking his head in the negative. He wondered aloud, "What the fuck have I gotten myself into?"

"Everything is ready," chirped Rahela, her boisterous announcement causing Jacob to start. Her apron was gone, replaced by a heavy overcoat and a hat. She risked a quick touch of his arm and added, "It is a dish that has been in my family for generations. I hope you enjoy it."

"You're not gonna join me?" Jacob queried despite expecting that Dr. Zhukova would pull another Hungarian out from under him. Rahela leaned into Jacob and spoke into his left ear.

"I *am* Hungarian, and the women in my family produce large families because they have twins without fail," whispered Rahela with great pride. Making no attempt to answer Jacob's question, she added, "I myself am a twin."

Jacob shivered. Rahela's soothing aroma and warm breath, as well as the prospect of her twin, sent Jacob's libido into overdrive.

"Enjoy your meal," said Rahela with shimmering eyes. Folding her hands in front of her in the same manner as Dr. Zhukova, she advised, "Leave everything after you eat. I will return to clean up later this evening."

Rahela whirled around and quickly followed in Dr. Zhukova's footsteps. Jacob restrained himself from following her but only with considerable effort.

"Okie dokie," Jacob said while riveting his eyes to the sways of Rahela's curvaceous hips. A neuron fired and he shouted after her, "Hey, what does drágaságom mean?"

Rahela stopped in her tracks and looked over her shoulder at him with an embarrassed smile and a glimmer in her eyes. She once again failed to answer his question, the blonde leaving Jacob behind. A freezing wind sent him scurrying into the house.

"I shoulda' went south," Jacob griped.

• • • •

JACOB'S LIMITED KNOWLEDGE of Hungarian culture fed his expectation of goulash for dinner. Rahela shattered that expectation by crafting a delicious two-course meal of *Krumplileves*, a soup of potatoes in broth with slices of sausage, carrots and turnips, and *Rakott Krumpli*, a potato casserole made with eggs, paprika, spicy sausage, thick bacon (which he later learned was called *szalonna*), quark cheese (or *túró*), onions, sour cream and breadcrumbs.

"Where the hell are they getting all this stuff?" Jacob said after polishing off a substantial portion of Rahela's meal. He indulged in a short nap before donning his winter gear and stepping out onto the balcony.

Community members buzzed around the grounds like bees, each one seemingly focused on the task at hand and oblivious to Jacob's presence. An occasional child flitted across his view under the watchful escort of an adult. Their activity continued even after the last light of the sun disappeared.

"She's hard-boiled, but she's still shaped like a woman," Jacob mused as Dr. Zhukova materialized from the mansion and began her walk towards the guest house. She walked with a determined gait and the slightest sway of her hips, the Doctor intermittently greeting Community members as their paths crossed. Jacob studied every step she took until she arrived at the entrance of the red-bricked path.

"It is time, Mr. Gottschalk," announced Dr. Zhukova in a strange, grave tone.

"For what, my execution?" Jacob asked. Dr. Zhukova sternly examined him at first but, after he simply gazed back with a small smirk, she relaxed her facial muscles into a begrudging grin.

"My apologies," said Dr. Zhukova. She folded her gloved hands in front of her and added, "The Community Council has decided we would like to meet with you tonight."

"All the suspects in one place," Jacob said to himself. He soon joined Dr. Zhukova in front of the guest house. She avoided the most direct route to the Visitor Center and escorted him there via the main road which, within the vicinity of the Community's center, was paved and cleared of all traces of winter.

"Our beliefs and our Community are decidedly Christian and based on the Bible Communism of John Humphrey Noyes. He founded the original Community at Oneida, New York in 1848. You will learn much of Father Noyes and Bible Communism in the coming days," said Dr. Zhukova as she abruptly launched into a tour-guide-like lecture. Despite his desire to do so, Jacob restrained himself and did not interrupt it. She cocked an eye at him and continued, "To answer one of your original questions, our denomination, at least in our own estimation, is Reformed Bible Communism. Given the negative connotations of the word Communism in the West, however, we call ourselves Reformed Oneidans."

"So they're communists," Jacob said to himself. Dr. Zhukova stopped on the main road and gazed proudly on the mansion house.

"The original Oneidans built their first mansion house at Oneida in 1849 followed by a second, larger one in 1862 with additions in 1869 and

1878," explained Dr. Zhukova. Turning and gesturing to the west side of the mansion house, she continued, "The 1869 addition was deemed the South Wing and, as you can see, we included a similar structure in our modern mansion house, which is much larger than the original."

"Why did you build it facing west?" Jacob asked as they continued their journey to the Visitor Center.

"Because we wanted the mansion house to face the beauty of Lake Oneida," answered Dr. Zhukova as if Jacob should have known the answer.

"Of course," Jacob replied.

"The Visitor Center is an exact exterior replica of the old South Wing, being built in the European 'Second Empire' style," explained Dr. Zhukova. Both South Wing replicas possessed red-brick walls and white-and-green trim. Both also had multiple-story towers housing the green double doors that formed the main entrance and a white-shingled mansard roof. Dr. Zhukova opened one of the front doors, politely held it for Jacob and gestured for him to enter, saying, "If you would, please."

Jacob hesitated. The only way to unravel the mystery of New Oneida, however, was to push onward so he stepped inside.

"You will wait in the public Council Room and I will summon you when the Council is ready," advised Dr. Zhukova as they walked through the Center. Its first two floors contained a museum chronicling the original Community founded by John Noyes and the genesis of the new Community.

"What's a cult without its propaganda?" Jacob said to himself. Their ascent to the third story led them to a cavernous meeting room similar to a city council chamber.

"Please be seated, Mr. Gottschalk," instructed Dr. Zhukhova as she motioned towards a chair just outside the double wooden doors leading to the private chamber. Holding her folded hands in front of her, she said with a courteous grin, "We will be with you shortly."

* * * *

"WE ARE READY FOR YOU now, Mr. Gottschalk," said Dr. Zhukova as she opened the deliberation room doors and waved her hand towards the Council's inner sanctum. An elusiveness in her tone sent a tingle down Jacob's spine.

"You sure about that?" Jacob replied as he stood up and followed her.

"You're not the first incorrigible man with whom we've dealt, I assure you," said Dr. Zhukova with a confident glance over her shoulder.

The Council's deliberation chambers made up the third story of the Visitor Center tower with three narrow, rectangular windows built into each of its other walls. Jacob turned his attention to the wooden conference table sitting in the center of the room, around which were six oversized chairs. Dr. Zhukova took the lone chair on the far end of the table and Jacob, without waiting for an invitation, claimed the chair opposite her. All but one of the Council members viewed him with reserved interest, mild disapproval or both. Dr. Zhukova introduced the friendly face first.

"We shall begin with introductions, Mr. Gottschalk. This is Edna Baxter, my very good friend and indispensable right hand," said Dr. Zhukova with a gesture to her right. Edna sat up proudly as the Doctor added, "She is our Director of Community and Individual Spirituality."

"Welcome to the Community, Mr. Gottschalk," said Edna, a petite schoolmarm of a woman. Edna's kind, mannish face, her ears, her nose and even the round lenses of her wiry glasses were small; her dark brown hair was remarkably devoid of gray and styled in a short, efficient manner. She examined Jacob with a faint smile as if she sensed the spiritual power within him, saying, "It is no coincidence that you found your way to New Oneida and I sincerely hope your stay will be a long one."

"I appreciate the sentiment but you may want to reserve judgment on that," Jacob replied. There was no doubt in his mind that Edna read his spirit like a written page though he did not know to what end.

"And this dear man is Dr. Malcom Frye," interjected Dr. Zhukova with a gesture to her immediate left and a measure of poorly-veiled affection. Next to her sat a balding elderly man with pale green eyes and a gauntness he seemed to share with her. His wispy hair and sparse, closely-trimmed beard were reddish blonde; his thin locks and the growth on the corners of his chin were tinged with silvery streaks. He possessed an unmistakable air of confident wisdom and seemed, at least to Jacob, to be English. Dr. Zhukova added, "He serves as our Chief Resources Officer and, as you can imagine, his is a critical role in the survival of the Community."

"Mr. Gottschalk," said Dr. Frye with a polite nod and a hint of a British accent. The Doctor wore a charcoal gray suit, a black shirt dotted in tiny, white circles and a matching tie and pocket square.

"The Englishman must rate to buck the dress code," Jacob thought. The two men vied for dominance with an exchange of stares, a contest in which Dr. Zhukova quickly intervened.

"Next, we have our Community Property Manager, and a Masters-level engineer, Meriwa LeClaire," said Dr. Zhukova as she motioned to the fifty-something woman on Jacob's right. He immediately felt a chill when Meriwa hawked him with her dark-brown eyes.

"Hello, Mr. Gottschalk," said Meriwa. Jacob sensed her detestation of his presence and she added pointedly, "It's been some time since an outsider has passed the gates of our Community."

Sallow-skinned and black-haired, she, as he would later discover, claimed both Inuit and French ancestry. Meriwa's rounded face rested in a permanent, smug smile that hung beneath prominent, fleshy cheeks. She was tall like Dr. Zhukova but, unlike her fellow councilmember, athletically built.

"Give me one of those vans and I'll pass right back through them," Jacob said with a grin. Meriwa was not amused. He studied her face briefly and thought, "Now there's a candidate for wanting me offed."

"Last, but by no means least, is Chidubem Sankara, our Chief Judicial Officer," said Dr. Zhukova. Despite wearing a dark blue suit, Sankara also broke with tradition by donning a white, gray and blue shirt bedecked with African designs. He was rangy with dark black skin, an engaging countenance, a bulbous nose and receding white hair. He also sported a beard and mustache of manicured stubble.

"Glad to have you here, Jacob, if I may call you Jacob," said Chidubem. They shared knowing grins and, despite Jacob's suspicion of the Council, he developed an immediate liking for Mr. Sankara.

"You could call me worse so why not?" Jacob replied. Chidubem chuckled.

"Now that we all know each other, let us address the reason why we are here today," stated Dr. Zhukova. Turning to Dr. Frye, she said, "Dr. Frye, if you would be so kind."

"Of course," said Dr. Frye. Standing up, he walked to the west side of the conference room and gazed out of the middle window.

"Thank you," replied Dr. Zhukova, their courteous dance garnering an eye roll from Jacob. Dr. Frye slid his hands into his pockets.

"Meriwa is correct, Mr. Gottschalk, that we have not had any visitors, at least to the Community proper, in many years," explained Dr. Frye. Turning to face Jacob, he tilted his head and continued, "Your appearance is quite unexpected and has caused a great deal of anxiety amongst our members."

"Look, I didn't just stumble in here," Jacob objected with a shake of his head. Pointing at the Doctor, he said, "Your people brought me here."

"After they rescued you from certain death," replied Dr. Frye in a politely-dismissive tone. Walking around the far side of the table, he said, "We are a Christian Community and we care for those the Lord entrusts to us. You were in no condition to travel on your own and, as I understand the situation, you never objected to being brought here."

"Where the fuck else was I gonna go?" Jacob asked incredulously. Chidubem and Meriwa recoiled while Edna squelched a gasp by placing her hand over her mouth. Dr. Zhukova remained unmoved.

"Your language, Mr. Gottschalk, is totally unacceptable and unnecessary," scolded Dr. Frye. Jacob slammed his fists on the table.

"Fuck my fucking language!" he barked as he rose to his feet. All five members of the Council froze and stared at Jacob in trepidation. Composing himself, he said, "Look, thanks for the help, but I'm leaving now."

Jacob bowed mockingly with his hands pressed together. Turning around, he started for the doors but one of them opened before he could reach it.

"Is there a problem, Doctors?" said a five-foot-eight-inch-tall woman with long, dark-brown hair, deep-brown eyes and a semiautomatic pistol aimed at Jacob. He guessed that she was of Mexican heritage and, though she dressed like them, a decade older than the Hungarians.

"Thank you, Juanita, but everything is under control," said Dr. Frye. Juanita nodded her assent and holstered her pistol. The Doctor looked to Jacob and asked, "Wouldn't you agree, Mr. Gottschalk?"

"Yeah," Jacob said with a grim face, "I'd agree. But we'll let Juanita stay just in case."

Pulling out his chair for Juanita, Jacob waited for her to take a seat. Dr. Frye, in the meantime, begrudgingly accepted Jacob's terms and motioned to the chair.

"Please," he said. An uncertain Juanita seated herself while Jacob closed the door. He pushed in her chair and walked to the window.

"Now, if you'll give me the floor, Doctor, I'll move this along," Jacob said as he leaned against the window frame. The tension in the room broke like a rubber band stretched too far and did not return. The other Councilmembers relaxed in their seats and Dr. Frye returned to his chair. All eyes fixated on Jacob as he began, "I'm from the City of Kaiser which is located in what used to be California. The Sierra Nevada Mountains, to be more precise."

Jacob looked at each face in turn. Juanita listened to his story with great interest and surprise but the Councilmembers were unfazed.

"So you already know about Kaiser," Jacob said.

"Yes, we do," replied Dr. Zhukova. She adjusted her glasses and said, "We have had business dealings with it on occasion."

Jacob wondered if the Council knew of Elizabeth. He decided to let the matter lie.

"I left Kaiser over six months ago to pursue my kidnapped stepdaughters," Jacob explained. A darkness passed over him before he continued, "They're dead. I had only one traveling companion, Sophie, but, as you know, she's dead. So, I'm now completely alone and no one from Kaiser – hell, no one period – knows where I am."

"We're going to need more information than that," said Meriwa to the affirmative nod of Dr. Frye. Juanita watched Jacob with growing pity.

"I told you what you need to know," Jacob said in irritation, "and left out the parts you don't."

"So what you're telling us is that you are no threat to the Community if we release you," said Dr. Frye.

"You got it, Doc," Jacob replied, "and I intend to forget all about this place once I leave."

"Where will you go?" asked Dr. Frye, the old man baffled by Jacob's refusal of the safety of the Community. Jacob punctuated his devil-may-care attitude with a wry smile.

"Not a clue, Doc," Jacob said, "not a clue."

The room remained eerily silent. Dr. Zhukova rose.

"Would you give us some time to discuss what you've told us?" inquired Dr. Zhukova.

"Sure," Jacob relented with a shrug. He looked at Juanita but she kept her head bowed.

"Thank you," said Dr. Zhukova. Placing her hands on the table in front of her, she added, "Please feel free to enjoy the museum while we deliberate but I must insist you remain in the building. Juanita, please see to that."

"Yes, Doctor," replied Juanita. She rose and opened the doors.

"Sure, whatever you say, Dr. Z," Jacob said with an exhale of resignation. Rotating around and leaving the Councilmembers at his back, he walked to the doors. Jacob paused in the doorway to allow Juanita to exit and said in as haunting a tone as he could muster, "The best thing you can do now is cut me loose, and soon. And if I were you, I'd tell your people to start locking their doors."

The Councilmembers exchanged troubled glances. Departing the chambers, Jacob closed the doors behind him and walked away.

• • • •

JACOB DESCENDED THE stairs to the second floor and began meandering around the museum. Little information registered in his consciousness, his mind too deep in contemplation to pay much heed to his surroundings. Juanita shadowed him but he soon lost track of her presence and she disappeared in the maze of exhibits.

"I know what this is and I'm not falling for it," Jacob prayed as he aimlessly wandered. Bristling in his spirit, he said, "You're setting me up to pull it all out from under me again. *Temporary blessings don't count.*"

The conversation ended when a woman's voice shattered Jacob's trance. He looked up and saw a familiar face.

"Hello, Mr. Gottschalk," said Boyka softly. She emerged from behind an exhibit displaying articles made and sold by the original Oneidans including travel bags and animal traps. Boyka appeared exactly as she had during their first meeting and Jacob was again struck by her beauty.

"What *the hell* are you doing here?" Jacob inquired sharply.

"Dr. Zhukova ordered that I return to the Community," inquired Boyka. She lingered at the corner of the exhibit's glass case.

"Was that before or after you told me you were going back to Station Genesis?" Jacob asked. Boyka bowed her head.

"I could not tell you the truth," replied Boyka feebly with growing distress.

"Yeah, that seems to be a habit with you," Jacob scolded her. Placing his hands on his hips, he leaned forward slightly and stated, "But that's gonna end, right fucking now."

A single tear ran down Boyka's cheek but she swiftly wiped it away. Jacob glared at her and, feeling the heat of his disapproval, she kept her gaze on the floor. Jacob pointed towards the Council chamber.

"Who on that Council wants me dead?" Jacob inquired.

"I told you," whined Boyka as she hazarded a glance at Jacob, "I do not know."

"Bullshit," Jacob replied, his ire causing Boyka to again lower her eyes to the floor. He moved towards her, saying, "*Who wants me dead?*"

"I do not know!" said Boyka defiantly as she retreated to the far corner of the display case.

"Okay, let's assume for a minute that you really don't know," Jacob said. He pursued Boyka around the case but she moved in unison with him until they returned to their original positions. A fuming Jacob explained, "There's something else going on here, too. Dr. Zhukova knows the fastest way to most men's hearts is through their stomachs and their cocks, and not necessarily in that order. You're young, beautiful and deferential and she's using you and your sisters to get me to stay here. She told all three of you to seduce me. I know it. You know it. So let's hear the plan. *All of it.*"

Boyka reversed course and walked to Jacob. He heard the gears of her mind spinning and, after a few quiet seconds, she spoke.

"Dr. Zhukova says the Holy Spirit abides in you," admitted Boyka, "and that it abides in me, and abides in my sisters."

"Go on," Jacob replied.

"She wants us to conceive children by you," continued Boyka, "and strengthen the Spirit within our Community through our children."

"Paliki and Rahela, too?" Jacob asked.

"Yes," confessed Boyka. She tried to place a hand on his shoulder but he dodged it. Boyka said awkwardly, "And there are others."

"That's totally fucking insane," Jacob said before becoming cognizant of his raised voice. Lowering its volume, he asked, "I'm not gonna be some holy breeding stud . . . well, depending on what the stud fee is."

Boyka did not understand Jacob's jest and sidestepped it. She tenderly grasped his cheeks.

"The Holy Spirit is with you, Mr. Gottschalk. Stay. Become a member of the Community. I will consent to interviews with you," replied Boyka, everything about her overture save her words feeling sexual. The libidinous energy crackling between them gave Jacob an instant erection. Leaning towards him, Boyka placed a kiss on his lips and said, "We will *all* consent, whenever you desire it, and bear you many children, who will be strong in the Spirit, like you are."

"What the hell's an interview?" Jacob asked as he glossed over the meatier aspects of Dr. Zhukova's plan. He then heard Edna's words and realized who else led the Hungarians' maternal efforts:

"It is no coincidence that you found your way to New Oneida and I sincerely hope your stay will be a long one."

The sound of someone walking down the steps from the third level grew louder. Jacob looked away briefly.

"I say too much," answered Boyka. Jacob attempted to grab her arm but she evaded him and took several backward steps.

"You don't say enough," Jacob chided her. She raised her finger to her lips and then disappeared behind an exhibit. The footsteps reached the bottom of the stairs and continued at a deliberate pace in his direction.

"That was fast," Jacob said as Dr. Zhukova entered the room with Juanita in tow. He rotated around and noticed she no longer donned her suit jacket. Juanita studied him closely.

"Is something wrong, Mr. Gottschalk?" asked Dr. Zhukova as she read his face.

"Nope, doin' just fine, Doc," he blurted unconvincingly. Jacob stuffed his hands in his pockets and stated, "And, by the way, I've decided to stay for a little while."

"Good. I will take you to your guesthouse now, and I suggest you retire early," said Dr. Zhukova with a penetrating gaze, "because we will leave before first light tomorrow."

"Perfect," Jacob said, "it'll be even colder then."

10

SARAH FELT PARTICULARLY vulnerable without Miriam and Darby and protested when Petra ordered the armored column's departure from Millers. All the vehicles had been fueled, however, and Petra had no intention of disobeying her commandant.

"They'll catch up," Petra brusquely reassured Sarah.

Miriam resurfaced first, the reformed demon announcing her presence with the clanking of her backpack chains. She found Sarah braving the chilly air, the nun wrapped in the emergency blanket and pacing back and forth outside the Humvee.

"Have we recovered from our little temper tantrum?" jibed Sarah as she stopped in her tracks. Longing for the comforts of civilization, she complained, "While you were flitting around the desert, I had the unique experience of squatting behind a boulder to pee."

"Well, unless a rattlesnake bit you on the cunt, we have bigger problems," Miriam said snottily. Feeling uncharacteristically spiteful, Sarah turned to her.

"I doubt God would have rescued you from the Abyss if he knew you would use such words upon your return," replied Sarah curtly. Miriam stifled a cry in response to her mention of the Abyss; instead, she emitted a jarring, high-pitched croak. Her eyes smoldered like black coals.

"She's back," Miriam replied, a demonic tone interspersed with her human voice.

"Who's back? Darby?" inquired Sarah. Her anger cooled.

"Wrong Nicks," Miriam growled through clenched teeth. Her arms fell to her sides and she balled her fists. She wanted to overturn the Humvee but squelched the urge.

"Miriam, what *are* you talking about?" asked Sarah with an eye roll. Miriam picked up a stone and crushed it.

"I wasn't the only one kicked loose from the blackness," Miriam answered, the one-time *daimoniou* unwilling to utter the word "Abyss". Pausing for effect, she picked up another stone and crushed it, uttering,

"The Master sent Lady Lizzie back as one of his own and she's got plenty of company."

"That's preposterous. Elizabeth is dead," scoffed Sarah. She shook her head in disapproval and opened the Humvee door, saying, "I am chilled to the bone."

Though troubled by Miriam's assertion, Sarah hid her concern and attempted to climb into the Humvee. Miriam grabbed the nun, moved her aside and slammed the door.

"We don't have much time, so listen," Miriam demanded. Pulling the blanket tight around Sarah, she explained, "Tonopah's an orgy of demonic activity and Lady Lizzie's running the show. Darby's biker runt was possessed by one of them and, if I get too close, she might sense me. I don't know what I'm giving off anymore, though Jacob, Jr. let me know I'm still at least part demon."

The baby kicked in Sarah's womb. She placed a hand on her belly and felt several more kicks. Miriam watched Sarah's hand and perceived the fetus's motion as if the hand were her own.

"You need to find Jacob," said Sarah, the protective instincts of motherhood burgeoning within her, "and we need to get as far away from here as possible."

"I don't want to leave you alone," Miriam said. She placed her hand over Sarah's hand and added, "Either of you."

"I may not have Jacob's power of exorcism," argued Sarah, "but our child seemingly has the same spiritual ward as its father. That, God willing, will protect us for now, but you must find Jacob."

"Who's going to protect you from material world?" asked Miriam. Sarah pondered the question but Miriam interrupted her by saying, "And don't say God."

"God acts through all the instruments he created, Miriam," answered Sarah, "and the instrument he has left us in this situation, albeit an imperfect one, is Darby."

"She does know I'll murder her if anything happens to you," Miriam conceded. Sarah chastised her with a disapproving look.

"She is our best hope for now," explained Sarah. She collected her thoughts and let them coalesce into a prudent course of action before saying,

"Darby has the resources to take me to this Jarbidge place and provide a stable home for us until you find Jacob. But you must do so quickly. If Elizabeth has revenge on her mind, the baby is in great danger."

"Okay," Miriam said. Her body tingled with the anticipation of seeing Jacob again. She declared, "I'll find him, and I'll check on you as often as I can."

Miriam opened the Humvee door and tucked the nun inside. Sarah caressed her face.

"Be careful," pleaded Sarah, "and stay true to Him. You were not saved to return to your old ways."

"I know," Miriam replied sheepishly as she looked away. She felt at that moment a great tearing within her as if the evil and the good fibers of her spirit forcefully pulled in different directions.

"And Miriam," said Sarah. Miriam looked back to her.

"Yeah," Miriam snapped.

"Tread very carefully with Jacob," advised Sarah. Miriam closed the Humvee door, momentarily stared at her through the window and then disappeared.

· · · ·

DARBY SPED TOWARDS the bay in the hills where Petra and the armored column awaited. Magg's motorcycle, which trailed Darby closely, suddenly accelerated and whizzed past her. Within seconds it was among the vehicles and heading straight for Petra's Humvee. She shook her head in disapprobation.

"Reckless little asshole," said Petra as she stepped between her Humvee and Magg's oncoming motorcycle. She folded her arms defiantly and sneered, "I'm not falling for it this time."

Darby stopped her motorcycle at the edge of the temporary camp. Ripping off her helmet, she glowered at Magg.

"I'm gonna kill that fucking twat," Darby growled, her tolerance of Magg's daredevil pranks at an end. The young woman unexpectedly jettisoned her helmet and released the handlebars. Darby dropped her own helmet and uttered, "Oh, shit."

Magg leapt from the motorcycle and, in a stunning display of strength and agility, landed on top of the Humvee. Her bike continued forward, struck Petra and rammed the side of vehicle. The crash rocked the Humvee but Magg easily maintained her balance.

"Stop her!" Darby bellowed as she dismounted her bike and charged towards the Humvee. Unholstering her fifty caliber pistol, she aimed it at Magg and emptied her clip. Several security personnel recovered from their initial shock and also opened fire on Magg with submachine guns. She ignored the bullets piercing her body and dove through the Humvee's metal roof as if it were water. The resultant noise was jarring.

"What the fuck?" said one of the Darby's officers in astonishment. She shoved him to the ground as she passed him and, upon reaching Magg's wrecked motorcycle, heaved it off Petra's motionless body. Darby's lieutenant was dead.

"Fucking cunt!" Darby roared as she foolishly threw open the car door. Magg screamed at Darby, her volume and pitch dizzying and nauseating all humans within earshot. Several of Darby's underlings went weak in the knees or vomited.

"Where's the nun?" roared Magg, the young woman's eyes black and distended and her teeth jagged. Staggered by the demon's screech, Darby grabbed the Humvee's door frame to steady herself.

"Fuck you," Darby gasped. Magg lunged forward and grabbed her with clawed hands.

"You're unkillable, but not untouchable," said Magg with a sneer and an odd gleam in her eyes. She headbutted Darby and knocked her unconscious. One of the officers came into view with his firearm trained on Magg. She released Darby, who slumped to the ground, and barreled into him before he could act.

"Get off him!" ordered another officer as a trio of them closed on Magg. She instead tore into her adversary, gutting him in a horrific display of spraying blood, tearing flesh and breaking bone. The officers fired several controlled bursts into Magg's head and chest, the direct hits ruining her physical form and sending her into convulsions. She fell next to her victim.

"We got 'er, she's dead," declared one of the officers. The trio inched forward with their guns aimed at the lifeless mass. Magg suddenly jumped to her feet and roared, the move sending Darby's minions scurrying for cover.

"No she's not!" shouted Magg with a hideous laugh.

"That's enough, demon," Sarah stated firmly as she walked around the front of the Humvee. Magg charged her but was immediately met with a spiritual field of force that hurled her backward. She struck the ground and tumbled away with Sarah on her heels, admonishing her, "Be gone now."

Rising up in a spidery posture, Magg hissed and shrieked at Sarah. Her body was a bullet-ridden mess and her face barely recognizable due to bleeding entry wounds.

"I'll rip that child from your womb and eat it!" barked Magg.

"You will do no such thing," Sarah countered as she confidently loomed over Magg, "and I suggest you inform your Lady that my child is well-protected and any further attempts on its life will utterly fail."

Magg collapsed and the demon fled her body, its screams echoing and lessening as if it traveled down a tunnel. Sarah shivered and felt dizzy, the nun walking to a nearby vehicle and steadying herself by leaning into its grill. Recovering twenty seconds later, she realized that all eyes were on her. She met every gaze before speaking.

"Wrap them in blankets," Sarah instructed, "so that we may provide them with proper burials."

Darby's officers obeyed, albeit slowly, and soon the entire camp was abuzz with activity. One of them roused Darby whose nose bled profusely.

"What the hell?" asked Darby as she regained consciousness and struggled to her feet. Her nose throbbed and she winced when she touched it, griping, "That little twat broke my nose."

· · · ·

THE WIND INTENSIFIED and the clouds thickened in the desert sky. Darby and Sarah supervised the interment of the dead, the former demanding haste and the latter requesting compassionate treatment.

"She was but a child," Sarah lamented when Magg's small, blanket-wrapped body was placed in its grave and covered with earth. She asked, "What was her name?"

"Magg," answered Darby.

"Short for Maggie, I presume," Sarah said.

"Short for Maggot," replied Darby. She kicked a stone into Magg's grave and expounded, "I pulled her filthy carcass out of the slums when she was a kid, running B and E's and selling drugs for a local dealer. She was a crafty little shit, and that kept her out of the prostitution rings at least."

Sarah pondered the rampant evil of Kaiser which in turn sparked thoughts of the rampant evil of the world. The death of the young woman intensified her belief that her child would always be in danger. She wondered how she would keep it safe and if it would suffer the same fate as Magg.

"I know it was an unexpected and difficult situation, and unfolded quickly, but had your response been less violent, we may have been able to drive the demon from her body and save her life," Sarah suggested gently while placing her hands on her pregnant belly. The guilt burgeoned within her.

Darby laughed as her officers used shovels to tamp down the last of the desert dirt and sand over the dead. She placed a heavy hand on Sarah's shoulder.

"You peacenik mother fuckers are something else," countered Darby with an incredulous smirk. Giving the nun's shoulder a hard squeeze, she said, "I was tryin' to save you and your kid, ya' dumb bitch, and here ya' are criticizing the way I did it. You may not realize this, but had you been in that Humvee, I'd be dropping the two of you in the ground right now."

Sarah surrendered.

"You're right, Darby, and for that we are grateful," Sarah said as Darby squirmed uncomfortably under the gratitude and withdrew her hand. Her underlings finished their work and lingered near the graves. Sarah commented to herself, "Pregnancy bladder is not always a curse."

"All right, it's over," announced Darby. She stuck her hands in her back pockets and walked to Petra's grave, saying, "We're leaving, so get 'em in formation and ready to rock."

"We are all in significant danger," Sarah informed Darby after the officers departed. A chorus of engines turned over and then hummed as they awaited the order to resume the northward journey.

"Miriam told you?" asked Darby. She moved her head on a swivel as if an attack was imminent.

"Yes," Sarah answered. The identity of the demonic presence in Tonopah precariously balanced on the end of her tongue, the words held back by the tendrils of her better judgment. She hugged her stomach and explained, "I sent her to find Jacob. We will need him to survive what this world is becoming."

"I've wasted too much of my life chasing that fuck," growled Darby, "and I'm not wasting one more fucking second."

"You won't have to," Sarah replied. Bracing for the expected explosion, she nonchalantly positioned herself on the other side of the graves and declared, "When Miriam returns, I will be procuring your release from service. We will need one of your vehicles."

"Are you fucking nuts?" asked Darby. In a rare moment of sympathy, she relinquished her incredulity and expounded, "Look, you try to drop that kid out here in the shit and it won't make its first birthday. Jarbidge, on the other hand, is a small fortress with medical facilities. That kid's already got the Gottschalk curse. At least come with me and give it a chance."

Sarah shook her head.

"Today was more that an attempt on my life, Darby, it was a reconnaissance mission," Sarah said pointedly. Completing her circuit around the graves, she gestured as she spoke and explained, "Next time, there will be more of them, and your people are no match for the minions of Ba'al Zeboul. If the three of us go with you to your fortress, you will all die or, worse, end up demonic puppets that murder others."

Darby crouched down. Taking a handful of loose sand from Petra's grave, she slowly let it fall from her fist and be blown away by the wind. She remained quiet for several minutes, Darby seemingly oblivious to the column of armored vehicles that awaited her orders. Sarah, despite her aching feet, indulged her vigil for her lieutenant.

"She was one of the very few who could be trusted to handle things without fucking them up, and the only one in this bunch," admitted Darby.

She stood up, motioned for Sarah to join her and said, "Well, she's free of this shithole now and we're not, so let's get moving. You're with me until Blondie gets back. And then you two can go wherever the fuck you want."

"I am so sorry for your loss," Sarah said as she tried to comfortingly grasp Darby's arms. Darby, however, whirled around and marched off before Sarah could touch her.

Minutes later the convoy was gone. All was quiet in the makeshift cemetery and the dead were left to the ravages of time.

· · · ·

"GOOD THING WE LEFT when we did," said Darby as she glanced into the rearview mirror. Her swollen nose ached and dark circles formed underneath her eyes. Sarah used the passenger side mirror to view the first traces of red light on the horizon behind them. Despite the ominous sign festering to the south, the first several hours of their journey north proved uneventful and the light gradually disappeared. There was no trace of anyone on the highways and the weather remained cloudy and cold without significant wind or precipitation.

Darby guided the caravan towards the Jarbidge Wilderness, a name it shared with a nearby small town and a river. There, in the lower elevations of a mountainous, lightly-forested area, Elizabeth built a walled fortress, a last bastion of civilization should Kaiser be compromised.

"I'll be glad when I can get my ass outta this seat," muttered Darby while steering the Humvee with one hand. Sarah lingered in a trance, her eyes dull and hazy as she stared into the floor. Darby poked a finger into her shoulder and asked, "You alive there, Sister Sarah?"

"Please just call me Sarah," Sarah replied as she slowly emerged from the darkened pathways of her mind.

"What the hell's the matter with you?" snapped Darby. Sarah raised her gaze and looked out of the windshield with narrowed eyes.

"It concerns me that Miriam has not returned," Sarah answered. Adjusting herself in her seat, she continued, "And it concerns me that the demonic world – perhaps even *the Abyss* itself – may be seeping into the material realm."

"Anything else bothering you, your eminence?" Darby asked in irritation. She instantly regretted engaging Sarah but, to her great relief, the nun did not reply.

Wild flurries swirled around them as they entered the Jarbidge Wilderness and rapidly strengthened into a heavy, wet snow. The column's progress slowed substantially on the narrow, winding roads as daylight failed. The ascent into Jarbidge reminded Sarah of the descent out of Kaiser despite its sparser tree cover and scrubbier underbrush.

The final leg of the journey to Jarbidge Fortress consisted of a single-lane road weaving through hills as it progressed into a small, narrow valley. Four inches of snow fell by the time the column reached the concrete and steel bunkers on either side of the approach. Armed with heavy machine guns, they created a forward kill zone intended to blunt any frontal assault on the fortress.

Darby reached for the radio receiver. She noticed that the rest of the column fell further behind them since the vehicles left the paved highway.

"All units halt. I'm gonna check on the bunkers," directed Darby. She proceeded ahead of the convoy but stopped her Humvee just before the road passed between them. Darby opened her door.

"Wait!" Sarah blurted, her exclamation causing Darby to throw her optical daggers.

"Yeah?" replied Darby.

"You don't know what might be in them," said Sarah gravely. Darby gave her a dubious look, exited the vehicle and slammed the door. Ignoring the falling snow and cold, she trudged up to each bunker and peered into it.

"'Saint Michael the Archangel,'" Sarah prayed as she folded her hands, bowed her head and mustered her faith. Her child stirred in her womb as she continued with eyes closed, "'defend us in battle. Be our protection against the wickedness and snares of the devil; May God rebuke him, we humbly pray . . . .'"

Darby heard strange sounds and felt errant currents of the wind rushing past her. She spun around to acquire the noises which she first attributed to the whistling air.

"Holy shit," said a trembling Darby, "they're screams."

"'And do thou, O Prince of the Heavenly Host, by the power of God,'" said Sarah while the baby leapt and kicked within her. The bizarre noises began to fade into the distance and the wind became less turbulent. She completed the prayer with conviction, saying, "'thrust into hell Satan and all evil spirits who wander through the world for the ruin of souls. Amen.'"

Whether due to Sarah's prayer or sheer luck, Darby returned to the vehicle untouched and unharmed. She shivered with cold and unease but, managing to compose herself, grabbed the radio receiver.

"We're buggin' the fuck out, so all units turn around and meet back at the highway," ordered Darby. There was no response over the radio and not one armored vehicle moved. Furious, Darby barked, "All units, turn around!"

Silence reigned as the snow quietly fell and not even the sound of static could be heard on the radio. Darby awaited a response for a few seconds before hurling the receiver at the dashboard.

"Fuck!" bellowed Darby. She punched the steering wheel, stifled her rage and said angrily, "So what do we do now, *Sarah*?"

"We go on to the fortress," Sarah answered matter-of-factly. She faced forward and would not look at Darby.

"You're fucking kidding, right?" countered Darby.

"I am not," Sarah said. She turned to Darby and advised with the utmost seriousness, "Whatever strength and grit and relentlessness you possess, Darby Nicks, muster it now, because what lies ahead will test you like you have never been tested, and you are about to make the most difficult choice of your life."

* * * *

JARBIDGE FORTRESS LOOMED above the road like a monster born of concrete and steel. Though small in terms of modern military installations, its green and grey walls rose to a height of twenty feet with equidistant machine gun turrets. The upper portions of its taller buildings appeared over the parapets.

The sinister red light seen at Tonopah now illuminated the fortress and the surrounding area. Though Darby perceived it as shining down from above, Sarah saw its true source. It emanated from the earth like the flame of a match burning upward through a sheet of pristine white paper and gradually spread outward as it consumed more and more ground.

"Where are you, Miriam?" asked Sarah when she noticed the fortress's great steel gates were open. There was no trace of humanity but evil hung heavily in the air.

"I think the kid's gonna be more help than her," remarked Darby as her gaze focused on the rearview mirror. The officers who peopled the armored column suddenly appeared over the hill, two lines of them walking towards the fortress on the snow-covered road.

"God save us," said Sarah. Each officer, whether male or female, possessed the hollow black eyes of the demonic kind along with serrated teeth and clawed fingers. The lines diverged as they marched past the Humvee and then came back together once they cleared the front bumper.

"That fucking asshole Aaron. He was planning a takeover the whole time," snarled Darby through clenched teeth. Her fury boiled beneath the surface but, with tremendous effort, she restrained it.

"It would be far better for us if it was Aaron's doing," replied Sarah ominously, "but it is not."

The lines diverged once again as they entered the fortress and a woman, tall and athletically-built, walked between them. A disgruntled Darby restrained the urge to push the gas pedal to the floor and run down her former officers and the woman. She instead rolled the Humvee forward, the proximity revealing the brunette was once a security officer assigned to Jarbidge.

"Well, that's not Adedewe," said a surprised Darby. She shifted the vehicle into park and asked, "But who the fuck else could it be?"

"Who indeed," Sarah said. The revelation of the demon's identity was imminent and inevitable.

"I'm going to find out right fucking now," said Darby carelessly as she exited the vehicle. The woman approached her and the two met halfway between the Humvee and the gates, Darby standing outside the light and her opposite number remaining within it. Sarah sat up and grasped the dashboard with white knuckles.

"I don't know who the hell you are, or where the hell you came from, but you need to tell Aaron to get his kids the fuck off my lawn," demanded

Darby. The woman laughed wickedly, her mirth sparking a sense of familiarity within Darby.

"I assure you that Aaron has no power here," the woman said arrogantly, "and soon he will have no power anywhere."

"Listen, cunt, let's dispense with all the bullshit before I shoot you in the fucking face," threatened Darby. She slowly unholstered her firearm and aimed it at the woman. Sarah winced at the combination of violence and vulgarity. The woman did not react.

"Oh, dear sister, how I have missed you," the woman said with a sinister grin.

"What the fuck did you just say?" asked Darby.

"What I did not miss is your foul mouth," the woman admonished Darby, "though at least your breath does not reek of whiskey."

Darby turned as white as the snow that descended lazily from the sky. The longer she studied the woman, the more she realized who she resembled. Darby's jaw abruptly dropped. She lowered her pistol and stumbled back a few paces.

"Liz?" gasped Darby. The woman examined herself briefly and smiled.

"This one was the least unsatisfactory choice," Elizabeth said disappointedly, "though, mind you, she is only a temporary host."

"What the fuck, Lizzy?" whimpered Darby. Flabbergasted by her sister's return, she regressed to a state she had not experienced since they were children.

"I've been revitalized, Darby," Elizabeth expounded as her host's body seemed to enlarge in the red light, "and sent back to do what we did with Kaiser, only on an infinitely grander scale."

"Sent back?" inquired Darby incredulously. Feeling like the doting younger sister she once was, she inquired, "Sent back by who?"

"Ba'al Zeboul, Lord of Demons," answered Sarah as she strode forth from the Humvee. Her strength burgeoned and she sensed the buttressing grace of the Holy Spirit. She also felt her unborn child vigorously rejoice in its presence.

"Hello, Sister Sarah," Elizabeth greeted the nun with mock pleasantness. Her haughtiness resumed and she sneered, "Unmarried and pregnant. So much for those sisterly vows you swore."

"Thankfully, my Master is merciful and forgiving," replied Sarah, her reference to God causing Elizabeth to squirm. Smiling proudly, she said, "And I warn you, tread very carefully. The child of Jacob Gottschalk does not like demons. One of your minions learned that the hard way."

Elizabeth's mood soured and she scowled at Sarah with cold, steely eyes. Sarah steadfastly met her gaze.

"I should have killed you long ago. It was a serious error in judgment not to do so," Elizabeth said. Returning her attention to Darby, she softened her countenance and launched her next verbal salvo.

"I need my faithful general again, Darbs," Elizabeth urged Darby. Offering her hand and speaking in a loving tone, she declared, "*I need my sister.*"

A shocked Darby looked at the face through which her sister spoke and then to her outstretched hand. Her host's fingertips seemed to gently touch the edge of the red light.

"Not too long ago I told you the winds were shifting, subtly shifting," began Elizabeth in an enrapturing voice, "but it is more than just the winds and it will not be subtle. The entire world will be ours . . . yours and mine . . . Vanessa's and Mallory's. We will usher in a new age."

"The girls too?" asked Darby. Her head reeled.

"Yes, they returned with me," Elizabeth replied. Retracting her hand and making a fist, she held it to her chest and implored Darby, "So come to me. Come to us. There is, of course, the awkward matter of you needing to die for this to work, but death is not as bad as you may think, and you will have the distinct advantage of repossessing your own body."

Elizabeth exhaled sadly.

"Unfortunately, mine was too mutilated for my tastes," Elizabeth said. She gazed at Sarah and, with a hideous grin of sharp teeth, remarked, "The work of another of Jacob's whores."

"So it was Sophie," said Darby. Concealing her next thought from her sister, she said to herself, "Miriam was telling the truth."

"I suppose I should thank that twisted soul," Elizabeth mused, "because she freed me from the hopelessness of my material prison and set me on the road to true freedom and power."

"True freedom," scoffed Sarah. Her disdain for the unholiness before her plainly evident, she stated, "Your Master is fickle and your leash is much shorter than you realize."

Elizabeth laughed.

"Your Master is renowned for blessings laced with curses," Elizabeth snapped, "and he will allow you to hang yourself with your leash."

"Shut the fuck up, both of you!" barked Darby. She desired more than anything else a fountain of whiskey in which to drown herself and her emotions. Unable to fully comprehend the decision laid before her, she said, "I can't deal with this right now. I'm leaving."

"Very well, Darby," Elizabeth replied condescendingly, "I will allow you to continue to cling to your mortal life, for now. My offer remains on the table but until you accept it, I cannot help you. Leave. And take your nun and her bastard child with you."

"Let's go," Darby ordered Sarah as she turned on a dime and returned to the Humvee. Sarah and Elizabeth shared withering glances before the nun complied. Darby snarled, "*Now*, Sarah."

The pair entered the Humvee without another word. Darby revved the engine, quickly turned the vehicle around and, with it sliding and slipping, sped off into the snowy night.

· · · ·

MIRIAM'S FORAY INTO the spiritual world proved unfruitful. Searching for Jacob's spiritual signature, which she could perceive but not locate, she twice mistook Sarah's child for him and ended up where she started. She quickly learned to distinguish its ethereal presence from that of its father and did not make the mistake again.

"I still can't *find* him," Miriam thought bitterly. Her search soon morphed into a meandering as she wallowed in self-pity and jealousy. Floating through an unworldly plane traversed by good and evil entities alike, she lost hope.

"Miriam!" beckoned a shrouded spiritual being. Miriam froze in response as the being again called out, "Miriam!"

Miriam recovered and hurled herself towards the entity but it fled. A small trace of Jacob's spirit suddenly manifested itself, appearing like a small, weak blip on a radar screen.

"Jake!" Miriam exclaimed in her spirit.

"He's here!" bellowed the being. Abandoning her pursuit of the mysterious entity, she immediately crossed the boundary between immaterial and material.

Miriam arrived in a small bedroom, cheerless and dark, with only a bed, a nightstand and a footlocker. A sickly ambient light shone through the window and the icy condensation forming on it, the faint illumination revealing that a long womanly form occupied the bed.

"Where the fuck is this?" queried Miriam in disappointment. The woman, who wiggled out of her sheets during the night, flipped onto her back. She wore only a floral tank top and panties; her ankle-length, plain nightshirt lay on the floor.

"Quiet," said Boyka as she lifted her head, looked at Miriam and then let her head fall back to the pillow. Realizing that an intruder stood in her room, she jumped straight up and stood on the bed in a defensive posture. Miriam pounced in the blink of an eye, the demon landing on the bed and grasping the lower half of Boyka's face with a clawed hand.

"I'll crush your jaw if you even blink," Miriam warned with a light squeeze, the pressure just enough to convey the extent of her supernatural strength. Boyka, afraid but composed, remained still as Miriam asked, "Is Jacob Gottschalk here?"

Boyka studied Miriam and gradually absorbed her demonic traits. Allowing the young woman to speak, Miriam slackened her grip.

"You are a, a . . . *démon*," Boyka said as she reverted to her native tongue.

"Yes," Miriam replied in her demonic tone. She then switched to her human voice and said, "And no."

A cloud of dread settled on Miriam when she realized the womb in front of her held the beginnings of another Gottschalk child. An evil, insidious desire arose within her, a desperate urge to slaughter Jacob's latest sexual conquest. She retightened her grip.

"You are hurting me," whimpered Boyka. The sound of approaching footfalls echoed in the hallway. Miriam plummeted to the bed while pulling the stunned Hungarian with her. Spooning Boyka tightly, Miriam made herself invisible to human eyes.

"Pull the covers over us," Miriam hissed. Boyka complied just as Meriwa LeClaire stopped outside the door to her room. Meriwa observed Boyka pretend to sleep for thirty seconds before continuing her journey down the hall.

"Where's Jacob Gottschalk?" Miriam whispered.

"Jacob Gottschalk?" said Boyka. Lying in an attempt to protect Jacob, she answered, "I do not know him."

"You're carrying his child so try again," Miriam said quietly through clenched teeth.

"I am pregnant?" asked Boyka excitedly before Miriam stifled her with a claw pressed into her cheek.

"Quietly, princess," Miriam admonished her. Meriwa's firm, deliberate steps returned. Miriam exited the material world.

"Boyka, are you alright?" asked Meriwa as she appeared in the bedroom doorway. Boyka sat up in her bed.

"I am sorry, Meriwa," answered Boyka as she hugged her knees to her chest. She forced a weak grin and said, "I had a nightmare but I am fine now."

"Are you sure?" replied Meriwa with a skeptical mien.

"It was just a dream," said Boyka. Meriwa noticed the discomfort that the barrage of lies caused the young woman and raised her chin. She studied Boyka briefly before attributing her disquiet to her dream. Meriwa's face and suspicion softened.

"Sleep well, child, and may God bless you with good dreams," said Meriwa with rare compassion. She nodded at Boyka and proceeded down the hall. Miriam reappeared at the foot of the bed.

"I know he's been here, and not too long ago either," Miriam asserted. A hesitant Boyka trembled but mustered her courage.

"Be gone, *démon*," demanded Boyka. Glaring at Miriam, she declared, "New Oneida is the Lord's community and no place for your kind."

Miriam experienced the spiritual equivalent of nausea. Boyka - youthful, beautiful and strong – reminded her of a younger version of Elizabeth and she now, just like Elizabeth before her, carried Jacob's child.

"I wouldn't be so snarky, bitch," Miriam sneered. She indulged in Boyka's troubled expression and said with sinister delight, "Your precious Jake's spread his seed over a thousand miles and you're just another one of his cum dumpsters."

Boyka gasped in response to the vulgarity. Tears rolled down her cheeks.

"You are liar," snarled Boyka. She defiantly wiped away her tears and uttered, "I said be gone."

Defeated by Jacob's promiscuity and deterred by his potential wrath if she harmed Boyka, Miriam ceded the round to the Hungarian. She retreated into the spirit world with the one spoil she took from the battlefield.

"At least I know he's here," she said to herself.

11

JACOB TOSSED AND TURNED throughout the night, New Oneida's newest guest haunted by the implications of Dr. Zhukova's spiritual breeding program. He groaned when Rahela's breakfast preparations roused him from sleep well before dawn. Sitting up in bed, he rubbed his face with both hands.

"Time to find out what the good Doctor has in store for me today," Jacob sighed as he began dressing in the clothes provided by the Community. Checking out his new look in the mirror, he scowled at his navy-blue pants and white, collared shirt. Jacob shook his head and exited his room, grumbling, "If Miriam saw me dressed like this . . . ."

Jacob shivered. Miriam was ever present in his thoughts and occasionally forced her way to the front of his mind.

"Good morning!" exclaimed Rahela when Jacob entered the kitchen, her greeting returning Miriam to Jacob's mental backburner. She dressed as she always did in her New Oneidan uniform and a navy-blue apron but wore her hair in a ponytail.

"What, no drágaságom?" Jacob replied with feigned annoyance and outstretched arms. Rahela quickly turned away and pretended to be busy with her preparations.

"I am becoming too attached to you, and that attachment threatens my growth in the Spirit and my love for God and the Community," droned Rahela as if Dr. Zhukova herself said the words. Jacob knew she struggled mightily, the Hungarian caught between her infatuation with him and the counter-directives of the Doctor.

"Do you really believe all that bullshit?" Jacob inquired as Rahela served his meal.

"Love without laying claim is the truest love," declared Rahela. She poured him a cup of coffee and said, "It is that love I should strive for. It keeps us from jealousy and the marriage spirit."

"The marriage spirit?" Jacob said with lighthearted incredulity. Rahela dodged the question and began cleaning a pan.

"You should finish your breakfast quickly," advised Rahela, "because Dr. Zhukova will arrive soon."

"I spoke to Boyka yesterday," Jacob said. Digging into the eggs Rahela forked onto his plate, he said through his food, "She said you'd be willing to engage in an interview with me whenever I want. You tell her that?"

Jacob's words hit Rahela hard and she froze. He studied her and hoped the weight of his stare would force her to reveal the Oneidan meaning of "interview". Regaining her wits, however, she grabbed the butter dish and placed it on the table.

"An interview? What is that?" asked Rahela with a puzzled grin. Her performance, while not convincing, was enough to give Jacob pause.

"Hell if I know, kid," Jacob replied. He contemplated the siring of a brood with the young Hungarian as he ate and Rahela resumed her tidying of the kitchen. Swallowing another mouthful of eggs, Jacob turned to his coffee and sent the first wave of caffeine into his veins. He struggled free of his daydream and thought, "Yeah, like I'm gonna turn into some moral Mormon fuck with fifty kids. I need to holster my dick for a while and get the hell outta here. But where do I go?"

· · · ·

DR. ZHUKOVA, AS PROMISED, led Jacob from the village before dawn and into the wilderness. Heavily equipped and wearing snowshoes, they trekked for several hours in the cloudy yet snowless morning. The sun was rising towards noon when they arrived at their destination, its rays occasionally escaping the clouds.

Stepping from the thick tree line, Dr. Zhukova entered a clearing. Masterfully carved in a rock wall at its far side was a recessed porch with four support columns. A large wooden door, heavy and ornate, permitted entry into the mountain.

"Is this where the ritual sacrifice takes place?" Jacob asked. He stopped a pace behind the Russian and chuckled. Dr. Zhukova glared at him over her shoulder.

"You are a very disrespectful man," commented Dr. Zhukova. The sharpness and gravity of her response erased the grin from Jacob's face.

"Says everyone who tests my low bullshit tolerance," Jacob sneered. Leering at Dr. Zhukova, who turned towards him, he continued, "Everything about your *Community* leads me to believe it's a cult. So, if you want me believe it's not one, then convince me it's not one. And while you're at it, convince me why I should put up with one more ounce of your cultist bullshit."

Dr. Zhukova bowed her head as she collected her thoughts. Jacob pointed towards New Oneida.

"Otherwise," Jacob said, "I'm walking right back the fucking way we came and out your front gates. For good."

"Give me one afternoon, Mr. Gottschalk," Dr. Zhukova replied with a sincerity that disarmed Jacob's anger. She alluringly nestled in his personal space and continued, "One afternoon of civil conversation and answered questions."

"All right," Jacob agreed. He allowed her to lead him onward.

"Take off your snowshoes, please," instructed Dr. Zhukova as they arrived on the porch. After they removed them, she produced a long, burnished key and unlocked the door. It creaked on its huge hinges as Jacob pushed it open and the pair stepped into a rectangular room.

"Who made this place?" Jacob asked. The room, hewn out of the mountain to form stone benches along the left and right walls, contained a wide doorway in its far wall and beyond it a natural passageway that led into darkness. Dr. Zhukova pulled free of her backpack and slung it onto one of the benches.

"Members of the Community, many years ago," answered Dr. Zhukova while she rummaged in her backpack. Jacob lingered in the doorway so she said, "Please, come in, and lock the door behind you."

Jacob reluctantly complied but, as he cast the room in darkness, Dr. Zhukova clicked a flashlight to life. Standing to the left of the door, the Doctor then inserted a large battery into a device on the wall.

"Holy shit," Jacob gushed as gold lights, placed at regular intervals and connected by thin wires, illuminated the room.

"Mr. Gottschalk, please, your language," scolded Dr. Zhukova as she stowed the flashlight. Jacob ignored the correction and walked into the middle of the chamber. Dr. Zhukova watched him and asked, "The lights provide a certain sacredness, do they not?"

"What is it with powerful women and weird lighting?" Jacob replied as he noticed the high humidity and heard drips of water. Dr. Zhukova began removing her winter gear and stacking it neatly on the bench. Jacob followed suit.

"Forget your shoes, Doc?" he inquired when he noticed Dr. Zhukova stood in bare feet. She removed and stowed her glasses.

"I never wear shoes here. I love the feel of the stone," Dr. Zhukova said while showing, for the first time in their short acquaintance, an endearing humanness. Stepping into the tunnel and wriggling her toes on the floor, she said, "Give me your hand."

The Russian kept her eyes forward and her mouth closed as she led Jacob deeper into the mountain. Their gaits seemed to mesh perfectly as they sauntered down the tunnel.

"Welcome, Mr. Gottschalk, to my spiritual sanctuary," announced Dr. Zhukova as the tunnel ended. She released Jacob's hand and permitted him to marvel at the sight before him. A massive natural cave housing a steaming pool of water dwarfed its human guests. The golden lights flickered beneath the water's bubbling surface, the agitation caused by hot springs feeding the pool. The water was accessed by a beach of smooth, wet stone running down to its edge. Drips echoed throughout the chamber and played a soothing song as Dr. Zhukova stated, "It is where I speak to God."

• • • •

CRESTING A RIDGE TO the west of Dr. Zhukova's hideaway, Juanita shielded herself from view behind a cluster of rocks. She raised her binoculars to her eyes and examined the clearing. It was empty but the trail made by Jacob and Dr. Zhukova could be plainly seen.

Juanita stowed her binoculars and cautiously picked a path through the trees. Upon reaching the edge of the clearing, she hid behind a trunk and surveyed the porch. No one was there but she noticed two pairs of snowshoes resting against its inner wall. She drew her pistol from its insulated holster and, retrieving a silencer from one of her many jacket pockets, affixed it to the gun.

Moving quickly across the clearing, Juanita kept her pistol trained on the door. When she arrived at the porch, Miriam appeared behind her. Juanita's spine tingled.

"Behind me," thought Juanita as she hesitated. Miriam simultaneously sensed Jacob on the other side of the door, albeit at some distance from the entrance, and saw Juanita standing in front of her.

"And where do you think you're going?" Miriam inquired. Juanita spun around and fired a tight cluster of shots into her chest, the silencer reducing them to pings that echoed off the side of the mountain. The bullets harmlessly passed through Miriam and struck the trees on the far side of the clearing. Juanita paused but then mastered her fear and fired two more shots at Miriam's head.

"Trust me, that never works," Miriam advised Juanita. She vanished from sight and reappeared behind her. Miriam whispered in her ear, "So I'd just put it away."

Juanita immediately threw an elbow at Miriam's face which she blocked. She attempted to tumble away but Miriam grasped her by the throat. Spinning Juanita around, she rammed her into one of the stone columns. She winced and moaned but managed to empty her clip into Miriam's face, the bullets again screaming off into the trees.

"You're lucky I've jumped on the Jesus train," Miriam said in irritation. Juanita struggled to breathe as she added, "But I'm barely hangin' on so I wouldn't push it."

"Who ... Wh, Wh, Who ...," gasped Juanita as her feet dangled several inches above the ground. Miriam kept her pinned to the column.

"Who am I?" Miriam asked. She took Juanita's pistol and crushed it in her left hand, repeating, "Who am I? That's a long, complicated story and I don't have time for that. Ya' see, I need to know if Jacob Gottschalk is on the other side of that door."

Juanita's eyes widened.

"So he *is* in there," Miriam said. She looked at the door longingly but Sarah's warning echoed in her head:

"My point is that Jacob may not readily accept you back into his life and, if he doesn't, you may have to . . . be patient."

"Y-y-yes," Juanita replied. Miriam lowered her to the ground and released her neck.

"You know I can kill you, right?" Miriam said. Rubbing her aching neck, Juanita shot Miriam a look of poorly-concealed hostility. The former demon answered that look with a punch that knocked Juanita to the ground.

"What do you want?!" yelled Juanita while holding her hand over the eye that Miriam struck.

"Was there anyone else with him when he got here?" Miriam inquired. Anxiety suddenly plagued her as she awaited an answer. Juanita's expression morphed from hostility to puzzlement.

"They said there was a girl with him," said Juanita while scooping up some snow and holding it to her throbbing face, "but she was killed in the plane crash. I don't know who she was."

Miriam's anxiousness eased and the faintest of smiles came to her face. She moved to Juanita and loomed over her.

"Get the fuck outta here," Miriam ordered as Juanita recoiled, "and tell whoever wants him dead they'd better reconsider."

• • • •

JACOB STOOD ON THE stone beach with his hands in his pockets. Dr. Zhukova walked in the shallows at the pool's edge, the water occasionally lapping at her skirt and soaking its hem.

"The heat of the water is magnificent," said the Russian.

"What's an interview?" Jacob queried, Dr. Zhukova's delayed explanations irking him. She left the water and walked to him.

"It is a sexual encounter between a male member and a female member of the Community and arranged through a Councilmember, usually the Director of Community and Individual Spirituality," said Dr. Zhukova. She halted just before Jacob and further expounded, "You see, we cherish God's gift of sexuality and see it both as a spiritual expression and a means to spiritual growth. We do not, however, allow the unfettered lust of human nature to run amok among our members, hence the Council's regulation of the sexual relations of the Community. Unsanctioned sexual encounters of any kind are forbidden."

"So mousy little Edna is the 'Minister of Who Gets to Fuck Who'?" Jacob said before engaging in a hearty laugh. Dr. Zhukova delivered a stinging slap to his cheek.

"You are a man of great sexual energy, yet you have allowed it to become corrupted and transform you into a deviant," chided Dr. Zhukova as a seething yet quiet Jacob glared at her. Going face-to-face with him, she stated firmly, "What you need now is a guide to assist you in purifying that energy and developing your full sexual, and hence spiritual, potential. After that, my dear man, there is *much* you can do here."

"Like siring a brood of holy bastards?" Jacob inquired sharply. Dr. Zhukova's countenance leaked a miniscule amount of concern before she sealed the breach.

"Perhaps we should start at the beginning," suggested Dr. Zhukova. She began unbuttoning her blouse and explained, "Father Noyes said our times are 'a chaos of confusion, tribulation and war,' yet, like Father Noyes before his heavenly commission was revoked for his sins, God 'has set me to cast up a highway across this chaos, and I am gathering out the stones and grading the track', not 'as fast as possible', but instead at a deliberate pace as dictated by the Lord."

"What the hell does that mean?" Jacob asked.

"No more profanity. Not in this place," ordered Dr. Zhukova gravely. She slid out of her blouse and dropped it to the wet floor.

"But you digress," Jacob uttered with a scowl. Her blatant attempt to seduce and distract him heightened his anger.

"New Oneida was the beginning of that highway," continued Dr. Zhukova, the redhead standing before him in a modest bra and the long skirt which she began to remove. She dropped it to the floor and said, "Leaving behind the Perfectionism endorsed by Father Noyes – *'If we say that we have no sin, we are deceiving ourselves and the truth is not in us'* – we formed a community of love and symbiosis where the love of God and others is placed above love of self and earthly possessions." (1 John 1:8).

Dr. Zhukova stepped away from her skirt. Despite her pale, thin form, she still aroused Jacob. He smirked.

"Why? Just why?" Jacob asked as he gestured towards her state of undress.

"I wish to engage in an interview with you," answered Dr. Zhukova bluntly.

"But I'm not a member of your holy Community," Jacob objected though his erection became obvious to Dr. Zhukova.

"All you need do is agree to join us, here and now," replied Dr. Zhukova while unfastening her bra and letting it slide to within a centimeter of her nipples. Holding it stationary, she stated matter-of-factly, "The Council voted to allow you to enter the Community on the usual probationary basis of one year. You may leave the Community at any time and the Council may expel you at any time. There is no risk . . . for either party."

"Who voted against it?" Jacob quickly queried. He had eliminated Dr. Zhukova and Edna from his list of suspects and presumed any other "yes" votes would narrow the field.

"That is not important," replied Dr. Zhukova. Her ample breasts dropped and bounced as she released them and let her bra fall to the cave floor. Grasping her panties with both hands, she slithered out of them with a sensuality foreign to religious leaders. Naked yet completely comfortable, Dr. Zhukova asked, "What is your decision, Mr. Gottschalk?"

"So I join and I get to fuck the boss?" inquired Jacob sardonically. Dr. Zhukova rushed him with a raised hand but he grabbed her by both wrists and held her at bay.

"Your filthy, foul language must stop!" screamed Dr. Zhukova.

"Fuck you!" Jacob snarled. Swiping out her legs, he lowered her to the ground roughly and pinned her to the stone surface. Placing his face threateningly in hers, he said, "I've had enough of this coy bullshit. You're going to tell me – right here, right now – what you're up to."

Dr. Zhukova relaxed her body in a sign of submission and closed her eyes in anticipation of a kiss. Jacob, though greatly desiring to take her at that moment, stopped himself. Scooping up the Doctor's lithe body, he walked into the pool and hurled her into its depths. She screamed in midair before splashing into the water.

• • • •

LURED BY HER FIRST substantial taste of Jacob's spirit since their acrimonious separation, Miriam appeared in the antechamber of Dr. Zhukova's sacred haven. Her proximity to Jacob stirred a longing in her spirit and she could not suppress it.

"You shouldn't be here," Miriam admonished herself. She placed one foot in front of the other, proceeding step by step, and said, "You need to get back to Sarah and the kid. You're not ready for this."

Loathing and loving every inch of progress, she entered the natural tunnel. She gently scraped her claws along the wall to her left and followed it forward, Jacob's spirit dragging her to him. She stopped when she heard his voice.

"*Fuck you!*"

A commotion followed.

"*I've had enough of this coy bullshit. You're going to tell me – right here, right now – what you're up to.*"

The echoes of a woman's scream followed by a splash emanated from further down the tunnel. Miriam vanished and instantly appeared at Jacob's side. Seeing him caused her to swoon.

"Where the hell is she?" asked Jacob. The period of time that Dr. Zhukova hid in the waters seemed like an hour when, in fact, it was less than a minute. Jacob remained rooted to where he stood with the water bubbling around his knees. He knew his future hung in the balance, the roads before him leading off in many directions with no indication of the correct path.

He suddenly felt another dark presence - Miriam's presence - in the cavern. She recognized it and backed away from him.

"Who's there?" Jacob asked as Dr. Zhukova broke the surface. Her return proved to be ethereal, her milky skin illuminated by the golden lights and her hair darkened by the water. She resembled the ghost of an aging mermaid matriarch and the vision of her distracted Jacob from further consideration of the unseen guest.

"You are an indecisive man," taunted Dr. Zhukova, her tone accusatory. She hugged herself to conceal her breasts which hung just above the water line. A covetous Miriam roared, though in a manner inaudible to human ears, and charged Dr. Zhukova. The Russian was spared when Miriam fled into the spiritual realm at the last possible millisecond.

"I'm a careful man," Jacob countered gravely, "especially when dealing with religious cults and their beautiful yet devious leaders."

"Come now, Mr. Gottschalk, where else would you go?" scoffed Dr. Zhukova. Jacob turned and sloshed his way to the shore. She called after him in desperation, "The spiritual flame of New Oneida is dying."

Dr. Zhukova's confession stopped Jacob's flight. He turned and waited for her to speak.

"I hope you're worthy of the truth," Dr. Zhukova said. She backstroked to shoulder-depth so that only her head and neck were visible and, with her hard eyes trained on Jacob, began, "The Community, like the faith of many of its people, is decaying. There is a faction that advocates for many ungodly changes to our rules – primarily greater personal freedom and especially unregulated sexual encounters – and the support for it grows every year."

Jacob laughed.

"Ya' can't suppress human nature, Doctor," he remarked.

"You, despite your numerous vices and faults, are the key to the survival of this Community," declared Dr. Zhukova ardently, "and to its expansion throughout the world. You carry God's favor and a tremendous gift of the Holy Spirit."

"So, Paliki spilled her guts," Jacob uttered. Internally, he wondered if he still held God's favor and, if so, for how much longer he would.

"Do not blame her," said Dr. Zhukova as she watched Jacob through the wafts of steam, "because, after God, her chief loyalty is to me. To keep your talents a secret from me would have been the crime, not breaking a confidence to an outsider she just met. Nevertheless, I sensed the power of the Holy Spirit from the moment I first laid eyes on you and that is why I brought you here."

"Yeah, for a fucking human breeding experiment," Jacob countered with a sneer. Dr. Zhukova kept her gaze on him and her focus on her arguments.

"Father Noyes called it stirpiculture," replied Dr. Zhukova. She swam forward a few feet and then said, "The selective breeding of the spiritually strong to propagate better and more resilient Christians. They are the workers who will build the great highway across the chaos and prepare the world for Christ's arrival."

"Okay, setting that wild assertion aside for a minute," Jacob said with a wave of his hand, "what made you choose the Hungarian hotties as the vessels for turning my spiritual water into wine?"

"They are from a group of small villages in a remote area of northeast Hungary," explained Doctor Zhukova, "and were orphaned at young ages. A Community member, guided by the Spirit to their orphanage, adopted them. They are truly extraordinary young women and the wellspring of the Community's future. As for their physical appearance, it is mere coincidence and of little relevance."

"And another red flag is unfurled," Jacob thought. The adoptions made sense from a cultist perspective. Adopt children without families and fill the void with the cult, the religious community becoming their new family, their new future and their new hope. Jacob asked with skepticism, "The wellspring of the Community's future, huh?"

"They have a tremendous capacity for the Spirit, though it is unrealized at this stage of their lives," said Dr. Zhukova. Running her hands through her hair to wring the excess moisture from it, she continued, "They have been instructed in our brand of Christianity since their adoptions and love one another as sisters, though I am still teaching them love without claim."

"You've still got a helluva lotta work to do," Jacob advised with a shake of his head. Underscoring his point with a serious look and raised brows, he said, "They're as green as it gets and the world is a lot less forgiving than it once was, which wasn't much."

"Not when it comes to their faith in God," argued Dr. Zhukova, "and I can sculpt anyone who possesses great faith into a spiritual pillar of the Community."

"I don't know, Doc," Jacob stated, "I just don't see why I should get involved in all this shit."

"If Boyka is pregnant, then you are already involved," reasoned Dr. Zhukova. Jacob shrugged and gestured to grudgingly concede the point.

"Given her *exuberance* for becoming a mother, she probably is," Jacob said while rubbing his right side. It was still sore.

"From now on I will call you Jacob, and you will call me Irinushka," Dr. Zhukova stated, her name the most seductive word Jacob had ever heard. He considered revealing the plot against him but decided instead to let it unfold of its own accord. The Doctor smiled at him and beckoned, "Come to me."

Dr. Zhukova swam as Jacob disrobed. Leaving his clothing and shoes on the beach, he walked with a determined pace towards her. He dove into the water once he reached waist depth and surfaced in front of the Doctor. The move achieved its desired result: she flinched. She recovered and inquired softly, "Will you join us?"

"I'm in," Jacob said, ". . . for now."

"Of course you are," replied Dr. Zhukova with a measure of conceit. She ran a single finger down his chest and asked, "As I said, where else would you go?"

"Oh, there's a place, Doc," Jacob countered. Dr. Zhukova's countenance became puzzled as he said, "But I'm sure they'll hold my reservation for a year."

The unlikely sexual partners, after gazing on each other briefly, hurled themselves into one another. They engaged in an ardent tongue-kiss while Jacob massaged the Doctor's bare, dense breasts and ran his hands over the curves of her hips. She, in turn, manipulated his penis and they soon passed into the throes of sexual intercourse and a multitude of sexual positions. Their lovemaking continued unabated for nearly an hour.

"Hold me close," ordered Dr. Zhukova as she spun around and jumped into Jacob's arms. He complied with her wishes by holding her afloat in the water, re-entering her and embracing her tightly. She gasped in his ear, "*Closer.*"

Succumbing to the forceful constriction of Jacob's arms, Dr. Zhukova experienced her orgasm with heavy, intense breathing and undulations of her body. He prepared for his own orgasm with the tensing of his muscles, a groan and the grabbing of Dr. Zhukova's buttocks. Thrusting herself backward by pushing Jacob away with her legs, she detached from his body and swam into deeper water.

"Where the fuck are you going?" Jacob demanded with a failed attempt to grab her. He pursued her but, proving to be a strong swimmer, Dr. Zhukova circumvented him and returned to waist-level depth.

"As a member of the Community, you are expected to practice male continence unless specifically approved by the Council for procreation," answered Dr. Zhukova as she stood up and again hugged herself to conceal her breasts. The Russian made a spectacular recovery from her intense physical exertion and her passion cooled. She added pointedly, "And my child-bearing days are over."

"Male continence?!" Jacob exclaimed, his sexual frustration fueling his wrath. He charged towards Dr. Zhukova but she matched him step-for-step in a tactical retreat. He yelled, "What the fuck is that?!"

"You must cease intercourse prior to your ejaculation," replied Dr. Zhukova coldly. The water lapped at her pelvis and provided a fleeting view of her vagina. Satisfied that he would move no closer, she added, "Also, you must not masturbate as it is a waste of your seed."

"You mean I gotta knock somebody up to blow my load?" Jacob asked slowly and incredulously. The prospect of release denied or children sired, at first, seemed repugnant but then he remembered the museum exhibit memorializing the communal raising of children by the original Community. Pondering his predicament and his blue balls, Jacob muttered, "We'll see about that, *Doctor.*"

"We must return to the Community," Dr. Zhukova said. Departing the pool, she called out, "I will then escort you to your guest house where Rahela should have your dinner prepared by the time we arrive."

Standing naked in the water, Jacob seethed while watching Dr. Zhukova collect her clothing in a business-like manner. She swiftly disappeared into the tunnel.

"Sneaky bitch," Jacob grumbled. Instantly focused on revenge, he planned a retaliatory ravishing of Rahela. A sinister grin on his face, and an uncharacteristic confidence in his heart, Jacob uttered, "Male continence my ass."

• • • •

DARBY PULLED THE HUMVEE in front of an unassuming block building disguised to appear as an old storage garage. It was, in fact, one of the supply depots Darby and Elizabeth established on a northern escape route into Canada and the second one she utilized since leaving Jarbidge Fortress.

"Stay here," Darby directed Sarah. She opened her door, glanced at the nun and said, "I'll make sure there are no uninvited guests waiting for us."

"Can I at least stretch my legs?" begged Sarah, her body stiff from the hours upon hours of travel. Darby scanned the vicinity and listened carefully. The surrounding area was nothing but rising mountains blanketed with evergreens and snow and only a faint afternoon breeze could be heard.

"Yeah, whatever," Darby mumbled. She had not slept in over two days and the emotional strain of her demonic sister sapped her physical strength. Failing to draw her gun, she zombie-walked to the structure.

A horrendous roar akin to a jet engine erupted throughout the valley. Sarah leapt from the vehicle and cast her eyes to the sky but Darby dropped her head and slouched her shoulders.

"What the fuck now?" Darby said. Sarah watched a small dark blur appear from behind one of the mountain peaks and careen out of the sky. It struck the ground like a meteor, the object cratering the earth and throwing up rocks and dirt. When the dust settled and the last of the debris rained down only wisps of steam arose from the hole. Sarah lumbered toward it.

"I take it your reunion with Jacob went poorly," said Sarah, the nun sporting larger, darker circles under her eyes and a drawn face. Darby breathed a sigh of relief, massaged the radix of her nose and then walked off to check the building.

"I'm gonna rip his fucking cock off," snarled Miriam with full demonic force. Feeling exhausted and filthy, Sarah clumsily lowered herself to a dry patch of ground and sat down upon it. She supported herself with her arms outstretched behind her and her legs spread out before her.

"What happened?" asked Sarah with a trace of irritation. She inhaled the fresh air deeply and relished the feel of the cold on her aching muscles.

"I don't want to talk about it," snapped Miriam. She remained hidden in her crater.

"Miriam, I'm mentally and physically spent, dirty, sore, fat and carrying another human being inside me," stated Sarah matter-of-factly. Closing her eyes, she drowsily uttered, "So either tell me what's going on or I'm going to pee, eat and then sleep, in exactly that order . . . unless I fall asleep right here."

"He's at some religious community way north of here," Miriam said. Sarah opened her eyes and sat up.

"Voluntarily?" inquired Sarah.

"Maybe," Miriam answered with uncertainty, "but I don't know."

"Well, how is he?" asked Sarah anxiously.

"Alive and kicking," Miriam said. Heartened by the demise of her rival, she added, "Sophie's dead, though."

"*Miriam*!" scolded Sarah.

"Relax, *mother*, I didn't do it," Miriam countered snottily. She crushed a stone in her hand as she said, "She died in some plane crash."

"Oh," replied Sarah with a measure of guilt for her premature accusation. She rested a hand on her stomach and commented, "That's odd, especially in these times."

"What's not odd is Jake sticking his dick in anything that moves," Miriam griped. Empathizing with Sarah, she expounded, "You've got competition. *Younger*, stunningly-beautiful competition."

"What are you talking about?" asked Sarah.

"How he does it, I have no idea, but Jake is a tremendous ass magnet," Miriam replied. She stood, peeked her head over the rim of the crater and looked at Sarah, saying, "He knocked up some twentysomething piece of ass already and I caught him getting ready to fuck this red-headed bitch."

A thought struck Miriam. She narrowed her eyes and examined Sarah.

"She kinda reminds me of you," Miriam said thoughtfully.

"I am neither red-headed nor a bitch," snapped Sarah.

"You sure about that last part?" Miriam said with a smirk. Sarah maneuvered out of the tense moment.

"So I take it you and Jake fought," said Sarah, "and that caused your explosive little tantrum."

"He didn't even know I was there," Miriam responded, her mood souring, "though he will soon."

"Please tell me-," began Sarah.

"I didn't kill anyone," Miriam interrupted her with a pointed finger. She lowered her gaze and kicked a rock, saying, "And it's a fucking miracle I didn't."

Sarah and Miriam sat quietly for several minutes, ending the conversation as if by silent agreement. Each woman became lost in her own thoughts as thick, gray clouds passed overhead.

"The building's clear," grumbled Darby as she stumped towards them. Both Miriam and Sarah watched her as she continued, "You two can sit out here yacking like fucking idiots in the cold but I'm going inside to sleep for at least a day. Good fucking night."

"Regardless of Jacob's predicament, or how either of us may feel about his sexual proclivities, we must travel to this community," said Sarah as Darby departed.

"I know," Miriam conceded. She jumped out of the hole and helped Sarah to her feet. Following Darby to the building, they walked hand-in-hand to a much-needed respite from the world.

12

DAYLIGHT CONTINUED to fade as Jacob and Dr. Zhukova trudged towards the Community. Neither of them spoke, their silence providing him much in the way of think time.

"It's a good thing I fucked her already," Jacob thought with a smirk and an internal chuckle, "because I'll probably be a permanent resident in her doghouse."

Jacob accepted his unsatiated carnal appetite and moved on to more important matters. One such matter was how to remain at the Community without becoming entangled in the snares employed by Dr. Zhukova. Identifying and neutralizing his would-be murderers was another.

"And then, of course, there's the Hungarian fuck squad," Jacob said to himself. Nearing the mansion house, he heard the dulcet tones of a small orchestra and an accompanying choir. He shook his head slowly at the religious hymns and muttered, "I hope the sex, safety and security is worth all this happy Christian bullshit."

Jacob could not deny the beauty and serenity of the Community's grounds even as the last vestiges of a harsh winter blanketed it in snow. The effort and care of its members were reflected in every aspect of the compound, from the meticulously managed roads and lanes to the buildings and interior designs.

A Community member joined Jacob and Dr. Zhukova on the last leg of their journey, the older man determined to present his minor issue to her. Rahela saved him from the monotony.

"Mr. Gottschalk!" called out Rahela. She rushed towards him but the tackle-embrace he anticipated did not materialize. Halting two feet from him as if telekinetically stopped by Dr. Zhukova, she said, "Your dinner is ready."

Jacob studied the young Hungarian's comely face and felt the warmth of her infatuation as she led him away from Dr. Zhukova and her prattling companion. He smiled and caressed her chin with his finger. Rahela averted her eyes and trembled.

"Did you miss me, Rahela?" Jacob asked with all the seduction he could muster.

"Please do not ask me such questions," begged Rahela despite her gaze answering resoundingly in the affirmative. The twentysomething was firmly on the hook though Jacob wondered if he or Dr. Zhukova baited it.

"You didn't eat with the rest of Zhukova's minions?" Jacob asked when louder waves of music poured forth from the mansion house and drifted about the grounds.

"No, I was excused to prepare your evening meal," answered Rahela with an eager smile. Jacob briefly contemplated what a perfect wife she would make but then crumpled up the idea and threw it away.

"Then you're going to stay and eat with me, kiddo," Jacob instructed her as he offered her his arm. Rahela reluctantly took it and, as they walked to the front door, she suffered intermittent bouts of shivering. Guiding her across the porch, Jacob said, "I'm gonna take a quick shower. Back in five."

"I should go to the mansion house," said Rahela nervously. She fidgeted and uttered, "Dr. Zhukova told me to return there upon your arrival."

"But ya' gotta eat," Jacob replied as he nudged Rahela towards the kitchen. She uneasily followed his direction and began the final preparations. Leaving her to her work, Jacob ascended the stairs and entered the bathroom. One minute later he was wallowing in a hot shower and washing Dr. Zhukova from his body. He considered another interview with her and mused aloud, "She was a damn good fuck."

The water pressure was strong and the water hot. Jacob began considering the rarity of such conveniences in the wilderness but his thoughts were disrupted by someone entering the bathroom. The intruder was far too quiet to be Rahela.

"Thank you for that assessment, Mr. Gottschalk," said Dr. Zhukova with much disapprobation in her voice. Her pause was clearly intended to prickle him and, for good measure, she added, "You were . . . adequate."

"I'm not as into older women. Your Hungarians are more my style," Jacob taunted as he resumed his shower. He heard a creak as she leaned against the vanity. His penis rose to the occasion and yearned for a second encounter with the good Doctor even as he asked, "Besides, you came, didn't you?"

"You may engage in another interview with Boyka, to which she has consented," replied Dr. Zhukova sternly, "but Rahela and Paliki are off limits for the time being."

"Lighten up, Doc," Jacob teased her with particular relish. Pouring it on thick, he added licentiously, "Why don't you hop in here with me and we'll go another round before dinner? Maybe Rahela could join us."

Jacob marveled at the way his confidence and his mood improved since his abduction by the New Oneidans. He felt his very essence changing.

"The table has been set for one and I sent Rahela to the mansion house with a warning about your propensity for sexual deviance and earthly attachments," said Dr. Zhukova sharply while ignoring Jacob's illicit proposition. Throwing open the shower curtain, she focused on his face and advised, "She will return at 6:00 o'clock tomorrow morning to clean up and prepare your breakfast, which will be ready at 6:30 am. Your first meeting, as a new member of the Community, is with our Membership Director at 8:00 am. That should occupy most of your day. Tomorrow evening you will be introduced to the Community."

"I wanted her to stay for dinner," Jacob complained, "ya' know, for some *lighter* conversation and company."

Steam floated around them as he glared at Dr. Zhukova and she looked at him icily. The conflict between them, however, kept Jacob fully engorged.

"Good night, Mr. Gottschalk," said Dr. Zhukova. Intrigued by how they crawled under each other's skin, Jacob smirked as she instructed him, "Please bring an open mind and a better attitude with you tomorrow. May you sleep with His blessings and protection."

Dr. Zhukova pulled the shower curtain closed and Jacob heard her exit the bathroom. Feeling sleep creeping over his eyelids, he soaped his testicles, enjoyed the smell of goulash and set his sights on day two at New Oneida. His past seemed to be fading in its emotional impact on his present.

"I'm starting to like it here," he said.

· · · ·

JACOB APPROACHED THE mansion house through the frigid morning air and the crackling of snow under his boots. The night sky faded into varying shades of hazy grays as the sun neared the horizon. Rahela did not arrive to prepare his breakfast as Dr. Zhukova promised but he managed to cobble together a meal.

"What have we here?" he thought as he stepped onto the main drive. Sitting on one of the long, green benches near the entrance was a woman. The shadows created by the yellow outdoor lights of the mansion hid all but her long legs. They were clad in a blue snowsuit.

"You're late," scolded the woman with a voice deeper than normal for most women. Jacob stopped in the middle of the driveway and grinned.

"You sure as hell don't sound like an Oneidan," Jacob replied while trying to pierce the shadows with his eyes.

"Neither do you," countered the woman. She was in no hurry to reveal herself so Jacob took the initiative by crossing the second half of the drive and ascending the porch steps.

"Jacob Gottschalk," Jacob said. The woman came into view: a classic brunette with a simple hairstyle and what appeared, at least in the glare of the lights, to be brown eyes. She sat to one side with her legs crossed and her right arm thrown over the back of the bench. Figuring that she was the Membership Director, Jacob conceded, "But you probably knew that already."

"I did," said the woman. The more Jacob studied her, the more she came into focus. Dark circles hung beneath her eyes and, though mildly attractive, time and perhaps undue stress bit into her face like an unforgiving winter wind. The woman stood up and continued, "I'm the Membership Director and the bane of your existence for the next several hours. I really hate to tell you this, but you and I have some paperwork to do and *a lot* to go over today."

"I thought this was a religious community," Jacob replied. He moved closer to her and asked with skepticism, "Shouldn't I be meeting with the *Director of Community and Individual Spirituality* first?"

"Your spiritual capability has already been judged, or you wouldn't even be here," explained the woman convincingly as, moving past him, she walked to the front doors and opened one of them. She held it for Jacob and said, "But there is much more to a person than spiritual capability. And Dr. Frye also likes to know what services you can best offer the Community. We still have to survive."

"That guy's a huge asshole," Jacob commented with a sour expression. He walked through the door and into the mansion with the woman on his heels. She closed the door.

"He certainly comes off that way sometimes," replied the woman, her deep knowledge of Dr. Frye evident, "but I'd ask that you keep any negative opinions about him to yourself. He *is* my husband after all."

"Whoops," Jacob said while turning around. He shrugged his shoulders and added, "Sorry."

"Carol Frye," said the woman with an extended hand and a grin. Despite Jacob's disparaging of her spouse, she remained good-natured.

"Fan-fucking-tastic," Jacob sighed as he took her hand.

• • • •

THE PAIR DRAINED TWO pots of coffee during a tedious meeting where Jacob discussed his career, social and medical histories and expounded on the skills he could possibly offer the Community. The experience was akin to a deposition and a mortgage application process in one rigorous exercise, the only good parts being the coffee and their bantering back and forth across Carol's desk.

"Well, that should about do it," sighed Carol as she wrote a few final notes and then closed a file folder. She leaned back in her chair, removed her glasses and tossed them on the desk, saying, "I just have one more question."

"Ask away," Jacob said before yawning and rubbing his eyes. His thoughts had been on lunch and Boyka for the past forty-five minutes.

"Will you consent to an interview with me?" inquired Carol with a straight face. Jacob laughed.

"Frye already hates my guts," Jacob said with the assumption Carol was joking. Clasping his hands on his stomach and crossing his legs, he added with a smirk, "Banging his wife would really put me on his shit list."

Carol did not react in the slightest to Jacob's jest and remained serious. His smile faded and he sat up.

"What if I told you it wouldn't?" asked Carol with a knowing look. Jacob blinked repeatedly and shook his head to clear it.

"Wait, are you seriously asking me for an interview?" Jacob replied with raised brows and palms. It was Carol's turn to be amused.

"We Reformed Oneidans practice complex marriage," explained Carol while Jacob gaped at her with a stunned expression, "where any member of the Community may have sex with any other member of the Community as long as the parties consent and the Council approves the union. And yes, Jacob, I'm seriously asking you for an interview."

"You've had sex with other men while married to Frye?" Jacob inquired in disbelief. The prospect of complex marriage and its practice in a Christian community fascinated him.

"That's right," answered Carol, "and Malcom has enjoyed the company of other women while married to me. Every member of the Community is married to every other member. Malcom and I wed prior to its formation so our nuptials were grandfathered in."

"*Grandfathered* is the right word for it," Jacob muttered with horrid thoughts of Dr. Frye having sex with Carol. Standing up, he chased them from his mind, walked to the window and gazed out of it, saying, "Zhukova left out a few things when I asked her about interviews."

Carol showed no inclination to comment on the methods of Dr. Zhukova and instead watched Jacob carefully. His mind generated a thousand questions but he settled on a select few and turned to interrogate her.

"Do you guys allow multiple partners at one time and homosexual sex, too?" Jacob asked. He wondered how far the New Oneidans pushed traditional Christian morals and the concept of communal marriage. He also wondered if Carol was bisexual.

"The original Oneidans didn't take it that far, and neither do we," answered Carol, "at least not yet. But those issues have been discussed by the Council and the membership as a whole. *Hypothetically*, of course, although there are some of us who think it's hypocritical to hold that sex is a form of worship, a blessed sacrament even, and then limit the forms in which that love may be expressed. With the exception of children, of course. There are strict and separate rules for those under eighteen."

"Tell me you're not letting old guys fuck kids or I'll fucking leave right now," Jacob asserted forcefully.

"Absolutely not," answered Carol while taking great offense to Jacob's insinuation. The pair exchanged sharp gazes until she backed down and asked, "Were you told about our Founder, John Humphrey Noyes?"

"Yeah, the Doc told me a little," Jacob replied. He folded his arms and leaned his back against the wall, continuing, "I know he started the whole thing back in the eighteen hundreds."

"Yes," replied Carol. Leaning back in her desk chair, she expounded, "It was he, along with higher ranking members, who primarily regulated sexual encounters in the Old Community, much like Dr. Zhukova and our Council here at New Oneida. One tenet of his was ascending fellowship, or the pairing of the younger, less-spiritually developed members with older, more-spiritually-developed members."

"That doesn't answer my question," Jacob interjected pointedly.

"You're certainly an impatient man," said Carol as she brushed aside Jacob's interruption. She, too, folded her arms and continued, "In any event, the purpose of ascending fellowship was the mentoring of the younger members and encouraging their growth in the Holy Spirit. Noyes, *in a practice we neither condone nor continue*, would introduce twelve- and thirteen-year-old girls to sex and guide them in their early sexual development. Likewise, older women – usually those past menopause - would first sleep with teenage boys and school them in sexual relations."

"So Noyes founded an entire Christian denomination so he could fuck pre-pubescent girls," Jacob concluded. He placed his hands on his hips and walked back to the desk, saying with anger, "*Nice.*"

"No one is perfect, Mr. Gottschalk," said Carol with annoyance, "which is why we rejected the Perfectionist teachings of Noyes a long time ago. However, when it comes to children and sex, we believe his intent was pure even if his actions were wrong. No child of this Community may have sex, *with anyone*, until age sixteen. Between the ages of sixteen and eighteen, the Community Council stands *in loco parentis* in judging whether the teenager in question is mature enough to begin complex marriage and ascending fellowship . . . but only if the child expresses a sincere interest. And no one here holds a monopoly on introducing our teenage members to sex, not even Dr. Zhukova. We protect our children as God protects his children."

Jacob shivered when he considered that the woman with whom he had intercourse the night before may have done the same with sixteen-year-old boys. He pondered the bizarre beliefs of the Reformed Oneidans in silence. Carol read the dismay on his face.

"I'm thirty-eight, Mr. Gottschalk," she assured him, "and the youngest man I've ever had sex with was twenty-one . . . when I was thirty. We can discuss the sexual rules of the Community as much as you would like but, right now, I'm just asking for an interview."

Jacob exhaled and returned to his seat. He offered Carol a muted grin.

"Sure, I'll *consent to an interview* with you, *Mrs.* Frye," Jacob said.

"Since you have Dr. Zhukova's ear, will you submit our request to the Council?" asked Carol. She was, by far, the most candid and down-to-earth Community member Jacob had met.

"Yeah, yeah, sure," Jacob replied. The air crackled with the sexual energy between them and he thought, "I bet this one's a sack demon. She's gotta be."

· · · ·

"I HAVE TO ADMIT, I thought that would be worse," Jacob told Carol as they exited the mansion house and she escorted him back to the guest house for his lunch. It was a cold day and the clouds migrating across the sky often blotted out the sun.

"We're just suckering you in," replied Carol with a feigned devious tone. Her sunglasses made her appear like a police detective. Making her way to a flagstone path leading down the hill, she guided Jacob towards the main road. A sidelong glance followed and she said, "You know, drawing you closer so you let your guard down and it's easier to brainwash you."

Carol laughed boisterously. Jacob forced a smile but knew, unlike Carol, that Dr. Zhukova and her Council of cronies were doing just that. He shivered despite the sudden appearance of the sun and the warm greetings of New Oneidans. Jacob politely returned them all but retained his suspicion of their motives.

"So, you joining me for lunch?" Jacob asked in an effort to change the subject. He expected an answer in the negative as shifting females seemed to be one of Dr. Zhukova's favorite strategies.

"No, sir," said Carol as they reached the bottom of the hill. They paused to let two four-wheelers pass as she explained, "I'm just making sure you don't wander off. Oh, and by the way, at 7:00 o'clock, you're meeting with the entire Community in the mansion hall."

Carol attempted to step out onto the road but Jacob stopped her by snagging the sleeve of her coat. She allowed him to pull her back.

"Yes?" asked Carol with an expectant expression. Jacob released her arm.

"Why the meeting with the entire Community?" he inquired.

"I don't know. Maybe just to introduce you. We don't get much fresh blood anymore," answered Carol. The expression on her face told Jacob she knew something he did not. He could not be certain, however, what she knew.

"You don't know or you're not telling me?" Jacob asked slowly and firmly, his demeanor darkening as he questioned her.

"Relax, Mr. Gottschalk," said Carol with seriousness and compassion. Taking his gloved hands in her own, she locked her gaze on his face and assured him, "It's all gonna be okay. Just go with the flow. Trust me, it's worth it. We're allowed to be real people."

Carol's attempt to put Jacob at ease temporarily succeeded as to the Council's intentions. He disentangled himself from her.

"You're not finking on our interview, are you?" asked Carol. She poked Jacob in mock disapproval.

"No," Jacob replied, "I'm not finking on our interview."

"Good, because you'd regret it," taunted Carol. Nodding towards the guest house, she suggested, "Let's go."

Carol proceeded to the guest house. Jacob shamelessly watched her do so and studied every inch of her body.

"What the hell is she doing with that old fuck Frye?" Jacob asked himself. Responding with a shrug, he followed Carol and turned his mind towards food.

• • • •

RAHELA WAS NOWHERE to be found when Jacob arrived at the guest house. She had ostensibly been there, however, as the breakfast dishes were gone and lunch was waiting for him. Jacob ate in contemplative silence.

"Am I really gonna stay here for a year?" Jacob asked himself. Desiring the wisdom only found at the bottom of a bottle of whiskey, he nonetheless pondered his future without it and reasoned, "Zhukova's built a thriving, secure community, it's far enough off the radar to avoid unwanted attention and no one knows I'm here. Maybe this could be home."

An uncomfortable tingle rippled down Jacob's spine as he said the word "home". He grimaced.

"I've made that mistake before," Jacob said aloud. He took the final bite of his meal and pushed away his plate. Pouring himself a cup of coffee from a carafe on the table, he allowed his mood to lighten and complained, "And I'll have to get used to that shitty cherry wine . . . or find some fucking whiskey."

Jacob chuckled quietly but an unexpected knock at the door interrupted his ponderings. He pushed himself away from the table.

"Enter," Jacob called out as he stood up and dumped his dishes in the sink with a clatter. He wondered which one of Dr. Zhukova's rotating beauties had arrived to mess with his head. He also found himself hoping it was Rahela.

"Hello, Mr. Gottschalk," said Boyka as she gracefully swept into the room.

"Of course it's her," Jacob thought while appraising the raven-haired beauty. He quickly noticed the distress on her face and bleariness of her eyes. Watching her bottom lip twitch repeatedly, he asked, "What's wrong?"

Boyka slammed into Jacob and embraced him. She broke down instantly, the Hungarian desperately clinging to his body and sobbing.

"Hey, hey," Jacob said as he wrapped Boyka securely in his arms. He encouraged her, "You're gonna be all right."

Boyka refused to be consoled and continued crying. She rested her head on his chest and soaked his shirt with her tears.

"Come now, Boyka, aren't we being a little dramatic?" asked Edna as she entered the kitchen. Supremely calm and confident, she looked to Jacob and explained, "She learned of your interview with Dr. Zhukova."

"I see," Jacob replied. He felt morally slimy. Boyka, meanwhile, refused to show her face and kept it tucked into Jacob's chest. He gushed, "I'm sorry, kid. I fucked up. I shouldn't've done it."

"You did nothing wrong, and she'll be fine," asserted Edna pejoratively. She approached the intertwined couple and placed a hand on Boyka's arm, instructing her, "Now, go into the bathroom and compose yourself."

Boyka hesitated. Edna waited patiently for her and, with some physical guidance from the older woman, she detached herself from Jacob and hurried to the bathroom. He ran his hand over his tear-stained shirt.

"I would like to speak with you, Mr. Gottschalk, about a matter of great importance," advised Edna. She gestured to the living room as if their meeting was mandatory.

"Sure, what the hell," Jacob replied. He took two steps towards the living room, stopped and then glanced over his shoulder, saying, "You didn't happen to bring any of that cherry wine, did you?"

"I did not," said Edna with a raised eyebrow.

"Yeah, I figured," Jacob muttered. They circumvented a couch and seated themselves in chairs flanking a stone fireplace. Jacob eyed it and said, "Care for a fire?"

"No thank you," replied Edna. She was so petite that, to Jacob, it felt as if he spoke to a child dressed as a middle-aged woman. That impression was buttressed by the large, plush chair in which she sat. There was, however, nothing young about her wise eyes and Jacob knew her penetrating mind uncovered the deeper meanings of his words.

"Shouldn't you check on her?" Jacob inquired with a nod towards the bathroom. He occasionally heard movement within it.

"As I indicated, she'll be fine," countered Edna. She explained with frankness, "Unfortunately, the two of you had an unusually intense introduction and that tends to fuel infatuation, especially in the young . . . and men like yourself."

"Men like me, huh?" Jacob objected with a sneer. He suspected that Edna knew the truth of Charles's death and his sexual tryst with Boyka. Jacob decided to veer the conversation in a different direction and queried bluntly, "So, Edna, what's on your mind?"

"Given that you've spent extended time with both Irinushka and Carol," began Edna, "I believe you've learned this Community is deeply divided."

"Dr. Z used the word *decaying*," Jacob responded. He leaned back in his chair, crossed his legs and set his arms on the armrests.

"The Community is her life's work," said Edna, "and her love for it obscures her normally sound judgment. There is no decay, just dissension in the ranks. The original Oneidan Community experienced the same convulsions."

"The old 'good of the one versus the good of the many' conundrum," Jacob commented. Edna smiled and nodded her head as he added, "The Community versus the individual."

"Exactly," answered Edna.

"So who's winning?" Jacob said.

"No one, as long as it all continues," said Edna. She scooted forward, set her feet on the floor and said, "The Council, save Meriwa on occasion, is firmly behind Irinushka and her orthodoxy but Carol has a large following among the rank-and-file members, especially the younger ones, who yearn for more freedom and, paradoxically, more attachment. They both battle for Dr. Frye's allyship and his oscillation between them has created a stalemate, though whether it's an intentional strategy to balance their influences or his inability to reconcile the roles of husband and father figure, I do not know."

Boyka made a composed entrance, her eyes puffy and her face pale. She watched Edna expectantly and received a warm smile in return.

"I'm glad to see you're feeling better, my child," Edna greeted her. Waving her hand in the direction of the kitchen, she directed Boyka, "Now, if you will, please make us some fresh coffee and attend to the lunch dishes."

"Yes, ma'am," replied Boyka. She disappeared into the kitchen without acknowledging Jacob. His attention wandered as he compared Boyka and Rahela as potential mates.

"Mr. Gottshalk," beckoned Edna. Her tone prickled him.

"Just tell me what you want from me," he demanded as he returned to the present. Edna studied him closely, the Community elder evaluating his spirit one final time.

"To father children with our Hungarian women, as many as you are able," stated Edna firmly.

"Do you hear how nuts you sound saying shit like that?" Jacob asked with an emphatic gesture.

"Perhaps I am, as you say, *nuts*," conceded Edna. She placed her hands in her lap and said, "And there is much I do not know. What I do know is that the Holy Spirit has descended upon you and God has granted you considerable power over the demonic world."

"I think the bigger question is why?" Jacob interjected. Edna drew herself up and seemed to grow in her chair.

"Don't you see, you foolish man?" snapped Edna. Her eyes blazed as she stated, "The purpose of your gift – *your purpose* – is to father a generation of spiritually superior humans, the first such generation, that will spread from here to the four corners of the earth and prepare it for Christ's triumphant return."

"Don't *you* see, you goofy broad?" Jacob countered as he rose to his feet. Boyka drifted into the doorway and watched him as he launched into a tirade, barking in a flurry of words and hands, "This selective breeding bullshit isn't as surefire as you and the good Doctor think it is. Sure, you could get your 'spiritually superior humans', or, much more likely, you'll get a bunch of Jacob Gottschalks."

Edna observed him with serious eyes. Jacob smirked grimly.

"A bunch of vulgar, angry, horny, drunken Jacob Gottschalks," he continued with a scowl. He waved a pointed finger and then pointed it at his chest as he said, "And nobody – not even me – wants that."

Boyka rushed Jacob and smacked him hard across the cheek. He stared at her in disbelief.

"Our children will not be that way. You will not be that way," Boyka admonished him. Cowing him with an all-consuming passion for God, she declared, "You will become a better man and we will raise them to love and serve the Lord."

Boyka let her fiery eyes linger on Jacob long enough to make her point before whirling around and departing. She stopped in the doorway.

"You will not have any of us until you become a man of God," announced Boyka as if she addressed the entire Community. She exited the living room. A dumbfounded Jacob simply gaped at her.

"Well," said Edna as she stood up and patted Jacob on the shoulder, "this went better than I expected. I will see you tonight at your introduction to the Community. Have a pleasant afternoon, Mr. Gottschalk."

"What, you're not gonna take a shot, too?" Jacob asked while motioning to his cheek.

Edna offered him a dubious expression and then proceeded in Boyka's wake. Jacob chewed the callous on the inside of his mouth as she left the guest house.

"I need a drink," Jacob sighed.

13

SARAH'S SPIRIT WAS rejuvenated. She slept late into the morning, prepared a meal consisting of unprocessed food and communed with her Master for two hours. Basking in the sunlight of an unusually warm spring afternoon, Sarah sat in a long, low chair and enjoyed the songs of twittering birds.

"Thank you for my strength and forgive me for my weakness," Sarah prayed. The surrounding slopes sparkled with intermittent drips of melting snow as the sun's rays struck them, the twinkles matching the tears of joy in her eyes as she appreciated the gift of her unborn child. It kicked when she hugged her stomach and said, "We must take courage, my little one, and follow the paths appointed to us."

"Damn it," griped Darby as she struggled to open the building's garage door. Achieving her task, she grabbed another of the chairs, walked over to Sarah and clunked it down next to her. Sarah wiped her eyes with the blanket that warmed her body.

"Good afternoon," Sarah greeted her. Darby plopped into the chair with a power bar and a tall, nondescript mug. She ripped the wrapper off the bar and bit into it, her actions prompting Sarah to suggest, "I made breakfast this morning, Darby."

"I know," replied Darby while chewing her food, "and I already ate the rest of it."

"Good," Sarah said with a motherly smile. Darby drank from her mug from which came the distinctive aroma of alcohol. Sarah offered Darby a dubious grin and advised, "I also made coffee."

"There's coffee in this," countered Darby. So great was Sarah's spiritual revival that Darby's vices floated away into the brilliant blueness of the sky above them. The incorrigible ballbuster looked around and asked, "Where's Blondie?"

Miriam materialized in front of them but said nothing. Darby sighed in irritation.

"Oh, great, she's here," muttered Darby.

"How are we feeling this beautiful afternoon, Miriam?" Sarah inquired.

"If God was going to give Jake to someone else," answered Miriam, "he should have left me in the fucking Abyss."

She shuddered at the mention of Ba'al Zeboul's realm but her longing for Jacob proved greater than her fear of it. Darby rolled her eyes.

"As much as I am enjoying your melancholy company," Sarah said, "the two of you need to turn your eyes to the future, grasp whatever strands of hope you can – they do exist, mind you – and pull yourselves out of the depressive pits in which you wallow."

"What future?" snapped Darby. She stood up, loomed above Sarah to intimidate her and added bitterly, "There's nothing left. Kaiser's a clusterfuck, or soon will be, my entire family's dead or demonic and humanity's on its way out. We'll be lucky if we live six months let alone long enough to find this bullshit future of yours. And you're dropping a kid into this shithole. You should feel the worst outta all three of us."

"And how do you feel about the future, Miriam?" Sarah inquired, the nun once again possessed of her steadfast patience.

"She's right. There's nothing left," agreed Miriam. Feeling the old evil struggling to gain entry into her spirit, she asked defiantly, "If I can't be with him, then what's the fucking point?"

Sarah stood up, let the blanket fall from her body and placed a gentle hand on each of their shoulders. They both squirmed under her loving touch but uncharacteristically failed to pull away from it. Sarah's eyes sparkled with spiritual intensity.

"Even if everything you said is true," Sarah said in a compelling manner, "God has set a purpose before each of you, both figuratively . . . ."

Sarah placed her hands on her pregnant belly and caressed it. Darby and Miriam watched their movement as if she were hypnotizing them.

". . . and literally," Sarah continued. Her face became grave but determined as she explained, "Elizabeth is about to unleash great evil into this world, greater than any it has experienced before, and only those like Jacob and his child have the power to combat it. I hope there are others – I pray desperately there are others – but, regardless, we must focus on what we can do, here and now. I need you to help me find Jacob and protect our baby while it is at its most vulnerable."

Miriam and Darby cast sidelong glances at each other. They then indicated their agreement by offering resolute gazes to Sarah.

"The forces of good are in serious fucking trouble if me and Blondie are their only hope," replied Darby. She downed her drink and picked up her chair, saying, "I got some work to do on the Humvee before we go, though some asshole left a broken jack here so it'll take time."

"I can help with that," stated Miriam. Walking over to the garage, she grabbed the underside of the Humvee with one hand and lifted it up. Miriam waited patiently with flat affect.

"Let's get started then," said Darby with a shrug. She lumbered towards the garage.

"Praise God for good days," Sarah said quietly with one final tear.

· · · ·

THE DIN OF HUNDREDS of voices caused Jacob to stop just outside the doors of the Community Hall. Carol looked to him sympathetically and, after a brief pause, took him by the arm. Leading Jacob forward, she squeezed it tightly.

"I don't like this at all," Jacob muttered though Carol either did not hear him or feigned that she did not register his remark.

The two-story Community Hall – called the Big or Family Hall in the original mansion – contained two banks of Windsor-styled, spindle-backed benches on its main level with one on either side of a wide main aisle. The balcony level took up three sides of the Hall's second floor and offered fixed-bench seating. Together, the levels provided enough room for several hundred Community members. A high-arched stage area dominated the far end of the Hall with three huge, rectangular windows towering over those who stood upon it.

Community members packed the hall and many stood around the outer edges of the room. The Council occupied seats on the stage with Dr. Zhukova sitting in a throne-like center chair. A slow wave of silence rolled over the auditorium as Jacob passed each row.

"Like a mother fucking queen on her mother fucking throne," Jacob thought as Carol escorted him to the area beneath the stage. Walking up the aisle, he noticed adult and teenage Community members of all ages watching him like a freak show attraction. Leaning towards Carol, he asked quietly, "Public execution?"

"You'll be fine," whispered Carol as she left Jacob at the front of the Hall and took a seat to his right. Scanning the audience, he picked out a few other familiar faces, including Juanita, Rahela, Paliki and Boyka. Dr. Zhukova rose when Jacob hesitated and motioned to a lone chair below the stage.

"Please, Mr. Gottschalk," requested Dr. Zhukova as her voice echoed throughout the chamber. Whispers rippled across the audience but were quelled by the Russian's stare.

"Why don't you tell me what the hell all this is first?" Jacob said. He walked to his chair and set his hand upon its top rail. The Doctor returned to her chair and seated herself with her arms on its armrests in true queen-like manner.

"We have brought you here today for what we call mutual criticism," explained Dr. Zhukova. Jacob felt the weight of many eyes upon him as she crossed her legs and explained, "We use it to curb unseemly behavior and encourage the development of more spiritual habits. All members of the Community are subject to it and, today, you will undergo your first session."

Jacob smirked. He remained standing and folded his arms intransigently.

"Do you usually do your grilling in front of the whole damn Community?" Jacob inquired.

"No, we do not," replied Dr. Zhukova, "but you have many ungodly behaviors that will require the focus and spiritual weight of the entire Community to correct."

Jacob unfolded his arms and pushed over his chair. It hit the floor with a startling crack.

"Fuck this," Jacob said, his profanity met with a chorus of startled gasps. Storming down the center aisle, he dramatically cast open the Hall doors and disappeared behind them.

Nearly every set of eyes in the hall watched Jacob's departure. Dr. Zhukova, however, made eye contact with Rahela who obeyed the Doctor's unspoken command and pursued him. Boyka jealously hawked her sister's steps.

"Mr. Gottschalk will need our collective spiritual strength to guide him down the heavenly path," announced Dr. Zhukova, the congregation turning its attention to her as she spoke. Juanita ignored the sermon into which Dr. Zhukova launched and followed Rahela.

• • • •

"I CAN'T STAY HERE," Jacob said aloud as he descended the front steps of the mansion house. He quickly crossed its drive and marched towards the village, muttering, "Esoteric Christianity's one thing but this Bible Communism bullshit is too fucking much."

"Mr. Gottschalk!" shouted Rahela as she pursued Jacob onto the main road. She called frantically, "Mr. Gottschalk, stop, please!"

Jacob, against his better judgment, stopped and allowed Rahela to traverse the distance between them. He sneered, exhaled and, with his hands on his hips, turned to face her.

"We all undergo mutual criticism," pleaded Rahela as she squeezed Jacob's arm. Pulling him in the direction of the mansion house, she said, "The Council is not singling you out. I promise you that."

"I need a favor, sweetheart," Jacob said bluntly. A suspicious Rahela became visibly anxious and he knew she was torn between her loyalty to the Community and her infatuation with him. Jacob disentangled himself from her grasp and assured her, "Relax, Rahela. I just need your help in prepping for a little hiking expedition tomorrow."

"Hiking expedition?" asked Rahela with a quizzical expression. Jacob placed his hands in his pockets.

"That's right," Jacob said. Nodding and walking towards the guest house, he added, "Starting with hiking boots. Size eleven."

Rahela watched Jacob walk away and then bounded to catch up. Her demeanor dimmed and she lowered her head.

"Where are you going?" asked Rahela. She proved remarkably easy to read and, as always, Jacob played on her naivete.

"For now, nowhere," Jacob said. Rahela's eyes grew wide and she froze in her tracks. He sensed the raging conflict within her so, lifting her chin with the knuckle of his right index finger, he explained, "But I've got some heavy shit to figure out so I'm going walkabout to clear my head."

Jacob and Rahela resumed walking and remained silent until they reached the guest house's red-bricked walkway. They turned towards one another.

"I cannot go with you," whimpered Rahela.

"I didn't ask you to," Jacob curtly replied. Rahela dropped her head after the rebuke so, in response, Jacob softened his tone and said, "I just need you to get me a few things. That's it."

"Okay," said Rahela. Refusing to raise her chin, she explained, "I will come early tomorrow with what you need and make you breakfast."

"Sounds like a plan," Jacob said. He kissed her forehead and then ascended the lone porch step. Disappearing into the guest house, Jacob sighed, "See ya' in the morning."

The door clicked closed. Rahela watched it with intense yearning and, after a brief hesitation, she stepped onto the porch.

· · · ·

JACOB UNDRESSED SLOWLY in the dark. The desire to remain at the Community and the urge to flee it battled within him though neither one gained the upper hand. He sat on the bed facing the door.

"Tomorrow," Jacob declared. Removing his t-shirt and tossing it to the floor, he stated steadfastly, "Tomorrow I make the decision and then that's it."

"Let me help you make the decision tonight," cooed Rahela as she appeared in the doorway. The light from the downstairs hall filtered around her and cast her in a strange light.

"Boyka said you're all off limits until I stop being such an asshole," Jacob replied. Rahela offered him an embarrassed smile.

"My sister does not speak for me," replied Rahela.

"Is that so?" Jacob asked with a mischievous smirk. He laid her on the bed and slowly undressed her while taking care to brush his hands against her most sexually-sensitive areas. Rahela trembled with every calculated touch and she shivered as he said, "What about Dr. Zhukova and Edna?"

"I should not be doing this without permission," said Rahela unconvincingly after Jacob stripped her down to her bra and panties. Saying nothing, he proceeded to the balcony's French doors and closed the curtains.

"You're free to leave at any time, sweetheart," Jacob replied while motioning to the open bedroom door.

"Come here," instructed Rahela. Wiggling her right index finger at Jacob, she rose to her knees, unfastened her bra and let it drop to the bed. The bouncing revelation of her bulbous breasts supercharged Jacob's sex drive.

"This is gonna be an incredible fuck," Jacob said to himself. He moved to the edge of the bed.

"Take off your underwear," ordered Rahela. Jacob swiftly obeyed and, by the time he finished disrobing, she had removed her panties and stood on the bed. She hugged his face into her breasts and kissed the top of his head.

"Lay down," Rahela directed him. He eagerly complied with her wishes, any resistance he felt wiped away by the scent of her honey-hued skin and the spongy flesh of her bosoms.

"Whatever you say," Jacob said with a shit-eating grin and his hands behind his head. Rahela hovered over him and began circling her hips in a hypnotizing manner. The erotic display lasted for thirty seconds before Rahela mounted Jacob and buried his entire length within her. He grabbed her breasts and moaned, "Holy fuck."

Rahela swirled her wide hips slowly as she rode Jacob. He found her technique exquisite and ceded all control to her. It was if she sought to coax his seed into her with all the sensuality she could muster. Jacob alternated between shamelessly massaging her heavy breasts and grasping the curves of her broad pelvis but, despite the intense pleasure with which she inundated him, he felt guilty.

"This'll kill Boyka," he thought.

"Wait for me," said Rahela when she sensed Jacob nearing his orgasm. He clenched his pelvic muscles to ward off his ejaculation and waited for Rahela to reach her own orgasm. Several minutes later they climaxed together and Rahela collapsed on him.

The paramours spent the next five minutes sloppily tongue-kissing one another until Jacob was ready for another round of lovemaking. This time, however, he took the lead during their energetic coitus and maneuvered

Rahela into numerous positions. He finished on top of her and then rolled off to the side.

"I never expected that from you," Jacob said amidst heavy breaths. They clasped hands and he added, "That wasn't your first time, was it?"

Rahela placed her finger over his lips.

"Sleep now," said Rahela. Sleep soon overwhelmed him and, with Rahela clinging to his body and ceding her own consciousness, he fell fast asleep.

• • • •

JACOB AWOKE AT 4:30 am to the sound of a digital clock's alarm. He detached it from its power cord and hurled it across the room. His attempt to silence it proved futile and it continued to sound well out of his reach.

"Fuck," Jacob grumbled as he slowly vacated the warm, comfortable bed. Twenty-minutes later he descended the stairs ready for his journey into the wilderness. Rahela was already buzzing about the kitchen and preparing his breakfast.

"Good morning, drágaságom," Rahela greeted him, the Hungarian grinning widely and warmly before returning to a pan of sizzling sausage.

"I thought you weren't supposed to call me that," Jacob replied. Rahela flashed him a mischievous grin, the Hungarian free of the chains of Dr. Zhukova and the Community.

"Everything you requested is in the living room," said Rahela with a nod. She sent Jacob off well-equipped, well-fed and with a enthusiastic kiss after a quiet breakfast.

"Thanks, kiddo," Jacob said.

"Do you call Boyka this *kiddo*?" asked Rahela jealously.

"No," Jacob replied before he departed into the morning darkness. Rahela's smiling face followed him until he disappeared from her view.

Ducking into the woods north of the main road, Jacob followed its meandering course at a distance until he cleared the Community. He then dropped south and followed the frozen river to avoid getting lost in the unfamiliar expanse of the forest. The first light of the sun crept ever so slowly over the horizon and gradually illuminated his journey. The forest remained shadowy.

Jacob's legs ached after several hours of hiking; his body perspired and he breathed heavily. Traveling through the urban sprawl of Kaiser did little to prepare him for the arduous hike from the Community. He followed a path up to a cliff overlooking a bend in the river, however, and the spectacular view wiped away the soreness.

"It is beautiful country," Jacob said aloud. He slid off his backpack, slung it to the ground and seated himself on a large, flat rock near the cliff's edge. Tracing the line of the river as it curled like a white ribbon into the distance, he reasoned, "It doesn't matter what I do. Now that Sophie's gone, it's just me anyway. If I fuck up and die, I fuck up and die."

The import of his words struck him. He closed his eyes and said a silent prayer for Sophie.

"Poor kid," Jacob said as he finished the prayer and opened his eyes. His use of the word "kid" prompted him to think of his own child. Unaware of its true fate, he believed it struggled to survive in Kaiser.

"If she made it," Jacob said sadly. He shook his head and uttered fiercely, "Bullshit. She has Liz's tenacity. She made it."

He paused and smiled.

"*Autumn* made it," Jacob said with swelling pride, "and if my little girl has the strength to survive the mistakes of her parents and a demonic attack then the least I can do is get her the hell outta Kaiser."

Jacob pictured he and Rahela raising his daughter and her future siblings at the Community. He also pictured Dr. Zhukova objecting to that arrangement.

"Maybe I can help Carol push for some of those personal freedom reforms," Jacob suggested. Hope burgeoned within him and, as he began pondering the finer details of a plan, he declared with satisfaction, "That's it. That's the plan. Once I get things squared away here, I'll go get Autumn, bring her back and raise her . . . in this weird religious cult."

• • • •

JACOB INDULGED IN THE solitude of the Canadian wilderness while ruminating over his plan and considering contingency after contingency. A cold wind brought him back to the present.

"I'll have to get acclimated to this fucking cold," Jacob mused aloud. His comfort in the natural setting suddenly became discomfort.

"Used to this wasteland," scoffed an old, gravelly voice. It yelled derisively, "Ha!"

Jacob spun around in a sitting position to find an elderly, grizzled man staring at him. He leaned on a gnarled walking stick.

"May I help you?" Jacob asked. The man looked like an unkempt Earnest Hemingway though his dirty, white beard was much longer and scragglier. His physique was worn down by life in the wilderness but he was by no means gaunt.

"Don't see too many people on the river anymore," remarked the mysterious man, his contempt for outsiders obvious.

"Hunted them to the brink of extinction, have ya?" Jacob retorted. Despite his remark, he sensed no danger.

"You're not from the Community," growled the man. He placed both hands on the top of his walking stick, leaned on it and speculated with an exasperated sigh, "No, you're from much farther away than that."

"Look, Gandalf, I just wanna be alone today, so get lost, will ya?" Jacob griped. He hoisted his backpack onto the rock and began searching for his lunch. The old man eagerly watched him pull a wrapped sandwich from the main compartment.

"Care to share that with a hungry old man?" asked Jacob's unexpected visitor, the elder's mood improving with the prospect of food. Jacob smiled and shook his head.

"That depends, old man," Jacob said as he slowly held up his sandwich. The old man's eyes followed it as it rose.

"On . . . on what?" asked the old man, his gaze riveted to the sandwich.

"On what you have to offer in return," Jacob answered, his proposed deal merely a jest. He doubted the man possessed anything of value but asked nonetheless, "Quid pro quo, yes or no?"

The old man said nothing and ogled the sandwich, his silence causing Jacob's smile to fade. He lowered the sandwich and the old man's eyes went with it.

"Yes!" exclaimed the old man. Sensing that his uninvited guest teetered on the edge of sanity, Jacob decided to have mercy on him.

"Enjoy your free sandwich, ya' goofy old bastard," Jacob replied. He threw the old man the sandwich with a flick of his wrist. The old man snagged the spinning sandwich from the air with uncanny skill. Retrieving the second sandwich Rahela packed for him, Jacob pleaded, "Now *please* get the hell outta here and leave me alone."

The old man promptly sat down on a smaller nearby rock, unwrapped the sandwich and began devouring it. Jacob watched him with disgust as remnants of the tojáskrém, or Hungarian egg salad sandwich, became entangled in his beard and tumbled into his lap.

"Tojáskrém," said the old man through a mouthful of sandwich. His knowledge of the Hungarian word grabbed Jacob's attention.

"How the hell do you know that word?" Jacob inquired. He studied the old man carefully as he continued to eat.

"Zhukova's poppets," answered the old man thoughtfully as he pointed a crooked finger to the west.

"Wait, you're of the New Oneidans?" asked Jacob in utter surprise. The naming of the group irritated the old man and he struggled to his feet with the help of his walking stick. He nearly fell several times but somehow managed to maintain his balance.

"Irinushka never told anyone the truth about her precious Hungarians," claimed the old man. He turned his finger on Jacob and expounded without pause, "How they came to her attention because they were receiving regular visions of the Virgin Mary. How the Blessed Mother told them of their destinies as mothers of a new spirituality. How days after Irinushka rescued them from the orphanage, it was destroyed by an earthquake. She is a deceiver to rival the Devil himself."

The old man seemed to lose the ability to perceive Jacob. Finishing the sandwich, he crumpled up the wrapper and stuffed it in his jacket pocket.

"I'm not telling you anything else!" bellowed the old man suddenly. He made several swings at the air with the stick and, after nearly tumbling down the path, he barked, "I told you to stay away! Go away!"

Before Jacob could respond, three silenced gunshots rang out. Three bullets struck the old man in the chest and killed him instantly.

"Fuck!" Jacob shouted as he rolled off the rock and sought cover behind it. Two bullets whizzed past him and missed their target by inches. Jacob frantically searched his backpack for a weapon but, finding none, he grabbed it and prepared to hurl it at his attacker. He said, "Guess Charlie's co-conspirators came to finish the job."

Jacob peeked over the top of the rock. He managed to catch sight of Juanita walking towards it with her pistol aimed at him.

"I would like to do this cleanly and painlessly, Mr. Gottschalk," advised Juanita as she approached, "but it if you resist, I can't do that."

Jacob tightened his grip on the backpack and tracked the sound of Juanita's footsteps in the snow. She stopped several feet from the rock.

"Can you at least tell me who wants me dead?" Jacob asked. He positioned his body to allow for maximum thrusting power.

"I suppose I could do that," replied Juanita, "but you'll need to stand up with your hands on your head."

"I guess this is it," Jacob thought. Before he could launch the backpack at Juanita, however, Miriam fell upon her in one of the most savage and gory attacks of her demonic career. Jacob heard the tearing of flesh and breaking of bones and leapt to his feet.

"Holy shit," Jacob uttered in disgust. The reappearance of the beautiful demon he once cast into the Abyss flabbergasted him more than her horrific slaughter of Juanita. He interrupted her murderous fury by calling out, "Miriam?"

Miriam ceased her annihilation of Juanita and rose to her feet. The pulverized body tissue and splattered blood glazed most of her body and soaked her hair and clothing. Glancing at the destroyed heap of humanity that was once Juanita and the corpse of the old man, Jacob grimaced and looked at Miriam.

"Hey," Jacob said, the word the only one he could marshal.

"Hey," replied Miriam. The moment for which she waited had arrived but she was unprepared for it.

"So you're back, huh?" Jacob asked.

"Yeah, I'm back," answered Miriam.

Their feeble conversation died and they simply observed each other. Miriam finally broke the silence.

"Where's Sophie?" she queried.

"Dead," Jacob answered.

"Is that why you're fucking the old redhead?" asked Miriam accusatorily.

"Don't start that bullshit now," Jacob scolded her.

"Bullshit?" Miriam questioned. She said with disdain, "Only you could walk into the wilderness and stumble into a nest of pussy, and you just can't keep your cock out of the middle of it."

"Let's not do this," Jacob said with his right hand raised in parley. Miriam growled and kicked a chunk of Juanita's femur.

"Did ya' fuck this one, too?" she snapped in her hybrid voice.

"The old man? Yeah," Jacob replied with considerable angst.

"Fuck you," Miriam said, her own angst acute and palpable. She calmed herself and shook her head, saying in a completely human tone, "I can't do this."

Jacob knew Miriam well enough to know what would happen next. The reformed demon refused to look him in the eyes and faded into nothingness.

"Well, that complicates things," Jacob said.

• • • •

JACOB DRAGGED HIMSELF back onto the Community grounds in the early evening, his legs aching and his mind set squarely on Miriam. Dr. Zhukova ambushed him as he walked west on the main road.

"Fuck me," Jacob muttered as the redhead stormed up to him with raging fire in her eyes.

"No member of this Community is permitted to leave it unless explicitly given permission by a member of the Council," stated Dr. Zhukova sternly, the Russian's patience with Jacob wearing thin. Poking a long, threatening finger into his chest, she berated him, "Your penchant for violating Community rules does not bode well for your continued stay here."

"You need to relax, my ragin' Ruskie ginger," Jacob replied. He sidestepped her and zombie-walked forward. She watched him for a few seconds and then scurried to catch up.

"You will undergo mutual criticism for this," said Dr. Zhukova, "and it will be *tonight*."

"What would you say if I said I know all about the girls' Marian visions?" Jacob queried as he stopped in front of the porch. The shocked expression on

Dr. Zhukova's face, though it lasted for but a second, greatly pleased Jacob. The doctor went cold, her response prompting him to think, "I'll be damned. It's true."

"I would know you were concocting wild stories to discredit me," said Dr. Zhukova. She grabbed Jacob forcefully and admonished him, "If you are to become a Godly man, it will take years of work, by you and the Community."

Jacob scooped up Dr. Zhukova and threw her towards a snowbank. She crashed into it.

"Stop doing that!" Dr. Zhukova screeched as she struggled to free herself from the deep snow. She ordered him, "Get back here!"

"Goodnight, Doctor," he said as he stepped onto the porch. The Doctor's outraged shouts followed him into the house and up the stairs.

"Jacob!" bellowed Dr. Zhukova. Ignoring her clamor, Jacob wearily pushed open the bedroom door. He saw the haphazard blood splatters first, the red streaks contrasting with the white walls and ceiling to create a gory painting. He immediately scoured the room with his eyes. Detecting no threats, he lowered his gaze to the bed. Rahela's mutilated corpse lay on its back with many large stab wounds marring her skin.

"*Miriam*," Jacob muttered as he processed the scene. Dr. Zhukova burst into the room.

"I'm speaking to you, Mr. Gott- . . . ," she trailed off with a pathetic squeak as she saw Rahela. Dr. Zhukova inhaled sharply and then emitted a single sob. Jacob caught her before she fell and guided them both to the floor as she said weakly, "*Rahela*."

The next several minutes proved some of the most surreal of Jacob's life. The usually stoic Dr. Zhukova clung to him and bawled in his arms as he stared at the mangled body of the woman to whom he made love just hours earlier. Jacob eventually came to his senses and returned to the moment.

"C'mon, let's get you outta here," Jacob urged Dr. Zhukova while lifting her to her feet. It took several attempts as her legs often gave way and her crying melted into a catatonic state. Guiding Dr. Zhukova to the door, he hazarded a final glance at Rahela and then escorted her from the room.

• • • •

"ONE NIGHT OF GOOD SLEEP was enough, my little one?" Sarah asked as she hobbled around the Humvee. The nun walked a circuit in the dark garage to stretch her cramping leg muscles. Heartburn also plagued her and the combination of pregnancy ailments made sleep impossible. She screamed when a bloodied Miriam appeared before her with her arms hanging limp at her sides and her head bowed.

"Miriam, you nearly scared me to death!" Sarah rebuked her. Bursting through the door into the garage, Darby charged forward and fired several shots into Miriam. They passed through her without effect and pierced the garage door. Sarah pushed down Darby's arm and yelled, "Stop!"

The shock of Miriam's bizarre appearance and the deafening blasts from Darby's fifty-caliber pistol caused Sarah to vomit. Doubled over with nausea, she wiped her mouth on her sleeve and placed a hand on the Humvee to steady herself.

"Sorry, instinct," apologized Darby as she holstered her weapon. Sarah raised her other hand in a sign of forgiveness.

"It's okay," Sarah sighed. Standing upright and turning her attention to Miriam, she said, "Who have you killed now?"

"I was protecting Jake," droned Miriam. She made no movement other than her lips and stared blankly at Sarah.

"Our reunion with Jacob Gottschalk has been too long postponed," Sarah declared with her hand on her belly and her fingers splayed. Adrenaline pumped through her veins and, already ruing an early morning start, she said, "You're taking us to him . . . *now*."

14

JACOB BECAME ACUTELY aware of the security presence at New Oneida in the hours after Rahela's murder. Much like Kaiser's security personnel, male and female Community members belonged to the ranks of those tasked with protecting their comrades.

Dr. Zhukova swiftly recovered from her sorrow and rushed to the first such security team member to appear, the Russian issuing orders for the lockdown of Jacob's guesthouse and the Community itself. More armed members emerged from the shadows and hurried off to execute their superior's wishes. She then escorted Jacob to the mansion house and squirreled him in an out-of-the-way storage room.

"Why the fuck do I have to wait in here?" Jacob objected when she presented the cluttered area to him.

"Never before has there been a murder in this Community," answered Dr. Zhukova gravely, "and, as the only newcomer here, all suspicion will fall on you. I simply do not know how my people will respond."

Jacob capitulated with a two-handed gesture. Dr. Zhukova closed the door and, to his surprise and chagrin, locked it.

"Hey!" Jacob shouted.

"You will be safe here. Please, trust me," Dr. Zhukova replied in a raised voice. She offered Jacob a look of pity which he did not see and added, "And stay quiet."

Jacob placed his hands on his hips and rotated to view his surroundings. The room contained shelving units stuffed with boxes of all sizes and labels. Though larger and better illuminated, it reminded him of the day he encountered Miriam in the Church of St. Cyril's storage room.

"Man, did that day change my life," Jacob said while experiencing a kaleidoscope of emotions. A grey stone hand, with its palm upturned and its fingers pointing at the floor, wrested his attention away from his feelings. It was part of a shrouded, four-foot-tall statue in the corner. Jacob, his interest piqued, approached it and queried, "What do we have here?"

Forgetting his troubles for the moment, Jacob cleared debris from around the statue. He then grabbed hold of the thick, dusty shroud and revealed what lay beneath it.

"Well, that's different," Jacob said. The meticulously detailed statue portrayed a slender female angel motioning to the floor in front of her. Her hair was wavy and laid upon her shoulders. She wore a gown with half sleeves tied with sashes just above her elbows and an over-garment that covered the right half of her body. Embroidered with berry-laden holly branches, the over-garment was tied to the angel's waist with a wide belt of cloth and at the shoulder with a clasp formed of holly leaves. Jacob studied the winged figure and commented, "Seems a little Catholic for Dr. Z's tastes but I guess that's why it's in here."

Jacob focused on the angel's smooth, unblemished face. He at first thought it to be comely but, upon leaning towards the statue, realized its face was plain and somewhat androgynous. The angel's eyes and mouth were closed and its head bowed as if in prayer. Jacob smirked.

"You're a little mannish for my tastes, sweetheart," Jacob said in jest. The angel's eyelids popped open but, instead of eyes, light of indescribable purity shone from her sockets and blinded Jacob. He tumbled over backwards yelling, "Fuck!"

Sprawled on the floor and surrounded by the debris he had just moved, Jacob blinked repeatedly and shook his head as his sight slowly returned. The intense light of the angel's eyes lessened so that he could once again see her.

"Jacob Gottschalk! Behold!" cried the angel with dramatic gesticulations. The light emanated from her mouth as she spoke, announcing loudly, "The Abomination of Desolation stands in the holy place and the great tribulation is upon you!"

An astonished Jacob struggled to his knees and observed the angel with awe. Its declaration of the end times terrified him and he trembled. His spiritual visitor became angry.

"Because of your wicked ways and your wavering faith, you will not enter the kingdom of God!" the angel admonished Jacob. He grimaced and swayed as if accosted by an unseen assailant. The hostility in the angel's tone ceased and she stated firmly, "The Lord requires your services nonetheless. You will here establish a sanctuary for the elect and, with the spiritual power of your house, keep and protect them from evil until the tribulation has ended."

Jacob's fear subsided as the Holy Spirit surged within him. It buttressed his confidence and he risked a question.

"What about the Hungarians?" asked Jacob, his mind racing and turning over the angel's use of the word "house". Wishing to stand but remaining on his knees, he said, "It is said they have seen the Blessed Mother and carry her favor."

"It is I who appeared to them," the angel answered, "and they carry my favor. Beware! To shepherd them carries great responsibility! Are you, Jacob Gottschalk, capable of such a task? Or will the minions of Ba'al Zeboul seduce and corrupt you, and drive you forever from the narrow way, to the ruin of many?"

"Shepherd how?" Jacob inquired in frustrated confusion. He rose to his feet and gestured wildly, asking, "And what about Miriam? Why was she released from the Abyss?"

"Remember!" the angel bellowed, the volume of her voice causing Jacob to recoil. Returning her hands to their original positions, she said, "Those who endure to the end will be saved."

"What about Miriam?!" yelled Jacob. Her final message delivered, the angel departed and the statue reverted back to its lifeless form. Jacob shivered and his spine tingled.

"The tribulation in my lifetime, a spiritual draft notice into the armies of light," Jacob said with a heavy heart, "and a baby struggling for life in the middle of it. *Fuck*."

Jacob winced and shot a glance at the angel. It showed no signs of life or animation.

"Sorry," he said.

• • • •

AN HOUR AFTER THE ANGEL'S intercession, Dr. Zhukova unlocked the door and entered the storeroom. Jacob sat opposite the door on an old wooden chair, his elbows on his knees and his hands clasped in front of him. He kept his gaze on the floor.

"The Council wishes to speak with you," said Dr. Zhukova as she observed the lines of care on Jacob's face.

"You tell Boyka and Paliki yet?" he asked.

"No," stated Dr. Zhukova. Taking several careful steps towards Jacob, she said, "They've been returned to duty at the Stations."

"You're not gonna tell them, are you?" Jacob inquired despite knowing the answer to his question.

"She is not and neither are you, Mr. Gottschalk," interjected Dr. Frye as he entered the room with the rest of the Community Council in tow. Two suit-clad New Oneidan men remained in the hallway. Dr. Frye walked past Dr. Zhukova and to within two feet of Jacob, saying, "And frankly your role in all of this is highly suspicious."

"Malcom, please, he had nothing to do with it," protested Dr. Zhukova as she stepped forward.

"Juanita is missing, Irinushka," advised Dr. Frye. Jacob raised his eyes to meet the Doctor's withering gaze.

"I'm sorry, but she's dead, too," Jacob admitted, his expression soured by the memory of Juanita's violent death. Raising his hands with palms outward, he stated, "It wasn't me ... but I know who did it."

"You did not come here alone, did you?" inquired Dr. Frye accusatorily. Jacob stood up and went nose-to-nose with him, his action prompting the security officers to draw their pistols and enter the room.

"Put those away," demanded Edna with a downward wave of her hand. She and Jacob shared a glance and she said, "There is no need for violence ... by *any* of us."

"Look, Doc, there's a shitload you don't know," Jacob asserted with an intensity that caused Dr. Frye to retreat a single step.

"Such as?" asked Dr. Frye. He haughtily thrust his hands in his pants pockets and cocked an eye at Jacob.

"Such as your precious Juanita whacked some goofy old fuck and was trying to do the same to me when she was killed," Jacob growled. His assertion stunned the New Oneidans. Edna gasped.

"Preposterous," said Dr. Frye dismissively. His disdain for Jacob turned to satisfaction as he announced, "By a four-to-one vote, the Council is expelling you from the Community immediately."

"Chubidem? Edna? You really think I killed Rahela and Juanita?" Jacob asked in mild disbelief. Edna shook her head in the negative. Her face was pallid and sad.

"I speak for Edna when I say we do not," responded Chubidem, "but, regardless of your involvement in these heinous murders, we agree you must leave. I'm truly sorry."

Jacob snickered.

"Well, ya' see, we've got a little problem," Jacob said. Returning to his seat and folding his arms in defiance, he stated flatly, "I'm not leavin'."

"You most certainly are," Meriwa interjected sharply with a scornful expression on her sallow face.

"Sorry, kids, but the angel told me I have to stay," Jacob answered with a nod to the statue. It remained uncovered in the corner of the room to his far right and all gazes fell upon it.

"Is all of this theater necessary, Mr. Gottschalk?" scolded Dr. Frye as he placed his hands on his hips and approached the statue. He observed it with disapprobation and said, "I never liked this statue. Perhaps you could take it with you when you leave."

The angel's eyes again popped open but this time its eyeballs were like polished coal and oozed a black, viscous material. It grabbed Dr. Frye's head with two black-clawed hands, its thumbs pressing into his eyes and its other fingers splayed. The sudden violence paralyzed all who watched the dreadful spectacle unfold. Jacob recovered first.

"Frye!" Jacob shouted as he leapt off the chair. Dr. Frye screamed in pain and fell to his knees as the angel buried its thumbs in his head.

"Malcom!" cried Dr. Zhukova as she watched the angel gradually crush Dr. Frye's skull.

"Be gone, demon!" Jacob barked as the Holy Spirit detonated within him. The demon managed to destroy Dr. Frye's head in a sickening spray of gore before Jacob cast it from the old man's body. The statue exploded in a hail of stone shards as the malicious spirit fled, the force knocking Jacob's body to the floor.

The security officers finally reacted and scrambled towards Jacob. He struggled to his feet, his forehead bleeding from a wound caused by the flying stone. Chubidem assisted Edna from the room but Meriwa still lingered in a trauma-induced trance.

"You're a little late, guys, but I appreciate the thought," Jacob said as he dusted himself off and walked to Dr. Zhukova. She shoved him away.

"Arrest him!" exclaimed Dr. Zhukova. The waterworks which Jacob expected did not come and instead she seethed with wrath.

"Arrest me?" Jacob replied. The words prodded Meriwa from her stupor and she nodded her head in agreement as Jacob pleaded, "Irinushka, come on."

"Do not ever call me that ever again," snarled Dr. Zhukova. The security officers obeyed her command, one producing handcuffs and the other keeping his firearm trained on Jacob.

"I cast the demon out of him!" Jacob protested.

"That is not what I saw," said a grim Meriwa while boring into Jacob with her eyes, "and even if you did, by who's authority did you do it?"

"Spoken like a true Pharisee," Jacob snapped. He allowed himself to be handcuffed.

"Your arrival has led to three deaths in twenty-four hours which has never happened in the entire history of this Community," said Meriwa as Jacob was led past her.

"Oh, just wait," Jacob muttered.

. . . .

UNABLE TO ENDURE THE tediousness of mundane travel, Miriam left Sarah and Darby to their long drive north to the Community. She instead sought out Jacob and found him in the Council's deliberation chambers.

"So, whaddaya wanna talk about, Doc?" Jacob asked with a full measure of disrespect. The chamber exuded a coldness absent during his first visit. Curtains were drawn over its narrow, rectangular windows and the light fixtures overhead emitted a sickly glow. Jacob sat at the wooden conference table as he did before; however, he now sat at the end opposite the entry doors. Two armed Community members stood behind him.

"We are here to decide your fate, Mr. Gottschalk," announced Dr. Zhukova, her eyes full of wrath. She was seated at the other end of the table with Edna and Chubidem to her right and Meriwa to her left. A third armed guard stood by the doors.

"I thought we settled on expulsion," Jacob replied. All of the Councilmembers possessed bleary, tired eyes and drawn faces. He felt the weight of their stares but kept his eyes on Dr. Zhukova.

"Balls deep in trouble as usual," said Miriam with an eye roll as she noticed his handcuffs. Uncertain of her next move, she stood behind him with her hands grasping the top of his chair. Her spirit fluttered; simply being near him made her happy.

"Please wait outside," Meriwa instructed the guards gruffly. They swiftly obeyed her order and vacated the room. Meriwa then unholstered an automatic pistol, chambered a round and set it on the table. She glowered at Jacob and said, "I know how to use this, and quite well at that."

"Whoopty fucking do," Jacob replied. Meriwa's eyes narrowed.

"Since your arrival at the Community, three members have been brutally murdered and another was killed in a freak accident," stated Meriwa as if reading a list of charges. Miriam looked to Jacob with a wistful grin on her face.

"Just like old times," reminisced Miriam. Jacob said nothing.

"Are they all the result of the demonic scourge you've brought upon this Community?" asked Meriwa, her question ratcheting up the tension in the room as everyone awaited Jacob's answer. He delayed his response to toy with them, his silence prompting Meriwa to shout, "Were they all killed by demons?!"

Jacob looked to Meriwa and, holding her in his unapologetic gaze, again dallied. She fumed.

"All but one," Jacob said thickly. He added sardonically and falsely, "Poor Chuck just fell off the bridge."

"Your flippant attitude on these matters is reprehensible," said Dr. Zhukova in disgust. Chubidem leaned forward in his chair and folded his hands on the table.

"We have children in this Community, Jacob. How much danger are we in?" asked Chubidem ardently. Jacob's respect for the old man cooled his impudence.

"Kick me out or kill me," Jacob answered cryptically, "and it'll buy you some time."

"What did the angel tell you?" demanded Meriwa.

"He didn't speak to any angel," snarled Dr. Zhukova. Jacob, infuriated by the Doctor's overt hostility, raised his handcuffed wrists and threw an accusatory finger at her.

"I warned you," he said in a raised voice. He then glanced at each Councilmember in turn and continued, "I warned all of you. You should've kicked me loose. But you didn't and now you're paying for it. So enough of this bullshit."

Jacob raised his wrists higher. Miriam moved to his side.

"Get these fucking handcuffs off me and let me go," Jacob insisted.

"This Community is in an uproar, Mr. Gottschalk," said Edna, her emotion and her tone heightening. She battled tears and continued, "They're frightened and deeply saddened by these tragedies."

"They may just burn you at the stake," Meriwa growled. Before her fellow Councilmembers could correct her, Jacob leapt to his feet.

"Fuckin' let 'em!" Jacob shouted. His dramatic opening froze the Councilmembers and even startled Miriam. Lowering his voice, he became fey and expounded, "They won't be far behind. You see, we're all in a world of shit. I'll tell you what the angel said. She informed me that the Tribulation has begun. That's right. Not *a* tribulation. *The* Tribulation. You see, these murders, they were just collateral damage in the shitstorm that is the life of Jacob Gottschalk. Hell, I'm used to it now. But the shitstorm of all shitstorms is coming, and regardless of what the fuck you do with me, you'd better get your people ready for it."

Astonishment gripped every soul in the room and everyone present gaped at Jacob, including Miriam. A shadow fell upon him and he let his arms hang limp.

"The world is about to become a very evil, horrible place," Jacob stated with authority. His captivated audience listened with fear as he quoted the Gospel of Luke 21:34-35: "'Be on guard, so that your hearts will not be weighted down with dissipation and drunkenness and the worries of life, and that day will not come on you suddenly like a trap; for it will come upon all those who dwell on the face of all the earth. But keep on the alert at all times, praying that you may have the strength to escape all these things that are about to take place, and to stand before the Son of Man.'"

• • • •

"WE'VE GOT PROBLEMS," Miriam announced as she materialized in the Humvee, her sudden appearance startling Sarah and Darby.

"Honestly, Miriam!" scolded Sarah. The demon kneeled between the front seats with a hand on the back of each one.

"Fucking twat," muttered Darby. She kept her eyes on the road.

"He's been there less than a week and there've already been three murders," Miriam said. She tilted her head and added, "Well, maybe four."

"That's terrible!" exclaimed Sarah. She looked upon Miriam with wide, disapproving eyes and asked, "What have you done!?"

"Hey, I only killed the one bitch," Miriam objected incredulously, "and she was fucking shooting at him. What was I supposed to do?"

Sarah placed both hands on her distended stomach. She worried about Miriam's resort to murder but other concerns loomed larger.

"Are there others?" asked Sarah, her words stabbing Miriam.

"If you mean demons," Miriam replied with a wounded mien, "then yeah."

Sarah gazed out the passenger window. Darby went cold.

"You said we'll be there tomorrow, correct?" asked Sarah as she turned to Darby.

"Yeah, if we don't run into any trouble and that last supply depot is still there," answered Darby, her tone dubious. She pressed the accelerator and said, "Otherwise we won't have the gas to make it."

"God is with us," Sarah said with a hopeful smile. Darby faked a smile in return, looked to the highway and drifted back into her pessimistic thoughts.

"You'd better hope so," Miriam said.

"Excuse me?" replied Sarah.

"Jacob said he was visited by an angel," Miriam explained with particular relish, and, mocking the words of Christ, "and she told him the Tribulation *is at hand*."

• • • •

THE ORIGINAL ONEIDANS were proponents of the Turkish bath and the Reformed Oneidans zealously adopted a modern form of the practice. The Church Council had an elaborate Turkish bath built on the grounds of the Community for that purpose. It resembled the other buildings but differed in its long, one-story design.

Intended to be a place of physical and spiritual renewal, the bath instead served as Jacob's prison. He was kept at the Visitor Center until nightfall and then secretly transferred to it by Meriwa and the three security officers. She departed soon afterward but the officers remained, the trio guarding Jacob as he slept fitfully on a couch in the building's lobby.

Dr. Zhukova and Edna arrived at the building the following morning with breakfast for Jacob. Both women, though still appearing worn and distraught, were better for the few hours of sleep they were permitted.

"Report back to the Community," directed Dr. Zhukova. Jacob stood up and offered the New Oneidans a dubious look as she added, "Meriwa awaits you at the mansion for debriefing and breakfast."

"But Doctor, what about Mr. Gottschalk?" asked one of the guards. Dr. Zhukova marched up to Jacob and smacked him hard across the face. He grasped his cheek. Edna winced.

"What the fuck was that for?" Jacob objected.

"You're going to behave yourself, aren't you, Mr. Gottschalk?" asked Dr. Zhukova sharply. Jacob dropped his hand, observed her stonily and then nodded his head.

"Yeah," Jacob reluctantly conceded, "I'll behave."

"Excellent," Dr. Zhukova replied as her malevolence evaporated. Turning her attention back to the security officers, she said with a weak grin, "You see? Everything is under control. Now, you have had a long, exhausting night so go, enjoy a hot meal and get some sleep. You have most certainly earned it."

A chorus of mutual appreciation and respect followed. Jacob plopped back down on the couch and endured the pleasantries with a sour mien.

"We have precious little time," warned Dr. Zhukova while watching the security officers depart. She closed all of the curtains in the room before rotating around to face Jacob.

"Fuck you," he snapped.

"Please, Mr. Gottschalk, hear her out," pleaded Edna. She seated herself next to him on the couch and took his hands in her own. Glancing at Dr. Zhukova, she said, "Irinushka has much to tell you."

"Indeed I do," acknowledged Dr. Zhukova after a pronounced swallow. Trembling and uncertain, she explained, "I owe you not one but two apologies. First, I am sorry for my recent mistreatment of you. Please know it was merely a ruse. Any sympathy I showed for you would have been instantly fatal to my leadership. The vast majority of our people want you expelled immediately, as does Meriwa, and more importantly, Carol. That alone gives her the momentum to have me removed, perhaps by force, if I advocated for you in any way."

"So this is all about your bullshit politics?" Jacob inquired. His suspicion softened when he saw the distress on her lean countenance.

"Not anymore," said Dr. Zhukova as she retrieved a square cooler she earlier set on the floor. She quickly served a hot meal to Jacob while Edna poured his coffee, explaining, "Which brings me to my second apology. I never should have lured you into this Community with sexuality and treated you like an animal to be bred. I exploited your weakness for my gain and, for that, I am also sorry."

Dr. Zhukova faltered. Edna attended to her and guided her to a nearby chair. The older woman then moved behind Dr. Zhukova and placed a reassuring hand on her shoulder. The last of Jacob's anger melted away and he pitied her.

"So, with my apologies made," said Dr. Zhukova, "I ask you simply, Jacob Gottschalk, what do you want?"

"It never seems to be about what I want, frankly," Jacob said. Concerned though he was, his hunger and caffeine dependency diverted his attention and he attended to his meal and coffee while pondering Dr. Zhukova's question. She and Edna waited eagerly yet patiently for his answer. Jacob, after ravenously completing his feast, downed the last of his coffee and said, "Okay, I'll tell you what I want, but there are a few things you should know first, and I'm gonna start with an apology, too."

"What do you mean?" asked Edna.

"I killed Charles," Jacob admitted. Edna squeaked and raised her hand to her mouth to stifle it. Dr. Zhukova remained stoic as Jacob said, "But not intentionally, even though Carol instructed him to put a bullet in my head and throw me off a fucking bridge. And, believe it or not, I'm sorry for that."

Jacob's assertion disturbed Dr. Zhukova and she grimaced. Edna retreated to a chair and slumped into it.

"Was Boyka involved in the plot?" asked Dr. Zhukova.

"Yeah, but she was a minor player and she wasn't gonna let Charlie off me," Jacob replied. He poured himself more coffee.

"She resisted her pairing with Charles in the beginning," advised Dr. Zhukova with palpable regret, "and we pressured her so much so that she probably afforded him more deference than he was due."

"She's a strong kid and she made the right decision in the end," Jacob said after a gulp of coffee. He advised gravely, "But you've got bigger fish to fry. I'd keep a close eye on Carol and her minions, especially with Dr. Frye gone."

"Did you kill Rahela?" inquired Edna gingerly. Dr. Zhukova's body shook as she asked the question and she struggled to compose herself.

"Of course not," Jacob answered. He, too, trembled as he remembered the woman who called him drágaságom but, burying his sorrow deep, he bit his lip and then continued, "She ran afoul of an old demon girlfriend of mine – don't ask – and that was that. Miriam killed Juanita, too, but that was to save my ass from a date with a bullet compliments of Carol."

"What's happening to our Community?" queried a perplexed and frightened Edna.

"In less than a year, I've gone from being oblivious to the existence of demons to hunting and being hunted by those assholes," Jacob replied. He rested his elbows on his knees and folded his hands in front of his face, saying, "So I have no doubt the Tribulation is upon us. You asked me what I want? I want you to let me go. The Community will be better off with me gone, anyway."

"Boyka will follow you," protested Dr. Zhukova, "and Paliki will follow her."

Jacob's eyes flipped up to Dr. Zhukova. Their blueness stunned her.

"There's a little baby girl in Kaiser who has the misfortune of the last name Gottschalk," Jacob stated firmly. He rose to his feet and declared, "I'm going to get her, whether you like it or not."

"You know, as do I, that those young women and their progeny are the key to the Community's survival," countered Dr. Zhukova. She leaned forward and implored Jacob, "I've already lost Rahela. Must I lose her sisters, too? Please, *stay*."

"I can't do that," Jacob countered though her pleas rattled his heart.

"If what you say is true, and the Tribulation is indeed upon us," argued Dr. Zhukova, "then there will be demons beyond count assailing my people."

"That's right," Jacob replied as he watched Dr. Zhukova concoct her plans. Her shrewdness reminded him of Elizabeth.

"With the press of the demonic world, we will need more people like you, and what better way to do so than to proceed with my original design with, of course, one important change," continued Dr. Zhukova. She spoke with a conviction that inspired Edna and stated, "Instead of missionaries and teachers, my people will be exorcists and protectors."

Jacob squirmed. Stirpiculture seemed morally wrong and he weighed Dr. Zhukova's plan against his knowledge of Scripture. Reading Jacob's doubt, Dr. Zhukova stood up and confidently approached him.

"I will protect you until you conceive children with Boyka, Paliki and their sister, Magdolna," offered Dr. Zhukova. Jacob noticed a dubious look on Edna's face but, when she realized he saw it, she concealed it. Dr. Zhukova looked at Jacob hopefully and continued, "Once the deed is done, as they say, I will equip you with anything you need and speed you back to Kasier. With my help you could be there in a week."

"Bullshit," Jacob said.

"I swear this to you before God Almighty," Dr. Zhukova assured him. Jacob hesitated but thoughts of Autumn permeated his mind. He shook his head in the affirmative.

"All right," Jacob said, "you're on, Doc."

"You will start immediately . . . with Magdolna," stated Dr. Zhukova as she began pacing and realigning her plans.

"How ya' gonna handle the free love movement?" Jacob queried. He wondered how ruthless Dr. Zhukova would be particularly when it came to Carol.

"Leave that to me," replied Dr. Zhukova.

"I knew you'd say that," Jacob said skeptically.

"This is God's will, Jacob," said Edna.

"Sure it is," Jacob replied with a shit-eating grin. He grabbed his face with his left hand and sighed, thinking, "And if it's not, I'm going to Hell anyway."

15

JACOB WAS AWOKEN BY the sound of the bathhouse door opening. Dr. Zhukhova entered first, the physician walking with her usual strong gait and obscuring the tall woman behind her.

"Jacob, this is Magdolna, the young woman of whom I spoke," said Dr. Zhukova with a waving gesture. The young woman stepped into view as the Doctor advised, "She is the youngest of the Hungarian sisters."

Clad as Boyka but clearly uncomfortable in the New Oneidan uniform, Magdolna swept up to Jacob and went nose-to-nose with him. The aggressive Hungarian brunette stood five-feet-ten-inches tall with greenish-brown eyes and lengthy, tightly-curled locks. Dr. Zhukova remained stone-faced as she observed them.

"He is too old, and American," complained Magdolna as she contemptuously studied Jacob. He would never forget those words and chuckled when she demanded, "I hate Americans. I want younger man."

"This matter has been settled, Magdolna," scolded Dr. Zhukova calmly. Amused and aroused by Magdolna's brashness, Jacob smirked and studied her body. The Doctor folded her arms and declared, "You are a wellspring of this Community's future, and he is a man endowed with the Holy Spirit. We must not waste this opportunity. It could vanish in an instant. Boyka already carries his child."

The Doctor's announcement of Jacob's paternity was sobering. The whirlwind incursions of the spiritual world had driven that possibility from his mind until he heard it spoken.

"*Magdolna*," Dr. Zhukova rebuked her. She gradually bottled up her anger with great difficulty, her harsh glance the last expression of her emotion to disappear. Sternly gazing at the younger woman, the Doctor patiently waited for her to act. Magdolna faked a pleasant smile.

"I am pleased to meet you, Mr. G-g-goss-shak," stated Magdolna haltingly and as if reading from a cue card. She reluctantly embraced Jacob, pecked him on the cheek and then retreated. Her detestation was palpable and it festered like an infection beneath her skin.

"Likewise, Maggie," Jacob replied while holding his ground. He felt a creeping attraction to Magdolna despite her distaste for him.

"No Maggie," snapped Magdolna, the firebrand meeting the nickname with a horrid scowl. Jacob instinctively stepped back as, bristling at the moniker, she snarled, "Magdolna."

"Magdolna has prepared dinner for the two of you," Dr. Zhukova interjected. She held the same cooler in which she brought Jacob's lunch. Magdolna fidgeted.

"Well, that was nice," Jacob replied with uncertainty. Nodding to the next room, he asked, "A word, Doctor."

"There is no time for that," countered Dr. Zhukova. She moved to the door and explained, "I've sent for Paliki and she will be here tomorrow, so I suggest the two of you take full advantage of that time."

After a pause, during which she held him with her hopeful eyes, Dr. Zhukova departed. Magdolna folded her arms and sighed in frustration.

"Why must I get old American?" she thought.

• • • •

WHEN ENGAGING IN A Turkish bath, a New Oneidan would start in a relaxation room heated by a continuous flow of hot, dry air meant to induce perspiration. He or she would then move into a hotter room if they so desired. A Community member assigned to the bath would wash his or her comrade in cold water and perform a full-body massage before a visit to the cooling-room for another period of relaxation.

"Helluva view," Jacob sighed as he sat in a heated relaxation room. The gentle snowfall outside reminded him of his youth and the joy of watching snowfalls from the comfort and warmth of his childhood home. Magdolna, despite Dr. Zhukova's strict orders, refused to engage with him in any way and remained in the lobby after they engaged in a quiet, awkward dinner.

Jacob heard footsteps outside the chamber and concentrated on the sounds as they echoed in the hall. Deciding that they were not the determined steps of Dr. Zhukova or the softer, graceful paces of his other paramours, he tensed. The footfalls ceased just outside the door. Whisking up his towel, Jacob covered himself.

"Hello?" called an obscured female voice. Jacob relaxed somewhat as the prospect of another male entering the room evaporated.

"Who is it?" Jacob replied suspiciously. Several seconds of silence followed without a response. He again queried, "Who is it?"

"Magdolna," answered the irascible brunette with conflict evident in her tone. Jacob rolled his eyes.

"And how may I help you this fine evening, Magdolna?" Jacob inquired in a tone of mock cordiality.

"I will wash you now," advised Magdolna slowly, the young woman's voice conveying her discomfort.

"That's great," Jacob countered uneasily with little confidence in successful copulation with Magdolna. Leaning against the bench behind him, he watched the burgeoning snow and said in a raised voice, "But I don't think we're allowed to fuck in here."

"No fuck!" barked Magdolna, her wicked tongue causing Jacob to wince. Prickled by his insinuation and frustrated by her difficulty with communication in English, she slammed her fist against the door.

"Forget the wash," Jacob called out. Magdolna exhaled loud enough for him to hear it before he added, "I'm not forcing you into anything no matter what Dr. Z wants."

"I wish to speak at you," said Magdolna.

"At me. Typical woman," Jacob replied. He shook his head and beckoned, "Well, get in here and speak at me."

Magdolna complied. Glancing to his right, Jacob watched her cautiously open the door and glare at him.

"Damn she's well-built," Jacob thought as he gawked at her willowy form and the green, silk bathrobe that covered it. The sight of her beautiful body aroused him and the question of whether she wore anything underneath the robe caused him to forget all else. He gestured at her and said, "Come. Sit. Speak."

Remaining mute, Magdolna untied her bathrobe and let it swiftly slide from her body. She wore nothing beneath it. Jacob went pale.

"Well-built indeed," he said to himself. Emboldened by the effect of her physicality on Jacob, Magdolna kicked her bathrobe out of the room, closed the door and walked to within a few feet of him. Jacob watched her every move and considered the imminent possibility of coitus, thinking, "Looks like you're gonna get your way, Dr. Ginger."

Sitting four feet apart, Magdolna and Jacob watched each other warily with wisps of rising steam between them. Small strands of Magdolna's dark hair became saturated with sweat, her once-tight curls loosening and sagging, and beads of it formed over her body. Their stalemate lasted for nearly a minute and the tension between them thickened.

"You don't like me very much, do you?" Jacob asked after the awkward interregnum. She searched for the right words in her mind.

"You are . . . asshole," said Magdolna sternly yet without anger, "and too old."

"You are . . . bitch," Jacob replied with a dubious expression, "and too young."

The quick rejoinder caused Magdolna's countenance to soften and the slightest of smiles came to her face. The tension between them eased. Jacob rose to his feet and held out his hand.

"You might just enjoy it," Jacob coaxed Magdolna. His judgment compromised by his arousal, he foolishly added, "Your sister did."

"You think of Boyka!" shouted Magdolna jealously, her shrill accusation wresting Jacob from his sexually-induced trance. Lunging at him, she errantly swung her right fist. He dodged it and caught her left fist as it careened towards his face.

"Stop, damn it!" Jacob demanded. Spinning the feisty Hungarian around, he twisted her left arm behind her back and grabbed her right arm. Their bodies pressed together and his erection became apparent to her. The moment lingered and Jacob assured Magdolna, "I wasn't thinking about Boyka."

Jacob turned the touching of their bodies into an embrace. Magdolna pretended to indulge in it long enough to set the trap.

"No fuck!" bellowed Magdolna before swiftly lifting her leg and slamming her heel into Jacob's testicles. The intense pain caused him to release her and she fled his grasp. Jacob dropped to his knees.

"You are old, American asshole!" screamed Magdolna as she fled the chamber and scooped up her bathrobe. Jacob heard her stomping away and ostensibly cursing in Hungarian. Cradling his aching testicles, he clambered onto the bench and moaned in agony.

"A happy, young Christian she is not," Jacob groaned.

• • • •

GIVING MAGDOLNA'S ANGER time to cool and his testicles time to recover, Jacob closed the door and returned to the bench. He chucked his towel aside and stretched out his legs.

"Now there's no one to give me the cooling bath," Jacob griped. He took several breaths and allowed himself to relax, saying, "Enjoy it now, pal, before the world goes to shit."

"Hello?" called the obscured female voice again.

"Of course," Jacob muttered. He wiped the sweat off his face from forehead to chin and said, "In or out, *Maggie*, choose one."

Magdolna failed to appear or make any noise. Frustrated by her games, Jacob jumped off the bench and hurled open the door. He was met with a sickening scream of intense pain and the swing of a knife.

"Fuck!" Jacob yelled as he retreated far enough to avoid a fatal wound. The large kitchen knife sliced into his skin nonetheless and he began to bleed.

Wielding the blade, Sophie shrieked like a banshee and slashed wildly at Jacob as he backpedaled. Most of her body was marred by burns of varying degrees, including half of her face, while the unburnt portions were ravaged by frostbite. Jacob whisked off his towel, caught Sophie's arm in it and wrapped it up. Despite the pain caused by his laceration, he hurled her into the far wall as burnt flesh sloughed from her arm. She crashed into it and crumpled to the floor.

Jacob groaned with a wince and examined his injury. He then turned his attention to Sophie.

"Come out of her!" Jacob demanded. No demon was forthcoming so he repeated, "Come out of her!"

Sophie suddenly rose up, powered not by muscle but by an evil spirit and displaying the black eyes and claws of a demon. She roared and charged Jacob but was repelled by his swirling, spiritual field of force. Flying backward, she again struck the wall but, instead of falling, she stuck to it like a fly.

"Gottschalk!" hissed Marcion, the demon causing Sophie's scorched carcass to cling to the wall. Jacob kept a close eye on him as he wrapped the towel around his midsection.

"Damn it!" Jacob shouted with a grimace as he tightly cinched the towel. Gently pressing his wound, he asked, "Didn't I throw you into Hell already?"

"The gates are open! The gates are open and we are loose!" declared Marcion with sinister delight.

"Yeah, I already heard, you burnt bastard," Jacob sneered.

"More will come for you, even if this one couldn't get the job done," replied Marcion angrily. He frothed at the mouth and lamented, "Even with her pain tolerance, she only had twenty seconds left in her!"

"And here I thought Miriam did it," Jacob said as he noticed the bloodied knife. Picking it up and glancing at it with disdain, he said, "Why? Why kill the poor kid?"

Marcion dropped Sophie's body from the wall but landed on her feet. He snickered as he indulged in Jacob's emotional angst.

"She didn't like you banging the black-haired bitch . . . or the redheaded bitch . . . or the blonde bitch . . . so I made her a deal," said Marcion as he held up a singed finger. Dancing around with his usual bizarre flair, he explained in a ridiculous song, "I kill the blonde for her, she kills you for me. No demon for Sophie, no protection for Gottschalk."

"But ya' failed *again*, asshole," Jacob snapped harshly. Gripping the handle of the knife, he taunted Marcion, "Ba'al Zeboul won't be happy about that."

"Gottschalk!" screeched Marcion with a threatening but harmless swipe. Overcoming the use of his Master's true name, he warned Jacob with growing haughtiness, "More will come for you, and for those you love, and they will all die! All die, Gottschalk! Some are already dead!"

Expecting more information to be forthcoming, Jacob withstood the fierce urge to cast Marcion from Sophie's body. He opted for hurling the knife at her. It stuck in her stomach and Marcion, with a hideous laugh, grasped it with both hands and pulled it further into his host.

"Come, now, Gottschalk, I have another surprise for you!" Marcion urged him while dancing out of the steam room and beckoning with his middle finger.

"I send 'em down and somebody keeps sendin' em' back," griped Jacob. Burying his sadness over Sophie deep under adrenaline and hatred, he followed Marcion and muttered, "This can't be good."

• • • •

"IF I NEVER SEE A *fucking* demon again!" Jacob barked as he entered the lobby wrapped in a fresh towel and with a makeshift, blood-soaked bandage haphazardly placed on his wound. He stopped with wide eyes and exclaimed in surprise, "Boyka!"

The Hungarian princess stood bawling in front of him while a Marcion-possessed Sophie stood behind her with the knife's blade across her throat. Magdolna and Paliki sat quietly and sad-faced in chairs behind her. Boyka held an old, ragged doll by its hand.

"You are hurt!" exclaimed Boyka when she noticed the bandage.

"Just a scratch," Jacob said with a weak grin. Making a quick play in hopes of surprising Marcion, he implored Sophie, "Soph, if you're in there, drop the knife."

"She's not," snapped Marcion in his demonic voice, "and she died hating you, so she wouldn't do it if she was."

"All right, then, Marcion, what's the price?" Jacob asked grimly.

"You must tell her what I did," Marcion said in Sophie's voice. He laughed mischievously, adding, "And what you did! Or I slice open her throat!"

Boyka cried out and sobbed. Jacob choked down his anger and pondered his next move.

"Sure, cocksucker, why not?" replied Jacob as he decided to take an unexpected tack. Looking directly and reassuringly at Boyka, he said, "This isn't gonna be easy for you to hear, Boyka, but I need you to trust me, and I'm so sorry to tell you this . . . Rahela was murdered."

"Rahela is dead?" squeaked Boyka. Both she and Paliki erupted into tears after the last word passed her lips. Magdolna held her tears at bay and fell into a bitter mood.

"Yeah, and she and I . . . we had sex before it happened," Jacob stated matter-of-factly.

"You hate him now, too, don't you?" insisted Marcion in Sophie's voice, the demon irked by Jacob's composure during his blunt revelations. He shouted again, "Don't you?!"

Jacob's stomach churned so much so that he temporarily forgot about his knife wound. He looked gravely at each Hungarian.

"The world's going to Hell, girls . . . no, it's *becoming* Hell, and has been for longer than I thought," Jacob said. He continued to divide his empathetic attention between them, continuing, "Evil's been creeping out of the spiritual realm and into our own for years, and it's arrived at New Oneida."

Jacob paused. His explanation drew horrified yet engrossed expressions from the Hungarians.

"Your sister was murdered by a demon, Boyka," Jacob informed her gently, "and I know it sounds crazy but it's true. I fucking swear it."

"Lying small-dick American! You did it!" roared Magdolna as she leapt up and hurled a wrathful finger at Jacob. Paliki's face hardened and she glared at him. He absorbed their disdain and patiently waited for Boyka to take her turn.

"I want you to have this," Boyka said calmly. She held out her doll to him and whimpered, "So you will remember me."

"Remember you?" Jacob queried uneasily.

"We were not allowed to have dolls as children," explained Boyka. She pushed the doll at him several times before he took it, expounding, "But she was with me, before I even met my sisters. Dr. Zhukova wanted me to burn her, like the other girls did with their dolls, but I hid her, and kept her safe."

Marcion wailed and dropped the knife. Tumbling over backward as if struck by an unseen force, he hit the floor and cowered.

Boyka, meanwhile, propelled herself into Jacob's arms and wept. He attempted to comfort her but she grabbed the back of his head and pulled him into a forceful kiss. It felt like no other she had given him. Before

Jacob could shove her away, Boyka punched him in his knife wound and he doubled over in pain.

"*You*," groaned Jacob as he hobbled away from a laughing Boyka. Magdolna and Paliki joined her mirth, all three of them cackling like teenagers pulling a sadistic prank. Marcion cautiously uncurled his body and watched Boyka like a whipped dog watching its master.

"Hello, Jacob," said Boyka in a cunning voice, her naivete and her accent absent.

"Here we go again," Jacob said under his breath. His mind screamed at him to flee but he knew flight was futile. He asked, "How?"

"I don't think you're quite ready for *that* explanation, my dear," replied Boyka. She drifted into a memory and then mused, "*My dear*."

Boyka sighed.

"Old habits die hard, I suppose," said Boyka. Jacob's face grew dour. He lowered his head but kept his gaze on her.

"Is she alive?" Jacob inquired. His blood boiled as he asked, "Are any of them alive?"

"I have to admit, you found yourself one gorgeous plaything," said Boyka as she examined her body. She held up her arms and let her eyes caress them one at a time.

"*Is she alive?*" Jacob growled. Marcion slithered towards the door but Paliki stomped on his hand and pinned it down. He yelped.

"She is," answered Boyka with a sly smile. Jacob's eyes moved from Boyka to Magdolna to Paliki and back again. Visibly reveling in his astonishment, Boyka asserted, "And she can stay that way – they all can - *if* you behave yourself."

"Still trying to control me, even in death," Jacob snarled. Overcoming his shock, he took a step towards Boyka and glowered at each demon in turn.

"Please do not pretend you still possess your old spiritual abilities," Boyka scoffed as she took a step towards him and said, "I know that the dog has returned to his own vomit."

"And the sow's back to wallowing in the mire," Jacob countered angrily, "but don't kid yourself, Liz, I'll still torch your demon ass."

Boyka laughed, not in her usual, mirthful manner, but in a cold, devious one. Her body transformed, her eyes becoming black and wicked claws forming on her fingers. Her fellow Hungarians followed suit.

"Was there really any doubt that you and I would return to our old ways?" taunted Elizabeth in her own voice.

"I suppose not," Jacob said. Thoughts of Mallory and Vanessa sobered him and he asked, "What about the girls?"

"Let's just say you no longer need to search for them," answered Elizabeth pridefully. Reading the lack of distress on her face, he knew his stepdaughters suffered the same fate as their mother. She continued, "I am proud of you, Jacob, for at least you did not abandon them, corpses though they were. Of course, your penis distracted you as it always does, and you failed to properly lay Vanessa to rest."

"It's only a matter of time," Jacob grumbled. The jarring reminder of Vanessa's continued possession allowed him to remember their unborn child and he asked desperately, "What about the baby?!"

"In the arms of the *aggelos*. Safe from both of us and far above the fog of the war we will wage," stated Elizabeth with clear contempt for her spiritual enemies. She turned and motioned to Sophie, saying, "In fact, it was that whore of yours who killed my earthly body and smashed your unborn child beneath her foot."

Sophie's wanton destruction of his child's life staggered Jacob. He stumbled to the couch and fell onto it. His mind reeled with sorrow and guilt over the unchecked violence and senseless deaths.

"Planning your next sexual conquest now that I'm stealing away your latest trollop?" asked Elizabeth without mercy or remorse.

"Liz, what do you want?" Jacob asked. He felt nauseous as he spoke.

"Besides torturing you by stealing the holy vessels you sought to fill with your seed?" asked Elizabeth with considerable hauteur.

"You always want something. Demons always want something," Jacob replied. He stood up intransigently and said, "And now *you* are a *demon*. So stop wasting my time and just fucking spill it."

"If it is indeed true that you still carry His favor," replied Elizabeth curtly, "your aimless wandering and wielding of your so-called power would be a considerable annoyance."

"More than an annoyance, sweetheart," Jacob warned her. Realizing he cared little for crusades, a fact Elizabeth knew well, he conceded, "Fine. Deal. Keep them alive, and I'll stay out of Kaiser. Now get the fuck outta here before I change my mind. And take the burnt bastard with you."

"Good bye, *Daddy*," Paliki mocked Jacob in Vanessa's voice. She sliced into him with her words, saying, "Guess you don't love me as much as Mallory. You *saved* her."

Jacob seethed and bored into Elizabeth with fiery eyes. She offered him a sly grin.

"You twisted bitch," Jacob admonished her.

"Daddy loves me better than you!" sang a suddenly bubbly Magdolna in Mallory's teenage voice. The display sickened Jacob as his stepdaughters departed with their humanly vessels. They took turns kicking Marcion like a dog as he scampered out the door.

"Move, maggot," ordered Vanessa.

"Thank you for locating strong, fresh bodies for us, though I suppose you are all alone now," said Elizabeth with feigned gratitude. Before turning on a dime and exiting the room, she nodded to the doll and said in an uncharacteristically crass manner, "Maybe you could fuck her."

• • • •

JACOB AWOKE ON THE lobby couch, feeling woozy and bleeding on the cushions. Girt only in his towel, he made a wobbly ascent to his feet and stumbled to the door. Throwing it open, he was slapped in the face with frigid air. He stepped outside into the falling snow.

"Mr. Gottschalk!" gasped Dr. Zhukova, her exclamation followed by those from the assembly of members that stood behind her. Carol and the Council were among them and all watched Jacob with deep concern. His skin was pale and sickly.

"What? No pitchforks and torches?" Jacob asked with a laugh. He moved and spoke as if drunk. Taking a few more unsteady steps forward, Jacob added, "Don't you know I'm an evil bastard? The angel said so."

"You need medical attention immediately," protested Dr. Zhukova and she rushed to him.

"No!" Jacob barked with an outstretched palm, his gesture freezing Dr. Zhukova in her tracks.

"Jacob, *please*," begged Dr. Zhukova in a hushed tone, "you have lost far too much blood."

"It doesn't matter!" Jacob shouted, the forcefulness of his response nearly causing him to fall. He regained his balance and his composure, informing the Community, "My little one is dead, the gates of Hell are open and few of us if any will survive the Tribulation to come."

"This is ridiculous, Irinushka. He's bleeding out and having delusions," said Carol. She motioned to two security officers who accompanied the group and directed them, "Get him inside."

"NO!" Jacob bellowed before vomiting and nearly falling again. He steadied himself on a nearby bench, exhaled and expounded, "Don't you get it, you vicious twat? The demonic world is overrunning us. Demons killed your husband and Juanita and Rahela. All of them. *Gone.*"

Gasps and murmurs broke out in the crowd. Jacob closed his eyes.

"How dare you?!" shouted Carol.

"How dare I?" Jacob inquired as his eyelids popped open. Pointing at Carol, he said, "This from the woman who ordered Boyka and poor little Charlie to execute me and throw me off a bridge."

"That's preposterous," rejoined Carol with incredulity.

"You're preposterous!" Jacob shouted like a child. He swayed and his eyes lost focus. Regaining himself, he said, "But I showed Charlie. I killed *him* and threw *him* off a bridge. Asshole."

Jacob bowed his head and his face became forlorn. His murder of Charlie wracked him with guilt and dredged up memories of the others he slayed.

"This man is clearly mentally compromised and bleeding to death," insisted Carol.

"Those are very serious allegations, Jacob, and not to be made lightly," Chubidem advised as he stepped forward. Offering Jacob his hand, he said, "Perhaps we should discuss this when you are of sounder mind and body."

"It doesn't matter what I do, what any of us do," Jacob replied with a shrug. Tugging at his bandage but no longer feeling the pain, he explained, "I said the Tribulation is underway. *The* Tribulation. A time of demonic slaughter and terrible atrocities against the living. Don't say I didn't warn you."

"Jacob, where is Magdolna?" asked Dr. Zhukova, the Russian suddenly cognizant of her absence.

"My ex-wife took her," Jacob stated matter-of-factly.

"Who took her?" asked Dr. Zhukova in disbelief.

Meriwa, who amazingly remained silent and unmoved during Jacob's outburst, stepped forward from the crowd. She waved the security officers forward.

"Carol is right. This has gone on long enough," declared Meriwa. Taking a pair of handcuffs from one of the officers, she marched to Jacob. They drew semiautomatic pistols and followed in her wake.

"Carefully, Meriwa, he is injured," objected Dr. Zhukova as she interposed herself between Jacob and Meriwa.

"Yes, and this delusional rant is going to kill him if the cold doesn't first," countered Meriwa. Jacob's eyes became hazy again and his vision blurred. He perceived the end of his life and began slowly removing his bandage.

"Jacob, stop," demanded Dr. Zhukova. He ignored her and pulled it from his skin.

"I'm going to die now, and skulk in the shadows of heaven, and try to catch a glimpse of my daughter," Jacob announced with a sad smile. Second later he lost consciousness and collapsed.

· · · ·

JACOB WOKE TO FIND himself reclining in a hospital bed. The room, the same one in which he first met Dr. Zhukova, was dimly lit by the same small lamp in the right far corner.

"That was one hell of a dream," Jacob said aloud. His eyes slowly focused on the familiar silhouette of a dark, blurry figure sitting at his bedside. He said with a weak chuckle, "You must be giving me some serious mind-fucking drugs, Dr. Z."

"Only an antibiotic, which you are fortunate they have here," replied Sarah with a hint of disapproval. His eyesight returned and he saw Sarah dressed in a long, navy-blue dress over a white collared shirt.

"Sarah!" Jacob exclaimed. He attempted to get out of the bed but his body was weak and his knife wound ached. Jacob squirmed in pain and asked, "How the hell did you get here?"

"You and I have much to discuss, Jacob," said Sarah as she raised a hand to calm him, "and much of it is unfortunate news."

"Yeah, I know," Jacob sighed. Thoughts of Autumn arose in his mind and his face quivered with sorrow. His knife wound, now stitched and tended, throbbed.

"Today, however, we will only discuss positive news and provide a weary man of God with the hope he needs," advised Sarah with a sanguine smile. Jacob gave her a confused look. Standing up and placing a hand on her distended stomach, Sarah proudly revealed her pregnancy to Jacob. She chuckled and said, "I know, I said it couldn't happen. As usual, God had other plans."

She took Jacob's hand and placed it on her belly. The baby instantly kicked. His eyes lit up.

"She's been a bundle of energy since I told her we were going to find you," stated Sarah happily. Squeezing his hand, she said, "Your spirits *must* be linked."

"She's healthy and everything's okay?" Jacob anxiously asked.

"Yes, she is doing splendidly," answered Sarah. She returned to her seat but Jacob kept his hand on her belly as she stated, "And, to her mother's great surprise, she has already demonstrated her father's spiritual gift."

"You were attacked?!" Jacob exclaimed with a grimace as he tweaked his laceration. He withdrew his hand and forced himself into a more upright position.

"No, no, settle down," scolded Sarah. She regretted her overzealousness in discussing their baby.

"Then how do you know she's got the power to kick demon ass?" Jacob queried suspiciously.

"Just a misunderstanding, that's all, and she was never in any danger," replied Sarah as she stood up again. Helping Jacob into his original position, she corrected him, "Now, no more profanity in front of the little one, Daddy."

"Was it Miriam?" Jacob asked. Sarah hesitated to discuss the issue of Miriam given Dr. Zhukova's order to keep him calm.

"Yes," Sarah finally conceded, "but I wouldn't be too hard on her. She meant the baby no harm and, without her, we never would have found you."

"Is she here?" Jacob asked.

"Yes, but-," began Sarah.

"I want to see her, *now*," Jacob demanded.

"Jacob, we need you at full strength to protect us from the coming storm," Sarah said while readjusting his pillows. She caressed his forehead and continued, "Assuming that Dr. Zhukova permits it, you can probably see Miriam tomorrow. Now, I have enough on my plate trying to keep *her* away from *you*, so please, dear man, just rest."

Jacob relented and placed his hand on Sarah's stomach again. The baby jumped in her womb. He grinned in adoration but the smile quickly faded.

"What does this mean for us?" Jacob asked as he took Sarah's hand.

"One relationship at a time, Jacob," she answered hauntingly as she squeezed his hand but then released it. Quickly disguising her concern, she switched topics and said with a grin, "I think, instead, it's time to discuss her name."

16

"GOOD MORNING," SAID Dr. Zhukova brusquely as she walked into Jacob's room rolling a small medical supply cart. She pushed it to the foot of his bed, saying, "It's good to see you alive, you foolish man. You almost left your unborn child fatherless."

"But I didn't," countered Jacob. Dr. Zhukova rolled his tray table aside which contained the dishes from his breakfast. Jacob stretched gingerly and said, "And I wasn't exactly firing on all cylinders during that whole episode, either."

"Next time, I suggest you do not fall asleep with a bleeding laceration," said Dr. Zhukova with an expression of playful disapproval. Her mood warmed and she said, albeit stiffly, "Congratulations on the baby."

"Thanks, but let's get her born first," Jacob said uneasily. He shifted in the hospital bed and stated adamantly, "I've played along so far but the good patient act ends today. I've got a lot to unfuck in a short period of time."

"Very well," said Dr. Zhukova, her exasperation with his profanity evident, "but I'm going to check your stitches first."

"Go for it, Doc," Jacob said as he placed his hands behind his head. Doctor Zhukova rolled a low stool to his bedside along with the medical cart. Snapping her surgical gloves into place, she pulled up his shirt and removed his dressing.

"Your wound is healing nicely," commented Dr. Zhukova as she ran a finger underneath the line of Jacob's stitches. She discarded the gauze into a small bag hanging from the cart and added, "You no longer need a dressing but you will need to keep your stitches clean and dry."

"Whatever you say," Jacob replied with raised eyebrows. The morning brought many things to his remembrance and he sought to address them all. He began with Boyka's missing doll, insisting, "I want Boyka's doll back."

"I am sorry but I cannot do that," advised Dr. Zhukova. She removed her gloves and disposed of them before asserting, "The doll should have been destroyed long ago."

"You know, the burning starts with dolls, and books," Jacob sneered while pulling down his shirt, "but it usually ends with bodies."

"That is a ludicrous and unfair comparison and you know it," snapped Dr. Zhukova. Standing up and pushing away the stool with her foot, she argued, "Dolls induce a frivolity in children that stunts their development in Christ. Treating them like real human beings is a lie - a 'species of idolatry' according to Father Noyes. It fosters a possessiveness in girls that, as women, they transfer to their real children. They then love those children before God."

"That's fucking ridiculous," Jacob chastised her. Surprising her by deftly swinging his legs off the bed and onto the floor, he demanded, "Give me the fucking doll or I won't tell you what happened to Boyka and her sisters."

Dr. Zhukova bristled with anger, the Russian unaccustomed to the blatant assaults on her authority. She wished to slap Jacob but could not bring herself to strike a patient.

"I adopted those girls, Jacob," confessed Dr. Zhukova as tears arose in her eyes, "and they are my daughters."

"Then you've got much bigger problems than a damn doll," Jacob said. He and the Doctor waged a bitter optical battle before she finally relented.

"See, you can be reasonable," Jacob said with a haughty smile. Dr. Zhukova whirled around to depart but Jacob stood up and grabbed her arm. She permitted him to hold onto it as he implored her, "Just wait a minute, Irinushka."

"Yes," replied Dr. Zhukova sharply. She refused to turn back to him.

"Since the day that angel dropped the T-bomb on me, I've been working out how to survive what's to come," Jacob informed her, "and saving your daughters from Liz's evil grasp is a part of my plan. I'm not ready to divulge the details so don't ask."

"What do you need from me?" inquired Dr. Zhukova without hesitation. Jacob released her arm.

"More trust than you're probably willing to give," Jacob responded gravely. Dr. Zhukova rotated to face him as he asked, "What's the situation on the ground?"

"As I expected, Carol is calling for a new, democratically-elected Council and most of the Community is with her," answered Dr. Zhukova. She motioned for him to sit with her on the bed and he complied. Folding her hands in her lap, she said, "I have peopled the Stations with those loyal to me, though Carol will learn of that soon if she does not know already. I have also kept your friends here to keep them safe. That Darby is quite a character."

"Fuckin' A. They brought her?" Jacob complained.

"She is a difficult and disagreeable person to say the least," said Dr. Zhukova. She offered him a smirk and added, "She reminds me of you."

"Nice," Jacob said. He chewed on the callous inside his mouth and asked, "Carol made any demands yet?"

"No," answered Dr. Zhukova.

"Good, it'll make your suggestion to her less of a concession," Jacob said. His use of the word "concession" garnered a look of doubt from Dr. Zhukova but he continued, "Tell Carol you've come to the conclusion that the vast majority of the Community no longer supports Bible Communism and that, because of that lack of support, the Community needs new leadership."

"And live under her tyrannical yoke?!" exclaimed Dr. Zhukova. Her eyes blazed and she objected, "Never!"

"I didn't say that," Jacob said. He took her left hand and squeezed it, urging her, "You and your followers must leave to build a new Community somewhere else but will need time to find a new place to establish it. Your people will move into the village, continuing to practice their version of Christianity, while Carol receives the rest of the Community, where she and her free love movement can practice theirs. And I wouldn't wait long. The sooner, the better."

"That is a most bitter pill," replied Dr. Zhukova. She extricated her hand and queried, "Where will we go?"

"Leave that to me," Jacob replied.

• • • •

MIRIAM MATERIALIZED at the foot of Jacob's bed late in the evening, her head bowed like child who expected to be chastised for her misbehavior. Jacob slept but, despite her quiet arrival, he soon stirred and awoke.

"Miriam, to be honest, I never expected to see you again," Jacob said. His whirlwind of love interests prickled his conscience.

"You almost didn't," replied Miriam, her spirit fluttering in his presence. The two would-be lovers stared at each other longingly but cautiously, neither one certain of what the next several minutes would bring.

"Yeah, thanks for that," Jacob replied as if grateful for a trivial favor. Miriam climbed over the footboard and seated herself on the corner of the bed with her legs folded beneath her. Jacob moved to avoid her touch.

"What's next?" asked Miriam, her trepidation concerning their future evident. Chewing on the callous inside his mouth, Jacob collected his thoughts and considered his options. Miriam began fiddling with her claws.

"If we're gonna have that discussion," Jacob began as Miriam looked away from him, "then I need you stay here, with me, for all of it. If you run, we're through, whatever that entails. Got it?"

"Got it," pouted Miriam after a pause. Jacob looked at her but his eyes clouded.

"The Tribulation's been going on for years, and probably started when you . . .when the *demons* were sent back after the fall of society," Jacob explained, "but now Ba'al Zeboul's opened the gates of the Abyss and demons are pouring into the world. It's bad. It's really fucking bad."

"I know," said Miriam as traces of her demonic voice seeped into her human one. She scowled and seethed, uttering, "I can sense them."

"So you probably know my ex-wife is one of his field marshals," Jacob said. He and Miriam refocused on one another.

"Yep," advised Miriam bitterly, "and I know she and her bitchlings hijacked all your little fuck toys."

"Don't get all sensitive on me," Jacob grumbled. Guilt-ridden over his promiscuity, especially given his proximity to Miriam, he protested, "I thought you were gone. *Forever.*"

"It doesn't matter," sneered Miriam dismissively. She crawled on all fours so that she hovered over Jacob, her nose nearly touching his own and her hair hanging around his face, and ranted, "I don't care about the fucking Tribulation, or demonic Lady Lizzie, or your fucking fuck toys, or any other bullshit. All I wanna know is *what's next.*"

Miriam watched Jacob like a predator. He used all his willpower to refrain from kissing her.

"All right, I'll skip to the ending," Jacob relented. "Despite my many and constant sins, God's still giving me the power to cast out demons, and apparently my kid takes after her old man. But that doesn't help us against material threats. So, no matter what happens, no matter how fucked I am, or how much you want to be with me, you're gonna stay with Sarah and the baby."

"No!" objected Miriam in a high-pitched voice.

"What are you, fucking six?" Jacob scolded her. Miriam grabbed his chin and pushed his mouth closed.

"I'm not leaving you again," declared Miriam.

"Miriam, I can't watch them every second," Jacob pleaded, "and you're the only one I trust."

"I'm just the only one who can do it," snapped Miriam. Exhaustion overcame Jacob and sleep lay heavily on his eyelids.

"Help me up," Jacob requested weakly. Miriam instantly complied and moved both of their bodies into a sitting position on the edge of the bed. Wrapping an affectionate arm around the demon, he absorbed the pain as she clung to his injured torso and laid her head on his shoulder.

"Who's gonna watch *you* when the bad guys aren't demons?" asked Miriam.

"That's my next meeting," Jacob said uncertainly. Sensing each other's weariness, they became quiet and took refuge in one another's arms.

· · · ·

DARBY IMMEDIATELY SLUGGED Jacob in the face. Stumbling backward out of her room, he fell into the hallway and grasped his face.

"What the fuck was that for?" Jacob shouted as his head spun. He lay sprawled on the floor and rubbed his aching jaw. Darby appeared in the doorway.

"Do you really want that list?" replied Darby with a glower.

"No, we don't have the time," Jacob quipped. Sitting up and resting his forearms on his knees, he grimaced and asked, "Are we even now?"

"Not hardly, asshole," answered Darby. Dr. Zhukova and several Community members emerged from doorways on either side of the hall with concerned faces. Seeing him on the floor, the Doctor hurried to him and knelt at his side.

"What is it? Your stitches?" asked Dr. Zhukova with concern. She attempted to lift his shirt.

"I'm fine, I'm fine, just a fist to the face," Jacob said as he warded off Dr. Zhukova. Darby leaned against the doorframe and folded her arms. The Doctor leapt up and thrust a finger at her.

"If you have opened them up you will answer to me," threatened the Russian. Darby laughed with a gleam in her eye.

"Can you stitch with a broken finger?" asked Darby with a smirk. Dr. Zhukova closed her hand into a fist.

"Enough!" Jacob shouted. His yell garnered the attention of both women. Addressing Doctor Zhukova first, he assured her, "Like I said, Doc, I'm fine, but I'll come down in a few minutes and if you wanna check my stitches, you can check my stitches. I just need to talk to Darby."

Dr. Zhukova hesitated. Jacob nodded back to the room from which she came.

"Very well," Dr. Zhukova replied as she regained her composure. She swiftly turned and marched down the hall. Darby watched her disappear and then extended a hand to Jacob.

"It's pathetic but you're the closest thing to family – *human* family – that I got left," Darby said. Jacob accepted her offer and she pulled him to his feet, continuing, "Plus you're the only non-fetus I know who can deal with demons. So I've decided to stick around . . . at least until I get a better offer."

"I'm surprised your sister hasn't made you one yet," Jacob said. Darby failed to take the bait.

"So what's this favor you want?" Darby asked as she walked back into her room. Jacob followed and closed the door behind him.

"It's more of a mutually-beneficial arrangement," Jacob countered.

"Bullshit," snapped Darby. She plopped onto her bed while still wearing her boots.

"It's not bullshit," Jacob said. He suddenly realized her once long, dark hair was short and blonde. Deciding to avoid any commentary on her new hairstyle, Jacob stated firmly, "I need you to keep the human assholes off my back and, in turn, I'll keep the demon assholes off yours."

"Can't your demon whore do that for you?" asked Darby. She unholstered her pistol and ejected the clip.

"She's not a whore," Jacob replied while Darby slowly removed each bullet from the clip, "and besides, she's not getting paid for it, so she'd be a demon slut, not a demon whore. But she's not a slut either."

Jacob paused. Darby threw him a nasty look.

"I think I might have a concussion," Jacob said while touching his jaw.

"I really fucking hate you," griped Darby. She returned to the task at hand.

"Miriam's on the kid's security detail so I need you on mine," Jacob said. He leaned against the wall and said, "Do we have a deal or what?"

"Yeah, sure, we got a deal," answered Darby. Finished with the removal of bullets from the clip, she began reinserting them and asked, "What about all these civilians?"

"Sarah and the baby come first," Jacob replied. Darby read his grim countenance and knew the hopelessness of their situation. Though he hated to say it, he added, "Other than that, follow what little you have of a conscience. Do whatcha' can."

"Can you trust Zhukova?" queried Darby.

"I think so," Jacob replied, "but even if we can't, I've got enough leverage to keep her in line. Short term, anyways."

"So then, asshole, what's the first move?" inquired Darby.

"We have a delivery to make," Jacob said determinedly, "*tonight.*"

"The Doc's not gonna like that," remarked Darby. She clicked the clip back into her firearm.

"If she doesn't like it," Jacob grumbled, "then fuck her."

"Whatever you say," said Darby.

· · · ·

LIGHT, FLUFFY SNOWFLAKES swirled wildly in the wind as midnight approached. Using Miriam's unique talent for covert operations, Jacob directed the stocking of a cargo van for the return trip to the Community.

"Man, Darby's punches are liked getting kicked by a mule," complained Jacob as he massaged his jaw.

"She's lucky I'm being a good girl now," snarled Miriam, her demonic voice interspersed with her human one. She sat on Jacob's bed with one leg tucked beneath her and the other hanging off its edge.

"Let it go, Mirry," Jacob corrected her. He finished packing a duffel bag and said, "Darby and I've committed so many crimes against each other that even I'm not holding it against her."

"So?" sneered Miriam in a snarky tone.

"You drug the kids?" Jacob asked as he zipped his duffel bag.

"Yes, master," answered Miriam in a fake tone of obedience. She vanished, reappeared behind him and pulled a punch to his kidney, saying, "The secret ingredient tonight was sedative. Half of them fell asleep in their dinners."

"Damn it, Miriam," Jacob protested, the punch wounding his ego if not his body. Before she could utter another sardonic remark, he whirled around, grasped her shoulders and kissed her on the forehead. The affection paralyzed her. Looking Miriam in the eyes, Jacob said, "I couldn't do this without you."

Miriam's frustration melted away and she indulged in the intense blueness of Jacob's eyes. He took her chin in his right hand.

"Go tell Sarah and Darby it's time," Jacob instructed Miriam. He examined her from head to toe, grinned and said, "And get some better clothes."

"You know it doesn't matter," replied Miriam with a grin of her own. She, without thinking, flippantly said, "I could walk out there naked and it wouldn't fucking matter."

"Oh, is that an option?" asked Jacob puckishly. The innuendo and its implication of sex, an activity of which Miriam believed herself to be incapable, seared her heart and she faded from his grasp. Jacob chided himself, "Fucking stupid, Jake, fucking stupid."

Giving his room a final once-over, Jacob cautiously opened his door and peeked outside. The hallway was empty and quiet so he stepped into it. Darby, followed by Sarah, soon joined him and the threesome made its way to the front doors. Miriam awaited them there.

"I disposed of the night watch, too," advised Miriam. A sharp look from Sarah prompted her to add in annoyance, "They're still alive. Everybody's still fucking alive."

"Stay here with Sarah while Darby and I bring the van around," Jacob directed Miriam.

Darby pushed Jacob aside and opened the door. The cold wind burst into the building.

"I got it, dumbass," said Darby as she swiftly exited. Jacob turned his attention to Sarah and gripped her arm.

"You feeling alright?" Jacob queried. Miriam sourly watched their interaction.

"I am fine," Sarah assured him with a heartening smile, "and so is the little one. Everything will be fine, Jacob."

Jacob forced a smile. His heart, however, felt uneasy.

. . . .

THE FIERCE WIND MASKED the rumbling of the van as Darby brought it to a halt before the doors. She gave Jacob a thumbs up.

"Here we go," Jacob said as he rushed Sarah outside. She struggled to maintain his pace.

"Jacob, please, not so fast," replied Sarah. Miriam followed in their wake with her arms at her sides and her fists clenched. The wind stopped and all grew still.

"Come on, Sarah, we gotta move," Jacob urged her. Darby opened the rear doors from within the van and held out her hand to Sarah. Jacob wrapped his arm around her to lift her up.

"What took you so long?" Jacob questioned Darby.

"Fuck off," snapped Darby.

"Where in Heaven's name are you going?!" shouted Dr. Zhukova as she marched down the front steps. Halting at the bottom, she yelled, "And what did you do to my people?!"

"Shit," Jacob muttered with an exhale. Glaring at Miriam, he said, "Looks like you forgot one."

"I will handle it," said Sarah as she extricated herself from him. Miriam shrugged to convey her indifference.

"Sarah, wait," Jacob pleaded. She pushed away his hand.

"I said I will handle it," countered Sarah. She walked to Dr. Zhukova.

"Fuck," Jacob griped. Lowering his voice, he nodded at Dr. Zhukova and instructed Darby, "If she tries anything, shoot her."

Darby hopped out of the van, drew her huge pistol and held it at her side though she seemed unsettled. Jacob placed his hands on his hips and waited impatiently.

"The Community is a dangerous place for you now and you should not go there," Dr. Zhukova warned. She folded her arms to warm herself and shivered, saying, "At least here we can quickly escape if they come for you."

"My child is in danger no matter where she is, Doctor," Sarah explained as she hugged her distended stomach. Offering Dr. Zhukova a sympathetic look, she said, "I apologize for Jacob's methods and I swear to you that your followers are unharmed. However, he believes our baby will be safest in the village and I agree with him."

"We don't have time for this bullshit," Jacob growled impatiently as he made his way to Sarah. Miriam's eyes widened and she shrieked.

"Jake!" bellowed Miriam. The baby suddenly lurched in Sarah's womb just as a sense of overwhelming evil slammed Jacob.

"And it begins," Jacob stated eerily. The Station's lights died and several shadowy forms appeared on the roof. They hurled themselves at Sarah and several others crashed through the nearest windows. Miriam threw herself into the fray and knocked two demons from their trajectories while a spiritual pulse from Sarah's pregnant belly dispatched several more. A straggler barreled towards her, knocked Dr. Zhukova to the ground and pounced on the nun. Jacob shouted, "Sarah!"

Jacob's wrath exploded from him in a wave of spiritual force that wracked each demon and thrust it from its host's body. Sarah's assailant suffered the same fate but, as Jacob knelt beside her, he realized its claws found their mark.

"No, no, no," Jacob said as he saw two clusters of jagged puncture wounds from Sarah's clavicles to the bottom of her sternum. The slightest traces of blood appeared near the lowest puncture.

"J-J-Jacob," whimpered Sarah fearfully with tears in her eyes. Darby charged up to them while sweeping the vicinity for threats and looked helplessly at her pathetic form. Jacob pointed at an unconscious Dr. Zhukova.

"Get her up, Darby," Jacob ordered. Darby quickly complied but several shakes and slaps failed to rouse the Russian.

"She's out," Darby said. The wind kicked up and, as if infused with evil intent, carried away her words. She yelled, "She's out!"

"Keep trying, damn it!" Jacob shouted. He held up his hands but found no use for them, snarling, "Fuck, fuck, fuck!"

Oblivious to the commotion, Miriam rose to her feet and wandered in a trance amongst the bodies of the demons' hosts. Unconscious yet alive, they lay scattered on the snowy ground.

"They're members of the Community," said Miriam as she surveyed their ripped and tattered clothing.

"Miriam!" Jacob bellowed. Hearing the panic in his voice, she instantly travelled through the spirit world to him and, seeing Sarah, cried out. Jacob ordered her, "Blankets, in the van!"

Shocked to her core by Sarah's condition, Miriam found herself unable to respond. The nun opened her eyes and seemed to look past Jacob.

"You! Help her!" Sarah called out in desperation.

"Sarah, don't talk," Jacob begged her. He turned to Miriam and yelled, "Get the fucking blankets!"

"She's awake!" shouted Darby. She dragged a woozy Dr. Zhukova over to Sarah.

"Irinushka, please, save them," Jacob pleaded. Shaking the cobwebs from her mind, Dr. Zhukova swiftly examined Sarah.

"We have to get her inside immediately," instructed Dr. Zhukova as adrenaline flooded her bloodstream.

"Please!" shouted Sarah again, the volume of her voice causing her great pain. Her eyes seemed to lose their vision and Jacob sensed that she peered into the spiritual world.

"Sarah, stay with me," Jacob implored her as Miriam crawled to Sarah's side and tenderly took her hand, "you've gotta stay with me, okay."

"You," said Dr. Zhukova authoritatively as she pointed at Miriam. She asked, "Can you get her inside?"

"I've never tried that before," Miriam answered. She saw the anguish on Jacob's face and, determined to remedy it, she declared, "Yes."

"Done what?" inquired Jacob.

"The medical room, quickly," replied Dr. Zhukova. She jumped up and ran into the Station.

"Where the fuck are you going?!" Jacob yelled after her. Miriam scooped Sarah into her arms and immediately dematerialized with the nun. Jacob shouted again, this time addressing Miriam, "Where the fuck are you going?!"

· · · ·

WHEN JACOB CRASHED into the medical room, he found a gloved Dr. Zhukova cutting off Sarah's blood-stained coat and a transfixed Miriam standing next to the examination table. He stopped and watched the scene in abject fear as Sarah writhed and screamed in pain.

"Hold her!" Dr. Zhukova ordered, the volume of her voice tweaking her attack-induced headache. Miriam restrained Sarah while she quickly filled a syringe with a sedative. The Russian inserted the needle into Sarah's arm, the sensation raising her consciousness and causing her to scream again.

"What is that?" queried Jacob. Sarah's movement slowed and her cries subsided.

"A powerful sedative," Dr. Zhukova answered. Resigned to her course of action, she said, "I have nothing else to give her. This room, this Station, was never intended for surgery. It will have to do."

"Who said anything about surgery!?" asked Jacob in a panic. His wound prickled him but the adrenaline coursing through his veins masked it.

"Help me remove her coat," Dr. Zhukova directed Miriam. Sliding her arms underneath Sarah, she effortlessly lifted her from the table. The Doctor raised her hand and admonished Miriam, "Be careful!"

Miriam said nothing and glowered at Dr. Zhukova who, ignoring the demon's ire, carefully pulled the coat from Sarah's limp body. The former *daimoniou* then gently placed Sarah back on the table so that the Doctor could perform a quick visual examination of the nun's injuries. A puzzled expression came to her face.

"Do demons harbor bacteria?" Dr. Zhukova asked Miriam. Sarah faded into even deeper levels of unconsciousness.

"No, but the humans they possess do," replied Miriam.

"We need to stop the bleeding and then clean and dress these wounds," Dr. Zhukova said. She dexterously cut Sarah's blouse down the middle, peeled back both sides and then cut off her bra. Her efforts revealed that each puncture bled; the tenth, however, broke through Sarah's sternum and bled more than the others.

"What can I do?" asked Jacob. His emotion left him and he became stoic as he felt his future hanging by a tenuous thread.

"Wash your hands and pull two surgical gown sets out of that cabinet," Dr. Zhukova answered as she nodded to the other side of the room. Opening a cupboard with her elbow, she grabbed a package of square wound dressings and returned to Sarah's side. The Doctor then tore open the package and placed one pad on each of the minor wounds.

"Don't take them," Jacob prayed as he rummaged through the cabinet, "*please*, don't take them. I can't lose another family."

"Use your fingers to apply pressure to each pad," Dr. Zhukova directed Miriam. She splayed her fingers and nervously held them above Sarah's wounds, her hesitation prompting the Russian to demand, "Now, Miriam!"

"All right!" responded Miriam, her efforts plugging each puncture and temporarily stopping the bleeding. She sensed Sarah's life force ebbing and said, "Something's wrong."

"Whaddaya mean something's wrong?!" demanded Jacob as he whirled around. He held a surgical gown set in each hand.

"The claw wound in her sternum is deeper than the others," Dr. Zhukova stated as she glanced at him. Returning her attention to Sarah, she said, "It may have struck her heart."

"Ah, fuck," Jacob uttered. Miriam studied Sarah's pallid, drawn face with sorrow.

"Very good, Doctor," announced an invisible Assarion. Jacob felt her presence skulking around them as she expounded, "The claw pierced her heart . . . her right ventricle wall, to be exact."

"Fucking *cunt*!" Jacob yelled. He intended to drive Assarion from the room, barking, "Not you, not now!"

"Whatever she is, leave her be!" Dr. Zhukova commanded Jacob as she removed her gloves, balled them up and deposited them in a garbage container. She shoved him out of the way and began scrubbing her hands and forearms, instructing him sternly yet calmly, "Help me with my gown."

Jacob fumed over Assarion's presence but obeyed Dr. Zhukova. He first donned his surgical apparel and then assisted her in doing the same.

"Do you need a break?" Dr. Zhukova asked Miriam as she prepped the medical cart for surgery. Jacob winced when she produced a sternal saw.

"I'm fine," replied Miriam. Minutes later, Dr. Zhukova rolled the cart beside the medical table. She, after swiftly placing drapes over Sarah's body, efficiently cleaned and dressed the nine superficial wounds in her chest before washing and disinfecting the incision site. Mesmerized by the process, Miriam removed her fingers one by one as Dr. Zhukova addressed each puncture and watched every movement of the Russian's hands.

"You ever done this before?" inquired Jacob uneasily. The Doctor did not look at him but continued disinfecting Sarah's skin.

"No and, in all honesty, I am taking a tremendous risk in operating under these conditions," Dr. Zhukova answered bluntly.

"These conditions?!" objected Jacob while Dr. Zhukova marked the dimensions of the surgical site. The reality of the impending surgery prompted Jacob to relent, "Never mind. I don't wanna know."

17

"THIS IS SUCH FUCKING bullshit," Darby grumbled as she threw an unconscious Community member over her shoulder and carried the woman towards the Station. Jacob, on his mad dash inside, ordered her to get the possession victims out of the cold. Darby climbed the front steps, opened one of the doors and griped, "Slingin' around all these fucking dead-weight, drugged-up Christians."

Darby laid the member in the foyer before venturing back out into the windy, snowy night. She opened the door and stepped onto the station's porch.

"Are you Darby Nicks?" deadpanned a female voice saturated with disinterest. Darby drew her gun with blinding speed as she noticed a waifish woman standing before her. She let her finger fall from the trigger at the sight of soulless black eyes.

"If you're gonna kill me, I'd do it quick before Jake gets back," Darby said as she holstered her firearm. Descending the steps, she felt an unusual twinge of sadness and muttered, "Especially if you killed his kid."

The demon smiled mechanically, almost as if it were a reflex, and revealed a toothless mouth of rotting gums. Dressed in a dirty, ragged sweatshirt and ripped, oversized jeans, it wore no shoes and was smeared with filth and grime. Its grin vanished.

"I'm not here to kill you," said the demon in its monotone voice. Darby noticed its fetidness as she passed it and moved to the next community member. The demon turned and advised, "I'm here with a message from Lady Lizzie."

Darby paused.

"She hates that name," Darby said. She lifted a large male community member into a fireman's carry with a grunt.

"Whatever," responded the demon with a shrug. It brushed several matted strands of hair from its face, its locks mottled with blonde and brown patches. Darby again ascended the steps as the demon informed her, "She wants you to return to her, to your family. They all await you at Jarbidge, far away from the Son's rabble."

"What? She hasn't retaken Kaiser yet?" Darby replied snidely. She opened the door, deposited the man inside and then returned to the top of the steps. Placing her hands on her hips, Darby caught her breath and eyed the demon closely.

"No, she hasn't," said the demon with no intonation. It did not further elaborate.

"You can tell my sister that I ain't interested in dyin'," Darby said thickly. The demon's mien remained emotionless as she continued, "I may hate Jake's guts but at least he ain't tryin' to kill me."

"That's because he hasn't fucked you yet," replied the demon.

"I said I'm not interested, cunt," Darby countered angrily. She walked down the stairs and towards the nearest Community member.

"There is no reason to stay here," said the demon without regard for Darby's slur. It approached Darby and, as if reading from a script, said, "Your hatred for Jacob is undeniable. He and his whores brutally murdered your sister and your nieces and brought about the downfall of Kaiser. Their home. *Your home.* A place where you exercised power and authority, a place where you were respected and, more importantly, *feared.* Yet thanks to Jacob Gottschalk, you now toil to save those you don't even know, and everything you knew, and everything you are, is gone. Forever lost."

Darby clenched her teeth and contemplated the demon's dispassionate yet compelling argument. It moved closer to her, its stench tickling her nostrils.

"Unless," said the demon, "you choose a wiser course than the one you currently tread. You can be your sister's right hand once again and wield the power and authority you once did, but on the grandest of scales . . . ."

Darby looked at the demon. Its arguments were uncomfortable reminders of the sins of her current allies and the rewards offered by Elizabeth.

". . . and I guarantee you, Darby," added the demon with the slightest increase in pitch, "*you will be feared.*"

The demon came too close and its putridness overwhelmed Darby's sense of smell. Her moment of doubt passed.

"You're a shitty saleswoman," Darby said as she lifted another community member. The demon smiled another misplaced smile but, as before, it quickly vanished.

"The Lady's offer remains," advised the demon, "though she warns you once again that her patience is not infinite."

"Neither is mine," Darby replied. Marching towards the steps, she glared at the demon and growled, "Now get the fuck outta here before I go get numb-nuts to hurl your skanky, meth-whore ass into hell."

"Okay," said the demon as it faded from view.

"What the hell was that?" Darby asked herself. She laid down the woman she carried inside the foyer. Reaching into her jacket, she retrieved her flask, unscrewed the top and took several gulps from it. She uttered with a grin, "Ahhhh. That's better."

Darby felt the heat of the whiskey flow into her chest and then rolled her shoulders. Stowing her flask, she returned to the task at hand and again braved the chilling wind and blowing snow.

· · · ·

JACOB AND MIRIAM LINGERED in a state of mild shock as Dr. Zhukova elucidated the surgical procedure, the limitations under which she labored and their roles in the operation. Jacob wore a full surgical outfit but Miriam, standing at the head of the table, did not, her hands affectionately holding the sides of Sarah's head. Forgotten for the moment, a silent Assarion flitted about the edges of the room and spectated with great interest.

"Are you sure this is a good idea?" asked Jacob nervously. He gazed dubiously on Sarah, the nun's body covered with surgical drapes save for her chest.

"Their lives most likely depend on it," Dr. Zhukova answered, her tone serious yet sympathetic. Glancing at Miriam with her green eyes, she motioned to a small monitor on a stand and said, "The monitor should alert us if there are any issues with Sarah's vital signs, but I have nothing to measure the fetus's vitals so that falls on your shoulders, Miriam."

Miriam nodded in the affirmative. Dr. Zhukova turned to the table.

"Let us begin," Dr. Zhukova announced. She held out her hand and instructed Jacob, "The ESU, please."

During Dr. Zhukova's surgical preparations, she introduced him to the ESU or electrosurgical unit - a device that uses high-frequency electrical currents to cut tissue. Jacob hesitated and looked from Sarah's pale yet unblemished skin to the ESU and back again. Dr. Zhukova indulged him until he removed it from its nonconductive holster and handed it to her.

"Thank you," Dr. Zhukova said in kindly tone. She announced for Jacob's sake, "I will make a subcutaneous incision along the midline as I have marked it."

Jacob inhaled sharply as the ESU sliced into Sarah's flesh. The current flowing through the instrument minimized her blood loss but Jacob was still required to suction some of it out of her incision. Miriam remained still and silent, her attention riveted to Jacob as he followed Dr. Zhukova's instructions with cautious, deliberate movements.

Throughout the surgery, Dr. Zhukova performed and described subtle steps such as identifying veins or marking certain areas. Jacob, however, heard few of her words as he concentrated on his own tasks. He watched helplessly as Sarah's incision grew deeper.

"Next, I will divide the interclavicle ligament," Dr. Zhukova said while continuing her work. She occasionally probed into the incision with her fingers and moved tissue. Jacob snapped to attention when the Russian said, "It is time to open the sternum so I can access her heart."

Despite Dr. Zhukova's efficient surgical technique, the sawing of Sarah's sternum grated on Jacob's nerves and, to him, seemed an eternity. He could not look at Sarah's pregnant stomach.

"First swab, Jacob," Dr. Zhukova directed him after the cut was complete. He provided a large, cotton swab which she placed over the right edge of the sternal bone to reduce blood loss. She then placed an identical swab on the left edge and used a diathermy to cauterize the inside of the incision.

"How is she?" Jacob asked as he ventured a glance at Miriam. She faked a hopeful mien.

"She seems fine," replied Miriam while sensing the beating of the baby's heart. Dr. Zhukova glanced at the monitor's screen to check Sarah's vitals.

She noticed, but did not bring attention to, the fact that the nun's heartbeat and blood pressure, while stable, were weak.

"They are both doing remarkably well," Dr. Zhukova interjected in an effort to keep Jacob even-keeled. She handed him the diathermy and changed her gloves before requesting, "The retractor, please."

Jacob handed the sternal retractor to Dr. Zhukova. She positioned its prongs inside the severed sternum bone and slowly cranked open Sarah's chest.

"Holy shit," uttered Jacob when he saw Sarah's beating heart. Dr. Zhukova, demonstrating an iron will, immediately examined her right ventricle.

"Assarion was right," Dr. Zhukova said. Reenergized by the relatively minor nature of the puncture, she immediately prepared to suture it, saying, "This is not a deep puncture. Sarah was blessed."

"If she was blessed that demon would have missed her heart," replied Jacob sourly. He immediately regretted his statement. Letting his anger evaporate, he said feebly, "Sorry."

Dr. Zhukova said nothing in response and he watched her masterful performance in awe. He spent the next few minutes assisting her as she deftly sutured the wound on Sarah's beating heart.

"These pledgets will buttress the sutures and help prevent them from tearing through any tissue," Dr. Zhukova said as she worked. Permitting herself an exhale of relief, she completed the last suture and declared with satisfaction, "The wound is repaired. We can close her sternum."

Heartened by the successful heart surgery, Jacob's body relaxed. He helped Dr. Zhukova insert drain tubes and a protective towel between the sternal halves. The Doctor changed her gloves for the next stage of the operation.

"God is with us today," Dr. Zhukova said. She began wiring together the two halves of Sarah's sternum using forceps and stainless-steel wire, saying, "There was no reason for us to have this wire yet, by His grace, it was here."

The repair of Sarah's sternum was tedious. Dr. Zhukova inserted and tied off each wire but the process was time-consuming even with Jacob's assistance in holding and tying. Eventually, the wiring was complete which allowed her to clip off the extra lengths and twist the ends to pull the sternal halves tightly together.

Dr. Zhukova, once finished with Sarah's sternum, closed her pectoral fascia with one line of running sutures followed by a second line for the subcutaneous tissue. She then clipped her skin together, cleaned the incision with iodine and covered it with a visible plaster.

"Thank you, Lord Jesus," Dr. Zhukova prayed aloud after applying the last of the plaster. Jacob shed a single tear but fought off the others.

"Thank you, Doctor," said Jacob in earnest. Their weary eyes met and he declared, "I take back every last curse and slander I ever uttered against you."

"Thank God," Dr. Zhukova suggested as she applied the final touches, "for without his guidance, my efforts would have come to naught."

"I will," promised Jacob. He smiled at Miriam and she quickly forced a grin in return. However, the second Jacob looked away, her face became grim and her spirit burdened.

· · · ·

JACOB FELT THE TIREDNESS in his eyes but the adrenaline rush of Sarah's surgery had yet to subside. He closed the door to the medical room and left Dr. Zhukova to clean up the last details of the operation. Darby waited for Jacob in the hallway and immediately noticed his blood-smeared surgical gown.

"She live?" asked Darby with her usual tactlessness.

"Yep," Jacob answered.

"And the kid?" inquired Darby with raised eyebrows.

"Uh-huh," Jacob said. Darby withdrew her flask from her jacket pocket, unscrewed the top and took a swig for herself. She then offered it to Jacob.

"Congratulations, Dad," replied Darby. Jacob accepted the flask and drained it. He grimaced due to the whiskey's strength and felt the burn slide into his stomach. It also cleared his mind.

"I sure as fuck hope you have more of this," Jacob said. Handing her back the flask, he asked, "How's it going out here?"

"I'll show you," Darby began bitterly as she snatched the flask from his hand. She stuffed it into her jacket, turned around and gestured with her finger, adding, "This way."

"Please tell me *they're* alive," Jacob said. Darby walked to the foyer and he followed several paces behind.

"You'll see," responded Darby. She led him to the foyer, opened the door leading into it and held it. Jacob leaned his head inside.

"Did you lay eggs in 'em yet?" Jacob asked in a disturbed tone. The once possessed members lay in a straight line on the floor, each one neatly packed into a sleeping bag. He returned his gaze to Darby and commented, "Damn, that's just creepy."

"They're still drugged," countered an irked Darby. She let the door close and added, "I didn't wanna just leave 'em on the fucking floor, ya' savage."

"I'll be damned, Darby," Jacob said with a shit-eating grin, "you're becoming a real human being."

"Fuck off," growled Darby. She placed her hands on her hips and said, "It was easier to take the sleeping bags to them than drag 'em all back to their rooms."

"Take it easy. Ya' did just fine," Jacob said. Shifting topics to avoid Darby's wrath, he removed his gown and asked, "What shape is this place in?"

"Just the broken windows. I closed the storm shutters so they're not a problem," replied Darby.

"So we're good for awhile," Jacob said. He massaged the radix of his nose and exhaled. Darby folded her arms while Jacob settled into a plastic-and-metal chair.

"Are you ever that lucky?" queried Darby with a dubious expression.

"Nope," Jacob said, "so let's hear it."

"Even if you can keep them away from us," Darby explained, "all they'd have to do is fuck up the power and wreck the vans. We'd all eventually freeze to death . . . or have to trek outta here on foot, and then freeze to death. They could contaminate the food and water, starve us out, or just keep us here. Turn this place into a prison . . . or a mass grave."

"Well, aren't you a bowl full of fucking sunshine," Jacob griped.

"You think I'm wrong?" said a surprisingly composed Darby. Jacob hesitated before answering.

"No," he said with a shake of his head. Resting his elbows on his knees and clasping his hands in front of him, he stated, "Cuz' even if we try to run, they've already shot us in the leg."

"Wonderful," commented Darby.

"There's no way Sarah's gonna be able to travel before she pops," Jacob said, "and maybe not after, at least for a while. And then we'll have a newborn with us."

"So, Jesus Genius, what the fuck do we do?" inquired Darby, her tone one of annoyance.

"'We' only includes Sarah and I," Jacob said. Staring into the floor, he expounded, "Everyone else better clear the fuck out before the demon shit hits the fan. And that includes you. You did your good deed. You got her to me and now you can go wherever you want. Hell, back with your sister, though I advise against that. But regardless of where you go, you've earned it."

"Fuck that," Darby objected. Jacob looked up to her as she insisted, "I'm staying. And if the blonde bulldog hears you spewing all that bullshit you're in for one hell of an asskicking."

Jacob smiled. It comforted him to be under Miriam's fierce protection again. He remembered her words from months ago:

"There is no me. There is no you. There is only us."

"So, I ask again Jesus Genius, what the fuck do we do?" inquired Darby loudly.

"I don't know," Jacob answered as he stood up. Before Darby could reply, they heard Sarah scream.

• • • •

MIRIAM FOUND HERSELF unable to leave Sarah so, for the privilege of remaining in the room, she collected and disposed of the refuse from Sarah's surgery. The nun's vitals remained weak but stable.

"I should administer more sedative," said Dr. Zhukova. Seconds later, Sarah's body lurched and she screamed.

"Assarion!" Sarah bellowed. She cried out in agony, "Now!"

"Hold her!" shouted Dr. Zhukova as she prepared another dose of sedative. Miriam rushed to restrain Sarah but stopped short when she felt Assarion hovering above her.

"Wait, don't!" Miriam yelled.

"Miriam, please!" replied Dr. Zhukova as she attempted to inject Sarah with the syringe. Assarion's spirit plunged into Sarah and she lurched again, the force hurling the Doctor backwards. Miriam raced through the spirit world and caught her before she struck the wall.

"Just wait," Miriam urged as she hugged Dr. Zhukova to hold her in place. Jacob burst into the room with Darby in tow. She halted in the doorway.

"What's wrong?!" Jacob exclaimed. He rushed to Sarah's side when he saw her body lying lifelessly on the examination table. Her eyes popped open.

"Sarah is dying, Jacob," answered Assarion with Sarah's mouth. Jacob's usual angst-fueled profanity failed him and he could only muster a single word.

"What?" he asked.

"Sarah is dying," Assarion replied, "and I have possessed her to save your child."

"You opportunistic bitch," snarled Jacob hatefully.

"It was not her decision, Jacob," Sarah said. Two small bloodstains formed on the front of her gown. Jacob looked to Dr. Zhukova and pointed at the spots.

"She's bleeding," said Jacob. Dr. Zhukova recovered from her shock and, after being released by Miriam, approached the table. Sarah's spirit waned and she appeared to lose consciousness.

"She probably pulled the staples and maybe even the sutures," Dr. Zhukova said concernedly. She attempted to examine Sarah's chest but the nun woke and gently blocked the attempt.

"Thank you for saving my child, Doctor," Sarah said, "but please, as Miriam suggested, wait."

"Wait for what?!" asked a distressed Jacob. He took her hand but his heart sunk when he felt its coldness.

"We have little time, so you must listen," said Sarah through a weak smile. Her skin resembled that of a corpse but she continued, "I will be of infinitely more benefit to our child if I watch over her from the next realm."

"Don't start that Obi Wan bullshit," Jacob admonished her. He addressed Dr. Zhukova, saying, "You can keep her alive, right, Doc?"

"It is too late, Jacob, and you know that," stated Sarah. She closed her eyelids tightly and then opened them, beckoning Jacob hoarsely, "Come closer."

Jacob moved closer to Sarah and leaned into her. She coughed up a small amount of blood which Jacob tenderly wiped away with his sleeve.

"I must go but she must stay," Sarah advised in a low voice. Jacob's countenance darkened as he sensed Assarion's presence intertwined with Sarah's spirit. She squeezed his hand and explained, "My spirit is not strong enough to keep my body alive. The Devil is the ruler of this world, of the flesh, and his agents have greater powers over the flesh than we do. Assarion's spiritual presence is enough to sustain my body until the baby is born."

"Are you sure about this?" Jacob asked. A great spiritual weight fell upon him as if someone laid a great material burden on his shoulders. He understood Sarah's desperate decision but found it difficult to condone. She tightened her grip.

"*It is the only way,*" Sarah insisted, the nun amazing her onlookers with her inner strength. Jacob felt the anticipatory stares but kept his gaze on Sarah as she said, "She was there at our baby's conception, she will be there at her birth."

Sarah again lost consciousness but Jacob patiently waited for her to return. She abruptly gasped, opened her eyes and stared directly at Jacob with a pointed expression.

"*She knows what to do,*" Sarah said. Jacob acknowledged his understanding with several subtle shakes of his head.

"Okay," Jaob conceded ruefully. Sarah pulled free of his hand and, in one last motion, caressed his face.

"Goodbye, Jacob . . . God is calling me home," whispered a weakening Sarah. Her hand fell and she said, "Name her Dinah . . . and . . . tell her about me . . . when she is ready."

"I will," Jacob replied. Sarah, in one final burst of energy, grabbed his arm in a painful, vice-like grip.

"Do not neglect your own salvation, Jacob," said Sarah in a commanding voice. Her abrupt admonishment gave everyone in the room pause and Jacob did not respond. Sarah's grip on his arm loosened and failed and her eyelids fell. Jacob remained still for several seconds and then stirred.

"Goodbye, Sarah," Jacob said. Stunned by Sarah's demise, he allowed his tears to fall. Jacob placed his hand tenderly on her head and kissed her, the gestures causing Miriam to boil like a cauldron. Jacob straightened up.

"Well, that's that," he said.

•   •   •   •

MIRED IN SOPHIE'S BURNED corpse, Marcion appeared next to the van. He raised his right hand to slash its rear, dual tires with his claws.

"I wouldn't do that if I were you," warned Elizabeth's messenger demon in her monotone voice. She materialized several feet away from Marcion and watched him with malicious eyes.

"Fuck you, Athaliah," Marcion snapped but, despite his defiant words, he lowered his arm. He began pacing restlessly and whining, "This is bullshit! Bullshit! They're vulnerable and we should destroy them all!"

"Gottschalk has the favor of God," rejoined Athaliah. She shuttered and spat on the ground before continuing without affect, "We can't approach him, or his child, and the slaughter of the innocents would only provoke him to action. The Lady does not want him running amok with revenge on his mind. He and his retinue are to remain untouched."

Athaliah smiled her brief, inveterate smile. Marcion swiped at her but she did not flinch.

"He still has to eat, and drink," Marcion argued. He jumped on top of the van and commenced one of his bizarre dances, saying, "We can strand them here and wait for them all to succumb to hunger and thirst. Yes, hunger and thirst."

"Including Lady Lizzie's sister?" asked Athaliah in a neutral tone. Marcion glowered at the Station.

"She and I have unfinished business," Marcion said. Any emotion he displayed melted away and he repeated, "Unfinished business."

"Why are you here?" asked Athaliah.

"The Lady wants to know Darby's answer," Marcion replied.

"You're lying," said Athaliah. She turned to the Station and perceived what occurred within it, continuing, "Now tell me why you are here or I will tell Lady Lizzie that you've slipped your leash."

Marcion scowled and lingered on the van. Resigned to Athaliah's advantage, he stepped off the roof and floated to the ground.

"I am here to see Assarion," Marcion admitted grudgingly. Turning to face him, Athaliah raised her chin and examined him closely.

"Why?" inquired Athaliah.

"There is someone who wishes to speak with her," Marcion answered in a monstrous voice. He wrinkled his nose and thrust a charred finger at Athaliah, declaring, "I will say no more."

Athaliah smiled again.

"It is always advantageous to have options," she said with a miniscule increase in pitch. Marcion smiled in return.

"Yes, it is," he responded, "*yes, it is.*"

· · · ·

JACOB AND MIRIAM QUIETLY watched Dr. Zhukova repair Sarah's torn staples while Darby leaned against the doorframe with folded arms. Assarion, now possessing Sarah's draped body, laid patiently on the examination table with her arms behind her head.

"So what's the verdict, Doc?" Jacob asked as Dr. Zhukova assessed her.

"I have never before conducted a post-surgical assessment of a, a . . . ," said Dr. Zhukova as she struggled for the right words. Assarion's proximity unnerved the Doctor, her nervousness standing in stark contrast to her confidence during the surgery.

"Demonically-possessed patient," Assarion offered in Sarah's voice.

"Yes," Dr. Zhukova replied with a troubled expression. Removing her exam gloves, she tossed them in the waste basket and addressed Jacob, saying, "And I am not an obstetrician."

"Just like you weren't a surgeon?" Jacob queried with a smirk. The Russian returned it.

"They're both alive, Sarah is stable and the baby is healthy," Dr. Zhukova announced happily. Jacob's exhale of relief was audible.

"Thank you, Irinushka," Jacob said. Slumping into a chair, he looked at Assarion through tired but suspicious eyes and asked, "And spiritually?"

Jacob folded his arms and crossed his ankles while Miriam moved to his side and placed an affectionate hand on his shoulder. Darby rolled her eyes.

"Sarah's spirit has departed the earthly realm," answered Assarion in her own voice. Jacob studied her closely as she rubbed her pregnant belly and said, "But your God permitted me to take its place and the baby's spirit is still here as well. She is strong."

Assarion's presence irked Jacob and he glowered at her. Dr. Zhukova cleared her throat.

"I would like to conduct an ultrasound when . . . if we return to the Community," advised Dr. Zhukova. She looked to Jacob for permission and said, "It would be prudent."

"That won't be necessary, Doctor, but thank you," said Assarion. Jacob's blood pressure rose as she stated confidently, "I assure you the child is fine."

"You're getting the ultrasound whether you like it or not," Jacob interjected sternly. Standing up and pointing at Assarion, he insisted, "End of discussion."

"As you wish, Jacob," replied a pleasant and compliant Assarion. Dr. Zhukova helped her into a sitting position and said, "I will defer to you in all decisions regarding our child."

"Good," Jacob said with a sneer. Miriam fumed. He returned to his seat and uttered acerbically, "You can start by never calling her 'our' child again."

"It is settled then," said Dr. Zhukova, the Russian wishing to break the uncomfortable tension between Jacob and Assarion. She avoided eye contact with both of them.

"May I get dressed now?" asked Assarion in mock deference. She unabashedly sat up straight and thrust out her exposed breasts, the movement sending her surgical drapes to the floor.

"Knock it off," Jacob chastised Assarion. The sight of Sarah's breasts would normally arouse him yet, in the horrible circumstances in which he found himself, they did not.

"Be careful!" scolded Dr. Zhukova. She used a fresh drape to cover Sarah's nakedness and insisted, "You must try to move as little as possible."

"I have a goodwill gesture to prove my sincerity in carrying this child to term," said Assarion. Jacob was relieved that she spoke in her own voice and moved very unlike Sarah.

"I know your intentions aren't blatantly evil, at least, or my daughter would've booted your demonic ass already," Jacob grumbled. He took a single bite of the callous in his mouth and said, "I assume you're going to tell me where Vanessa's body is . . . unless you gave it back to her."

"I most certainly did not," said Assarion with distaste. Dr. Zhukova helped her stand up while she explained, "I know you're returning to New Oneida and I hid her body along the route there. Quite close to Mallory's pyre, in fact. I will take you to it so you may properly lay her physical body to rest."

"Why the most recent change of heart?" Jacob inquired with skepticism dripping from his tongue. He buried his sorrow over Sarah's death and his stepdaughters' corruption deep but quickly recycled it as hatred for all *daimoniou*.

"My days with Marcion soured me on the company of demons," answered Assarion, "but, even more so, I feel like the child is somewhat mine, not in the sense of possession but of parentage. I feel a responsibility for her."

Jacob laughed boisterously and, though he did not know it, the baby's spirit stirred in Sarah's belly. Miriam fumed.

"Despite what Sarah said, you weren't there at her conception," Jacob corrected Assarion harshly. He returned to his feet and approached her. Dr. Zhukova felt the heat of his anger as he continued with growing vitriol, "You were there when we fucked, sure, but I cast your evil, conniving spirit from Sarah's body well before one of my little swimmers rang her bell. She's as much Darby's kid as she is yours."

"If there ever was a child damned to Hell," quipped Darby.

"There's no need for the hostility," Assarion assured Jacob, "because I have made my choice and I know which side of the Tribulation I stand upon."

Jacob's face became grim. The gears of Dr. Zhukova's mind spun as she processed the new information about Jacob's past.

"Yeah, and what side is that?" Jacob snapped snidely. Hankering for the relief only alcohol could bring him, he asked, "I need another drink. Where's the whiskey, Darby?"

"Once a drunk, always a drunk," replied Darby.

"Go get it," Jacob demanded. Sympathizing with Jacob's situation, Darby complied with his wishes and left the room.

"I will get her settled into one of the bedrooms," replied Dr. Zhukova. She walked to the cabinet and procured another a patient gown.

"Don't bother," Jacob said with a glower at Assarion, "because we're not staying."

• • • •

"THIS IS A TERRIBLE idea," Dr. Zhukova castigated Jacob as she assisted Assarion in dressing. The trio stood in the same recovery room in which Jacob met her and made ready to depart for New Oneida. Unhappy with the decision to leave immediately, Dr. Zhukova argued, "Her body has undergone significant trauma and she is in no condition to travel. You are placing both of them in serious jeopardy if you leave."

"Can you keep Sarah together, Assarion?" asked Jacob crassly. Dr. Zhukova helped her don a man's sweater as her pregnancy ruled out most of the clothing at the station.

"Yep," answered Assarion with uncharacteristic brevity.

"And what of my people?" Dr. Zhukova pressed Jacob, the Doctor on the verge of tears. Jacob suddenly realized the exhaustion on her face as she asked forlornly, "Are you simply going to abandon us here?"

Jacob offered her a look of kindly pity. He embraced her and she eagerly accepted his compassion.

"I'm so sorry, Irinushka," said Jacob. Pulling away from her but maintaining his grip on her forearms, he said, "Of course we're not abandoning you. And you've gotta be fried right now."

"I am tired," Dr. Zhukova admitted in an obvious understatement, her condition betrayed by the darkened circles under her eyes. She grew uncomfortable in Jacob's grasp and disentangled herself from it. Fiddling with the bedding, the Russian said, "First, however, we must get her settled. Sarah's body needs time to recover regardless of her spiritual status."

"Let me worry about that," said Jacob. He attempted to interrupt her efforts but she persisted. Assarion studied her new form in a long wall mirror and ran her hands over her distended stomach.

"Her body seems fine to me, perhaps weak, but she did just have heart surgery," commented Assarion, the flippancy in her voice irritating Dr. Zhukova.

"Is that one of your demonic powers, medical diagnosis?" Dr. Zhukova replied.

"All right, all right," said Jacob with a raised hand. He pointed at Assarion and then to the reclining hospital bed, saying, "You, in bed, now."

"Yes, Dear," cooed Assarion puckishly. She pulled down the covers and slid into the bed.

"Carefully, please," Dr. Zhukova pleaded with a wince. Jacob turned and pointed at her.

"You, get some sleep and something to eat, in whatever order works for you," ordered Jacob. He nodded over his shoulder at Assarion and inquired, "Can she eat or drink yet?"

"No, not yet, but soon," Dr. Zhukova answered. She moved to Assarion and tucked her into bed, saying, "She can attempt clear fluids and some chicken broth tomorrow morning and, if she can tolerate them, solid foods later in the day . . . assuming we're staying that long."

"We'll be here in the morning at least," confirmed Jacob. He gently grasped her shoulders, rotated her around and nudged her towards the door, insisting, "Now go get some sleep."

"What about you?" Dr. Zhukova asked with concern. Jacob planted himself in a chair in the corner of the room and folded his hands in his lap.

"I'm staying with the kid," replied Jacob. Miriam materialized next to him and startled Dr. Zhukova.

"He's such a good daddy," said Assarion with sparkling eyes. Jacob and Miriam threw a barrage of optical daggers at her.

"Fuck off," grumbled Jacob. Miriam, pleased with Jacob's response, said nothing.

"Well, with that, good night," Dr. Zhukova said, the Russian discomfited by the demon's presence. Breezing out of the room, she hung a left and departed with fading footfalls.

"We've got company," Miriam stated with flat affect.

"I sensed them as well," added Assarion. Miriam's anger burgeoned with each word she spoke.

"Just lie there quietly and don't say another fucking word," snarled Jacob with a threatening finger directed at Assarion.

"Just trying to help, my Dear," taunted Assarion, her cheek causing Jacob to raise a fist as if to punch the air. She chuckled and settled into a restful state. Jacob returned his attention to Miriam.

"How many?" inquired Jacob. His eyelids grew heavy.

"Marcion just showed up," Miriam answered, "and there's a new one, too. It's been creeping around for a while."

"Reconnaisance at best," Jacob uttered with disapprobation, "and, at worst, who the fuck knows what havoc they're wreaking."

Much to Jacob's surprise, Miriam sat on his lap and laid her head on his shoulder. He tensed at first but, enjoying the physical contact, relaxed and wrapped his arm around her waist.

"Believe it or not, there is a silver lining to Sarah's death," said Jacob. A spasm of pained anger passed over his face before he composed himself and continued, "We can move her now, and the baby. We need to get them back to New Oneida."

"You can worry about it tomorrow," Miriam said. She placed a protective hand on his chest and said, "I'll keep an eye on the baby. You need to sleep. You've been cut, too."

"Thanks," Jacob muttered as his drifted into light sleep. Thirty seconds later, he slumbered heavily. His dreams, however, were strange and filled with red light and the laughter of children.

18

THE MORNING DAWNED sunny and bright and the air warmed quickly. Despite their prevalence in Jacob's dreams, the demons did not harry the group overnight. Their absence and Assarion's improving physical condition buttressed his decision to leave late that morning.

Three vans and Darby's Humvee left Station Genesis, the vehicles glinting in the sun as they proceeded east. Darby, much to her chagrin, drove the first van with Jacob, Miriam and Dr. Zhukova in passenger seats and Assarion secured in a makeshift medical bed.

"You're an asshole," Darby chided Jacob when he convinced her to surrender the Humvee's keys to a member of the Community. Jacob slapped the side of the van.

"This thing's carrying some precious cargo, Darby," replied Jacob. He placed a hand on her shoulder and said earnestly, "I need you at the wheel. Just please keep the drinking to a minimum until we get to Station Exodus."

"You first, cocksucker," Darby shot back with an extended middle finger.

The convoy arrived at the bridge unmolested, the sight of its towers kindling Jacob's memories of his passionate night with Boyka. While they waited for a tall, burly Community member to open the gate, Jacob pondered aloud.

"Do we close it behind us to keep unwanted visitors out or leave it open in case we gotta haul ass in the other direction?" he asked.

"You'd need something big and armored to breach it without wrecking whatever you hit it with," Darby advised, "and you probably don't have anything like that at your Community, do ya', Doc?"

"We do not," confirmed Dr. Zhukova. The vehicles rolled forward through the open gate.

"I can open it," Miriam said confidently. Jacob considered all the possible scenarios involving the gate and decided flight from New Oneida was least likely.

"Closed it is," said Jacob.

The caravan arrived at Station Exodus as the sun sunk in the west. Its rays struck thick, intermittent clouds that overtook the convoy late in its journey but, instead of a breathtaking array of reds, purples and pinks, the sky glowed an eerie, oppressive orange.

Jacob, as his first priority, ensured that Assarion was safely settled into Station Exodus's recovery room. He admonished her to properly rest in his absence before guiding Miriam into the hallway.

"This may seem a little risky but I think we're okay for tonight, believe it or not," said Jacob. Miriam nodded her head in agreement when he added, "Keep your eyes open anyway."

The unlikely pair embraced and he placed a quick kiss on the top of her head before marching down the hallway. She watched him lovingly and then, with a last twinge of regret, returned to his child.

"There is much consternation among my people over abandoning the Stations," Dr. Zhukova informed Jacob when he met her at the front doors.

"Did you tell them the alternative is a demonic buttfuck?" countered Jacob sharply. He immediately regretted his tone and said, "I'm sorry. I've got a very unpleasant task in front of me and it's making me more of an asshole than usual."

"One you should not face alone," Dr. Zhukova said as she walked him to the van waiting in the driveway. Disquieted by what she considered an unnecessarily dangerous journey, she begged, "Let me go with you."

"I need you here in case anything goes wrong with Sarah," replied Jacob, "as do your people. They'll listen to Darby grudgingly but they're not happy about taking orders from the Queen Bitch."

Appearing as if summoned by the use of her name, Darby exited the Station and walked up to Jacob and Dr. Zhukova. She held a black book in her right hand.

"Hey, you said you'd stay," said Jacob, his emotions rising in anticipation of a battle with Darby.

"Relax, dickhead, I'm staying," Darby replied. She stated with an unusual measure of wisdom, "I'll have my own reckoning with Nes' soon enough. But I think it's time you took this back."

Darby handed Jacob a Bible, the same one which he gave her upon his exit from Kaiser. He recognized its faux-leather cover.

"Thanks," said Jacob as he took the Bible and suppressed the urge to needle her about the gesture. He climbed into the van and, within seconds, trundled down the drive.

"I have prayed many prayers that he will return," Dr. Zhukova said as Jacob turned onto the main road.

"Don't worry," Darby assured her, "that asshole always turns back up."

. . . .

ASSARION DESCRIBED for Jacob the location of Vanessa's body and, even in the dark, he recognized the vicinity of Mallory's pyre. Taking with him a gas can, waterproof matches, a flashlight and his Bible, he left the van and trudged through the snow towards the clearing. He clicked on the flashlight and aimed it forward.

"Let's get this over with," Jacob said with a blast of steamy breath and the snow crunching beneath his boots. The temperature dropped quickly after the setting of the sun and the air was frigid. He shined the flashlight into the clearing, shivered and complained, "Fuck it's cold out here."

The flashlight revealed that Paliki's long, lanky form awaited him, the Hungarian dressed in a full-length navy skirt and a white blouse. She stood in front of a neatly stacked pile of logs and, as Jacob approached her, he saw Vanessa's decomposing corpse lying upon it.

"Get the fuck outta here," Jacob snarled. Paliki tilted her head and pretended to pout.

"It was *my* body, Daddy," reasoned Vanessa in her own voice.

"Don't call me that," Jacob growled through clenched teeth. Anger flashed in Paliki's black eyes.

"I'll call you whatever the fuck I want!" barked Vanessa in monstrous voice. She straightened up as the spiritual force field exploded around Jacob, its multitudinous wisps of spiritual protection circling him at high speed.

"Fine, stay. I don't fucking care," Jacob uttered with a dismissive wave. He proceeded towards Vanessa and caused her to retreat, the field waning with each step she took. Jacob unscrewed the cap of the gas can and carefully soaked Vanessa's corpse in gasoline, saying with a smirk, "It's your funeral."

"This one was here when you destroyed Mallory's body, wasn't she?" asked Vanessa. The spiritual ward weakened enough for her to slither closer to Jacob while he observed the charred remains of Mallory's pyre.

"You know she was here," Jacob replied as he tossed aside the empty can. He rankled under his deal with Elizabeth and wished with every fiber of his being to cast Vanessa from Paliki's body. He and Vanessa knew, however, that the gates of the Abyss stood wide open and she could easily return.

"You haven't had her yet," said Vanessa sensually. She sauntered towards Jacob and added, "She's so long, so tall . . . and I know you'd love to climb her."

"Ya' know if I knocked up Paliki her baby'd be capable of casting you out," advised Jacob matter-of-factly though he had no intention of copulating with her.

"How strong's your pullout game, Daddy?" Vanessa queried with a seductive grin. She began unbuttoning her blouse and said, "Just think, you'll be doing her and me at the same time, and I know you've wanted me from the day you saw me."

Vanessa's moral decay saddened Jacob so much so that it overwhelmed his anger. He prayed there was some decency left in her.

"It's not too late for you to repent, Nes'," pleaded Jacob. Gesturing emphatically, he implored her, "You're responsible for your own life, your own spirit. You don't have to follow your mother. I can help you."

"You?! Help me?! You're responsible for what I am!" Vanessa bellowed in a hybrid voice.

"You're right, kid," Jacob said. He struck a match and tossed it on the pyre. It erupted in high, raging flames and cast the entire clearing in an orange light. Guilt-stricken, Jacob pulled a metal water bottle from his coat and swigged from it.

"You know you want her, and me, so take us!" shouted Vanessa as she stripped Paliki down to her bra and panties.

Jacob ignored Vanessa's desperate attempt to beguile him and tossed the matchbook into the fire. Producing his Bible, he used the light of the roaring flames to locate a verse. The crackling of the burning wood echoed in the silent, cold night.

"Fuck me, Daddy! Fuck me!" yelled Vanessa while ripping off her remaining garments and charging Jacob in the nude. The spiritual field of force surged and repelled her, its power hurling her to the edge of the clearing. Turning from libidinous to wrathful, she rose up, shrieked hideously at him and ran into the woods. Jacob did not watch her and instead focused on his Bible.

"'Brother will betray brother to death, and a father his child; and children will rise up against parents and cause them to be put to death,'" Jacob droned. Vanessa's screeches echoed in the distance as he recited, "'You will be hated by all because of my name, but it is the one who has endured to the end who will be saved.'" (Matthew 10:21-22).

Jacob closed the Bible. He stared into the dancing fire and felt its rippling heat. It consumed the corpse of the uncorrupted Vanessa he once knew and he watched it burn long into the night.

. . . .

"WAKE UP, SLEEPYHEAD," Miriam cooed with a mischievous grin. She opened the curtains and light streamed into one of Station Exodus's bunkrooms.

"What the fuck?" groaned Jacob as he opened his eyes. He was in the clothes he wore the night before though someone removed his cold weather gear. Realizing Miriam was not with the baby, Jacob sat up and exclaimed, "Where's Sarah?!"

"*Assarion* is down the hall, resting as you ordered. She was even able to eat solid food this morning," Miriam replied with a strange optimism. Jacob's head throbbed and he felt grimy. Miriam offered him two large aspirin and a half-full glass of water, adding, "And the little one is doing fine, though she's a little pissed due to all the commotion."

"How did I get back here?" asked Jacob. Miriam dropped the aspirin into his upturned hand and then gave him the water.

"You took a ride on Air Miriam," Miriam said. Jacob swallowed the aspirin and then drained the glass of water in several gulps.

"That's turning into a damn convenient trick," Jacob said. He set the glass on a small bedside table and inquired, "But what happened? Was I attacked?"

"Only by the whiskey," Miriam said. Giving him a look of rebuke, she explained, "You, like a drunken dumbass, passed out in the snow. You're lucky the fire kept you warm . . . and that I left Baby Gottschalk for a few minutes to find you."

"Dinah," Jacob corrected Miriam, the naming of his child making him oddly uncomfortable.

"What?" asked Miriam.

"Her mother named her Dinah," Jacob replied. Miriam wrinkled her nose.

"You know what happens in that story, right?" inquired Miriam.

"Yeah, I know," Jacob said sourly. Miriam moved towards him with the intent of sliding into the bed but Dr. Zhukova's angry entrance interrupted her.

"You stupid, stupid man!" barked Dr. Zhukova, her loudness tweaking Jacob's headache.

"Fucking take it easy," Jacob said with a raised palm.

"As a supposed man of God you should never use such language," scolded Dr. Zhukova.

"Fuck, fuck, fuck," Jacob said bluntly. Looking around the room, he waved his hand and said, "See, nothing fucking happened. And I never said I was a 'man of God.'"

Miriam stifled a chuckle. Jacob rubbed his aching temples.

"Damn I'm getting old," he complained. His stomach growled.

"So much depends on you and yet you still shamelessly wallow in a mire of sin," asserted Dr. Zhukova.

"Oh, trust me, there's plenty of shame," said Jacob. He climbed out of bed and steadied himself by placing a hand on the top bunk bed, saying, "I burned the rotting corpse of my stepdaughter last night who, by the way, is now a demon and possesses your daughter. And guess what *she* did last night?"

Miriam squeezed Jacob's arm to cause him the slightest twinge of pain. He took the hint and stopped speaking. Her presence calmed him and he let his angst gradually bleed away.

"Do you think you are the only one who has lost, Jacob?" queried Dr. Zhukova sadly. She, with watery eyes, stated, "The scourges of self-love and lust pulled at the seams of the Community before you arrived, but you came to us with evil nipping at your heels, and now demons tear at those seams. The minions of Ba'al Zeboul have murdered my beloved people and kidnapped my daughters, who I love second only to God."

"And yet you have given selflessly to save my daughter, and I thank you for that," Jacob lauded her. Dr. Zhukova waved away the praise.

"That is irrelevant to this conversation," countered Dr. Zhukova. She stepped forward and drew herself up, asking ardently, "How can I trust you to protect the people I love when you act as irresponsibly as you did last night?"

Jacob's voice delivered the answer to her question but it was not Jacob who spoke. The words flowed effortlessly from the past.

"I walk the line between good and evil, Mirry, and the side on which I stray varies by the day. The alcohol, the sex, the profanity . . . the violence. I'm completely unworthy of the Holy Spirit . . . but it still haunts me, and sometimes directs my steps. So despite all the fucking garbage in my life, despite all my fuck ups, the yoke of God is upon me and I take whatever grace He provides . . . albeit reluctantly at times. I don't know why, but while I may be a fucking poor servant, and whether it's through deeds of evil or of good, I'm still His servant."

Jacob and Dr. Zhukova looked upon Miriam in amazement as the last word passed her jagged teeth. She wrapped an affectionate arm around Jacob and offered Dr. Zhukova a stalwart mien.

"I'm getting some breakfast and a shower, Doc, and then *my* people are leaving today for New Oneida," Jacob advised Dr. Zhukova. They locked eyes as he said stoically, "What you and your people do is entirely up to you."

• • • •

A THICK BLANKET OF cheerless gray clouds slowly rolled out of the south late in the morning and overshadowed Station Exodus. Noon arrived without the sun and the world grew unnaturally quiet. No one spoke as the vans were loaded for the final push to New Oneida.

"Are we going to a funeral?" queried Assarion when she exited the Station and witnessed the sullen mood of the group. Jacob glowered at her and she quickly said, "My apologies. Ill-timed jest."

Jacob returned his attention to the Dr. Zhukova's beloved loyalists as they boarded the vans. He realized they were all older, able-bodied adults and thought of the Community's children.

"What's wrong?" asked Miriam worriedly as she clung to Jacob's side.

"I'm starting to figure out how this is gonna go," Jacob said without looking at her. Miriam waited expectantly for him to elaborate and, when he did not, she tugged on his coat.

"And?" asked Miriam in irritation.

"Just stay with Dinah," Jacob answered.

Four additional vans joined the caravan as it departed from Station Exodus. Despite Darby's desire to speed to their destination, Jacob kept the line of vehicles moving at a modest, consistent pace.

"It'll be dark when we get there," complained Darby, her wild eyes conveying her displeasure. They bored holes in Jacob, who sat in the front passenger seat.

"No, it won't," Jacob replied with the utmost conviction. He kept his gaze forward and did not speak again. When the convoy passed his stepdaughters' pyres, a dark shadow fell upon him and he bowed his head.

Darby's skepticism grew as the veil of clouds concealed the sunset and the light uniformly bled away. Her doubt disappeared, however, when she saw the familiar, amorphous curtain of light in the distance. Darby brought the column to a halt when she reached its edge.

"God save us," uttered Dr. Zhukova as she gazed on it in terror.

"God save us, indeed," Jacob said.

"Has it occurred to you, Jacob, that perhaps we are heading in the wrong direction?" asked Dr. Zhukova. Her trepidation was palpable and Darby's face clearly indicated her concurrence with the Russian's desire to retreat. Being content to rely on Jacob's guidance, Miriam said nothing while Assarion squelched a smile. The humans' fear stoked her demonic instincts.

"Drive on, Darby," Jacob replied without explanation. His gaze remained on the road ahead and, with the matter settled, Darby accelerated into the unknown.

• • • •

"I GOTTA ADMIT," JACOB said with uncertainty in his tone, "I thought there'd be a *lot* more destruction. And, I don't know, maybe some demons."

The entrance to New Oneida looked exactly as it did the day that Jacob first passed its gates save for its immersion in the eerie red light. The arched, polished sign reading "Welcome to the New Oneida Community" was in perfect condition, the square, red-bricked columns were intact and the gates were firmly attached to their hinges. Disconcerted by the lack of ruin, Jacob began mauling the callous inside his cheek.

"They were just waiting for us," said Miriam as she knelt in the space between the front seats. Looking to Jacob with a resigned expression, she said, "They're all around us, Jake."

"I told you it was a set-up," grumbled Darby. Her eyes burned.

"Of course it's a fucking set-up," Jacob snapped. Noticing movement at the edge of his vision, he announced, "And here comes the architect right now."

Moving with strong, confident steps, Carol walked down the center of the road. She wore New Oneidan garb but, despite the cold, donned no winter gear. Jacob exhaled.

"All right, you kids sit tight and I'll see what Mrs. Frye has to say," Jacob said as he shifted his weight to exit the van. His attempt was foiled when Miriam locked his arm in her iron grip.

"This is a bad *fucking* idea," growled Darby, her words matching the expressions of Miriam and Dr. Zhukova.

"Let go, Mirry," Jacob said.

"No," refused Miriam.

"She can't hurt me," Jacob replied.

"Are you bulletproof now, too?" asked Darby snidely. She rested her arm on the steering wheel and said, "Because she's packing."

"'I was watching Satan fall from heaven like lightning,'" said Assarion in Sarah's voice. Its use garnered the rapt attention of the van's inhabitants as if it cast a spell upon them. The child leapt in Sarah's womb when Assarion continued, "'Behold, I have given you authority to tread on serpents and scorpions, and over *all* the power of the enemy, and *nothing* will injure you.'" (Luke 10:19).

Jacob read no deceit on Sarah's face. He also felt an intense spiritual connection with his unborn child.

"'Nevertheless, do not rejoice in this, that the spirits are subject to you, but rejoice that your names are recorded in heaven,'" Jacob recited in completing Jesus's words. He wondered where his name was recorded but did not share his concerns.

Feeling the power of the Holy Spirit within Jacob, Dr. Zhukova surrendered her doubt and relaxed in her seat. Miriam reluctantly released her grip on Jacob's arm and Darby's face settled into a sneer as she averted her gaze.

"'Do not be afraid, only believe,'" Dr. Zhukova said, her own faith strengthening as she spoke. (Mark 5:36).

• • • •

"WELCOME BACK, JACOB," said Carol as she watched Jacob approach. He detected a haughtiness in her beyond her normal confidence and it caused him to stop ten feet away from her. Standing in the middle of the road between the pillars, she smirked and asked, "Still up for that interview?"

"Sure. Right here in front of everyone?" Jacob countered.

"Actually, I was going to have them slaughtered like pigs first, including your unborn child," Carol said. She unexpectedly maintained her distance, which Jacob took as a sign she feared his spiritual defenses, but continued, "And then, when their blood darkens the snow and their innards litter the forest, I will rape you as my creatures hold Miriam and make her watch."

"Ya' can't rape the willing, sweetheart," Jacob replied with a grin. Carol cackled evilly and the sound of her sinister laughter chilled the heart of every human who heard it. She drew a pistol from her belt, chambered a round and aimed it at Jacob.

"We both know you're not willing," scolded Carol.

"What's with the gun?" Jacob asked. He folded his arms and said, "Afraid to get your claws dirty?"

"The Helper may repel claw and tooth," said Carol, "but does It repel bullets?"

Jacob chuckled.

"Do you know how often people point guns at me?" Jacob asked with a shake of his head. He taunted Carol, gesticulating emphatically and saying, "Hell, Liz actually did shoot me once. But I'm still fucking here. So go ahead, *Carol*, take your best shot. Go on. Do it."

Carol's demonic host roared. Her eyes flooded with black and her fingernails elongated into wicked claws.

"Jake!" yelled Miriam as she prepared to rush to his side. Darby slowly drew her pistol.

"Do not interfere, Miriam!" shouted Assarion as Sarah, the nun's voice again proving enough to hold Miriam in check.

"C'mon, Carol, shoot me!" Jacob barked as he pointed at himself. The adults of New Oneida emerged from the trees on either side of the road with a cacophony of screeches and roars, each one dressed neatly in the New Oneidan way and toting a firearm. The children appeared with them, shrieking and hissing, waving their claws and snapping at the air with their serrated teeth.

A long, terrifying wail pierced the air and sent a shockwave through demon and human alike. Jacob, however, stood unmoved as Athaliah materialized between he and Carol.

"Put the gun away," Athaliah ordered Carol in her characteristic disinterested tone. Watching from the driver's seat of the van, Darby widened her eyes and tensed her muscles in response to the demon's abrupt appearance. Miriam sensed her reaction.

"This is my territory," insisted Carol in a monstrous voice. She lowered her firearm and said, "I will do with these intruders as I see fit, Athaliah."

"Athaliah," Jacob whispered. The demon seemed to hear its name and turned its attention to Jacob. She smiled her quick toothless smile before readdressing Carol. Her stench washed over Jacob and his countenance turned sour.

"You have no territory," advised Athaliah in monotone, "and you will do as the Lady commands."

Carol began to protest but, when Athaliah turned away from her, she stopped. Holstering her gun, she swallowed the bitter pill of Athaliah's admonishment and waited like an iniquitous yet doting servant.

"Jacob Gottschalk," said Athaliah. Speaking as if each word wearied her, she instructed him, "You will take your people into New Oneida and dwell in the buildings south of the road. There you will stay, under the protection of the Lady."

Jacob laughed heartily. His energy irritated the demons and they squirmed while moaning and crying.

"Under the Lady's protection, huh?" Jacob replied.

"Yes," confirmed Athaliah, "but any who leave, human or otherwise, will be exterminated."

"What of the children?" Jacob inquired as his mirth ended. Athaliah rolled her eyes. She kneeled down and motioned for the nearest child to come to her.

"Come here," she beckoned. The four-year old child obeyed and stood before them. Athaliah poked the boy in the back of the head with a claw and said, "Say hello to Mr. Gottschalk."

"Fuck you, Gottschalk!" shrieked the child. It snapped and swiped at him without contact and shouted, "We all hate you! Die! Die, Gottschalk!"

The other children hopped up and down and repeated shouts of "Die! Die!" Jacob glanced over one shoulder and then the other to view their hatefulness and then patted the child on the head.

"Great kid, thanks," Jacob said. The boy recoiled from him and snarled.

"Do you still want it?" inquired Athaliah as if she offered him a stray, grizzled dog with a bad temper.

"You realize I can just cast all your little beasties out of these kids, right?" Jacob responded. Athaliah looked at Jacob with exhausted eyes. The children, in unison, screamed and growled as they fled into the forest.

"If you can catch them," droned an undaunted Athaliah. Jacob withdrew inside himself and prayed. A minute passed as he calmed his mind and heart and allowed the will of God to guide him.

"Okie dokie," Jacob said. Athaliah flashed him her trademark reflexive grin. He walked back to the van, climbed inside and said to Darby, "Drive on."

"Are you fucking crazy?!" objected Darby. Miriam slithered into his lap and cuddled into him. She was content to merely be with Jacob and deferred to his wishes.

"Darby, we're surrounded by hundreds of armed demons," Jacob reasoned. He threw a finger forward and said, "The only way is forward so drive on or get out."

"There is no amount of whiskey that can make you tolerable," grumbled Darby. She started the van and shifted into "D". Rolling forward, the van proceeded slowly into the Community.

Carol stepped aside and watched the convoy move past her with restrained wrath. The children returned and, though unable to harm Dr. Zhukova's loyalists, they jeered them with threats and profanity. The crowd of demon-possessed members followed the vehicles east in a haunting procession.

"The Lady is weak," complained Carol. She punched a chunk out of a brick pillar and scoffed, "Allowing worshippers of the Holy One to defile the realm of the Master. I wonder what he thinks of such things."

"I'll be sure to relay your opinion," Athaliah said, her sudden reappearance behind Carol startling her. She smiled her sickening smile, let is vanish and then advised, "For now, watch and wait. You may just get what you wish."

· · · ·

RELISHING THE PHYSICAL contact with Jacob during a brief halt, Miriam momentarily forgot the perilous situation in which they found themselves. She wondered if "real girls" did such things as sitting on their boyfriends' laps. Darby noticed the closeness Jacob and Miriam shared and it made her more uncomfortable than the short sermon that Dr. Zhukova insisted on delivering to her faithful.

"God has guided us back home in the midst of the Satanic tidal wave of the Tribulation and He will protect us. Amen," Dr. Zhukova preached into the radio receiver. Each van driver echoed her "amen", their spirits buttressed by the Doctor's words.

"Thank you for indulging me," said Dr. Zhukova with gratitude. She handed the radio receiver to Darby.

"So now that we've tickled everyone's balls, what next?" asked Darby as she returned the receiver to its metal clasps.

"Your sister has graciously invited us to stay in New Oneida during our Tribulation vacation," Jacob said with all the sarcasm he could muster, "so we accept the invitation."

Matching Jacob's memory, the road plunged downward into the western end of the valley before turning east around the skirts of the mountain. It took a large turn south before again bending east. The red light bathed nearly everything in its evil glow, even the massive mansion, but it failed to penetrate one area: the village.

"Another setup?" asked Darby with a glance at Jacob. Miriam watched his face expectantly.

"No, I don't think so," Jacob said. Though he did not show it, he felt great relief in finding a haven for Dinah to be born. Remembering his past mistakes, he sought another opinion, asking, "What do you think, Doc?"

The Doctor surveyed the village which appeared exactly as it always had. She smiled nostalgically.

"As I said," answered Dr. Zhukova, "God has guided us back home."

19

DARBY HIT THE GROUND running upon arriving in the village. She immediately assigned some of Dr. Zhukova's people tasks such as unloading the vans while leading others in a meticulous sweep of the grounds and buildings. Freed by Darby's assumption of leadership duties, the Doctor settled Assarion into a suite in the small hospital building with Jacob hawking her every move. Miriam followed them at a distance and clenched her fists each time Jacob snuck a glance at Sarah's or Dr. Zhukova's bodies.

"Asshole pervert," she thought, "always thinking with his cock. Even at the end of the world."

Dr. Zhukova assisted Assarion in removing her clothing and checked the surgical site once in the suite. Satisfied with its condition, the Doctor helped her into a hospital gown and then her bed before attaching the monitoring equipment to Sarah's body. Miriam leaned against the wall with her arms folded and seethed but Jacob was too engrossed in his child's well-being to notice.

"The surgical site is healing well and her vital signs are normal for a pregnant woman," Dr. Zhukova said as she removed her examination gloves. Tossing them in the trash, she continued, "Both Assarion and Miriam sense that Dinah is alive and well so, after Assarion rests tonight, we'll do an ultrasound in the morning."

"Thanks, Doc," Jacob said. He sat down in one of the chairs and exhaled quietly, "We made it."

"I will assess her regularly, of course, but I will also assign some of my people to the hospital so she will be monitored twenty-four hours a day," Dr. Zhukova assured Jacob. He surveyed the room briefly and then shook his head in the negative.

"Not necessary," Jacob said. He grabbed the chair next to him and moved it around, saying, "I just need a cot, probably right here. I'll just move these chairs out."

"Why do you have to be in the same room with her?" complained Miriam with a few steps towards Jacob.

"Don't be jealous, Miriam," interjected Assarion. She adjusted herself in her bed and declared, "I have no romantic designs on him."

"Fuck you," snapped Miriam with an extended middle finger. Jacob shot her a look of disapproval.

"If you would excuse me, I would like check on how my members are faring," requested Dr. Zhukova, the Russian eager to escape the romantic tension. Jacob grinned tiredly and nodded.

"Absolutely, Irinushka, thank you," he replied.

"And you," said Dr. Zhukova while shaking a finger at Assarion, "keep your movements to a minimum. Rest, and I will return in a few hours."

"Yes, Ma'am," Assarion replied with a respectful smile. Jacob studied her face carefully but again detected no deceit.

"And you, Jacob, we will recheck your stitches when I return as well," advised Dr. Zhukova. Turning on a dime, she swiftly left the room.

"Look, Mirry, even if this place is demon proof, it doesn't stop them from sending in humans to do their dirty work," Jacob replied when the sound of Dr. Zhukova's steps faded away. Offering Miriam a coy smile, he added, "Ya' do know you can stay here, too, right?"

"Like a happy family," said Assarion with feigned joy, "daddy, mommy, baby and daddy's demonic girlfriend."

"Will you please shut the fuck up?" growled Jacob. The prospect of refereeing the interactions of Miriam and Assarion raised his ire. He buried his face in his hands and said, "And Mirry, will you please find us a cot?"

Miriam scowled at Jacob. He raised his head and threw up his hands in frustration.

"At least he said 'us,'" said Assarion. Glaring at her and giving Jacob the cold-shoulder, Miriam slowly faded from material existence.

• • • •

"YOU ARE TRULY INSANE," said Elizabeth when Miriam appeared before her, the former Constable of Kaiser still in possession of Boyka's body. Despite the windy, chilly conditions of the early spring evening, she wore a strapless, casual dress that accentuated Boyka's beautiful figure. Her long, dark hair blowing in the wind, she continued, "Coming here, and standing in *my* presence, without Jacob's protection."

The archenemies stood on the rounded metal spine that formed the highest point of Chinese Peak Casino, a towering, tubular skyscraper of glass and steel with a truncated apex. Once bathed in psychedelic, purple light, the building was now inundated with the demonic red light that infected New Oneida.

"Don't worry, I have something to offer," Miriam replied with a sneer. The vitriol the two spirits harbored for one another boiled beneath their emotional surfaces yet they both restrained their desire to act upon it.

"Had your fill of Jacob already?" Elizabeth queried with a vile snicker. Miriam growled.

"*You'll* never get him back," said Miriam, her demonic voice interspersed with her human one. Elizabeth's face hardened and they glared at one another.

"That ship has sailed, my little blonde harlot," Elizabeth said as she let her anger pass. Folding her arms, she stated matter-of-factly, "He is yours now, for as long as you can stand him. But I digress."

"The demon who runs New Oneida, Carol, is not as loyal to you as you might think," advised Miriam. Her anticipation of Elizabeth's response was palpable.

"Save for my daughters, no demon is loyal beyond the punishment I can inflict on it," Elizabeth replied, "and I am very aware of *Carol's* limitations."

Elizabeth raised her chin and smugly waited for Miriam's response. Miriam absorbed the initial defeat and parried.

"Marcion's been around, and talking a lot with Athaliah," said Miriam. Elizabeth's face remained stoic but Miriam sensed the slightest of stirrings in her spirit. She gently stroked her chin and pondered.

"Reports on Marcion's activities, as warranted, may be worth something, depending on what that something is," Elizabeth said.

"As long as it doesn't put Jake or the baby in danger," Miriam added firmly. Elizabeth nodded in assent.

"And what do you wish in return?" Elizabeth inquired.

"To speak to Boyka," answered Miriam.

"Why would I allow you unmonitored time with her?" Elizabeth scoffed.

"I didn't say *unmonitored*," snarled Miriam with contempt. Elizabeth motioned with both hands to indicate her assent.

"Very well," Elizabeth replied, "but keep it short."

Boyka's black eyes rolled back and her blue eyes reappeared. Her claws retracted and her teeth lost their jaggedness.

"*Démon*!" exclaimed Boyka in fear as she recognized Miriam and recoiled. Miriam grabbed her arm to steady her.

"Be careful or you'll fall," Miriam admonished her. Boyka realized the height at which she stood and her knees went weak. Miriam grabbed her by her upper arms and snapped, "Be careful!"

"Is Jacob here?" asked Boyka. Miriam read the desire in her eyes.

"No, and I don't have much time, so listen," Miriam demanded. She struggled with her emotions before explaining, "I don't know if any of us will survive what's coming, but if you do, *you* need to be with Jake."

"What?" whimpered a frightened and confused Boyka.

"You're better for him," Miriam continued with great difficulty. Applying greater force to Boyka's arms, she continued, "You can satisfy – you have satisfied – his sexual appetite. I can't do that, I'll never be able to do that, and I can't give him any more kids."

"We are not permitted such attachments," countered Boyka feebly, the Hungarian disbelieving her own argument.

"Bullshit," Miriam said. Boyka squirmed uncomfortably in her grip so she loosened it and stated, "You're already attached and you know it."

"I lost his child very early," protested Boyka sadly, "and he will want the nun because she carries his other child."

"You're such a slut, Jake," Miriam muttered to herself, her utterance drawing a baffled look from Boyka. Shaking the thought out of her head, she said, "Trust me, Sarah's not gonna get in your way."

The emotion of ceding Jacob to Boyka overwhelmed Miriam. Stifling her sobs, she released her.

"He may choose you," Miriam advised Boyka as her physical form wavered, "but that will never change the fact that I chose him."

Miriam vanished and Boyka's demonic traits returned. She looked to the north and was met with a gust that tossed her lengthy tresses. They moved like grasping tentacles in the wind.

"*Insatiably*," Elizabeth remarked.

. . . .

DR. ZHUKOVA MET JACOB at the doors that led from the Visitor Center's public Council Room into the Council's deliberation chambers. He held a tall, half-empty cup of black coffee in his hand and seemed in a daze.

"Jacob, thank you for coming," said Dr. Zhukova with a look of sympathy. She touched his arm and added, "I know you don't like to leave her."

"Let's just make this meeting efficient," Jacob replied with exhaustion in his tone. He loathed leaving Dinah but Dr. Zhukova had done so much for him he could not refuse her invitation.

"Of course," she said. Turning around, Dr. Zhukova opened both doors and walked inside. Jacob took a slug of lukewarm coffee and followed her.

"Where the hell've you three been?!" Jacob exclaimed when he saw Edna, Meriwa and Chubidem sitting in their chairs. The curtains were closed and covered the narrow, rectangular windows. Traces of the red light filtered into the room, however, due to the building's proximity to the road.

"Please, if you will have a seat, we will explain," said Dr. Zhukova as she pulled out the chair at the near end of the wooden conference table. Jacob voiced his displeasure with a dramatic sigh and dropped himself into the seat. Dr. Zhukova closed the doors.

"Thank you, Jake," said Chubidem. Dr. Zhukova walked to the far end of the table and seated herself as he explained, "God provided us with this sanctuary and, after the demons came, we fled here with a few of our members and hid ourselves. We would have spoken with you last night but we didn't want to disturb your . . . your child's . . . well, *her*."

"Don't feel bad," Jacob said. He drained his coffee cup and set it on the table, saying, "I've been trying to figure that one out myself."

"We are very sorry for the loss of Sarah," Edna said solemnly. Observing Jacob through her round, wiry glasses, she added in a more hopeful voice, "But we are thrilled for you that your child is safe and healthy."

Jacob averted his gaze and clenched his teeth. He had yet to process Sarah's death and his child's motherless future so he punted.

"I gotta ask this. How are you powering this place?" Jacob inquired as his eyes jumped from face to face. He picked up his cup and looked into it, saying, "I mean, I see the solar panels, but those can't be enough to keep everything running."

"River turbines," answered Meriwa. She explained, "We installed them years ago. They made the Community energy independent even before the disintegration of the world's social fabric made them a necessity for us."

"Well, let's hope the river doesn't run dry," Jacob said. He focused intently on Meriwa and asked, "What about the plane that started all this? Know where that came from?"

"A settlement on the West Coast which occasionally air drops supplies to us in exchange for an exorbitant fee," Meriwa answered. Surprising Jacob with her candor, she added, "It was late and off course. Why that was the case, and the reason for the crash, we do not know."

Jacob examined the three Councilmembers in turn and assessed them meticulously. They indulged his doubt and patiently waited for it to end. Dr. Zhukova intervened.

"Jacob, we are all in agreement that it was God's divine plan that you arrived here," Dr. Zhukova said. Jacob chuckled.

"Wasn't it you who said I showed up 'with evil nipping at my heels," Jacob replied smugly, "and then blamed me for all the Community's problems."

"I was wrong," Dr. Zhukova said with a contrite mien, "but I think I've earned your trust and your forgiveness for my mistake."

"You have, Doctor, many times over," Jacob relented, his respect for Dr. Zhukova evident in his tone and mannerisms. Edna rose, approached Jacob and took him by the hands. Her own trembled with excitement.

"We all agree now, Jacob, that we should proceed as you and I discussed," said Edna as she squeezed his hands and shook them. Jacob extricated them from her grasp as she declared, "We have been attacked by a horrible evil yet we now have the ability to match it."

"Things have changed a little bit since we had that conversation," countered Jacob. He looked around nervously for Miriam but did not see or feel any trace of her.

"Dinah will be, *is*, an exceptional child," said Dr. Zhukova, the Russian leaning over the table in her enthusiasm, "and, through you, we can create more exceptional children, God-fearing children of great spiritual power and faith. We can indeed cast up a highway across this chaos, gathering out the stones and grading the track."

Jacob grew grim. Edna reached out to touch him but, reading his mood, set her hand on the back of his chair.

"Join us, Jacob," Edna implored him. She launched into a passionate address, saying, "The Community has undergone tremendous loss and trauma. The shock of it has yet to wear off for many and, when they feel the full effect of that loss, they may lose hope and their faith in God. There will be hard times ahead, and threats both from within and without, and we need you. We want you join the Council and help our Community survive the Tribulation and the demons that beset us so that we all may see Christ's return."

Edna motioned to Dr. Frye's empty chair. Miriam suddenly appeared next to Jacob.

"All right, that's enough, Jesus freaks," interrupted Miriam rudely, her arrival startling the Council. Her crassness made Jacob cringe but he welcomed the rescue from the Council's pressure. Edna backed away as Miriam said, "He's got a lot on his shoulders and you don't need to make it worse."

"I'm fine, Mirry," Jacob said with a grin. Talking with his hands, he stood up and said, "Look, I appreciate the offer, I really do, and I'll think about it, but for now, Doc, you and the Council should run this place. Let's get everyone settled and figure out the basics – like how we're going to survive for the next few weeks – and then we can worry about the rest of it. Fair enough?"

"Of course," replied a visibly disappointed Dr. Zhukova.

"That makes perfect sense," Edna said, her ever-hopeful attitude shining through. Chubidem nodded in agreement but Meriwa appeared unmoved.

"Good," Jacob said. Taking Miriam's hand and grabbing his coffee cup, he declared, "Now, if you'll excuse us, I'm going to get another coffee and then my girlfriend and I are going for a walk on the beach."

Miriam smiled.

. . . .

THE TRIBULATION'S RED light did not sully Lake Oneida and, when the morning sun broke free of the clouds, its light settled on the water. Its rays shattered into millions of brilliant sparkles and stood in defiance of the evil illumination on the far shore.

"Though we do need to work on your people skills," Jacob said as he and Miriam strolled down the beach hand-in-hand, "thanks for getting me the fuck outta there."

"They ambushed you," griped Miriam. She refused to release his hand.

"How much did you hear?" Jacob queried with a sidelong glance.

"Enough," grumbled Miriam. Tamping down her emotions, she squeezed his hand and said, "But I don't want to talk about it."

"Good, 'cuz I don't want to, either," Jacob replied. He saw the faces of Edna, Chubidem and Meriwa in his mind and queried, "Are those three clean?"

"Yeah, they're clean, though Meriwa still doesn't like you," answered Miriam. The pair stopped near the waterline and gazed out at the lake as she said, "This place makes *me* uncomfortable, so no real demon is gonna dare set foot in here."

"I sure as fuck hope you're right," Jacob replied gravely. Miriam slipped underneath his arm and he wrapped it around her shoulders.

"I brought the gold," advised Miriam proudly.

"You did?" Jacob asked with a muted grin. Miriam shook her head in the affirmative.

"Yeah, it's in the Humvee," answered Miriam. The mention of the gold took Jacob into the past. His eyes became glassy and he stared at the sunlight reflecting off the lake's surface. Miriam allowed him to dwell there briefly before asking, "So what's the plan?"

"Long term, who the hell knows?" Jacob answered with a shrug. The clouds overtook the sun and it disappeared. He became cognizant of his absence from Dinah and said, "Short term, we hole up here, at least until Dinah's born. Speaking of her, I really need to get back."

"No, you don't," said Miriam as she held him in place. She leaned into Jacob and added, "Aunt Darby's babysitting right now."

"Never thought I'd hear that," Jacob said. He remained silent for several minutes as the gears of his mind spun at breakneck speed. Miriam finally nudged him out of his daydreams and he returned to her.

"You gonna go after Zhukova's Hungarians?" asked Miriam with the slightest hint of demonic tone in her voice.

"I'm gonna tell you the same thing I told the Council," Jacob said without looking at Miriam. She tightened her grip on him as he stated firmly, "Let's just see what happens."

"She did save your daughter, so . . . ." Miriam pressed him.

"Let it go," Jacob said. The potential conflict between Boyka and Miriam lay far in the future and he wished to keep it there.

"I'm not gonna turn into a real girl, Jake," Miriam said before pushing him away. She waited for his explosive response but it never came. He squirmed uncomfortably as his stitches prickled him.

"Well, I'm never gonna turn into a good man, so there ya' go," Jacob replied blithely. She watched him closely as he asked, "Remember when I told you I was a thirtyfolder?"

"Yeah," said Miriam. She barely restrained her desire to embrace him again.

"That was bullshit, my usual, guilt-ridden attempt to return to grace," Jacob explained. He thrust his hands into his pockets and explained, "I'm a dog among thorns, period. I'll do what I can here, especially for Dinah. Then, when she's ready to be on her own, I'll wander aimlessly around the world until I die, and then get a place just outside the gates of heaven, with the rest of 'the dogs and the sorcerers and the immoral persons and the murderers and the idolators, and everyone who loves and practices lying.' And maybe get to see my daughters once in a while." (Revelation 22:15).

Jacob laughed fatalistically. Miriam gave him a quizzical look. His eyes snapped to her.

"So you in?" Jacob asked. Miriam hesitated but for a moment.

"You know I always am," Miriam admitted. She charged him and leapt into his arms, saying as she lost herself in his brilliant blue eyes, "And now I'm a dog among thorns, too."

The unlikely pair, human and reformed demon, kissed each other deeply. Many disapproving eyes watched them express their intense affection for one another, eyes that they felt upon them. Yet, for that brief moment in time, they indulged in one another and left the rest of the material and spiritual worlds behind.

Epilogue

• • • •

STANDING AT THE SAME vantage point from which Elizabeth once surveyed her domain, Niu watched the sickly red curtain of light that surrounded Kaiser from his office balcony. It occasionally rippled, or ebbed and flowed, but it remained a permanent fixture on the city's borders. The balcony doors abruptly opened and one of Niu's suit-clad bodyguards strode through the doorway.

"Tā láile, xiānshēng," advised the bodyguard. Niu raised two fingers and motioned for his visitor to be admitted. His bodyguard bowed and departed.

A Chinese woman in an ostentatious wide-brimmed hat sauntered onto the balcony. The hat was white while her dress was an amalgamation of white and peach and festooned with peach blossoms.

"I am very pleased to see you," Niu greeted the woman. He did not look at her but said, "I was afraid you would not reach us."

"No one else would have," the woman replied without any trace of an accent. She exuded an aura of disinterest, one that Nui acutely sensed. The woman said dismissively, "Your demonic besiegers fled before me."

"There is someone I would like you to meet," Niu stated in businesslike fashion.

"Yes, I sensed his presence when I arrived," replied the woman. She moved to the edge of the balcony and scolded Niu, "It is incredibly foolish to invite one into your home."

"You are quite beautiful, for an exorcist, that is," said Aaron as the comely demon strode onto the balcony.

"Your pleasantries are wasted on me, *wangliang*," advised the woman with a hint of hostility.

"Yes, I know, you are a *fangxiangshi*," said Aaron condescendingly. His smile was impeccable and beguiling.

"Why have you invited me to a meeting with this *wangliang*?" inquired the woman sharply. Her eyes narrowed.

"Because the two of you will be working, if not together, in many of the same spaces," Niu explained, "and I want to make certain you both understand the contours of your responsibilities and that any *disagreements* are to be brought to my attention immediately. Now, Aaron's compensation has been negotiated and agreed upon but you have been silent on the matter."

"This is certain to be fascinating," commented Aaron while leering at the woman. Her ire vanished and she looked to Niu.

"I want the one about whom all the demons speak," the woman said. Returning her gaze to the amorphous curtain of evil red light, she insisted, "I want Jacob Gottschalk."

THE END

OTHER WORKS BY
JOSHUA R. FIELDS

THE MILLSTONE CRUSADE. *". . . but whoever causes one of these little ones who believe in Me to stumble, it would be better for him to have a heavy millstone hung around his neck, and to be drowned in the depth of the sea." The Gospel of Matthew 18:6.*

Shocking abductions of ones they hold dear unite Catholic teenagers Judas Trent and Ursula Baumé and thrust them into the evil world of human trafficking. Mentored by a whiskey-drinking, cigar-smoking priest, the headstrong psychokinetic and the disfigured healer lead their friends against a local sex-slave operation in Southeast Michigan and Northwest Ohio.

Together, Judas and Ursula take the fight to those who would harm and enslave children and score early victories against their enemies. Yet as the dangers of their Millstone Crusade against human trafficking increase and their feelings for one another are continually frustrated, they are forced to consider one simple question.

Can they stay together?

• • • •

'85 LOVE AFFAIR. Ten years after the unexpected and tragic deaths of their parents, siblings Elliott Warden and Emma Hastings enter 1985 in very different places. Emma, as matriarch of a loving family and owner of the successful club Johnny Dubs, prospers but Elliott, lost in a meaningless career and a sea of shallow relationships, flounders.

The return to Michigan of his high school sweetheart and her best friend, Donna, provides Emma the perfect excuse to intervene in her brother's love life. Her machinations quickly go awry after the arrival of a pretty, young waitress with a heart of gold and a vivacious, talented and beautiful musician with a soon-to-be fiancée. Believing Elliott to be courting romantic disaster with the younger women, Emma makes several risky plays to finally set him on the path to wedded bliss with Donna. Elliott has other ideas, however, and seems destined to make 1985 one hell of a year.